The Immortal Fate

Lillian's Story

The Immortal Fate

Lillian's Story

J.M. Merillo

The Immortal Fate: Lillian's Story

Cover Image: *To The Light* by Mel Gama,
a royalty free stock photo from dreamstime.com

ISBN-13: 978-0-6158-7645-0

For

Katherine Smith Cody, who inspired the physical beauty
and effortless charm of Rachel Kane (But possesses none
of Rachel's faults)

And

My beloved husband, Mario Merillo Jr., who changed my
life forever and gave me my very own happily-ever-after;
you are my world and my inspiration

❧1☙

Did you ever stop and think to yourself that your life was completely wretched?

You'll have to excuse my use of the word wretched as I've been reading Mary Shelley's *Frankenstein* lately, and I'm afraid its prolific use in that work may influence me to slip it in much more than I probably should. No one ever faulted Shelley for her over-abundant use of the word, so perhaps you'll forgive me as well.

The truth is even if I weren't reading *Frankenstein* at the moment the word wretched would have still come to mind to describe my life. Perhaps you don't understand the extent to which I mean the word wretched to be so perfect a description of my life at that point. Can you say you've ever stopped and thought, *What the hell was I born for? Why was I created to endure such a miserably insignificant existence?*

These were the exact questions I was contemplating as I sat on my bedroom floor, jotting down lines of poetry, and pausing every so often to look at my reflection in the mirror propped against the wall. I kept looking up at myself, as I decided on the next words I would write, and I couldn't help thinking, *Am I smart enough? Am I pretty enough? Do I matter at all, to anyone?*

Now when I look back it seems so childish that I ever worried about such things, but at the time I was nineteen, very naive, and unfortunately still living at home with my wretchedly over-critical, under-attentive parents. I believed at that time that I had nothing to offer and that my life would always be a waste so the only thing left to do was something drastic. I was waiting. I had been waiting three long, wretched years to be rescued.

Don't laugh.

Most teenage girls are waiting to be rescued.

The only difference was I knew who my rescuer would be; I just didn't know when he'd rescue me. That was why I was still living at my wretched home with my alcoholic parents, who on more than one occasion told me that I should be locked up. I don't mean in prison because I was a particularly bad child. I mean in a loony bin, a crazy house; complete with a straight jacket and heavy medications. To them I was cursed. I know it sounds like something right out of *The Omen*, but it wasn't exactly like that.

They'd always blamed me for the death of my uncle, Ben Thorne. They didn't think I actually killed him, just that his death was somehow my fault. They were convinced that whatever evil had touched him and led to his death had touched me as well, and I would bring nothing but grief to all those around me.

I guess that's why they never invited me along to family functions; wouldn't want me killing off Aunt Martha with my voodoo curse. I don't have an Aunt Martha if you were wondering if that was a joke.

I stopped writing and looked at my reflection. I thought I was pretty, in an old fashioned way. I had long straight strawberry blonde hair that curled softly at the ends, bright green eyes (my favorite feature actually), slightly on the tall side and thin, but proportionately curvy. I was paler than most girls my age, who spent their every waking moment of summer at the beach, and I didn't pile on loads of make-up or wear boy's sports jerseys and short shorts like most girls in my town. I tended to wear long dresses or skirts and the most make-up I ever wore was a little lipstick. I guess that didn't exactly help me from being an outcast.

I opened the bottom dresser drawer to my left, pulling the drawer completely out to find the picture I'd hidden beneath. I took the picture out, examining it, and comparing it to my reflection. No one knew that I had the photo and I made sure no one would find out, because it would only cause questions and most likely trouble for me. I looked back at the picture feeling a stronger connection to the stranger staring back at me than I felt to any living person. This was my family, the only person that truly felt like family. The picture was of my uncle, Ben.

I loved looking at the picture because every memory I had of Ben was filled with happiness, and it made me feel better to see those bright green eyes, so similar to mine, staring back at me. Most of my early memories were of Ben. He had been like a second father to me, well, more like a real father, because my own wretched father had been more interested in going to the wretched bar than spending time with me.

Sometimes I got angry at the picture. I would blame Ben for the way my life was. Would it have been different if he had lived, would people have accepted me? Would my wretched parents actually have looked at me with love in their eyes, instead of the disgust that they showed? Would I have never gotten tangled up in a dangerous world that changed me forever?

For whatever reason, I had been touched by something dark early in life that never seemed to leave me. It was more than just losing a beloved uncle to some mysterious force, it was something darker, more sinister, and somehow it caused people to instinctively avoid me. I don't know how people could sense it, maybe I was too quiet, maybe I put too much meaning into what I did say. Perhaps it was because I knew of a world that existed that no one around me knew about, and it made day to day life seem trivial. Whatever it was I always felt like an outcast, and I didn't know how to change that.

My only saving grace was my friendship with Rachel Kane. We'd been friends since I was fifteen, starting high school in a new town; Rachel was a year ahead of me and lived three houses away. She basically took me under her wing when I moved in, and although I was nothing close to popular, people didn't bother me, because I was Rachel's best friend. I never could understand what she saw in me. She had dozens of friends and every boy in our school wanted to date her, but she would ignore them all to spend time with me. She told me it was because she liked my sarcastic sense of humor and that I was much more interesting, because all her other friends were so painfully normal.

I looked back down at what I had written. I had worked lazily on the same poem for the past hour, too preoccupied with thoughts of the strange twists my life had always seemed to take. The final lines described the emptiness I so often felt...

I am a shadow,

I am a dark spot,

    - Just a blot

        - on the page

I had lost my focus for writing. I was going to start working on another one of the many poems I never seemed to find time to finish but decided my mind just wasn't in the right place. I thought perhaps a walk would clear my head. I was just putting the picture of my uncle back under the bottom drawer in my dresser when my plan was interrupted by the sound of a light tap on the window. In normal circumstances a person would be hesitant to check to see what had made that tapping noise, but as it had been the code Rachel and I had come up with to signal each other I was certain who was waiting on the other side of the blinds.

I was wrong.

Sort of.

My heart was beating out of my chest as I peered out my window into the dusky evening and saw not just Rachel but some unknown man beside her holding an umbrella over her head. The damp man standing beside Rachel had a stern look on his face and was motioning for me to hurry; as if I should have been ready for him to show up at my window any time of the day, unannounced, though I had absolutely no idea who he was. I could see the delirious look on Rachel's face and guessed that this was the rescue I had been longing for.

 I took one last look at my room and said goodbye, because I was fairly certain I wouldn't be back...ever. I thought momentarily about leaving a goodbye letter, imagining what my parents would think when they returned from dinner and realized I was gone, but decided it wouldn't make any difference to them. It would just be another inconvenience that I had provided them with to go along with the inconvenience I'd given them by being born.

Would they even notice?

Probably not.

They didn't really notice anything I ever did. I was just a mistake that had happened to them nineteen years ago, and after what happened to my uncle they looked at me like I was some kind of freak, if they looked at me at all. They probably wouldn't even tell anyone until after the weekend, wouldn't want my sudden disappearance to interfere with another two days to drink themselves into oblivion.

I didn't pack a bag. I just grabbed my poetry book, shoving the picture of Ben between the pages, and ran out the front door to the street in front of my house where a white limousine was parked; engine ready for our escape. When the car pulled away we were quiet at first, then I introduced myself to the man who was now sitting across from me, hoping he was going to tell me for certain that this was the rescue I had so longed for.

"I'm Lillian Thorne. I don't think we've ever met before."

He looked at me for a moment and sighed, then as if forced to speak he said, "I know who you are, Miss. I was sent by Mr. Cavanaugh."

My heart raced in anticipation. "Lex? Lex sent for us?" I asked excitedly, though, that had been my assumption from the beginning.

The man again reluctantly answered. "I'm sorry." He leaned closer. "You did know Mr. Cavanaugh was sending for you? You didn't seem very surprised when we showed up at your window. Unless you are used to people you have never met before signaling you through your window to get into their car."

I smiled politely, or as politely as I could muster at his unnecessary sarcasm. "I didn't know exactly what to think. Lex always told us one day he'd send for us, but it's been so long, and he never told us when. I was starting to think he didn't want us any more. When I saw you I really didn't know what to expect," I explained, adding, "But I did hope he had sent you."

"Well as for what Mr. Cavanaugh has told you, I have no knowledge of that. I am Mr. Cavanaugh's personal assistant, a steward or butler if you will. I run his household and do basically whatever else he needs. As Mr. Cavanaugh is so busy during the day he sent me, as he trusts me absolutely with all of his strange demands, to come collect you. You probably don't need to know but since you seem to insist upon it, my name is Bradley Spencer, and no we have not met before," he announced in a bored, I have better things to do than this, tone.

Bradley said he had been instructed not to speak with Rachel and me too much. I couldn't think why, except that Bradley had made it up so he wouldn't have to talk to us, but frankly I was too excited to care either way. Rachel and I were busy discussing how shocked everyone would be back home in Wilmington, North Carolina when they realized we'd left, well, at least how shocked they'd be to find Rachel had left. Rachel did admit that she'd told her parents she was planning on going away with me on vacation for the rest of the summer, so she would at least have a couple months before anyone became suspicious of her whereabouts.

When Rachel and Bradley fell asleep I pulled out the picture of Ben from my book, something I did when I was lonely or upset, which was often. As I looked at Ben's smiling face, wondering if I was making the right decision to leave my unhappy home, I was reminded of the first time I laid eyes on Alexander Cavanaugh, or Lex as he preferred to be called in those days.

I'm afraid Rachel and I fell foolishly in love with a self-indulged, ostentatious, impish, sometimes obnoxious, absolutely gorgeous and irresistibly charming vampire.

Yes, vampire.

Trust me, they're out there, and Rachel and I had stumbled upon them, quite accidentally, or so we had thought at that time. I'm getting ahead of myself, though. I was describing how our lives became entwined with vampires, and with Lex in particular.

Lex was, unfortunately for his ego, the embodiment of what one might call a perfectly beautiful man. He was tall with a slight muscular build, chiseled but somewhat boyish facial features, and shimmering black hair that came just above his ears and occasionally fell tauntingly across his vibrant blue eyes. He could have been a model or an actor from any era. He was as breathtaking in old-fashioned suits as he was in a t-shirt and jeans.

He was like looking at a perfect work of art; no one could deny his beauty. Even his skin was beautiful. It was a pool of the smoothest milk, no blemishes, no shadows, no contrasts of color. The whitest white you can picture, but it only added to his brilliance, making every other feature all the more defined. Especially those eyes. Those brilliant blue fire opals that could capture the light around them, almost making them appear to glow and swirl with every shade of blue as he moved.

Lex had been twenty-six when he had been turned, but his true age was two hundred and twenty-three. Lex looked like he could be a prince from a fairytale, but he was more like a villain. An irresistibly charming villain that you have a hard time blaming for his badness. He's like the big, bad wolf but with perfect hair, and eyes that melt you when they look at you. Yet for all his distracting beauty he is hungry...all the time, but it's not his fault. He's a big, bad wolf after all; what do you expect him to do?

Feed.

And he does.

Lex claimed that his appetite was vastly conservative compared with his younger days, aided not only by the length of time he has been a vampire but also by the consumption of some very ancient, powerful blood. The longer one is a vampire and the more powerful the blood that you drink the longer you can go without feeding. This gave me much greater confidence in spending so much time with Lex as he claimed to have a better command over his thirst than most due to the particularly strong blood he has had.

Lex was surrounded by his own kind; vampires trying to co-exist among humans without attracting too much attention. They created a council, a vampire government so to speak. They try to enforce laws among vampires in order to keep a low profile for their species and maintain some kind of generalized idea of right and wrong. Their coven, that's a gathering place of vampires for all you non-vampires out there, was in Lex's mansion in Florida.

Dangerous information for a mortal to have.

Each council is supposed to be made up of thirteen members, including any elders. The elders are treated more like kings and queens than just the heads of a council, but then the council itself is like a little government itself, setting rules and enforcing them within their region. For some reason The Council of the 7th Order, the council to which Lex was a member, had only been made up of twelve members for years. Although Rachel and I had only met two of these members, Giovanni Rossi and Mason Malone, we knew the rest by name, and had heard many stories about them from Lex.

Again, dangerous things for mortals to know, but for some reason Lex trusted us completely, perhaps naively. Of course, Lex had a habit of trusting people almost immediately and without any reason. I think he just couldn't imagine that anyone would ever, ever want to betray him. Part of his vanity I suppose. He assumed that everyone loved him the moment they met him. Most did.

Rachel and I first met Lex just a few days after I'd turned sixteen years old. Rachel and I were visiting Rachel's older cousin who lived in Florida at the time. One night when her cousin was working a night shift we decided to raid her closet and go out to a nightclub. Rachel talked me into wearing one of her cousins constrictive dresses that was cut so low that I couldn't wear a bra with it, thankfully it seemed to be designed in such a way that one was not needed, and it was so short I knew I'd be tugging at the bottom all night, though, the dress was so tight I don't think it budged even when I bent over. Rachel had also brought us both fake Ids from back home. Really badly made fake Ids, but we probably didn't need them anyway. If our looks didn't get us in Rachel would find a way; she always seemed to have a scheme for getting what she wanted.

Rachel and I had taken a taxi into the city where clubs lined both sides of a road closed for pedestrian traffic. We decided to sneak into a swing club called the Plum tree. As soon as we entered the main room I could feel all eyes turn to us. I have never been vain about my looks. I knew that men took notice of me, especially when Rachel dressed me up, but I didn't think any more than they did of any other girl. Plus, I always thought that Rachel was the beautiful one with her long flowing brown hair, beautiful blue eyes, and plump mouth. Although she was almost a foot shorter than I was, she had a much more voluptuous figure and she had learned how to use it to her advantage. Not to mention she was much more outgoing and flirtatious. I figured if I was with her most of the attention was directed at her, and I only received attention from men wanting to get closer to her.

I leant toward Rachel. "I think everyone is looking at us. Do you think they can tell we shouldn't be here?"

Rachel smiled slyly, always the confident one. "Lil, they're looking at us because we're like the best looking girls here. Don't be so nervous, you look beautiful."

Rachel and I went to the bar and ordered the only alcohol we had ever been allowed to drink, champagne. The man that was sitting to the right of me turned around and smiled.

"Hey, honey, let me buy you and your friend a real drink." His eyes shifted from my eyes to my body as he gestured to the bartender to come back and changed my order, "Make that two martinis, dry." Then he turned back to me and announced in a superior tone, "My name is Jerrod. This is my friend Jo."

I tugged Rachel so she would turn around. "I'm Lillian," I said softly and turned my head slightly to the left, "and this is Rachel."

Jerrod let his eyes flicker to Rachel who tried her most seductive smile on him. He was a beautiful man. Twenty-one maybe Twenty-five at most in age, with large brown eyes, and short almost curly dark hair. Jerrod was probably the most beautiful man I'd ever seen in real life at that point, but I couldn't help staring at his friend. For the first time in my life I felt my heart actually pound with the want of someone. I had never looked at anyone and felt that, I was absolutely transfixed by him.

Jo had deep brooding eyes that looked like gleaming liquid honey. His dark auburn hair was tucked behind his ears, just missing the tops of his strong, jawbones. He had full, savory lips that I couldn't help imagining kissing, but he seemed reserved, brooding, sullen even. When he looked at me something in him melted. His eyes lost some of their sadness and seemed more surprised that I was standing there, as if he'd forgotten he was in a club with countless people surrounding him. After a moment he seemed to remember where he was and that I was just another body in the room and went back to staring at what looked like a glass of beer in front of him.

Rachel moved around me to talk to Jerrod, who I could see was trying to charm Rachel to weakness, but she seemed to be trying to do the same to him. After a moment of waiting for Jo to come over to me, and even though I was a little nervous, I got up and walked around to sit on the other side of him.

"Are you all right? You look...upset. Maybe I could make you feel better," I said clumsily, trying my hand at flirting, though, I had very little experience with it.

Jo looked up from his beer but his eyes showed no sign of the dull haze that comes from drinking, and answered in a clipped accent, "Lillian? Lillian, I do not think you and your friend know what you are getting into."

I pressed my lips together in puzzlement. Was this how people bantered when they were flirting? I wasn't sure, but I wasn't very pleased with Jo's tone toward me.

I snapped at him, "We're just trying to have a good time. I'm sorry if I annoyed you. I won't bother you any more."

I got up to go back to my seat when Jo put his hand on my arm and said gently, "I should apologize. You are trying to be friendly and I am acting like il messaggerio della morte." He got up and extended his hand to me. "Would you dance with me, Lillian?"

"I don't really know how to swing dance," I stammered, standing in the middle of the dance floor with Jo.

He grabbed my right hand and slipped his arm around me, pulling me close. "I am called Giovanni, I hate Jo. Jerrod is the only one that calls me that. There was a time I was called Vann by my friends, if you preferisco." He pronounced the name as if it were spelled Vaughn. Then he brushed his cheek against mine as he whispered in my ear, "And you do not have to know how to do this dance, I will lead you."

After I got a hang of the basic three-step dance Vann started spinning and turning me. I was completely out of breath but he seemed to have unending energy. Finally a slow song came on and he pulled me close again. I liked the earthy, musky smell of his hair and closed my eyes to better take it in.

"I don't think I've ever danced so well. You're amazing, Jo...Vann," I tried to correct myself as I pulled away a little to look in his eyes.

He looked away and pulled me back close. "Lillian, I do not think you should leave your friend da solo for too long. We should go back." His face took on that sad expression again.

I tried to think of something to keep his mind off of whatever was making him sad. "You haven't told me anything about yourself. Where are you from? Do you live here, visiting? What do you do for a living?"

"I do not like talking about myself." He coaxed, "Come, let's get back, I will get you another drink."

I shook my head yes, realizing he wasn't going to change his mind.

After two more martinis I had to excuse myself to go to the

bathroom, and I hoped I didn't look too wobbly on my feet as I walked away. I had to pass through a cigar room in order to get to the bathrooms on the opposite side of the club. As I walked through the smoky room of couches and lounge chairs I noticed a man leaning against the far wall glancing at me and then turning away as if he didn't want me to know he was watching me. His dark hair was loosely slicked back and he had the most wondrous, piercing blue eyes. I tried not to stare at him, but couldn't help myself, his almost sheer white shirt hugged his body in such a way that I could see every ripple of muscle beneath and he left the three buttons at the top undone revealing a black leather and silver beaded necklace and the most luminously perfect skin I'd ever beheld.

Besides being distractingly gorgeous he also seemed strangely familiar, as if I had seen him before, perhaps in a dream. He brought to mind the memory of my uncle, Ben, and that strange beauty he had seemed to possess. The few memories I had of Ben's appearance and even the picture I kept of him made me think of a rock star; he seemed to have some kind of indescribable glamour surrounding him.

Still, I wasn't sure why this man would make me think of Ben. The man looked nothing like the picture I had of my uncle, but something about him reminded me of Ben. I felt my mind was trying to remember something, something from when Ben was alive, but I just couldn't seem to reach it. My head felt a little hazy from the martinis and I reasoned that the alcohol must have been playing tricks on me. How could some stranger in a nightclub have anything to do with Ben? I brushed the thought off. It was a ridiculous thought anyway.

As I kept walking it was hard for me to not look at the man. He was now looking straight at me, changing his mind apparently about letting me know that he was watching me. It was as if he were screaming at me from across the room just by looking at me. I knew what his voice would sound like, as if his eyes were revealing everything to me. Those burning blue eyes, so difficult to look away from, seemed to be locked on me with a strange look of curiosity. Finally, I forced myself to look away from him as I passed by.

"Lillian?" an intimate voice purred.

❧2❧

"Lillian?" the voice queried a little louder.

I slowly turned around. The beautiful black haired man was looking at me, smiling his devilishly hypnotic smile. "I can't believe it. It's amazing. You look exactly like-" he stopped short.

"Did you just say my name?" I asked, my lip trembling.

The man seemed to recover from his initial look of wonder and replied, "Yes, Lillian, I said your name. I was just wondering what a sixteen year old girl was doing in a place like this?"

I felt fear creeping into me. My heart was racing as I caught my breath. I didn't know what else to do; I turned and ran into the bathroom, and locked myself in one of the stalls. I waited a few minutes, my heart pounding, scared I was going to get into trouble just for being underage in a bar and even more terrified that the dark haired man was planning to do something to me. When I finally convinced myself he wasn't going to follow me into the bathroom I exited the stall.

I stood, my hands resting on the sink, looking in the mirror. "How the hell does he know my name?" I whispered to myself aloud. "He must have heard someone say it," I tried convincing myself, then grudgingly asked my reflection, "but how does he know how old I am?" I stared in the mirror at my own confused and frightened face.

Rachel was still out there! What if the man tried to go after her?

I shook my head at a loss for what to do. It felt silly to be so frightened of this man when all he did was talk to me. I reasoned that I would just go speak to him and there would probably be some logical reason why he knew my name. Maybe I did know him. *Though I think I would remember a man that looked like him.*

I walked out of the bathroom toward the place where the black haired man had been standing, but he was gone. I sighed with relief that I wouldn't actually have to confront him, and continued walking out of the cigar lounge toward the main bar. I was just turning the corner and could see the waves of Rachel's light brown hair when a hand fell gingerly onto my left shoulder, startling me.

"Lillian, don't be alarmed. I'm trying to help you." I didn't turn around because the man's lips were already pushed against my hair. He continued with his plush voice, whispering, "The men you're with are dangerous. I don't know what they mean to do, but I suggest that you and Rachel get as far away from them as possible."

I didn't want to look at him but I forced myself to turn my head. He didn't step back as I turned to face him even thought my nose very nearly touched his, but I didn't care how close I was to him. I was caught in his eyes. Those perfect pools of sapphire water made me forget my fear and timidity.

"What are you?" The words fell so naturally from my lips I didn't even realize what I was saying.

His eyes shifted and caught the light, making all the many hues of blue swirl. His hushed voice insisted, "Never mind what I am, Li-" He stopped abruptly as if he had been about to call me something other than my name and instead brushed my cheek and tenderly continued, "Little queen. I'm not important right now. I'm just trying to keep you and your friend from becoming someone's dinner."

I shook off the spell of his gaze. "Are you trying to tell me Jerrod and Vann are going to hurt us?" My voice had taken on a cynical tone, "Come on. Vann can barely talk to me, a young girl. What makes you think they would hurt us?"

"I know them, I know what they are." The man pulled me back a little. "Look, I know you won't believe me if I tell you the truth. They're the same as me. They are what I am. I can't explain to you right now. Giovanni is a good...man; I don't think he'd do anything to hurt you. On the other hand Jerrod..." He stopped and shook his head. "Jerrod is out of control. He's unpredictable, crazed, and I don't know if Giovanni could or would protect you from him. Just get away while you can. Promise me," he said, as he brushed my cheek once again, as if comparing it to someone else's.

I nodded solemnly and took one last look at the black haired man before I turned to go back to the bar. I kept repeating everything he had said in my head. I didn't know if I should believe him or not. It was too peculiar, and yet somehow it seemed I should know what was going on, as if I had dealt with things like this before. I should have been more scared than I was, but something deep inside me was a bit curious to see how things played out. It all felt so strangely familiar to me. I sat down next to Vann still a little shaken, but undeniably intrigued.

Vann put his hand under my chin and turned my face to his. "I told you the same thing, uccellino. You don't belong here, and especially not with us." He got up to persuade Jerrod to leave with him.

I sat in silence, watching passively as Vann pleaded for Jerrod to come along with him, trying to make sense of what the black haired man had said to me. Rachel was desperately trying to convince Jerrod to not listen to Vann and go out with us somewhere else, but in the end Jerrod gave into Vann's persistent tugging. Jerrod stumbled to his feet and kissed both of our hands. When he looked up from my hand I saw something in his smile that reminded me of what the black haired man had said about being someone's dinner. I shook the thought off and smiled at him as he was being pulled away. Before they disappeared around the corner I saw Vann twist his eyes back to me for a moment, as if he were trying to figure out a puzzle.

I was lost in thought when I heard Rachel's pouting voice complain, "I don't get it, weren't we having fun? That guy Jo was such a stick in the mud. I don't even know how you managed to get him to talk at all."

I looked at her and half smiled. "He doesn't like being called Jo. His name is Giovanni and I think, maybe, he just saved us from something bad. I can't explain it exactly, but there was something...dark surrounding them."

I lost myself in thought for a moment, because I'd always felt something dark surrounding me as well. Maybe that was why I'd felt so drawn to Vann. Maybe that was why I'd been inexplicably drawn to the black haired man.

Reluctantly I said, "We should probably head home. I think we've had enough excitement for one night."

Rachel and I went down the steps that led to a road crowded with pedestrians. We turned the corner, losing the crowd on the side street, and continued walking toward the bus stop on the next corner. I suddenly realized that something felt like it was missing. I turned around to see Rachel standing about twenty feet behind me staring into a small alleyway.

"Lil, come on!" she said gesturing to me and pointing down the alley. "Jerrod's waiting for us."

Then she disappeared into the alley.

I started running toward her, a feeling of dread filling me. "No, Ray! Rachel don't go!"

I ran into the alley where I saw Jerrod standing in front of Rachel, who was pushed up against the wall, a look of horror on her lipstick smeared face. She looked at me with tears streaming down her face, unable to move.

I tried to sound practical as I explained forcefully to Jerrod, "We have to go home, Jerrod. Rachel's cousin will be expecting us and she knows where we are. Come on, Rachel."

Jerrod turned to me with a broad, cruel smile on his face. I now realized what had caught my attention in the club that had made me think about being someone's dinner. As Jerrod smiled I could see two pointed teeth just slightly longer than his other teeth, like fangs, glinting at me from his greedy mouth.

"Don't worry, Lillian, there's enough of me to go around." He turned back to Rachel who was now trembling with fear.

I wasn't sure if I trusted what I had just seen, perhaps my fear was making me see things. Either way I knew I had to help Rachel. I ran at Jerrod thinking I could possibly knock him off balance and give us enough time to make a run for it. With one swift move of his arm he sent me crashing into the opposite wall. My head felt sore, certainly not as sore as it should have felt, but the alcohol probably helped with that. I was able to ignore my own pain, focusing instead on Rachel and how I was going to help her. I forced myself to stagger clumsily to my feet. Rachel was struggling to get free of Jerrod, kicking her feet and swinging her head side to side, but he was too strong for her. He pinned her arms behind her back and was pushing back her hair from her neck.

I was frozen. I didn't know what he meant to do. Well, I did...but I didn't want to admit it to myself. This couldn't be happening. People did not drink people's blood.

I kept thinking in my head, *someone's dinner. I'm trying to keep you and your friend from becoming someone's dinner.* In my mind I screamed for help. As ridiculous as it seemed, I screamed for the black haired man, whoever he was, to save us.

I couldn't let him do whatever he was trying to do to Rachel, so once more I ran at Jerrod, jumping on his back, and throwing my arms around his neck. "Run, Rachel!"

I saw Jerrod's hand go up, and heard as it struck Rachel in the face. I heard her drop to the ground. He then bent down low and flipped me over his back so that I flipped forward and ended up sprawled on the ground in front of him. Jerrod pushed me down onto the pavement and thrust his hand under my neck.

"I see you're very eager for my attention. I won't make you wait any longer; you can be first." He bared his fangs exaggeratedly to show what he meant to do.

I was paralyzed with fear. He pulled my neck toward him, his lips pressed against my skin, and then I felt a momentary surge of pain. His teeth were in my neck drawing out my blood. I felt delightfully dizzy. I knew I was going to die, but the pain was almost soothing, like a release from a lifelong pain. Perhaps pain wasn't exactly the right way to describe it. It was more like a burning sensation; a lovely, sensual, burning that I didn't really want to stop. I almost didn't care anymore what he did to me. I don't know if it was the effect of the martinis or what Jerrod was doing to me, but I felt light, almost euphoric, and though I couldn't see what was happening with my eyes I was experiencing visions of sparkling, swirling colors.

"Jerrod, Smettila! Stop!" I heard a voice yell from somewhere far off. I struggled to see and the voice spoke again, "Jerrod, you lied to me. You deceived me...just so you could drink from these girls? You are out of control! The council will not stand for your blundering ways."

My head was swimming but I knew the voice. "Vaahh...nn," I crackled.

Suddenly my eyes were open and I saw Jerrod's body flying away from me and into the opposite wall. I could barely keep my head up, but I forced myself to keep my eyes open and there was the black haired man from the club standing over Jerrod's sniveling body. I turned my head and saw Vann wipe a tear from his eye and walk away. My eyes were getting heavy, but I looked back at the black haired man who now had Jerrod's neck pressed to his lips. Jerrod was clawing at the man to no avail. He was as weak to the man as Rachel and I had been to him. I let my head fall against the wall and my eyes shut.

"Lillian, can you hear me? Little queen, are you alright?"

I opened my eyes and saw a bounty of tousled black hair swinging above me. When I realized what had happened and what the black haired man was, I screamed and scrambled away from him. He didn't move to stop me. He just stood there looking at me with a sad curiosity. I didn't know if I should scream for my life...or thank him.

He bent closer to me and pleaded sweetly, "Don't be afraid of me, please. I would never let anything hurt you. I swear it, on my soul." He leaned toward me and kissed my lips gently and I thought that I tasted strawberry. I felt his arms go around me and suddenly I was moving.

I was dazed, but insisted, "Rachel?! Where is she?! We can't leave her! She isn't dead! I know she isn't. Rachel! Rachel, are you alright?"

The man bent and kissed my forehead. "Rachel is right here. Giovanni is helping her."

I heard Vann's cool-toned tongue, "Lex, why are you so interessa in these two bambinas? What are we going to do with her?" He bent his head toward Rachel. "And the uccellino there?"

"I'm not a child," I slurred groggily, hearing the Italian word bambina.

Lex looked down at me and smiled as he ignored Vann's first question and answered, "We are going to protect them, watch over them, keep them safe. That is what we will do. For now we'll get them home so they don't get into trouble."

That was how it happened. Lex had saved our lives. Maybe he had been watching us for a while. Maybe he had just stumbled upon us that night. Either way he saved us and for some reason he loved us as if he had always loved us.

We kept in touch with Lex and Vann through letters, and during school breaks we usually took advantage of Rachel's cousin's invitations to stay in Florida with her. That is until she moved back to North Carolina two years later. We met Mason Malone, who had been turned by Vann, during our following visit, and struck up a close friendship with him as well. Three years we kept in touch with them, writing letters when we couldn't visit for extended periods of time, though Lex never gave us his address, but insisted we send our letters to a PO Box in another state. Rachel even tried convincing them it would be easier to just talk on the phone, but Lex insisted that it was too dangerous to have anything that connected us to him. We didn't even know exactly where he lived. Every time we visited he would come get us and take us out somewhere.

I had begun to think that Lex was growing tired of us. I thought all the secrecy was simply because he wanted to be able to cut ties with us easier. I wasn't sure how long I was going to have to wait before I gave up waiting for him and began putting together some kind of life for myself. I was terrified that I would end up having to spend my life pretending to fit in, pretending that vampires didn't exist, and pretending to not feel so completely disconnected from every single person I would meet. I can't even explain how relieved I was when Rachel and Bradley showed up at my window. My fears vanished instantly. Finally after all that time of promising to take us, Lex wanted us to be with him, for the rest of our lives.

At last, after about half a night of riding in the limousine we arrived in Florida. Rachel and I had fallen asleep, but someone managed to carry us to our room without waking us. I woke up in the darkened room confused at first about where I was, but after stumbling into another bed I remembered I wasn't in my room. I was able to find a light switch using the minimal glow of moonlight coming through the windows, and a lavish jeweled chandelier illuminated in the center of the room as if it were a grand ballroom. I noticed Rachel, still lying in bed, watching me. Although both of us were exhausted we decided to inspect our new dwelling.

The walls were a deep shade of royal purple with gold trimmed paneling across the barrel-vaulted ceiling and a matching wood-carved gilded border circling the room just below the ceiling. Within each panel on the ceiling were beautifully painted pictures of angels flying in blue, clouded skies. I had suspicions Lex had modeled our room to look like one from the Palace of Versailles. He was usually doing things in an over-dramatic, grandiose manner.

There were two cream colored, gold trimmed dressers, on opposite sides of the room from one another, a large wood dining table by the balcony doors, and a small empty mirror table by the window. Our enormous four-poster beds were fitted with plush silky comforters covered in large dark purple flowers. The beds were about eight feet apart from another and on the outer sides of our beds were small round purple-clothed tables with single dark roses in golden vases upon them.

The wall between our beds had a large oil painting of Rachel and me in Victorian-style dresses walking down a hill holding hands. There was a dark, menacing castle in the background, and beyond that it seemed the sky was made up of dark colors as if the painting were depicting a scene at night. I noticed the painting wasn't particularly accurate with our appearances. My hair was a much deeper, darker red and Rachel's hair was very long, curly, and black. I studied it for a moment, finding it strange that Lex would have a painting done of us with such inaccuracies, but then again he probably thought it was funny. As I got even closer I noticed the painting itself seemed aged, almost as if it really had been painted during the time period it depicted. Of course, Lex had enough money to get anything he wanted the way he wanted and probably found someone that could create such a look. Something about the painting haunted me, the castle in the background gave me a chill, as if something were hiding inside of its walls, watching me from one of those high windows. I almost convinced myself I might have actually been to the castle, but I had never been anywhere except North Carolina and Florida.

"Amazing, isn't it?" Rachel commented behind me and then exclaimed, "Let's check out the closet!"

The door to the closet was directly opposite the painting of Rachel and me. Once inside, there was a long hall which included first on either side a twenty foot long closet of clothes for each of us, then two dressing rooms across from each other, and two bathrooms at the very end.

While admiring the beautiful gilded mirror in my dressing room my hand lightly touched the symbol of a golden sun with sixteen points at the top-center of the mirror, causing the mirror to swing out, revealing a staircase leading down. Rachel had the same in her dressing room. We walked a little way down but couldn't find any lights so we decided to just wait for Lex to show us what was down there later.

Rachel and I soon discovered that our closets had almost all identical clothing in them only now and then in different colors. We found long silk nightgowns to wear to bed, each with a matching robe. My nightgown looked silver but when the material shifted it seemed to change color, Rachel's was bright red.

We went back to bed, now beyond exhausted, but were awoken about an hour later by the sound of loud music and people babbling. I thought I was still dreaming until I looked over and saw from the moonlight flooding in the glass balcony doors that Rachel was awake as well, and not looking very pleased.

"I know this is our first night and all, but if he's going to have a welcome party for us I think we should at least be invited, let alone awake," I joked groggily, and then added seriously, "Doesn't he know what time it is? Anyway we should find him and kill him; ya know before the sun does."

"I completely agree," Rachel said, yawning.

We whipped our robes on and stomped out of our rooms grumpily. We were not about to let Lex get away with keeping us up, even if he was a vampire. I was glad I had put my robe on when we reached the massive stairway and looked down onto a sea of people. I didn't normally wear such revealing nightgowns to bed to begin with, and felt more than just a little self-conscious to be in front of so many strangers dressed as I was. I wanted to run back to our room before anyone noticed me, but I could see by the look on Rachel's face she was determined to find Lex.

Out of the innumerable mass of people Lex danced toward us, smiling ear to ear. "Good morning, darlings! Like the party?"

Rachel and I looked at each other rolling our eyes. "No!" we yelled down to him pretending to be much angrier than we were, but I couldn't help smiling at his child-like charm.

"Lex, can we talk to you for a moment?" I asked, gesturing dramatically for him to come up the stairs so we wouldn't have to shout to him, drawing even more attention to ourselves.

He hopscotched up the stairs. "What?" he asked as if nothing were out of the ordinary.

"When are these people leaving?" Rachel asked dreamily.

"When ever they feel like it. Why?"

I gave Rachel a hopeless look. "Lex, we have been in a car most of the night and where as you are used to being up all hours of the night, we are not. You have to give us at least a few days to adjust. Anyway why are you having a huge party like this? Isn't it against your rules?"

"Plus," Rachel added, "the sun rises in about half an hour."

"Oh, I forgot about that small deal with the sun," Lex joked. "and I have parties like this all the time, the council doesn't mind. At least, I don't think they mind...but tonight is particularly special because you're here."

"We weren't even invited," Rachel spat in annoyance. "Just tell everyone to go home."

Lex pouted his lip dramatically. "But I don't want to kick everyone out. That would be rude."

I gave Lex a confused look. "But you're a vampire. And most of the time an obnoxious one." Then narrowing my eyes and patting his cheek like one would a small child, I encouraged, "I think you can come up with something. You are terribly clever."

Lex narrowed his eyes for a moment studying me, and getting that strange, sad look he sometimes got when he stared at me, and then he stated solemnly, "and you are terribly beautiful."

Within ten minutes of lying back into our beds, Lex came to say goodnight to us, obviously discovering a way to end his party quickly.

"I can't even begin to tell you how happy I am that you're both here," Lex said sweetly. He sat on the edge of my bed and brushed my cheek with the back of his hand and whispered, "It's amazing, every day you look more and more like-" He didn't finish.

I looked at him puzzled. "You started to say that to me when we first met. Who do I look like?"

Lex just smiled sadly and said, "I'll tell you one day, but it still brings up too many bad memories." Then he clasped my face in his hands and lamented, "All those years you suffered. All the unhappiness you endured. But I'm going to make it up to you. I should have found you sooner. I should have done more."

I smiled at him not really understanding what he meant. "Lex, you've done so much for us. I mean, you know how my family life was, and you really helped me get by. I would have run away a long time ago if I hadn't thought one day you'd come for me."

He seemed to avert his eyes guiltily. "You never deserved to be treated the way that you were treated. Your parents should never have blamed you for anything."

"Well like I told you I don't really remember what happened, but from the things my family has said...they think...they think I caused some accident...a fire, I guess, that killed my uncle. I think I would remember something like that, though. I guess in the end they figured that I was bad luck to have around." I felt all the years of guilt starting to well up inside of me. Guilt for something I couldn't even remember doing.

Lex kissed my cheek and I again thought I caught the faint scent of strawberry on him. "Don't think about it anymore. It's the past, and I know it wasn't your fault. Get some sleep, and remember whatever happened to you before or however you were treated, you're home now. I'll always look after you. I swear it, on my soul."

Lex left the room quietly trying not to wake Rachel who had passed out minutes after lying down. Unfortunately, I had trouble sleeping. I should have been exhausted, but Lex made me start thinking about the past and how so much of what was happening now seemed connected to that past. Lex's reassurance had the opposite effect than he'd intended. Instead of falling into a peaceful, worry-free sleep, I was anxious and felt a strange foreboding. I couldn't help going over and over the words Lex had said to me. Words which seemed to hint that things had been kept from me, secret things, things which Lex himself knew and was not sharing with me.

I climbed out of bed and took my poetry book over to the balcony doors where the moonlight was just bright enough to see by. I removed the picture of Ben and stared at it, feeling confused, and wishing Ben's image might ease my mind from beyond the grave. I had always had this feeling that Ben was watching over me, maybe he could somehow guide me, or at least console me.

Still restless, I pushed open one of the French doors quietly and stepped out onto the balcony. I sat with my book at the wrought-iron bistro set just to the left of the door. My mind was racing with feelings of déjà vu, so I began writing...

My desolation has unwound,

Calling to memory something I found

I paused looking out over the side lawn and past that into the dark maze of garden paths. I almost felt like I was being watched, but tried to ignore the feeling as I set Ben's picture next to my book and continued writing. My eyes lingered to the picture of Ben, hoping he could magically give me the answer to the one thought that preoccupied my mind, *Why did Lex sound like he was hiding something? Something important?*

J.M. Merillo

A NIGHT IN THE UN-LIFE...

Lillian got up from her laptop, reminiscing about those early days spent with Lex, and went to the kitchen, absently opening the refrigerator.

"Aughhh, I'm still doing it!" she yelled at herself, slamming the empty refrigerator closed.

After twenty years as a vampire she still made little human mistakes like that. Looking in the fridge when she was bored for a bite to eat (though she didn't eat), accepting lunch invitations for the middle of the day (though she'd burst into flames if she actually attended), and picking up ridiculously heavy objects in front of people (Did you know she'd won the "World's Strongest Woman Competition" in Istavislan. Twice! It's so remote you won't even find it on a map, and they don't really like the attention, so it's all kept very quiet). She'd never actually gotten caught doing anything that would give her away, but it made her angry that she still behaved like a fledgling, like a novice.

She went to the bathroom to splash cold water on her face. Another habit, because of course she didn't get tired or worn-out unless she hadn't fed enough, so splashing water on her face had no effect in waking her senses up. She liked the feeling of the cold water on her skin anyway, especially when she had fresh blood running through her veins. Everything felt better after she fed. Her whole body felt more alive, more awake, more...human.

Not that she didn't enjoy being a vampire, but she never realized how lonely it would be. She had thought her vampire life would have been spent with Rachel, Lex, Vann, perhaps even Mason, but things didn't work out that way. She was getting more used to that; to not expecting things to turn out the way she hoped they would. Every new place she went, every mistake that she made, causing her to leave and start again, it was like a game. Try to blend in or you have to leave. People started noticing things and then it was time to go before they got too suspicious and stumbled upon the truth. Plus, she had been on a mission that required her to keep going, keep searching. After twenty years, though, she decided she needed a break from her disappointing search.

That was why, finally, she had moved back to Asheville, North Carolina.

It was risky being so close to where her family still resided. From what she had found out they reported her missing, but no really strenuous investigation ever took place. After all she had been nineteen, and it would have been obvious that she hadn't had an ideal home life. Of course there had been a search for Rachel, her family didn't believe that she would just leave home, but in the end the disappearance of both of them and no leads on where they would have gone led both families to surmise that something unfortunate had happened to them on their vacation together. Still, there was always a possibility someone might recognize her even with all the changes she'd endured, but she needed to be back where it all began. Where she'd been turned, where she'd received The Immortal Fate, as it was sometimes called. She needed to write her story and feel some connection to her past.

Lillian touched the oval-shaped pendant resting on her chest, thinking about the past, and forced herself back to the laptop.

"This is your life now. All you have keeping you going," she stated blandly to the screen. She shook her head. "Wow, that's sad. A vampire, and my reason for living is this stupid story."

Then she thought back to everyone she had met and cared for, and many that she had lost. Maybe the story was for them. It was her gift to those that had touched her life, for good or bad, and gave her the life she had now. Whatever her life was now, it could have been much worse. She could have ended up like so many others: dead or even worse still...a traitor, working with the enemy.

"So stop whining and write, already!" Lillian scolded herself as she opened the document to start her third chapter.

ଋ3ଙ

The next day Rachel and I woke up late. It was already three-thirty in the afternoon. I suggested we go swimming, and hoped it would at least keep my mind off of the curious feelings I'd been having. We went to search for bathing suits in our closets. I found a brown crocheted one-piece with lining covering the top and bottom while Rachel was looking through her side of the closet.

"Lillian, you won't believe what I just found." Rachel turned around holding up a blue half-shirt and matching mini-skirt with zippers going up the front and they looked like they were made of rubber.

I couldn't help but laugh. "That is hideous. What in the world is it for?"

Rachel went through my closet and found an identical one in purple. She held it up for me to see. "I don't know but I think we should dispose of them before Lex gets any ideas. We'll have to keep an eye on him, always playing tricks and joking around," she said, laughing lightly.

"Speaking of Lex, did he seem strange last night? Guilty even? Like he was hiding something?" I asked remembering my conversation with Lex earlier that morning.

Rachel finally found a black patent-leather bikini as she answered in mock indignation, "He should have felt guilty for waking us up. Our first night here and he doesn't even invite us to our own party! He probably just didn't want us stealing the limelight from him."

I just smiled, not pushing Rachel to understand my meaning, as we got our towels and made our way down the main stairway. We were walking down the stairs when Bradley Spencer, the superior butler, appeared below us.

"Bradley, how are you?" Rachel asked sarcastically.

"I am doing well. You're going for a swim I presume?" he asked in his haughty manner.

"Yes, we were just about to try to find the pool," I answered, ignoring his rude tone.

"The pool?" Bradley chuckled.

"What's so funny? You do have a pool, don't you?" Rachel raised her eyebrows.

"Yes. Well no. Not *a* pool. Mr. Cavanaugh has several pools on the property," Bradley boasted as if they were his.

Rachel and I looked at each other and smirked. Typical Lex, always over-doing everything. As if one pool weren't enough. I wouldn't have been surprised if one was completely filled with champagne to show off to all his mortal party friends. Anything to impress, that was Lex.

We followed Bradley to what he called the luncheon pool. He led us out a door off the right side of the house into an enormous screened-in area. The pool was not as large as an Olympic size swimming pool, but was definitely larger than an average sized one. It boasted an irregular shape, most likely to accommodate its most prominent feature, the reason it was referred to as the luncheon pool, there was a large rounded area on the right side with tables and seats in it. There were six brick red, round tables coming out of the water about a foot and a half and surrounding each table were five round seats of the same color just barely below the water. Leading to each table from the side of the pool were a double set of what looked like toy train tracks, only they were too wide for a toy train. Rachel and I dove in and swam for a bit before sitting at one of the tables.

"Tea?" Bradley asked, appearing again out of nowhere.

"Got anything stronger?" Rachel asked playfully.

"I'll see what I can come up with," he answered as if bored, but I could see him smirk a little. "Would you like a bit of lunch as well?"

We nodded. Bradley turned to go back into the house and then stopped, as if he had just remembered something he wanted to tell us.

"One thing I might warn you about, I don't know what Mr. Cavanaugh has explained to you, but you'll probably find his daily routine somewhat odd. He stays out all day and does not get home until after dark." He stopped and walked closer to the pool, lowering his voice, "No one ever sees him come or go. I think he has a secret passageway into his room because he's paranoid someone may try to follow him." Bradley composed his excited expression. "But I thought I might mention it so that you don't expect to see him during the day. He is a very busy man." With that he walked into the house.

When Bradley left the screened in pool to get our lunch we burst into laughter. He had no idea what Lex was! Rachel and I had assumed he knew, especially after he had bragged about being Lex's personal assistant who took care of all his strange demands. Bradley must have thought Lex was nothing more than your average, eccentric millionaire.

"Ray, that must be why he wasn't supposed to talk with us in the car," I said giggling.

"Good thing we didn't talk about Lex in front of him. Not that he would believe such a crazy thing anyway."

After ten minutes a middle aged man dressed in a white short-sleeved dress shirt and black dress pants emerged from the house carrying a tray of sandwiches and iced tea. I started to get off my seat to get the tray but the man put his hand up and shook his head.

"No need, Miss," the man said as he set the tray of tea and sandwiches in his hands onto a slightly larger tray connected to the train tracks in the pool. The man pushed a button on a remote he was holding and sent the tray on the tracks slowly but smoothly gliding to our table. "Mr. Cavanaugh came up with the idea himself. If you need anything else here's a remote. I'll leave it on the lounge chair. Just push the button marked kitchen and someone will be right out." He smiled kindly and went back into the house.

After eating we swam a bit more until we decided to relax and lay on the lounge chairs drinking the ice tea Bradley had sent out for us. We couldn't decide exactly what was in it, but it was definitely more than just iced tea. Although I can say in all the time I knew him he was never polite, Bradley was excellent at getting people what they wanted.

Rachel was about to take another drink of our special iced tea when she stopped, looking past the pool, and said loudly, "Hi, can we help you?"

I looked up to see a muscular looking young man with dark short-cropped hair, wearing khakis and a pale blue button-up shirt (with a few too many buttons undone) walking toward the screen door of the pool

28

enclosure. He didn't look like one of Lex's staff; almost all of them wore the same uniform. He seemed to have come from the gardens beyond the pool, but by the resolute way he walked toward us I thought he might have been some kind of solicitor that had gotten past the staff. He didn't answer Rachel right away but waited until he was standing in front of us.

"I'm a friend of Lex's. I was at the party last night," he looked at me, staring for an uncomfortable amount of time as if he recognized me from somewhere else, then he turned to Rachel and in a sickly sweet voice said, "By the way red silk is very becoming."

I'd rarely seen Rachel taken in by a corny pick-up line, but she was blushing from ear to ear. He was attractive to look at, but something about his demeanor completely turned me off of him. He made me think of an army guy when I looked at him, like a life-sized G.I. Joe; I don't know if it was the buzz-cut hair style or the way he stood so rigid, as if he'd been trained to, or the unnecessary amount of muscle he possessed, or the way he spoke so firmly, or the way he seemed to be absently grasping for a weapon at his waist that wasn't there. Maybe it was because he made me feel like we were doing battle by just having a conversation. He had seemed to be headed in our direction on purpose, yet he was just standing there saying nothing. I waited for him to explain what he was doing there, but he seemed to be struggling to not look at me and kept smiling uncomfortably at Rachel. Rachel too just kept smiling back at him, as if she had suddenly lost the ability to speak, even though she was usually the one doing most of the talking.

Finally, as no one was offering anything else I introduced myself, "I'm Lillian Thorne, this is Rachel Kane. And you are?"

"I'm sorry, how rude of me," he answered in an accent I couldn't quite place. There was a touch of an English accent, but it obviously covered up another accent; perhaps an original foreign language that he'd spoken as a child. He stated, "My name is Osborn Hune." He pronounced his last name as if it were spelled Hoon.

"Osborn," Rachel repeated as she played with her hair. "That's a very romantic name. What is that, English?"

Osborn shifted uncomfortably as if he realized he had been staring at me for too long again. He quickly turned to Rachel as he smiled and remarked, "I spent much of my childhood in England, but I've traveled extensively. It can be a very lonely life, traveling all the time, but I've learned much."

I rolled my eyes at Rachel, but she didn't notice. I pushed for more information, "So where are you living now?"

"Actually, I live here," he answered me seriously, before laughing lightly and giving Rachel another winning smile. "I travel most of the time, but Lex lets me stay here when I need a rest. I value his friendship and it always lifts my spirits to be here." Osborn glanced at his watch and stated regretfully, "Ah, I'm afraid I have to leave you. I have an appointment at eight-thirty, but it certainly was a pleasure."

He bent and took our hands one at a time kissing them in farewell, but lingered uncomfortably over my hand as if he were going to say something more. I watched him go feeling like we'd just taken place in a stage rehearsal for some play I didn't know we were in. He turned momentarily, holding a small square object in his hand. He looked down at it and then to me; giving me a look of complete hopelessness. He waved at Rachel as if he realized how uneasy he'd made me and decided instead to move on to Rachel. When I turned to joke with Rachel about Osborn's bizarre behavior and abrupt arrival and departure I could see her watching him go with a faint, secretive smile on her lips. I'd never seen her look at anyone like that, not even Lex, who I had always suspected she was in love with even more so than I was.

As connected as I had always felt to Lex, I had tried to keep a respectful distance on Rachel's account, but now seeing this reserved, contemplative Rachel, I wondered if she really had cared at all for Lex. Then again, Rachel always had a habit of showing exaggerated fondness to people she just wanted attention from. I don't mean it meanly, only that as someone that was used to being popular, Rachel had learned how to draw people to her, and one of those ways was to flirt and show affections that she might not really feel. It was very useful among the high school lot, and apparently it worked on vampires as well, because Lex took to Rachel almost as quickly as he claimed to have loved me. Perhaps, they were two of the same; beautiful people wanting to be loved by everyone.

As we watched Osborn walk further and further from our view, so did the sun slide further and further below the horizon. Within a few minutes of the sun dropping out of view I heard the French doors open behind me. Rachel turned around to see who had come out and smirked to herself.

"Lil, you'll never guess what he's wearing," Rachel said putting her hands over her eyes, obviously back to her normal self now that Osborn was gone.

I turned around to see Lex in a leopard print Speed-o with matching leopard print fuzzy slippers!

I had told him, unfortunately, about a dream I had about him wearing exactly that, but in the dream we'd been out in public. I suppose I should have been grateful he only wore it now, to amuse us.

He smiled with childish pride, turning in a circle with his arms out, and asked seriously, "So, what do you think? I look amazing, right?"

I laughed and scoffed, "You look like something all right. I don't know if amazing is the right word, though."

Lex ran and dove into the pool, purposely splashing us as he did. He then jumped back out, came over to where we were sitting, picked us up in turn and threw us into the pool. We played, and yes I mean played, in the pool for about half an hour. There were many times when Lex reminded me of a kid, and that was one of them, he loved goofing off and laughing, and of course wanted everyone to laugh along with him. He would toss us and chase us until we got caught up in the game laughing so hard we could barely swim.

While Rachel and I were wrapping ourselves in our towels Lex put his arms around us and said nonchalantly, "You had better hurry up, you two have to get ready for the party tonight."

Rachel and I looked at each other raising our eyebrows.

"Oh, you're inviting us to one of your parties?" Rachel asked in mock surprise.

Lex pretended to sound offended, "No, actually I'm inviting you to one of your parties. The council is coming to meet you two. It's kind of a coming home party and..." he paused then said quickly under his breath, "they need to approve both of you in order for you to stay."

"Wait, approve us?" Rachel interjected. "What does that mean?"

I hadn't really been paying attention to the last thing Lex had said.

My heart was pounding and I felt myself smiling. "So will Vann be there? He's on the council, right?"

Yes, I still had a crush on Vann. The first is always the hardest to get over.

Lex had been about to answer Rachel, but turned to me instead and asserted, almost jealously, "Why? Are you in love with him or something?"

Rachel cut in before I had to answer, "Don't change the subject! Why do we need to be approved?

Lex looked at his wrist as if he were wearing a watch, which he wasn't. "Oh, look at the time. You better hurry along, don't want to be late. You only get one chance to make a good first impression. I'll see you in the Grand Hall." As he spoke he had been inching closer to the door until he finally dashed inside leaving us with no answer.

Rachel grabbed my hand, pulling me after her, and said, "We better get dressed then. We don't want to be late for our judgment."

We ran straight to our room to get dressed. I sat on my bed watching Rachel pick out a shimmering black satin slip dress. As she was changing in the open closet she noticed I hadn't moved from the bed so she decided to pick something out for me.

"This will be perfect," Rachel said walking toward me with her prize.

She pulled me to my feet and yanked a crimson silk dress with a sweetheart neckline over my head, pulling my arms through the straps, and tugging it straight so that it caressed the tops of my feet. Rachel pulled me to the door of our dressing room where a mirror was hung so I could watch as she pulled my long strawberry-blonde hair up in a partial French twist letting some of the strands fall in long soft curls. I looked at myself, hoping Vann would notice me, hoping he would finally let his guard down and show some kind of affection. I thought I looked pretty with my glinting green eyes, perfectly rouged lips, and cascading curls. Rachel had wandered off only to return with a ruby necklace and earrings for me.

I finally broke the silence, "Do you think Vann will ever want me?" I was still studying myself in the mirror, my confidence faltering, my fears of not being good enough to be wanted coming back.

"If he doesn't then he is out of his mind and I think you should just forget about him. I can't believe how beautiful you look, Lil. I mean not that you don't always, but that dress is just perfect for you. You look like an old-time movie star. If Giovanni doesn't fall at your feet then he must be blind." Rachel leaned her head against my neck looking at me in the mirror. "We've got to get approved by the council and you're worried about Giovanni!" Rachel squeezed me playfully.

I turned around and hugged her. "I know, Ray, I'm being silly. I wish I could be more like you, everyone loves you, and you're not afraid of anything. I'm glad you came with me. I don't feel so afraid with you here. I don't think I could face the council on my own."

I tugged on a pair of black suede heels and had just done up the ankle straps as Rachel grabbed my hand and pulled me toward the main stairway. Lex stood at the bottom waiting for us, his arms extended as if he meant for us to jump into them. Lex gave us each an arm and led us to the banquet hall.

The hall was massive, with high barrel-vaulted ceilings of gold, and walls of deep burgundy. Two ornate fireplaces were situated along one wall with what I assumed were alabaster statues on either side of them. The walls were covered with dark landscapes and mirrors trapped within gold frames. Lastly, my eyes fell upon the enormous banquet table, though the hall could have held a much larger table, the elegant linen covered table looked to easily seat sixteen. The copious crystal chandelier hovering over the table illuminated the red and gold place settings, and easily lit the remainder of the hall which was made up of leather arm chairs and sideboard tables. Lex gestured for us to stand just off to the right of the door. Obviously, to allow the council to greet us as they entered the room.

Lex looked at me for a moment and I heard his concentrated thoughts, *You look absolutely glorious, little queen.*

I glanced at him and quickly looked down, smiling to myself. I had never really allowed myself to be completely taken in by Lex, because as I mentioned before I had thought Rachel had feelings for him, but now that I saw her indifference toward him I felt a kind of giddy nervousness from his attention. I felt my cheeks flush at his comment, and hoped he hadn't noticed as he left the room.

Almost immediately after he left the room the doorbell rang. Lex came back in standing at the door introducing everyone as they came in, "The council is here. These are our council elders Malika and Tor. They are among the oldest of our kind."

The man and woman, both of whom looked as if they were of middle-eastern descent, walked in regally, smiling politely at Rachel, but as they passed me Malika paused.

She reached her hand out as if she were going to touch my cheek and whispered, "It can't be. You look-" she stopped and turned to Lex, sharing a troubled look with him, before she bit her lip and smiled warmly. "You look lovely," she corrected herself before taking her seat alongside Tor at the head of the other end of the table.

Lex continued introducing, "Council members: Kara, Una, Turin, Matthew, Sylvia, Glen."

All nodded politely as they entered, excepting the tall blonde Sylvia, she patted my cheek, smiling and exclaimed, "You are being very pretty."

Lex went on as if bored, "I believe you already know Giovanni, and of course Mason, and this is Demetrius."

Demetrius seemed to scowl at us for a moment and then must have realized by the look on my face what he'd been doing and switched to a greasy smile. "So this is what I have given up my night for. There seems to be quite a lot of fuss over you my dear," he stated darkly.

I immediately decided I didn't like him. He reminded me of a traveling gypsy, the kind you heard about in stories that went from place to place selling people turpentine as a remedy for a cough, and always snaking their way out of difficult situations. Perhaps that was a better comparison, calling him a snake, he certainly seemed to slither past and strike with his forked tongue.

Rachel and I were seated on either side of Lex at the opposite end of the table from Malika and Tor. As soon as everyone was seated Lex ordered the food and wine be brought out. I wondered if they always put on such a show for Lex's staff, having plates of food and bottles of wine placed on the table that no one would eat or drink. In addition to all that,

Lex had some special, unmarked bottles placed on the table as well and he even went around the table pouring out the thick red liquid from these into everyone's glasses.

I picked up my wine glass filled with the thick substance and looked dismayed at Lex. "This isn't what I think it is?"

Lex took Rachel's glass just as she was lifting it to her lips, and then mine, replacing them with clean glasses and pointing to an open bottle of red wine in front of us. He finally stood to address his company. Everyone followed his lead and stood. He raised his glass to Rachel and me, and again everyone followed. So far so good.

"You were going to let us drink that weren't you?" Rachel whispered nodding to Lex's glass.

He shook his head playfully and winked reassuringly. "I would like to make a toast. To Lillian and Rachel, I hope you will all come to accept and love them as I have. The circumstances of our meeting were out of the ordinary, just as our friendship has been, but I can honestly say they have proven remarkably at ease around our kind." Then he turned slightly to Rachel, then to me, raising his glass. "I cannot express how happy I am that my girls are finally home, where they should be...and safe."

"Safe?" Demetrius ticked with his slippery tongue. "Is this one of your new projects, Lex? Bringing young girls whom you think are in mortal danger to live among us? We shall be overrun with these unfortunate beauties, if you're given leave to do so." Demetrius laughed sarcastically, causing Una and Kara to snicker as well. "We'll have to find a new safe-house for the council to meet at to accommodate all your *charming* refugees."

Lex was fuming, but said nothing. He and Malika exchanged a strange look as if Lex were asking permission to defend himself to Demetrius.

Instead Malika cleared her throat, and looked pointedly at Demetrius reminding him, "You forget, Demetrius, you do not speak for the council, I do." Then turning to us she continued, "To Lillian and Rachel, the council welcomes you and hopes to enjoy more of your company."

Everyone raised their glasses to us and drank, then sat without any other comments. I thought it was rather a good sign that no one had demanded we be thrown out immediately, even considering Demetrius's comments. Plus, Malika had given me a compliment and welcomed us on behalf of the council, that had to count for something. All in all I felt pretty secure in the idea that the council would ultimately accept us, and allow us to stay with Lex, even if the gypsy, Demetrius, found our presence ridiculous.

I finally let my eyes shift over to Vann. His eyes immediately met mine with the old curiosity in them. I told Rachel I wanted to talk to Vann, to which she merely rolled her eyes and smiled sheepishly in reply. I got up and whispered in Vann's ear telling him to follow me. I went to a side courtyard just down the hall from the council's banquet hall to wait for him. A few minutes later Vann came out and sat on the bench across from me. His eyes were evasive. He seemed filled with immense displeasure.

I leaned toward him affectionately asking, "Vann, aren't you glad to see me at all?"

"Yes...and no. Lillian, you know I care for you. I cared for you the moment I saw you in that bar, but you should not have come here. You have so much of your life to live, why would you waste it with the dead?" Vann stopped, imploring me with his eyes.

"Vann, you're not dead. You're vampires, not zombies. All of you are more alive for me than any other creature on earth. You try so hard to convince me that you're evil or damned, but I know you don't want anyone or anything to feel pain. The one thing I was most happy about when I got here was that I would see you. Am I a fool to be so in love with you?" I moved to sit beside him, though, I was so nervous to even be saying what I was saying to him.

He didn't turn to look at me. Instead he stared at the ground, his hands dangling between his knees. "You are a fool, uccellino. You think this is some kind of game. You heard Demetrius; it makes no sense allowing mortals to live among us. We are murderers. We feed on your kind. What makes you think none of us would feed on you?"

I was horrified. I looked at him wide eyed, my mouth quivering for words. "Vann, you don't mean that you would..."

His eyes met my unbelieving gaze. "No, Lillian, I would not drink from you, but you are molto semplice, very simple, to think Lex brought you here for your *mortal* company. He has plans for you, whether you like it or not. It seems he has always had plans for you."

I shook my head. "I don't understand. What do you mean?" I stopped as I repeated his words in my head. *Mortal company. Of course.* "Lex means to turn us?"

Vann nodded his head. "Si, he wishes to give you The Immortal Fate. Haven't you seen the room beneath your own? The segreta passage through your dressing rooms?"

I thought a moment. "We found the passage, but we didn't go down. It was too dark."

"I'll tell you, uccellino. There is a room beneath your own with two coffins. Can you guess who the coffins are for? Can you guess why Lex wanted the council to meet you and Rachel? Or why he waited three years to bring you here? Three years to live your lives, because sixteen is too young to be turned. It's against our regolamento. You must be at least eighteen to be turned. His beloved darlings," he said with disdain.

I looked at him letting a few tears drop easily from my eyes. "If you care for me why don't you want to be with me? Don't you see?" I thought about what immortality could mean for me, even though I hadn't honestly considered it ever even being offered to me. "We could be together forever. You won't have to see me die and I won't have to part with those I love."

Vann took my hands in his, and moved so close to look in my eyes that I could feel his breath on my mouth. "Lillian, I would rather kill you with my own hands than see you immortale," he said as if it were an oath he would not break.

I felt my very world tumble at his wretched words. I loved him and he would rather see me dead than live forever. I had waited all this time thinking that one day Vann would want me. That he would want me forever. Instead of finally professing his love, Vann told me he'd rather see me dead.

Not exactly an encouraging courtship for a nineteen year old girl, and yes, I know my love for Vann at the time was childish and over-dramatic. Looking back on that time I can't understand why I was so determined for Vann to be passionately in love with me. He'd never given me any indication that he could feel that way for anyone, let alone me, but it was the first time I'd ever felt so strongly for a man and I had clung desperately to that feeling. It certainly wasn't the end of the world to have my heart broken for the first time, but when you're a teenager so many things *feel* like the end of the world.

Must be something to do with the hormones.

I tried to make myself hate Vann, perhaps to say something to him that would hurt him as much as he was hurting me, but at that moment Rachel and Mason walked into the courtyard. Vann and I were still holding hands. They saw the two of us looking straight into each other's eyes, but they didn't see the tears flowing down my face. They didn't see the anger building in my eyes, anger at myself for letting myself believe something so foolish, or the complete despair consuming me that I was once again not wanted.

Rachel smirked and pulled Mason toward us. "What were you two doing?"

I looked away from Vann wiping my tears. "Nothing," I answered simply.

"Uh, huh. So, Vann what were you two doing?" Rachel asked teasingly.

"It's none of your business! Why don't you leave me alone! You're always trying to fix me! Trying to make me more like you! I'm not you, Rachel, I can't charm men to fall in love with me, and then laugh about how I don't love them back. I have a heart! And mine doesn't work that way!" I screamed at Rachel.

Vann looked up at me, his amber eyes flooded with tears. It suddenly angered me that he was upset. That he had said such awful things to me and *he* was crying. I gave him one last loathsome glance and ran to my room.

I went straight to my dressing room, pushed the sixteen pointed sun symbol on the mirror, and pulled open the door that popped out. I found a light switch after a few minutes. It lighted fixtures along the curving stairway. I walked down the stairway that seemed coiled about a thick column until it combined with another set of stairs, which I assumed were from the other dressing room, producing a colossal staircase. The room at the bottom of the stairs was pitch black. I felt along the walls for some time before finding a switch to illuminate the grandiose chandelier in the center of the room.

I was taken back when the light came on. The room looked exactly like our room above, only there was a bar where the balcony should have been, and instead of beds there were two glistening gold coffins with purple velvet lining.

Gold coffins? Isn't that strange…and yet familiar. I thought I had heard of something like that before. Hadn't Ben once said something about a gold coffin? That didn't make sense, why would Ben talk about coffins at all with a child.

I felt my mind was trying to tell me something, but more important was the idea that Lex wanted to make us vampires and never even discussed it with us. He had plans for us, and we had no idea what exactly those plans were. I ran back upstairs and started packing a suitcase.

Rachel came in quietly and sat on her bed, watching me.

"What are you doing?" she asked softly.

"Packing. I have to leave. Why didn't he tell us any of this? And what else is he hiding?!" I was angry and not really thinking straight. I stopped and looked at the suitcase full of clothes. "Oh, this is silly."

"Exactly, there's no reason to leave. We can figure this out together," Rachel assured me.

I looked at her irritatedly, explaining, "No, I shouldn't be packing. None of this stuff is mine." I turned and walked out of the room.

I began running for the stairs when I heard the click of Rachel's heels behind me. As I was swiftly approaching the banister I turned, not breaking my fast stride, to tell Rachel to stop following me. When I turned around I saw her running toward me, much closer than I'd thought she was, a startled look on her face. She tripped somewhat trying to stop, hurdling right into me, and knocking me over the banister. I grabbed onto the bars as I flipped over the banister. I looked down at what seemed like a long drop, about thirty feet or so. Certainly worthy of a few broken bones or if I fell just right a broken neck. I looked up as Rachel lent over the railing.

"Oh, my God, Lil, grab my hand!" Rachel demanded extending her hand.

I took too long to consider how Rachel was going to pull me up and my fingers slipped from the banister sending me plummeting below. Fortunately, the council happened to be standing almost directly below me. They caught me easily, as if I were a feather floating down above their heads, and put me on my feet.

The tall blonde Sylvia laughed lightly and playfully scolded in a thick accent, "You are being not so careful, you know you are not vampire yet?" With that she poked my nose with her pointer finger as if I were a silly little child.

I didn't say a word, though my heart was beating wildly and I desperately wanted to cry. I walked calmly toward the banquet hall when Lex came storming out toward me. He stopped right in front of me and grabbed me by the neck, lifting me off my feet.

"Are you mad?! Are you out of your mind?! What were you thinking?!" he screamed right before throwing me across the room. "Were you trying to kill yourself?!"

Mason half caught me before I completely hit the floor and helped steady me to my feet.

"Yes, from a second floor banister I was trying to kill myself!" I said as I walked angrily toward Lex. I stopped to look him in the face. "Although I don't have to try to kill myself. You could do it for me. Or did you have something else in mind that you haven't told us?!"

Lex pursed his lips in guilt and muttered, "I swore I would keep you safe."

"Alexander!" Malika said warningly, shaking her head at Lex.

For a moment I was reminded of the first time I'd seen Lex. How he had made me think of my uncle Ben. How he had somehow been there to rescue me when I'd needed him. I shook off the feeling and ran past Lex, and past Vann as he came up behind Lex. I started up the stairs to go back to my room.

"What did you do to her?" I heard Vann ask.

"I didn't do a damn thing. You're so wonderful with her why don't you go ask her why she just tried to kill herself!" Lex sneered walking out of the room.

When I entered my room I saw Mason, the vampire Vann had turned forty years ago, sitting on my bed. He must have retreated to my room as I argued with Lex. Mason still retained the youthful expressions of a nineteen year old, which was the age he had been when he was turned. His black hair fell back from his dark eyes when he looked up at me. I slammed the door behind me, locking it hurriedly, as if that would keep out a vampire. Mason unclasped his hands from between his knees and sat up straight.

I stood in front of him, my eyes blurring with tears, and said, "I don't know what I'm doing."

He got up without a word and put his solid lengthy arms around me. He then led me to the bed and pulled me to sit beside him.

He held my left hand in his, studying it with curiosity. Finally, he answered me in his southern drawl, "Lillian, ya know I'd do anythin' for ya. Whatta ya want me ta do?" He didn't look up. Just continued playing with my hand.

"Will you stay here with me tonight? Make sure no one comes in? I'm just angry...and scared. Everything is so confusing and I feel like my brain is trying to remember something important, but I just can't reach it. Little bits of memory keep popping up, and I just don't understand what it all means. Please, will you stay?" I looked at him desperately.

He finally turned his head toward me and kissed my hand as he said simply, "'Course, sugar, I'll stay."

I then told him everything that had happened, the strange feelings of déjà vu I was experiencing, and he told me what he thought. I was beginning to doze off to the sound of his thick accented voice when Rachel knocked on the door. Mason looked at me with eyebrows raised.

"Oh, let Ray in, of course. I was so horrible to her," I said.

Rachel didn't yell at me or even glare at me, admittedly I would have deserved it for the way I'd treated her that night, instead she rushed to me and hugged me tightly.

"Are you okay? What is going on?" she asked, concern in her eyes.

I explained to Rachel what I had already told Mason, about Vann's hurtful words, that Lex was hiding things, and how I was starting to remember little pieces from my childhood that I hadn't before. I wasn't sure if it was connected, but it felt like it was. Rachel held my hand while I rambled and I was yet again thankful that I, at least, had her there with me. Rachel fell asleep soon after I'd finished telling her everything, obviously exhausted by the day's dramas, and Mason again promised he would stay the whole night to watch over us. I don't even know what time I finally fell asleep. I stayed up, agitated, and unable to slip easily into a calm enough state to close my eyes. So instead I wrote...

> *Look down*
>
> *Hang your head*
>
> *You've no reason to be happy*
>
> *Misery is your constant companion*

When I did finally drift off to sleep it wasn't for long. Perhaps less than two hours later I was startled awake.

"Damn, I'm a' be in trouble. I can' let ya in, I promised I wouldn'." Mason was staring at the balcony.

I followed his gaze to see Vann knocking on the balcony doors, and I could hear Lex pleading with Mason to open the door to our room. I went back to sleep but was awakened a half-hour later by loud bickering.

"It's your fault she tried to kill herself!"

"Oh, I'm sure it had nothing to do with the little talk you had with her in the garden!"

I looked down at the foot of my bed and could see Vann and Lex barely a foot away from each other arguing. I wanted to pull the covers over my head and ignore them, but they were becoming increasingly louder as they blamed the other for causing my bizarre behavior, and I knew if I didn't intervene they would most likely get physical. I leaped to my feet, still in my bed, and jumped between them.

"Get out of my room. If you want to fight about me do it

somewhere else. Rachel and I are trying to get some sleep. You know, like normal human beings!" I shouted toward Lex, suddenly angry. "I guess that's not what you want us to be," I added lowly, more to myself, but I knew they heard me.

Lex had this look on his face like he had just realized this was entirely his fault. "Lilly, little queen, don't be like this. Don't you want…"

"Just get out. I'm so tired and you are driving me crazy. I don't know how much more of this I can take. Get out, please," I stated almost in tears again, pointing to the door.

Lex looked at me with worry, biting his lip, but nodded and followed Vann, who had just hung his head, out of the room. I lay back in my bed, staring at the ceiling, confused about my feelings. I wasn't sure how I felt about becoming a vampire, especially when someone was already planning it without asking me what I wanted. I was also having these strange memories from my childhood, including memories of Lex. It didn't seem likely, though, that I'd met Lex when I was a child, he would have told me. Wouldn't he? I wasn't sure I could even trust the images that were popping into my head. Maybe I had been right to tell Lex he was driving me crazy; maybe I had made a mistake allowing myself to become part of this world, and now it was taking its toll on my sanity.

Then there was Vann. All these romantic ideas I'd imagined for us seemed so childish now. I couldn't even think why I had been so enthralled by him, except that being shy myself I must have been drawn to his dark, mysterious quietness. I had let my naïve romanticism create an idea of who Vann really was, if I could just get through to him, but it was all make-believe. He wasn't some dashing, romantic, misunderstood man secretly wanting to be loved; he was just himself, quiet, moody, thoughtful, but detached. Why had I let myself fall so foolishly in love with someone that just saw me as some kid to protect? I thought Rachel and I had always been quite mature for our ages. We'd always felt more comfortable being around adults than with those our own age, but I didn't feel so mature since we'd arrived. I knew living a life surrounded by vampires had obviously warped our sense of reality a bit and certainly being a teenage girl did not help matters, but I was beginning to feel like nothing more than a silly little girl.

∞**4**∞

I woke up the next day dreading the wretched light pouring in the windows. Yes, I used the word wretched again. Seriously, if you have never read *Frankenstein*, read it and then tell me if you think Mary Shelley wasn't just a bit obsessed with the word. I am still amazed her novel wasn't titled something more like *The Wretched Creature*. Admittedly it is a fun word to use, but I digress...

So...the wretched light was pouring in the windows. I turned over trying to avert the rays when I noticed an envelope with my name on it leaning against the vase on the table. I pulled myself from the bed and ripped open the envelope. The letter inside read:

Dearest Lillian,

I stayed as long as the sun would allow.

I know you understand. I'm sorry Giovanni

and Lex woke you; I did try to keep them out,

but they are much stronger than I am, and I

do owe my life to Giovanni. We will be coming

back tonight. Giovanni wants to talk with you.

Don't worry, everything will be fine. You know

that we love you and that is what is most

important. I know you're strong enough to

handle this little squabble. This will be over

soon. Stay strong, sugar.

Your servant,

Mason

I felt a little relieved to know someone was on my side, besides Rachel that is. I wanted to wake Rachel to tell her that Mason had said everything would be all right. I looked over and saw that a letter had been left on her table as well. Out of the corner of my eye I noticed Rachel was staring at me. I showed her my letter and urged her to open hers. It took for me to actually get the letter and place it in Rachel's hands, as she was still lying in bed rubbing her eyes. She reluctantly opened the letter with a great huff and read it. She didn't smile but sat up a little in bed as she read. I asked her to read it out loud.

"No, it's not important. Just the same as yours," she said.

"Ooooh, What does it say?" I said teasingly, not understanding why she wouldn't share the contents of the note. I grabbed the note from her hands without warning and plopped in my bed, facing her.

"Lil, don't read it," Rachel said without making a move toward me.

I started reading aloud, "Dear Rachel, I just want you to know that Lex and Giovanni are furious at each other over this Lillian thing. Lex is jealous of Lillian's feelings for Giovanni and upset that she nearly hurt herself, and Giovanni thinks Lex is just using Lillian for some selfish purpose. Lillian seems a little edgy. She told me a few things last night that seemed to border on paranoia. From what Giovanni told me she was really emotional about what he had said to her, granted he could have said it gentler. I know she said it was just an accident falling over the banister, but we're worried she may actually want to hurt herself. Please watch her. This is one of the reasons Giovanni is so worried about you two being here. Living among vampires can drive mortals insane or in the least influence their rational thinking. Giovanni and I are coming tonight to speak with the council. Certain council members weren't exactly impressed with last night's show. Not surprisingly most of the complaints originated with Demetrius. Until we get there don't let Lillian alone. Or with Lex for that matter. Giovanni is very suspicious of him and what he might do."

I threw the note down, hurt that Mason couldn't tell me what he really thought, and feeling foolish for actually believing things would be okay. When ever had my life been okay? Things always went wrong;

people always seemed to find reasons to not want me around. I thought I had found a place where I belonged, where I would be accepted. Instead, after only two days, I had proved myself to be an outcast amongst outcasts.

"Lillian, don't be mad. He just doesn't want you to get hurt. He's worried about you."

"He could have told me himself!" I screamed, as I ran out of the room and to the main stairway.

Bradley was waiting at the bottom of the stairs as I was running down.

"Pleased to see you using the stairs this evening, Miss. Is there anything I can help you with?" he asked.

"No," I said, quickly walking past him. Then I stopped, fury pulsing through me, and instead decided, "As a matter of fact you can help me. Do you know where Lex's bedroom is?"

"Yes, Miss, but like I said he isn't home during the day so…"

"Just show me," I sighed. "Please."

Bradley reluctantly led me down a hall just off to the left of the front door. There were so many turns I wasn't sure I would be able to remember my way back. I suppose it made sense for Lex's bedroom to be somewhat difficult to find. It would be almost impossible to just stumble upon it, just by the sheer number of turns you had to make, but once we actually reached the door I still didn't even see it. Bradley pointed to a dead end.

"That's the door to his room at the end of the hall. But as I already told you he isn't home and the room is always locked."

I looked at Bradley trying to decide if he was testing my sanity by pointing to a plain wall and calling it a door. He huffed impatiently and stomped over to the area of the wall he'd indicated, pointing at it again, but I still could not see it.

Bradley pointed to a piece of molding above the wainscoting on the wall. "It's a concealed door," he stated in annoyance, as if I should have known that. "There is a release handle hidden just below the molding here, which causes the door to pop outward. That is, if it weren't locked as it always is during the day."

"Oh...ummm...thank you," I answered distractedly as I waved Bradley away to examine the handle myself.

When I was sure Bradley was out of sight I squeezed the release handle with as much force as I could muster and pulled as hard as I could. The door didn't budge. I tried again, pulling with my whole body, and getting myself so angry that I actually pounded on the wall in frustration.

Then I heard Lex's voice in my mind like a lightning bolt, *What the hell do you think you're doing?!*

The pain in my head from his concentrated thoughts was excruciating, and it scared me. I sprinted out of the corridor. After about seven wrong turns, my panic rising, I finally found my way out and into the Grand Hall. I ran up the stairs to my room and threw open the door. Rachel was sitting on the bed, her hands folded impatiently in her lap.

"Lillian…" Rachel began.

I walked right past her. "Ask me later," I said opening the closet door.

I went to my dressing room, pushed the golden sun symbol at the head of the mirror, and pulled the mirror out when it popped open. I found the light switch, swiftly engulfing the entire room in crystalline light. I went straight to the bar, trying to ignore the conspicuous presence of the coffins. I was searching for something to wash away my fear. Rachel appeared at the base of the stairs looking in awe and surprise at the room.

Burgundy. I had always liked the sound of that. No idea what it tasted like, but into the glass it went.

"Lil, I think I'll wait upstairs for you," Rachel stammered seeing the coffins.

I continued pouring the alcohol into the glass and gulping down the smooth but full bodied wine. After greedily washing down four glasses of the burgundy I felt lightheaded enough to think about things, or at least I felt better equipped to think about the things I had to think about. I went back upstairs where Rachel was waiting for me. She looked at me questioningly, but the question she asked caught me off guard. Maybe the wine had more to do with that than her actually asking an unexpected question.

"What...did...you...do?"

I knew what she meant but I tried to evade the question. "I went and had an enlightening little drink. Though, I'm not sure if enlightenment agrees with me," I added feeling a little more tipsy than I had just moments earlier.

"Lil, I heard you ask Bradley to show you to Lex's room." Her face was twisted with worry. "You know their rules. If he tells the council, they could...they could," she couldn't say it, she just shook her head.

I knew what she was getting at. A vampire's safe-room, the place a vampire slept during daylight hours, was considered a sacred place. A place too important to be violated or treated with disrespect, and usually its location would not even be shared with other vampires. For a mortal to intrude upon such a place...well, let's just say they don't just slap your hand and tell you not to go there again.

I looked at her seriously, or as seriously as I could manage in my current state. "Yeah, I went to his room. I don't know what I meant to do. Maybe if I had gotten in I would have left him a nasty note or wrecked something, but I couldn't even get in so it doesn't matter," I slurred involuntarily. "But I have to leave. He knows what I did. I heard him. He knows I tried to get into his room and I know what he'll think. I have to leave," I lamented, not sure where I would even go.

"What were you thinking? Really, Lillian, what would you have done if you'd found him...sleeping?" Rachel asked, eyes wide in accusation.

I shook my head, my eyes tearing up, and in an almost offended tone I stated, "I would never hurt him. I was just angry, Ray, I wanted to make him as angry as I felt, but I would never hurt him. I love him too much," I admitted somberly, adding, "no matter what he does to me."

At that moment there was a knock on the door. I felt my head slowly register the thought to look out the window. I turned and saw the sky without a trace of any glow of sunlight. No hue of light or even wisp of gray.

It was night.

"Damn it!" I exclaimed, looking pleadingly at Rachel for what I should do.

I could see Rachel was scared herself. She simply shook her head at a loss and turned her shaky gaze toward the door. Lex walked in a moment later, strutting in like a king about to send a peasant to the dungeon, or in my case more likely the gallows.

"What were you thinking?" he asked slowly, authoritatively. "Do you know what you've done? What I must hide from the council, lest they punish you?" He grabbed my arm somewhat roughly and demanded, "Why are you doing this to me?"

My head was swimming with the alcohol I wasn't used to drinking. I pushed Lex away; he didn't fight me, but let me shove him angrily before I pushed past him without a word. I ran down the stairs knowing full well that Lex would follow and was much faster than I, if he wanted to be, but I hoped Rachel would at least try to distract him and give me a small head start. I still had no plan. Where was I going to go, how would I even get there? Then Bradley appeared at the bottom of the stairs.

"Where are you going, Miss?" Bradley asked in his superior manner.

"Away. Anywhere." I heard Lex coming so I said the first thing that came into my drunken mind. "I need car keys. Lex wants me to run an errand for him. Quickly!"

Bradley opened a closet by the front door within which was a locked safe. He slipped a small key from his collection on his belt into the lock and produced a set of keys for me. Either he had no idea what was going on or he really didn't care, but whichever it was he handed the keys to me without question.

I ran out the front door and realized I had to go back.

"Bradley, What car?!" I asked jingling the keys in midair.

"Mr. Cavanaugh's black Porsche," he said as if I bored him terribly.

Though I was scared out of my mind I did smile a little at the thought of driving a Porsche. Hey, I was a teenager and had only driven enough to pass my driver's test; the idea of driving a ridiculously expensive and fast car was too exciting for my teenage brain to ignore. I ran back out the door, jumped in the car, and shifted into reverse as fast as I could get it started. At the same moment that I floored the gas pedal Lex jumped behind the car. I felt the weight of his body as I hit him and I slammed on the breaks. I shifted into first and fishtailed, but was able to maintain control enough to not stall. I barely knew how to drive, let alone drive manual, but I'm sure you guessed that already.

I knew Lex would be all right, but I was worried I had hurt him so as I was driving away I looked back. I was struggling to see out the tiny rear window when a Range Rover came thundering into the driveway. Suddenly the car was stopped without me hitting the brakes. Glass was everywhere. Lex ran to the Porsche as Vann and Mason got out of the SUV.

"Get her out of there!" I heard Vann yell.

My getaway was not as brilliant as I had imagined it would be when my drunken mind had heard the word Porsche. Someone dragged me out of the rubble and laid me on the ground. Rachel came running out of the house and I could hear her screaming and raving, but Bradley grabbed her to stop her.

"Miss, you don't want see. It will only upset you more," Bradley was explaining almost tenderly to Rachel.

She was still screaming and punching at him to let her go. Finally she kneed him between the legs. I know that not because I saw it, I was quite incapacitated on the hard, rock strewn driveway, but because at the same moment I heard every man, yes they were vampire men, exclaim in the middle of all that was happening *Ow, that's got to hurt!*

"Sorry, Bradley!" Rachel screamed as she ran toward the car. She stopped short just before trampling my foot. "Oh, my God. She has to go to the hospital!"

Mason was crying, begging for someone to do something; I started throwing up. I got up and scrambled to the other side of the car so they couldn't see me; even in my dazed inebriation I was embarrassed to have everyone watching me get sick.

"Look! She's spitting up a lot of blood." Rachel looked harshly at them. "Do something!"

Instead of correcting everyone about how severe my injuries were, which really amounted to a few scratches, I moved back within view and held my breath. When everyone looked at me, seeming confused about why I was still walking around, I swallowed over dramatically. Don't wince, I didn't actually have anything in my mouth, I was just putting on a show for all the vampires who had seemed to forget that I'd just been in a pretty serious accident and were still arguing amongst themselves.

"Is that better?" I asked stumbling past them, toward the house. Then I yelled back, "Bradley, pick up my clothes!" I then flung my dress, which was splattered with dirt, blood, and the burgundy (not blood) that I had just thrown up. I walked back to the house wearing only my red lacy undergarments and my black suede heels. Bradley followed me into the house carrying my ruined dress just as I had instructed.

"Show me to Lex's room again," I ordered.

"I don't know if I…"

I scowled at him. "You'll show me to his room and you'll do it now!"

"Yes, Miss," he spat.

Bradley walked in front of me leading the way to Lex's room. When there were only a few more turns left he turned around to look at me as if he had just realized something.

"Miss, I think you should put some clothes on so…" He stopped, looked me up and down, and smiled. "So I don't do something you wouldn't want me to."

"Oh, how sweet of you, trying to make me feel like a helpless woman," I cooed dramatically and then pushed Bradley up against the wall, losing my usual timidity for the moment. "We both know you don't have an ounce of nerve in your body, so cut the crap and move your sniveling excuse for manhood down the hall! I don't think you quite understand that I am not in my right mind today! So get your ass moving before I do something to *you* that you don't want *me* to!"

"Yes, Miss," he said stuttering and pulling away from the wall.

We turned down a few more halls until finally I recognized where we were. I put my hand under the molding on the wall finding the catch and squeezed the handle. A section of the wall popped out slightly and I pulled it open wide to find a regular door behind it. I tried the knob and the door opened. Obviously Lex had been in too much of a rush to confront me to remember to lock either door. Before I entered I grabbed Bradley by the collar seeing he was trying to slip away unnoticed.

"You don't know where I am. Got it?" I turned him loose.

"Yes, Miss, I haven't seen you," he said as he ran down the hall.

I went into the room knocking pictures and vases onto the floor. "He doesn't even use these," I said ripping the sheets off the bed and throwing them out the window.

I went to Lex's massive walk-in closet, knowing his need for beautiful things I took an armful of obviously expensive clothing, and threw them out the window as well. On my way to get another handful of clothing I picked up a small framed picture of myself and threw it against the far wall as Lex walked in.

He grabbed me by the wrists. "Lillian, what are you doing?"

"I'm punishing you," I admitted, trying not to let tears form. "And I'm looking for…something."

"I've done nothing to you. Why would you want to punish me? Anyway, whatever you're looking for you won't find here," he stated too quickly.

I shook loose of his hold. "How do you know? You don't even know what I'm looking for. Maybe I'm looking for something you stole from me," *like my life*, "or…maybe I'm looking for something else."

"Lilly, I don't have anything of yours!"

"You know what I'm looking for so why don't you just tell me where it is." *I know your coffin is here somewhere.*

"No!" He scrunched his eyebrows as a disobedient child might.

I smiled triumphantly as I realized that, though Lex was far stronger and could inflict terrible pain easily on me, he was held back by some force stronger than himself. I realized looking at his helpless demeanor, that though his physical strength far outweighed mine, the emotional power I had over him was far stronger and it paralyzed him. If I hadn't still been tipsy I don't think I would have thought such a thing, my confidence did not allow me to believe that I held such power over anyone.

Knowing the power I held over him I taunted playfully, "Well then I'll have to find it myself. Or did you want this to be a game? I know how much you like games. Is it under the bed?"

"No! There is nothing under there," he said frantically.

I tried pushing the bed but it was unmovable.

Lex watched me without trying to stop me, but pleaded again, "There is nothing under there."

"Help me move it then. It would be a lot more fun if you helped." I went on pushing at the bed unsuccessfully, though even if I were to find his coffin I'm not sure what I would have done. At that point I was just exhilarated to be making Lex nervous.

Lex finally grabbed my wrists, roughly, but instead let go and pulled me close, whispering in my ear, "Why are you doing this? I love you too much to hurt you."

I caught that faint familiar scent of strawberry coming from him as I admitted, "I know." I looked at him, pretending to be caught in the moment, and said, "And I love you too much to throw all of your clothes out of the window."

Lex's eyes shot wide. "My clothes?!" he screamed as he ran to the window.

I took the opportunity to move swiftly out of the room and back to the Grand Hall, navigating the many turns much better this time. I saw Vann entering through the front door as I started walking up the main stairs.

"What did you say to Bradley?" he asked plainly.

I turned on the stairs, holding the banister for support. "Why?"

Vann looked down and smiled sheepishly. "He ran out of the house screaming, and he says that he quits."

I laughed to myself, not believing that I actually scared someone. "I threatened to skin him alive," I said jokingly.

I went to my room and noticed Mason was there once again, waiting silently for me, sitting on Rachel's bed. I sat on my bed turned towards him. He looked at me for a moment then went to my closet. He came back with a delicate white dress with yellow flowers on it. He pulled me to my feet, without a word, and slipped the dress over my head. Yes, with red undergarments on he put a flimsy white dress on me;

obviously he did not know much about woman's fashion, but I was too sluggish from the emotional and physical exertion I'd just endured to point this out to him.

"They'll be arriving soon, sugar," Mason said softly as he took my hand and led me downstairs.

Lex came out of the banquet hall leaving the doors open enough for me to see the council was already there. Lex stood in front of me, turned to Mason, and told him harshly to get me cleaned up. I guess he was a little upset about half his wardrobe being tossed onto the lawn. Mason just nodded his head and took me to the bathroom. He closed the door, turned the water on in the sink, and got a washcloth. He placed me in front of the mirror so I could see the dirt and blood from all the little scratches on my face and bare arms. Not to mention my impossibly snarled hair. After washing my face and brushing my hair Mason pricked his own finger with his teeth and began applying small dabs of his own blood to my wounds, causing them to heal within minutes, and wiped my face clean again. He then began putting lipstick on me.

"I can do that. I'm not incompetent," I said softly.

Mason pushed back his hair from his forehead. "Is alrigh'. I like takin' care of ya, sugar. Anyways ya had quite a full day as is, let me do what I can."

I looked at my reflection, held for a moment in those green eyes that were so like my dead uncle's, and I couldn't help wishing, yet again, that he could somehow help me. I felt so confused about things. I was starting to remember all these things that I didn't want to be true, because if they were the person that had ruined my life was the same person that I had thought was my rescuer. I wished Ben's ghost would just appear and explain everything to me before I did really go insane.

Mason wound his hand around mine; it was time to face the council. He led me back into the banquet hall where everyone was already seated waiting for us. I think Mason felt a little embarrassed because everyone stared at us when we walked in. Mason stood behind me as I sat at the head of the table. I asked that Lex and Vann be seated at the extreme opposite end of the table, partly because I knew it would hurt their pride to be moved, but mostly because I needed both of them to be far away from me, for different reasons. Mason and Glen sat in their places.

Malika stood and began speaking, "We, the Seventh Order of the Council of the Eternal, will now commence this hearing to deal with the occurrences surrounding the mortals Lillian and Rachel. More specifically to deal with the prospect of these mortals living amongst us and perhaps being allowed to one day receive The Immortal Fate."

I turned my head sharply toward Lex. "So that is why you brought us here! When were you going to tell us?!"

Malika interrupted before Lex could answer. "Lillian! We would like for you to explain, from the beginning, all of your dealings with Alexander Cavanaugh and Giovanni Rossi leading up to last night. Then we will better understand the nature of your relationships and how deep your knowledge goes of our kind." Malika sat, her eyes shifted momentarily to Lex as if she were nervous about something.

I told the council how Rachel and I had met and kept in contact with Lex before he'd brought us there to the mansion. Then I continued with the events of the night before, "During the gathering yesterday I excused myself so that I could speak with Vann alone, because unfortunately I thought that I was in love with him." Saying it out loud sounded so foolish and I could feel my own cheeks flushing with embarrassment. I looked down the table at Vann who turned his guilt-stricken eyes toward me. "Vann was behaving coldly toward me, more so than usual. I thought he would be as happy to see me as I was to see him. Instead he told me that Lex wanted to turn Rachel and me, which I knew nothing of, and that he would rather see me dead. I waited three years to be with you. I loved you every waking moment, well, I guess it wasn't really love, but more blind infatuation, but...but all you could say was you'd rather see me dead." I looked at him, my heart beating with anger at my own childish feelings, but hurt nevertheless for not being wanted.

He jumped to his feet defensively, his eyes filling with tears as well. "You did not have to try to kill yourself!"

I shook my head frustrated. "I didn't try to kill myself! Rachel accidentally fell into me and pushed me over the banister and I lost my grip. That's it! Anyway it was the second floor! You're acting like I fell off a building or something. Look I have better things to do than stay in this crazy house. I will go insane if I stay any longer. I had a lovely time but I think it's time I left. It's the conclusion you'll come to anyway, so I might as well just leave now. It's okay, I'm used to it. In the end I always end up on my own." I started walking slowly toward the doors.

Lex looked up from the table wide eyed with confusion. He blurted out, "You're thinking of him again."

I stopped, surprised, and turned around. "What nonsense are you talking about now?"

Lex shook his head as if he hadn't meant to say that out loud, but he had obviously been concentrating on reading my mind as I was walking away. Though, not all vampires had the ability to read minds, Lex could, and he didn't have to put as much effort into it as most.

Vann stood, staring hard at me as if he had gone into a trance, and finally pointed at me, obviously reading my mind as well. "You are thinking of Ben! You didn't know him, why would you think of him?" I could see that Vann was putting all his effort into probing my mind until he found what he wanted and I couldn't stop myself thinking it. "He was tuo zio? Your uncle?"

Mason looked at me curiously. "Ben was your uncle? Why didn' ya say somethin'? How could ya speak to Lex if ya knew?"

I started walking backward shaking my head at them, confused, because I was starting to put together all the little hints and whispers my mind had been struggling with. I was remembering, and I wasn't sure I could handle what I was remembering. I couldn't stop shaking my head, as if that would make the memories go away again.

Lex came toward me. "You can't hate me for something that happened a long time ago. I only ever tried to keep you safe. I only ever tried to help Ben."

I was shaking all over with the memories that were flooding back to me. "I'm beginning to think Vann was right. He's probably afraid you'll do to me what you did to Ben. I know it was you. You made him one of you. You used him, and he loved you. You used him like you use everyone, and you tried to change him." I looked at Lex accusingly. "But he wasn't like you! He couldn't be heartless or cruel." I turned to Vann. "He was full of love and loyalty."

Vann hung his head in guilt but Lex wouldn't let the subject go. "Lilly, forget about Ben. You think this will correct some past wrong?

You can't change anything. No matter how sorry you make me feel you can't change what happened to Ben."

"Is that why you were there that night in the club?!" I asked astounded. "You've been following me all that time just because Ben was my uncle?!" I screamed and turned to run up the stairs to get away from Lex before he saw me completely break down.

Rachel walked out of the banquet hall and yelled my name. I turned around, feeling guilty for not thinking about what she might be going through these first few days in our new home, but I could see nothing but sympathy and concern on her face. I knew whatever decisions I made, if I decided to just leave, would affect her, but I felt so overwhelmed by the disturbing memories flooding my brain.

"Lillian, don't weep for someone who didn't even..." Lex started, but corrected himself, "who isn't even here."

"It's your fault he isn't here. You killed him didn't you? You turned him and then tortured him to the point where he no longer wanted to live. Didn't you? Didn't you?!" I screamed losing my composure, and dropping to sit on the stairs I put my hands over my face and wept.

Rachel came and sat beside me, putting her arm around me. In an uneasy whisper she asked, "What did Lex do? Did he really kill your uncle?"

I wiped at my eyes. "It's a long story."

"I don't have anywhere to go at the moment," Rachel answered, squeezing me tighter.

Malika was now standing at the foot of the stairs as well, looking on nervously. "Lillian, I am going to ask that you come back into the banquet hall. I need to know what it is that you know."

Rachel put her arm around my waist and walked with me back to the table. I saw her give Lex a hard look, causing him to step back, hanging his head. Malika walked behind us, perhaps making sure that I didn't change my mind and try to make a run for it.

As we walked back into the banquet hall I caught the end of what Demetrius was telling the others in a hushed voice, "...he really thinks we're going to allow one of these girls to become the thirteenth member of the council, he is sadly mistaken."

Demetrius stopped abruptly as we entered, but I could see by the sly smile he gave me that he didn't care that we'd heard him. I could see that he viewed our presence as nothing more than a ridiculous spectacle, and though no one except Una and Kara openly agreed Demetrius, the others made no attempt to disagree with him. I couldn't understand why Malika took such an interest in what I was accusing Lex of, and so I felt a little foolish to explain everything to a room full of vampires that could care less what I had to say. If Malika hadn't made the request for me to return to the room I probably would have just left the mansion.

I could see Malika giving Lex a troubled look before she took her seat, and then she scanned the others around the table who seemed oblivious to her unease as she demanded, "I want you to tell me what you remember about your uncle, Ben Thorne."

"When I was five I remember him...changing," I began somberly. "I only remember I was five because it was soon after my birthday party. My uncle had planned it; I think he had always taken care of my parties. He was like a father to me; my own parents didn't really want anything to do with me. At that time my parents and I and Ben all lived with my grandfather in his huge house," I took a breath collecting my thoughts. "After my fifth birthday, it might have been days or weeks I'm not sure, Ben disappeared for awhile. When he did finally come home he would only stay for a few hours, barely talking to anyone, and then leave again for days, sometimes weeks, at a time. I overheard my parents say a few times something about drugs, that's what they thought, anyway. Months went by like that, my grandfather would beg him to stay, my parents would make cruel jokes about addiction, and I could do nothing but stare at his changed appearance. Then one night he showed up with another man. My parents remarked that it was probably his dealer that he owed money to, hoping to extract his payment from the family. I think he called himself Dannis, but I'm not sure." As I said the name I noticed Lex and Malika looking at one another again, troubled, but I continued, "I knew there was something strange about Dannis. I guess children always know. I didn't understand why people were entranced by him, or why he answered me when I hadn't said anything. My mother and father fought on the few occasions that he came to our house, I assume because my mother couldn't hide her attraction for Dannis. After a few visits I had made up my mind that he was a vampire. It wasn't a very hard thing for me to believe at the time. I mean I still believed in Santa Claus; believing that some evil man had been the cause of my uncle's transformation only made sense to me, especially because it had affected my uncle's attentions to me. I felt abandoned by the only person who had ever showed me love. My grandfather had always treated me kindly, but ever since my grandmother had passed he walked around in a daze and took little interest in anything. I knew Ben was trying to stay away from me to try to protect me from something, but it was hard to accept as a child.

"Ben never came to visit without Dannis after that first visit. He would sit or stand off in the shadows not saying a word, just watching, as Dannis would sit with me for hours. At times Ben would become agitated and beg Dannis to leave with him. Each time they came for a visit Ben's behavior became more and more erratic, even crazed at times. My own father, who was usually very well drunk by the time Ben and Dannis would stop in for a visit, actually called the cops several times because Ben became violent. Somehow Dannis convinced my parents to allow him and Ben to take me out, and I overheard my parents starting to say that not only was Ben doing drugs but he was having a relationship with Dannis. Obviously my parents were not that concerned about my safety because I recall several outings with my uncle and Dannis, even though they were convinced that they were doing drugs. The memories of the places we went are all so confusing. Dannis was always asking me if I remembered a certain place or would show me pictures and ask if I knew the people in them. Then on one of our strange visits, a castle that we had gone to a few times, something bad happened. I don't remember exactly, but I think Ben tried to hurt me, I think he almost killed me. I remember being terrified of both him and Dannis after that. I think when he realized what he had almost done he despised himself. He was overcome with guilt and loathing for himself."

Lex interrupted me, looking to Malika cautiously, before correcting, "Ben never hurt you. You don't remember. It was someone else-"

"That's enough, Alexander. You do not know the story, don't put words in Lillian's mouth," Malika warned and calmly directed at me, "Please continue, Lillian."

Lex's comment gave me pause, but I continued, "Ben woke me up early in the morning one day and told me we were going to church. He said he had to ask for God's forgiveness for himself and for protection for me. It must have been just before sunrise. We knelt together before an immense stained glass window as the sun began to pour in, illuminating the figures of angels, and spilling multicolored light over both of us. Ben told me to close my eyes and pray to God for protection. I prayed, but I didn't ask for my own protection, I prayed for Dannis to go away and let Ben and me return to our former life. When I opened my eyes...there was nothing there. Nothing but sunlight shining on a pile of dust. He killed himself because of Dannis. After that my parents shunned me even more and our extended family wanted nothing to do with a child that was sure to be demented by such experiences. I think they blamed me for Ben's death, but I didn't really understand what had happened. My grandfather came for me in the church, as if he had known what was going to happen. He told me that Ben was gone... forever."

"Non capisco, I don't understand. Why would you come here knowing what Lex did to your uncle?" Vann questioned.

I shook my head wretchedly. "I didn't know. Not right away anyhow. Little things were coming back to me, but it wasn't until after we had talked in the courtyard. I went to the room below mine and I saw the gold coffins. I hadn't even remembered the day Ben had died after all these years. I think something in my brain buried the memory. When I saw the coffins, though, it made me think of what Ben said to me once about someone being audacious enough to sleep in a gold coffin. Obviously, he was talking about the one who turned him. After that I started remembering everything. Right down to what Dannis looked like," I said the last pointing to Lex.

Lex turned exaggeratedly toward Malika opening his eyes wide and putting his hands up in frustration as if asking permission to tell his side, but Malika just shook her head sternly.

Vann was the first to say anything, "Ben Thorne. It has been molto tempo, long time, since I have thought about him. There were many questions about il suo morte..." Vann paused noticing Lex giving Malika an almost troubled look, but instead turned back to me and said gently, "I never meant to hurt you, uccellino. What I said in the courtyard, it was not meant the way it came out. I have known Lex too long to not think he is doing something for his own selfish purpose. I did not want you getting hurt. You know that I wouldn't ever want anything bad to happen to you."

I nodded my head, trying to smile as I scolded him playfully, "I

hate when you call me uccellino, little bird, it makes me feel like a child."
I took a deep breath and turned to Lex with miserable, questioning eyes.

He turned his cloudy eyes toward me. "I knew. I knew Ben was your uncle. I have been following you since...Ben's death. I didn't drive him mad. It's true he was troubled, but I never abandoned him. We were supposed to go to the council for help because...he was becoming reckless, like Jerrod." He paused composing himself before he went on, "When I found out what he'd done, and in front of you, I swore that I would watch you, try to protect you. And...I fell in love with you. I'm so unbelievably sorry. I should have told you all this a long time ago. I was completely wrong. I love you and Rachel, and all I want is for you to be happy...and safe."

Malika stood. "Alexander, Lillian, Rachel I think the best thing to do, in light of these past issues and present reactions, would be to put this on a trial period. It is very difficult for mortals to live among us and apparently some thought needs to be taken as to whether Lillian and Rachel actually want to live among us and perhaps be allowed to be given The Immortal Fate. I think it would be for the best to implement a few basic rules to be followed until you can learn to live with each other or decide that it is best to separate from one another. I also believe it would be wise to require Lillian and Rachel to reside here for at least one year before we will decide if they would like or should even be given The Immortal Fate. So these are the rules to be followed, and this goes for everyone in this room:

"First, no one may enter any other's private rooms. Meaning no mortals in an immortal's chamber and vice versa. We already know what kind of damage that can cause." Lex was vigorously shaking his head in agreement. Malika continued, "Second, there is to be no physical contact of any kind between you. That includes the exchange of blood, Alexander, and there will be harsh punishment to any vampire that attempts any harm on Rachel or Lillian. Third, and I'm sure this goes without saying, Lillian and Rachel, you are to discuss none of what you see and hear with anyone outside of this room. It is imperative that we keep what we are hidden from outsiders," Malika said pointedly looking at Lex, who suddenly seemed to find the table very interesting. "Lastly, the council is to be notified about any indecent behavior from anyone and will deal with it accordingly. Alexander, are you agreed?"

Lex looked at me somewhat deterred and back at Malika. "Of

course I agree. Anything to keep my little queen."

I smiled at his affectionate pet name for me. "I agree," I answered, deciding it was the best option I had to stay with Lex, plus I might be able to find out more about Ben.

The gathering was soon adjourned, and everyone poured into the main hall. I closed the doors before Lex could leave.

"I think in light of our new....... *predicament* we should raise the stakes. Just so one of us has more than authoritative pressure to keep us on track," I said raising my eyebrows and giving him a sly smile.

Lex looked at me as if he were offended. "Why, Lillian, are you suggesting that one of us would take this agreement lightly?"

"No," I answered shaking my head and grinning. "I'm suggesting that it would take more than an agreement to *your* elders to keep *you* straight. I propose a bet. Whoever breaks a rule first loses."

Lex pondered the notion, but I knew he had a weakness for such games. "What are the terms?"

"If I win you will first grovel for my forgiveness in front of all of your friends and second you will buy me my very own car. A model of my choice to be determined at a later time. What do you want, if a miracle occurs and you don't break a rule?" I asked sarcastically.

Lex thought a moment and then his lips slowly curved into a smile. "My request is far less painful than yours. It will only cost you your pride, not your pride and a ridiculous amount of money. Do you remember the rubber dress that you and Rachel tried to dispose of?" Lex had a look of triumph on his face. "I would love to see you having to wear that in front of a large room of people singing karaoke to a song of my choice...to be determined at a later time."

I narrowed my eyes and huffed at him for finding the wretched dresses we'd thrown in the garbage. I knew he'd want them for just such an embarrassing joke. I nearly protested until I remembered Lex's reputation for breaking rules. Reluctantly I said, "Very well. Shake on it."

We walked out of the room, our arms around each other. As we entered the Grand Hall everyone stopped talking. Vann was standing in the middle of everyone collecting money. They just looked at us dumbly.

I laughed. "You heard us?"

"Actually," Vann said shyly. "We were listening. We hear your bet and decide to make one of our own."

"How many are for me?" I asked glancing imperiously at Lex.

Everyone eagerly answered at the same time, "All!"

Vann shrugged his shoulders. "It is inevitable. Lex will break a regolamento first. The bet is *when* he will screw up."

"Oh thanks, Giovanni, I'm glad to see my friends have confidence in me," Lex said trying to sound outraged.

I threw my arms around Lex and kissed him on the cheek. Vann found me and I finally got what I had wanted from him. Sort of. He wound his arms loosely around me, turned my face up to his, and kissed my lips lightly. It wasn't passionate. It was just kind and affectionate.

He let his lips caress my cheek as he moved close, brushing against my ear. "Ti amo, uccellino," he whispered. "I love you with all my heart, my little bird."

I had waited so long to hear Vann say those words, but I realized I had already known they were true. I really didn't need him to say them anymore. I was finally discovering that there were many kinds of love, and as much as I'd wanted Vann's love for me to be passionate and reckless like in a romance novel, it never would be. He loved me, in his way, and I shrugged off the silly idea of a carnal love affair with him. I was no damsel in distress and he was certainly no knight in shining armor. It was time to put away such foolish things and just accept the different love I was being given by those around me. They were now my family after all, and so far the most loving one I'd ever had. As everyone said goodnight I felt perfectly content with my situation and I couldn't wait for the sun to set once more.

J.M. Merillo

A NIGHT IN THE UN-LIFE...

"Couldn't wait for the sun to set once more, indeed," Lillian announced smugly to the empty room.

She stood and stretched, though naturally her bones didn't ache and her muscles didn't get stiff. "Time for my favorite red delicacy," she joked to herself.

Lillian saved her document, closed the laptop, and placed her copy of *Frankenstein* over some notes she had made so they didn't get disturbed by the breeze coming through her cracked window. Before leaving her large apartment above the art studio she swung her thin black coat around herself, remembering that there was a slight chill in the air, and mortals would be dressed for the cool weather.

As Lillian crossed the street she turned around to see the man who owned the art studio below her apartment walking on the opposite side of the road.

I wonder what he paints in there, Lillian thought watching him.

She had never been particularly curious about the boy. Lillian had decided she would try to keep to herself this time. Try not to draw attention to herself. So she decided no searching for answers, no seeking out others like herself, and certainly no companionship with the mortal boy downstairs. Though, calling him a boy was far from accurate. He was obviously older than the age she'd been when she was made a vampire. She guessed he was around thirty, but she was never good about people's ages.

She wasn't even sure if people believed her when she told them she was twenty-five, which she wasn't. She had been twenty years old when she'd been made a vampire and it had now been twenty years since then. Obviously, she didn't age, but twenty years as a vampire had given her knowledge most twenty-year-olds did not possess. She had also learned early on that being a twenty year old woman had its limitations in the modern world, and over the years she had eventually settled on saying she was twenty-five. She found it to be the oldest age that people would accept of her by appearance, but it was also the youngest age at which people actually showed her respect and accepted that she might actually know what she was talking about.

Lillian continued watching the boy as he walked away from her and she entertained the thought of breaking into his studio for a peek at his paintings. Instead she turned, walked the opposite way, and thought about the first time she'd met him.

It had been the first week Lillian had moved into the apartment. She had been careless with the time while out hunting, and had fainted in the hall right in front of the art studio belonging to Asher Reed. He had found her lying on the floor and had carried her into her apartment. It had been a lucky coincidence that Ash had been there to save her from the sunlight, unbeknownst to him, but despite his kindness Lillian kept her promise to herself to stay away.

Coming around the corner she spotted her prey, a very plump man who was stumbling out of a bar. She easily picked the thoughts from his mind. His wife was dead, but he had a young stepdaughter that lived with him. Lillian saw jumbled images of the large, inebriated man forcing himself on his helpless stepdaughter.

Poor girl, Lillian thought shaking her head. *She won't have to fight him off* ever *again.*

Lillian walked swiftly toward the man and hooked on to his arm. "Mind if I join you?"

The man looked at her dazed from the alcohol. "Sweetheart, you're the finest woman I've seen in a long time."

Lillian stopped and stood in front of him. Turning toward him she let him kiss her roughly on the lips before pulling away a little to whisper in his ear, "Come this way."

Lillian led him into a narrow, dark alley and pushed the man up against the wall playfully smiling. The man pulled her closer, struggling to get her coat undone. Lillian pushed back his collar and caressed his neck with her hand.

As she was about to bite down the man looked up and grinned. "You're not any sort of vampire are you?"

"Maybe," she said smiling.

The man laughed, pulling her coat askew to kiss her bare shoulder.

What a silly question, she thought, then slowly inserted her small but deadly fangs into his soft fleshy neck.

Lillian let her senses reel from the intoxicating taste of alcohol in the man's blood. Despite what she'd ever learned about vampires, she could actually eat and drink as long as she'd fed on blood. The blood pumping in her body would just push it through her system, making it very inconvenient how quickly the food or drink escaped her body. It was a handy trick, being able to eat and drink in front of people, to make her seem more human, and she knew how to time it so as not to make an embarrassing mess. Still, the best way to enjoy these things was through the blood of others, and alcohol in the blood was one of the most intoxicating, even if the effect didn't last long. She felt a lovely calm enfold her body as she took in the last few drops of blood. The man fainted dead in her arms. He probably hadn't even felt her bite, because he had been so drunk. It had been a much too kind end for him.

Lillian removed a miniscule razor-sharp knife she kept in her coat pocket. After removing the man's wallet, taking his money, and throwing the wallet down a gutter she slit his throat. She put his body further down the alley under some pieces of cardboard. When the body was found the police would think it was just another robbery.

Lillian started walking home, stretching her senses to see if there were any others like her near. It was rare to find any vampires within a close radius of where she was, but she never stopped searching. In the last twenty years she had never stumbled upon any stronger than herself, and those weaker than her, even if they were older, ran from her in fear before she could even speak. Lillian continued back to her apartment, fumbling distractedly with the oval pendant around her neck and thinking about the next words she was going to write in her book…

ᴄ5ᴄ

I woke up with an awkward feeling. It had been about three weeks since the council had decided to let Rachel and me stay at the mansion as a trial run, until they or we made a final decision. Everything had actually been wonderful since then, with no fights or misunderstandings. I was spending a lot of my time with Lex, as Rachel seemed to disappear more and more often without any explanation. It was strange spending so much time alone with Lex. Ever since we'd met him, Rachel had always been there with me and Lex, and if Lex and I were alone it wasn't for very long. I had learned my lesson with Vann, though, or so I liked to think, and strenuously worked at not falling completely and utterly in love with Lex. Other than that things had been delightfully uneventful and simple, and Rachel and I were completely content with our situation. Still something didn't feel quite right.

My fear for the morning, or should I say afternoon, was not suddenly diminished by the absence of Rachel. There was no note and the door was left wide open. In normal circumstances there would be no need for alarm, but Rachel and I had made a promise to leave a note if we went anywhere and we never left our door open, especially if one of us was still asleep. After the events of our first days in the mansion we decided we had to protect each other. We were two mortals living in a house with a blood drinker, and although we wanted to trust Lex and the other vampires that had access to the house, we also knew we should be cautious. Even with Rachel's increasingly frequent absences she always let me know she was at least safe. I was worried; Rachel had been behaving more and more withdrawn and now she had simply forgotten a promise we'd made to each other to keep one another safe.

To quiet my uneasiness I got up and got dressed, choosing a light blue empire-waisted satin halter top dress that fell just above my knees. I exited the closet, pulling the front strands of my hair back and fastening them with a small butterfly clip, when I noticed a few things littering the floor just to the side of Rachel's bed. I looked at the scene before me, confused. The vase that usually sat on the table beside Rachel's bed was on the floor half-way to the door and the table itself was knocked over. Rachel's slippers were haphazardly scattered to the right and left of the bed and a glass that looked as if it had held some kind of liquid was lying on its side near the opposite wall.

This wasn't good, something was wrong, and I had to find Rachel. I grabbed my poetry book and walked around the house for awhile on the off chance I might run into Rachel, but found the house deserted. With my curiosity running wild, trying to imagine every possibility, I decided to take a walk in the garden to calm my mind and think more clearly.

I was probably getting worried for no reason; Rachel probably forgot to leave a note, that's all. She had probably left in a rush and knocked the table over causing everything to go flying. Rachel had been disappearing more and more as of late, and always seemed to change the subject when I asked what she'd been doing. Maybe she was getting tired of having to tell me every single time she was going somewhere and needed some space, maybe she felt there was no reason to be so careful in our new home. Maybe she was just getting tired of our friendship. She had been much quieter lately, even a bit more reserved in her behavior and appearance. Instead of the loud, wise-cracking, go-with-the-flow girl in a short skirt and low-cut shirt she'd become a quiet, moody, prude in a pencil skirt below her knees and dress shirt up to her neck. There was nothing wrong with her new appearance or even really her new behavior, except that it just wasn't her. She didn't laugh as loud, she barely smiled any more. Something had changed, and she was pulling further and further away from me.

I was walking toward one of my favorite parts of the garden. The multicolored flagstone-paved path opened onto a small open circle completely surrounded by over-sized tropical trees and plants, blocking out all other views and giving the spot a welcome, secluded feel. On one side of the flagstone-paved circle there was a lovely wood and wrought-iron bench where I usually sat reading, writing in my poetry book, or just staring at the photo of my uncle. Directly across from the bench was a four, maybe five foot tall wooden-looking statue of a Greek female warrior, I thought perhaps it was supposed to be Athena. She held a spear in her right hand and in her left she held some kind of staff that seemed to be wrapped in what looked like fabric. The fabric seemed to be attached to what looked like a spindle. About the girl's left side hung a terrifying shield with what I assumed was the image of Medusa's head. I wasn't sure why, but looking at the statue always made me feel better.

The reason I enjoyed the spot so much, besides the comforting feeling that the statue gave me, was due to its fortunate placement in the garden. The bench that I spent so much solitary time occupying was completely shaded from above by various palms and brilliant, violet-flowered jacaranda trees, and was also situated in such a way that even on the hottest days, which that had turned out to be, there was a refreshing tunnel of wind that blew through along the path and swirled around in the open area.

On that particular day, though, a well-groomed, sandy-haired gentleman occupied the bench, my bench, where I had hoped to calm my mind and convince myself that I was worrying for no reason. I thought the man couldn't have been more than twenty-five or twenty-six, but he held himself very confidently, as if he were older. His sandy-blonde hair was short and perfectly parted to the side. He had very subtle, almost feminine features with a soft jawline and slightly squared chin, but his face had traces of deliberate stubble giving him a look of seductive maturity. He was the only human I'd ever seen that I couldn't take my eyes off of; with his long, thick eyelashes over large, blue-green eyes, and salmon-toned lips that seemed to pout as he concentrated. Everything about him seemed elegant, from the way his graceful fingers turned the pages of his book, to the way that he shifted his long legs as he moved further back on the bench. He was dressed in navy blue dress pants, a white short-sleeved dress shirt with the top two buttons undone, and a yellow and navy argyle vest. I noted that the red, linen-bound book he was reading had the words *Lalla Rookh* printed across the front in gold lettering.

I thought it was strange to find someone dressed so formally on such a hot day just sitting in the garden reading, sitting in a vampire's garden none-the-less. After consideration I reasoned that Lex did make many friends (and enemies for that matter) from all walks of life. Maybe it wouldn't be so strange to find any manner of person hanging about. Plus, the stranger had obviously discovered that the spot, even in such brutal Florida heat, stayed comfortably cool, which was probably the only reason he'd chosen to sit out of doors dressed the way he was instead of taking refuge within the cool air-conditioned confines of the mansion.

"I thought I was dressed rather casually actually," the gentleman quipped in a soft, elegant English accent.

"What did you say?" I asked, surprised, because I was sure I hadn't said anything aloud about the way he was dressed.

The man put his folded finger to his lip as if he'd said something he shouldn't have, and then explained somewhat uncomfortably, "I apologize, sometimes I don't even realize I'm doing it."

I sat down on the bench next to the man not only curious, but wanting for some reason to be nearer. "Doing what?"

"It isn't easy to explain really," he began, looking at me for the first time, but then he seemed to forget to continue as he studied my face.

I looked down, uncomfortable at how openly he stared at me, and offered clumsily, "You've stumbled upon my favorite spot. I usually come here to be alone." I gestured to the statue and continued, "I don't know why, but that statue always seems to put me at ease. It makes me feel...safe."

"Perhaps because it's the Palladium," the gentleman offered, but when I gave him a blank look he explained, "The Palladium was a sort of sacred statue created by the Greek goddess Athena to honor the memory of Pallas, who was like a sister to her. During a fighting match Athena wounded Pallas, killing her, and because of her guilt she created the Palladium. The Palladium was also thought to have protected the city of Troy from its inception, until it was stolen, and I'm sure you know how that story ended."

I felt my cheeks flush as I realized he had stopped talking and I was still staring fixedly at him. I muttered shyly, "I suppose that must be why I feel so drawn to it. Maybe I feel it can protect me." I smiled, embarrassed, and changed the subject, "I don't think we've met. I think I would remember meeting someone like you. I mean...someone that looks like you...I mean someone," I paused, feeling my cheeks redden again and instead focused on his beautiful linen-bound book adding a little too enthusiastically, "with a passion for reading."

He smiled warmly and in his lovely accent said, "You must be one of the beautiful ladies I was told so much about." He held the book up for me to see better. "Are you a fan of obscure literature?"

"I have yet to make it all the way through that book, it's a difficult read, but I know what it's about. It's...very romantic," I answered shyly.

The man seemed amused. "Yes, very romantic. Falling in love with someone you're not meant to and then finding that they are exactly the one you were meant to fall in love with. Sometimes the road to love, though long and winding, is paved with unexpected, and pleasant surprises."

I smiled at the beautiful way that he spoke, but remembered my earlier confusion once more. "You didn't tell me...how did you know what I was thinking before...about the way you were dressed?"

"Oh, that," he said, sitting up a little straighter. "Well, I don't know if you'll believe me, but I...well, I have an ability to read people's thoughts, so to speak."

I laughed. "You're teasing me."

"No, it's true." He nodded earnestly. "Ever since I can remember I've just been able to pick up on certain thoughts. It doesn't always work, but over the years I've kind of trained myself to be more consistent."

"So...you could read what I'm thinking right now?" I asked, still not convinced.

"Maybe," he said, biting his lip. "It doesn't always work when I try, and sometimes it does when I'm not trying at all. I have learned that it is easier when someone is in an altered state of consciousness, like when someone is taking a narcotic or sleeping. It can also help if they are in a state of exaggerated emotion, such as the happy ecstasy when a man is marrying the love of his life or the utter unrestrained hopelessness when one has lost the love of his life," he said the last part slowly, and seemed to withdraw afterward.

"Are you all right? What's wrong?" I asked, worried I might have said something to upset him.

"Well," he said looking down at his clasped hands. "I've been here a few weeks, off and on, since Lex's big party, the night you arrived in fact. I've really enjoyed being here, and it is so lovely, but it doesn't seem to be helping me. Lex invited me to stay for as long as I like after my...Well, I shouldn't be bothering you with my problems. It isn't proper, I'm sorry."

He sounded depressed as he looked up at me with sad, pleading eyes, and though he said he didn't want to tell me, it was almost as if he were baiting me to ask him what was wrong. His eyes were locked on me as if they were begging for me to push him, just a little, to tell me everything.

I decided to give him the benefit of the doubt and trust that he was just sad and polite, and not trying to win me over with a sob story. I had heard stories from Rachel of men, well boys in our situation, pretending to be heartbroken to gain sympathy (and much more) from a girl. I didn't want to think that Dallen was just trying to make me feel sorry for him to get something from me, but I was just too naïve to know either way if he was. Plus it was hard to ignore those aquamarine eyes pleading me for comfort.

I wanted to embrace his warm body, but instead consoled softly, "You can tell me, it might make you feel better to say it out loud. I know you don't know me, but you can trust me. I've been through some pretty hard times myself."

"My brother died. It's been over a year, but...it was horrible. I can't get the picture out of my head." He stopped and closed his eyes. He seemed to be composing himself. Then he was perfectly calm. "You're right. It does feel better to talk about it."

I let my breath out slowly. I hadn't thought it would be anything that serious. I guessed he was having financial problems or trouble with women, and I'd be able to say something clever and funny to make him laugh. I never knew how to react to such serious things. Most of my life I'd been unhappy with my situation, but when people would try to comfort me I found their words more annoying than helpful. Which was why when I was faced with hearing some heartbreaking or unhappy news I never knew what to say. I always thought of how empty people's words sounded to me, and I certainly did not want to sound empty or fake to someone whose heart could barely beat for sadness.

He saw my loss for words or was able to read something from my thoughts. "I know you weren't expecting that. I should have warned you. I'm sure you can't wait to get away from me now."

I put my hand on his shoulder encouragingly, pretending it hadn't completely caught me off-guard, and changed the subject asking him as calmly as I could muster, "As a matter of fact I was wondering if you'd like to have dinner with me? It's so lonely eating by myself, and it seems to be happening more and more of late. I'd really enjoy the company."

He nodded his head yes while wiping at his eye.

"Good, because I would have been thoroughly insulted if you had said no," I said over-dramatically.

"Lex is so lucky to have such a beautiful, kind girl staying with him."

"Just don't tell him that. I'm trying to hide my caring side from him," I said giving him my most devilishly sneaky look. "You'll join me, then?"

"Of course," he answered with a handsome smile. "It's very rude of me; I should have asked immediately, you're Lillian, aren't you?"

I wanted to ask if he'd read my mind, but settled for answering, "Yes, I am. And now I feel silly I never asked your name."

"Dallen Gray," he said simply. "I noticed you're carrying a journal, may I ask what you write?"

I bit my lip, grasping my book protectively. "Oh, it's just..." I shook my head a little embarrassed. "I like to write poetry sometimes. It calms me."

Dallen didn't laugh, but smiled warmly and asked earnestly, "Would you allow me to read any?"

"Ummm, I suppose," I assented, then added quickly, "But only if you promise not to laugh."

He got up and offered his arm. "I would never laugh at you. Shall we?"

I took his arm and we walked arm in arm to a patio area, overlooking the large maze-like main garden below, where I was most often eating dinner alone. We sat at one of four round high-top stone tables. The tables were the color of pale pink sand and were mercifully fitted with large umbrellas to block out the late afternoon sun. After sitting for just a few minutes one of the staff came hurriedly to ask what he could get for us.

It was the same man that had brought mine and Rachel's lunch the day after we'd arrived. He stood with his hands behind his back and said,

"Good to see you again, Miss, it has been some time. I understand you usually have your dinner here; I'll let the kitchen know you won't be dining alone this evening. What would you like to drink?"

I glanced at Dallen who gave me an exaggerated look of being impressed. "You do have pull around here. What would you like, Lillian?" I loved the way he said my name.

I folded my hands under my chin thinking for a moment and then offered, "It's such a hot day, how about white sangria?" I asked Dallen and then turned to the attendant and asked hopefully, "Would you be able to make that?"

"I believe we should, Miss." The man smiled politely before leaving.

"It's quite unbelievable isn't it, all this wealth?" Dallen said as he watched the attendant retreating back to the house. "I don't think I could even dream all of this up if I tried." Dallen swept his hand through the air indicating the property.

We both looked out over the main garden made up of grand fountains and countless hedge mazes which led into smaller, flower adorned gardens. These smaller gardens encompassed both sides and the rear of the property, and were only broken up by such things as flagstone paths, lovely vine-covered arbors, countless benches similar to the one I was so fond of, decorative fountains and statues, and not to mention Lex's numerous swimming pools, which more resembled lavish ponds settled out in the middle of nothing but plants and trees. On one side of the mansion the gardens actually continued all the way around to the front where they were met by the curve of the driveway. As I've said before Lex always did things in a grand manner, and I wouldn't be surprised if his gardens weren't designed after the opulent and majestic gardens at Versailles. Never having been there, though, I can't say for sure.

Finally Dallen shook off his awe and asked, "What does Lex do that he could acquire so much?"

I didn't know how much Dallen knew about Lex so I decided to evade the question. "It must be something important to keep him away all day." Dallen's softly arched eyebrows came together questioningly. "What do you mean keep him away all day? You do know….about Lex? What he is, I mean?" he asked, as if he already knew that I knew.

74

I laughed to myself. "Yes, I didn't think you knew. I didn't want to go blurting out Lex's secret. Although, I guess it's really not much of a secret if he keeps telling people."

"Still being a vampire doesn't exactly explain how he came to possess this much wealth. I mean it would almost be impossible to steal all of this," Dallen replied sweeping his hand through the air again.

I lowered my eyes and said softly, "You don't know Lex very well do you?"

Dallen chortled, a wide smile creeping upon his handsome face. "I must admit, I have actually known him for quite some time, but until recently I...let's just say I had other obligations which didn't allow me to spend my time cavorting about with a free-spirited vampire. I believe Lex found my abilities...entertaining, but it does become a bit exhausting trying to keep up with Lex, and most of the time we've spent together has been at some party or another. Not exactly the time or place to have a serious conversation about his amassed wealth."

I explained, "I think Lex actually came from a wealthy family in Ireland and had invested his inheritance. I don't really know a lot about his past but I think he lived in England for a time and came into some money there as well. The rest he...well...he did kind of steal. He some way or another had documents drawn up to tie him to one of the wealthiest families in the South. The last relative died some seventeen years ago and everything went to Lex. He got their fortune, sold off the family's properties, and built this place."

Dallen shook his head, unsurprised. "How cleaver. I should have known he got all of this dishonestly," he jested affectionately.

"You only say that because he's Irish. Don't the English hate the Irish?" I asked, teasingly.

He seemed to drop his guard for the first time and relax. "I wouldn't say hate. There is a history of...disagreement between the two, but most of that is gone. There are some prejudices that remain, of course, and I probably do unintentionally express prejudices that were passed down from my parents."

"So you're friends with an Irishman, staying in his home and enjoying his hospitality, oh and you're reading a book by an Irishman to boot," I added.

"Yes, I'm sure my great-grandmother is, what's the expression...rolling in her grave," he laughed at himself.

The attendant came back carrying a pitcher filled with fruit and a yellowish liquid and two wine glasses. He poured the sangria into our glasses and placed the pitcher in the middle of the table. "Your dinner will be done shortly," the man said before leaving.

"May I take a look now?" Dallen asked, pointing to my book where I'd laid it on the table.

I handed it to him, gulping nervously, and I could see he found my discomfort amusing. I took the opportunity to swallow what was left of my sangria and refill my glass, trying to ignore the sound of pages turning from across the table. Dallen eventually came upon the picture of Ben that I had tucked into the book, and I felt compelled to explain that he was my uncle that had died when I was young. Dallen seemed relieved by my explanation.

"Some of these are very dark," Dallen commented, "but very beautiful. I can feel how much sadness you must have felt as you wrote these. This one is almost frightening "The Darkroom"."

"That's how I felt most of the time," I told him somberly, "like I was trapped...in darkness."

Dallen looked at me with soft sympathy in his eyes. "I hope you don't feel that any longer."

"Sometimes," I admitted, "but my life has gotten better since I've been here. I really don't know if I would have been able to lead a normal life, even if Lex had never found me. Anyway if I hadn't met Lex and moved here I would have never met you, and that's something I can't complain about."

Dallen took the wine glass up and looked out across the garden. "I truly wish I could stay here…" he turned and looked yearningly at me. "…with you. This has been one of the best days I've had...in a year...and it's because of you."

For a moment I felt nervous again. I wasn't used to anyone finding me charming and wanting to actually spend time with me, especially so quickly. Unless you counted Lex, who it turned out felt he owed it to my dead uncle to protect me. Other than that I didn't have a lot of experience with men, especially mortal men, and the premature interest Dallen was showing me made me suspicious. After all we'd only just met, and he seemed moments away from professing his love. Again I tried to convince myself that I was only uneasy because I had no experience with flirtation and romance, and that maybe this really was how people behaved when they first met and liked each other. I thought perhaps that I had become too used to the world of mystery and danger that I was immersed in to feel comfortable in what should have been a normal situation with an attractive man.

I shook off my uneasiness and instead focused on how much I enjoyed looking into Dallen's blue-green eyes and listening to his voice. "Why can't you stay?" I asked bringing the sangria to my lips.

"My work requires me to travel considerably. This evening I'm leaving for Cuckfield, I mean, I..." He looked down as if he hadn't meant to say that.

"Cook...field? I've never heard of it. Where is that?" I asked.

"Oh, it's just a small town in Georgia. I'm afraid I won't be able to come back here again, or at least not for a very long time. My work doesn't really allow for much leisure time." His beautiful blue-green eyes looked unsettled as if he'd just realized something.

"But you might come back? You don't know for sure that you won't?" I asked, trying to keep him talking about his work. After his obvious slip, I was very interested in what he was trying to hide, and why he should want to hide anything from me.

"Actually, I'm quite sure that I won't be able to come back here, ever," he stated sternly, looking away once again.

I pressed the subject, thinking that perhaps he had only pretended interest in me and now decided he needed an excuse to not follow through. "Why? What do you do that you can't come back?"

Dallen reached across the table and took my hands in his, either reading the uneasiness in my mind or mistaking my curiosity for more than it was. Well, okay I was a little interested, but mostly I wondered why he was trying to hide something from me. I was just a stranger he met today and would never see again.

"Oh, Lillian, I can't tell you. It is very important, though. Maybe one day you'll understand how important. I wish we had met...before. Things are so complicated right now, and I think it is probably for the best that I'm being called away. I would love nothing more than to spend time with you and get to know you better. Which would only complicate matters further; so, yes it is for the best that I'm leaving, even if I wish I weren't." His eyes beamed clearly and I could tell that he meant what he was saying even if he did seem to be showing an unusual amount of affection for someone he just met.

I pursed my lips into a smile and quipped, "You're right it is probably better that you're leaving, you'd just get bored with me if you stayed anyway." I paused, looking into his beautiful sea-swept eyes and added seriously, "I have really enjoyed this...talking with you." Then I laughed a little uncomfortably as I added, "This is kind of like my first date. I haven't spent much time around mortal boys...uh, men. And now you're leaving and I won't ever see you again. But it has been nice."

Dallen and I talked all through dinner. We talked about his brother, and about Lex, and about his trip to Georgia. He also told me his age, thirty-three. Have I mentioned I'm not very good at guessing ages? After dinner he had an attendant call a cab to take him to the airport, and I even helped him bring his bags out. I hesitated a moment, not sure how I should say goodbye, but in the end I hugged him and kissed his cheek. As he pulled away he seemed to pause, as if he weren't sure how to say goodbye either. It didn't seem like enough and yet we had just met, how much more of a goodbye could we expect of each other?

That was the last I would see of the handsome Englishman. Though I wished in my heart otherwise. It was nice to be with a man, not a vampire, and talk like any other man and woman might. I watched the car pull away, feeling divided about my choice to come live with Lex. My future seemed to already be decided, but what if I fell in love? What if I decided I didn't want to be a vampire after all? What if I wanted a normal life? Being with Dallen, even for just a few hours, left me daydreaming about what I would miss if I decided to accept The Immortal Fate: love, marriage, children, a home like I'd never known...

ಬ**6**ಇ

I went back to my room to find Rachel and tell her about my day with Dallen Gray. I walked into our room and was reminded of her absence by the litter of strange items across the floor and disheveled blankets and pillows on her bed. She had obviously not been back, and there was still no note.

I looked at the closet door. The only place I hadn't looked. I walked to the closet hoping Rachel wasn't where I thought she was. I knew how uncomfortable the room below ours was to her and if she was down there something bad must have happened. I opened the closet door, and started down the hall of clothes. I walked to the end, checking first both dressing rooms, and then moved toward the bathrooms praying that she would be in one of them. I tried the first door but it wouldn't open.

I banged on the door, yelling hopefully, "Rachel?! Rachel, are you in there?!"

"Go away, Lillian!" was the answer I received.

My heart sank with the bitterness in Rachel's voice, but at least she wasn't in the safe-room below. "Please, Rachel, open the door."

"He'll be here soon, just go away, Lillian!" Rachel screamed.

I wasn't sure what she meant but thought perhaps she was talking about Lex. "Rachel, Lex wants you to come out. He asked me to come get you," I lied.

"Tell Lex to rot in hell! I don't want him near me! Just leave me alone!"

Okay, that was apparently not the right thing to say. I didn't know what to say. I felt like I'd missed something.

Finally at a loss I uttered, "Rachel, I'll be here if you want me. I don't know what you're so angry about, but Lex told me to tell you that he's sorry and you were right and he'll make it up to you."

I turned to go, but heard the door crack open.

Rachel looked at me through the tiny crack and sneered, "Tell Lex that he can make it up to me. He can light himself on fire and when his wretched little body is reduced to ashes I'll be there to spit on them." Then the door was slammed shut.

My mouth dropped open and my eyes shot wide in shock. I didn't know what to say. Rachel wasn't a vindictive person, usually, and I had never heard her say anything truly mean to or about anyone. I couldn't even remember a time I had actually seen her angry, she was usually so easy-going, and only ever made smart remarks if someone annoyed her. She had been a little more withdrawn lately, maybe even a little more temperamental, but I couldn't understand where this was coming from.

I just shook my head. *What is going on?* I thought to myself as I tried to think of what mess Lex had so recently gotten himself into that Rachel hated him, but he had been perfectly good lately. I decided to leave it alone and ask Lex when he woke up.

When I walked back into our room I went to the window to see how close the sun was to setting. I was so frustrated that Lex couldn't be there right then and there to help me that I punched my right fist down in agitation. To my extreme luck the small round mirror table was there to catch my hand. The mirror was smashed and my knuckles were bleeding. It wasn't horrible, just a lot of little scratches, but it was certainly inconvenient. I ran back to the bathroom, that Rachel had not locked herself in, grabbed a hand-towel and wrapped it around my hand. I decided to start my trek to Lex's room even though the sun had not completely set, I would wait outside his door until he came out, but I only made it as far as the bottom of the main stairs when Lex emerged from his labyrinth-like hallway.

"Lex, something's wrong with..."

"I can't talk right now, Lillian," Lex stated as he turned toward the front door to leave.

Again I felt completely lost. *Was Lex angry at me?*

Things had finally started going well; I didn't understand what could have happened. I had been around either Rachel or Lex or both constantly the past few days. Even when Rachel wandered off on whatever secretive excursions she was having, I would spend time with Lex; there wasn't even a time they could have gotten into a fight without my being present.

"Rachel hates you!" I screamed trying to get his attention. I lowered my voice asking gently, "What did you do to her?"

His hand was on the door handle, but he turned back toward me with his head down. "She does?"

"What did you do to her?"

Lex looked at me, as if deciding something, and muttered, "Come with me. I'll tell you on the way."

We got into his new black Porsche (unfortunately the old one was beyond repair) and started down the winding driveway.

"What happened to your hand?" he asked, glancing down at my hand.

"It's stupid. I wasn't paying attention and I hit a mirror. See," I said, showing him my hand, still slightly wet with thin lines of blood where the glass had scratched my skin.

Lex stared blindly at my hand, sighing loudly and ignoring the road.

"Lex, the road!"

He pulled his eyes away from me and swerved the car back into the right lane.

"Now, "I said, catching my breath and wrapping my hand in the towel so it wouldn't distract Lex, "what did you do to Rachel?"

Lex looked at me for a moment and then reluctantly admitted, "Last night while you two were sleeping I came into your room."

"You broke a rule," I whispered to myself, triumphantly.

"What?"

"Nothing. Go on," I laughed softly.

"Well, I went to Rachel's bed and leaned over her to drink from her, but she woke up. She went mad," he paused, looking at me for pity, when all I did was raise my eyebrow he went on, "she hit me, and threw things at me. Then she ran for the closet. I don't know how you didn't wake up, but after that I couldn't bring myself to try to drink from you.

Even with how crazed I felt from hunger."

I took my right hand in my left thinking, *Lex, this is my hand and my blood, you can't have it!*

"Lillian I'm not going to lick your hand, or bite your hand, or bite you for that matter," he said thrusting the gear into fourth.

"Why did you go to Rachel? Were you going to drink from us both?" I asked, hoping his answer was going to be no to the latter.

"I didn't mean to go to Rachel. I thought that it was your bed that I went to, but I was so disoriented I didn't really know what I was doing," Lex stated simply.

My eyes grew wide; I could feel them protruding from the sockets. He had actually meant to drink from me, and saw nothing wrong with admitting it to me as if I might actually be flattered that he had wanted to drink from me. Don't get me wrong, it's wonderful to be wanted, but I preferred it were for something other than my warm, delicious blood.

"How could you, Lex? After everything that's happened, after what the council said? What am I supposed to think now? How can I even trust you?" It was a lot of questions, but I didn't expect him to answer any of them, I just didn't know what else to say.

"I'm sorry. You have to forgive me," he stated matter-of-factly. "You don't know the thirst. It affects everything; it reduces our will and even our sanity if we go without it for too long."

"Lex, I want to go home," I said resolutely. "I really don't want to drive around with you when you're...like this. Where are you taking me anyway?" I asked

"I'm going to feed so I can control my hunger, but I'm weak. I haven't fed since before you and Rachel arrived. It's been over a month. I may need your help," he said the last low as if he didn't want me to hear.

"No way! What do you think I am! I am not going to feed you like some kind of pet. You can do it yourself. I mean how weak can you possibly be?!" I yelled in outrage.

We pulled into a dark parking lot just off to the right of a little diner. Lex parked under a shady tree toward the back of the parking lot where there was no light from the road and few cars. He looked at me pleadingly. His body was rocking back and forth as if he were going through withdrawals. His head looked limp like it was too heavy for him to hold up. For the first time I noticed how perfectly gaunt and sickly he looked. I couldn't understand why he would have let himself become so weak. He'd obviously been preoccupied with Rachel and me living in the mansion, but there must have been something else, something that he wasn't sharing with us. He had told me on a number of nights that he was going out to feed and wouldn't come back for hours; obviously he had been lying to me, but why? What had he really been doing?

"Lillian, please I can't bare it any more. Almost five weeks since I've fed. I just need a little help. I'm not sure how much my strength has been reduced; I just need you to be there to make sure everything goes right. Please, Lillian," Lex pleaded, almost to the point of tears.

I saw how weak he already was. I had a feeling he was exaggerating a little, but I had never seen Lex so weak. It frightened me a little to see him so pathetically dependent. Whatever had caused him to go without feeding for so long must have had something to do with Rachel and me, and if he hadn't even slipped a little to tell us what was going on it must have been really bad.

"All right, Lex. Just this once, though. If you didn't look perfectly wretched I wouldn't even consider it. You are really going to owe me after this," I said reluctantly. "What do you want me to do?"

Lex replied, "I need you to lure someone out of the diner. That's all. Unless..."

Oh, I didn't like this. "Unless, what?"

He hesitated, then said in his sweetest voice, "Unless they fight me too much I might need you to intervene."

I almost choked, "Intervene?! What do you mean intervene?! You've got to be kidding?! I am not intervening in anything! I don't even know how you talked me into coming with you!"

"Little queen."

"What?!"

"Shut up and bring me a drink," Lex joked, trying to sound funny, "before your bloodied hand starts to look appetizing."

I was disgusted. "Appetizing! This is not funny, Lex! You are not going to talk me into this. I can't do it. I am not a murderer, and you are a bastard!"

"Murderess," Lex corrected.

I stared at him vehemently. "Well, then I am not a murderess and I am having serious doubts as to whether I could ever become a vampire. How can you just kill someone? It's too horrible to even think about. Plus, I'm not going to do something that I know you won't even be grateful for. You are the most ungrateful man on the planet!"

"I'm ungrateful! I'm ungrateful!" Lex protested as if he were offended, then stopped and thought about what I said. "I am ungrateful."

"I know. Bastard." I turned my head away smirking to myself.

"Lillian, will you stop calling me that; my parents were married. Please, please, please help me this once? Please?" he asked sweetly, pouting his lip and locking my eyes with his swirling blue fire opals. "Just this once and I'll never ask you for anything ever again."

"That will be the day," I said sarcastically. "Lex, you can't be that weak. You can get your own victim yourself. Why do I have to do it?"

Lex straightened his shoulders as if he were about to tell me something very important. "This is a lesson that's why. I know you don't fully understand what it means to be a vampire and I would like you to learn from this. Being a vampire takes more than just sinking your teeth into someone. You must be able to find your victim, the right victim, and be discreet from beginning to end. Death is horrible but necessary and the power can be very seductive, but we try to keep a balance. Pleasure should not come from the act of killing, only from the blood."

"You just made that up," I said annoyed with him and his theatrical rhetoric.

"Yes. Yes I did, but if you want to be a vampire someday you'll have to learn these things anyway. So here's your chance to get a jump start on your education."

I wasn't sure how I felt about becoming a vampire but I conceded, "Okay, fine. I'll go ask someone to help me with my car, but that's it! The rest is up to you, I am not intervening. Okay? So just stop trying to teach me your vampire lore," I said sourly, "I already know death is horrible. Remember *I* may still have to face it one day."

I walked slowly to the diner, feeling out of place and nervous, but as soon as I entered I spotted my prey, or rather Lex's prey. He was sitting alone staring at people as though they were monsters. *Little did he know.* I wasn't sure why he'd stood out to me, but something about him seemed off, like he didn't belong there. I walked over to the young man going over what I was going to say in my head. I stopped in front of him, and as he looked up at me the look of horror left his face momentarily, but was soon replaced with a look of suspicion. Up close he was actually handsome. Short brown hair, brown eyes, and a muscular physique. He smiled uneasily, almost mockingly at me, but said nothing so I sat down next to him.

"I'm sorry to bother you but my father isn't feeling well. He's very old. I need to get him home and my car won't start. Could you help me?" *Wow, I needed acting lessons!* I sighed thankful that I had said everything as I had planned I would and didn't stutter or suddenly stop and swallow like I did sometimes when I was nervous.

The man stood up immediately, walked in front of me and said in a low voice, "Let's go." He gestured a little impatiently with his hand for me to lead the way.

"My car is over this way," I said as we came out of the diner, thinking that had been much easier than I'd anticipated.

I felt something pushed into my side. I looked down in shock to see a small gun, half concealed by his hand, pressed up against my side. No wonder the guy had seemed out of place in the diner. Who knows what he'd been planning to do with that little gun before I gave him another option.

"We're not going to your car, precious," the man said as he lent down close to my ear and nudged me to the right, toward the opposite side of the parking lot. "Are you here with someone?"

"I told you I'm with my father," I stated nervously, looking around wildly for any sign of Lex.

"You said he's old?"

Despite being scared out of my mind, I had to snicker to myself. "Oh yes, very old," I admitted, "and he is going to be extremely pissed off that you threatened me."

"There's not much he can do about it though is there," the man said, letting his lips brush against my hair.

Lex still wasn't coming, and the man was steering me closer to a lone car parked almost directly across the parking lot from where Lex's car was. I was really starting to worry. This might be it. This guy was going to shove me into his car and speed off before Lex even noticed I was gone. Finally, I saw him walking toward us.

"It's about time," I muttered to myself. Then loud enough for the man to hear I said smugly, *"That*...is my father."

The man froze when he saw Lex, young and swift, advancing toward us. I took the opportunity to push the gun away and make a run for it. Before I had even taken three steps Lex had the man by the back of the neck and was leading him back toward the Porsche.

"I'm afraid I'm going to have to punish you for your rude behavior toward my girl," Lex said as he dragged the man behind the tree we'd parked beneath.

I didn't want to watch but somehow I couldn't help it. The man didn't even fight as Lex delicately sank his teeth in, his eyes closed as if he were enjoying a long, delicious kiss. The whole thing was horrific and yet tender. I was both disgusted and fascinated. Watching the ease with which the man accepted his death, I was curious how it felt. I barely remembered the way it had felt when Jerrod had drank from me for just a few moments and I was very nearly tempted to ask Lex to drink from me just to understand what the man was feeling; how he could be so calm and resigned. It did take away much of the romanticism of being a vampire, to watch a person die, to know that this would have to become a regular part of your existence. To learn to live with the guilt of taking a life, no matter how undeserving that person is of that life, and owning the responsibility of that choice. I watched Lex pull away from the now lifeless body realizing, that day, I had made that choice. I had chosen that man out of everyone in that diner to die and I would have to live with that guilt even if I hadn't actually killed him myself and even if he had been planning to do something horrible to me.

Lex took out his key-chain, which had a small ornate pocket knife attached and used it to make a gash where his teethmarks had been, and then emptied the man's wallet. He then rested the man up against the tree, half covering him with branches and leaves. I watched all this somewhat in a daze. Strangely, I had this feeling that I had witnessed something like this before, but the feeling was dream-like, detached, and it didn't cure me of the shock I was experiencing at that moment.

"Lex, you killed him. You really killed him," I whispered trying to hold my tears back.

"I know. I'm a vampire, that's what we do. It's okay," he said matter-of-factly. "Come on let's get out of here."

I want to explain something before going on. I don't want you to think that I was cold or indifferent to the taking of another human's life. I wasn't. I didn't want to help Lex, but it was also a life I was thinking about having for myself. Becoming a vampire. I couldn't turn my nose up at his means of survival when I could possibly be doing the same thing in a few years; should he turn me. Plus, I did live with vampires and just the acceptance of living in a world where vampires existed affected my view of things. Normal things almost didn't seem real. Everlasting life, eternal youth, immeasurable power, these things were real in the world I knew. Death, although always surrounding us, seemed so far away, no matter how we tempted it. When I saw the young man at the diner die I felt confused about how to feel. It had been disturbing to see, but it had also been so peaceful, so seemingly painless and easy. I did fight with my emotions, because I did feel guilt, I did feel revulsion, but I also felt this sense of "maybe it's not so bad to die".

As I walked in the front door, with Lex behind me, I noticed a dark figure at the top of the stairs.

"Where have you been?" Rachel asked imperiously.

I had forgotten that Rachel was furious at Lex and wasn't sure how she was going to react to anything I said so I simply said, "We just went for a drive."

Rachel walked down a few steps toward us. "A drive? With a blood thirsty vampire, very smart Lillian," she reprimanded.

I didn't want Rachel to be angry with me so I tried to explain, "I didn't know. Lex didn't tell me what had happened until after I'd gotten in the car. Anyway he went to feed so that it won't happen again."

Rachel walked down the stairs, slowly, letting each footfall sound like the end of the world. She stopped on the first step of the staircase looking from me to Lex. For a moment I was nervous that she was going to slap me across the face.

"You're lucky he didn't have you for dinner," Rachel sneered with a strange glint in her eyes.

"Hey, I would never-" Lex began defensively.

"Rachel-"I tried to talk.

"Shut up, Lillian!" Rachel yelled meanly at me. "It must be so nice to be the favorite. To not have to worry about anyone draining you in your sleep. I don't know why you even wanted me to come here with you! Everything is about you!"

"Rachel, please can't the three of us be friends, and stop hating each other," Lex pleaded.

"You didn't seem to think so last night. You know, when you tried to kill me," Rachel sneered.

I again tried to intervene. "Ray, you're right Lex shouldn't have done what he did. He was completely wrong and he deserves to be punished."

"Okay, Lillian, I'm not sure where you're going with this, but-" Lex interrupted.

I ignored Lex. "Rachel, please don't be angry with me. I'm not trying to make anything about me. I've never been the center of attention before and I'm sorry if I've been inconsiderate to you. Please, don't be mad. Lex, isn't there anything you'd like to say?"

Lex got down on his hands and knees in front of Rachel. Going all out, with an over-the-top apology, Lex-style. I bit my lip and shook my head at him, not sure that was exactly the right approach to take.

With his hands clasped tightly, he begged pitifully, "Rachel, please forgive me. I didn't mean to scare you or make you think that I would ever hurt you. I am sorry beyond reason. Please. I was just so hungry, I couldn't control my thirst. Under normal circumstances you know I wouldn't have even thought of asking for such a favor, and I was only going to take a little drink. Just enough to give me the strength to hunt on my own." He paused a moment to let his pouting eyes take effect. "If it makes you feel any better I meant to drink from Lillian."

I glared at Lex after he said the last part, but seeing Lex on his knees reminded me of our little bet. I thought, perhaps, I could at least get a laugh out of Rachel.

"Lex," I said, grinning and giving him a superior look. Then I turned to Rachel and said triumphantly, "Guess who already broke a rule, and will be on his knees begging for my forgiveness in front of everyone at the end of this week *and* buying me a car."

Rachel burst out laughing and weeping at the same time. "I'm sorry for being so mean to you, Lillian." She hugged me and I felt relief that our friendship was still intact. She pulled away and slapped Lex playfully on his arm, exclaiming, "You! You deserved it, I should tell the council and let them beat you unmercifully, and don't you even think those pouting eyes have any effect on me." She almost sounded like her old self.

"You're right he did deserve it," I agreed.

"So...you forgive me right?" Lex asked, flashing his big, boyish smile.

"I shouldn't, but..." Rachel shook her head yes grudgingly, and Lex hugged her for taking pity on him.

Rachel smacked him in the chest. "You're a bastard you know that!"

I raised my eyebrows at Lex playfully. "See? I told you."

Lex completely ignored me and asked teasingly, "So are you girls up for a bit of prowling?"

"That is not funny. Haven't you learned your lesson about mortals and blood drinking?" I asked, shaking my head. "We don't find it exciting in the least. Plus, I don't think I could ever go through that again. Lex, that guy...is dead."

"That is what happens when a vampire feeds," Lex replied smartly.

I gave him an agonized look. "Well, I am not a vampire, I'm human, so I'm sorry if watching another human die doesn't give me a trill."

Lex brushed my cheek. "Little queen, would it make you feel any better if I told you I saw what he had planned for you, and it included your death and he was plenty thrilled about it."

I knew the man had been disturbed, but I had tried not to think about what would have happened if Lex hadn't gotten to me before the man had gotten me into his car. Sadly I admitted, "I guess it has some relevance."

"Good. So no more of this guilt over the death of a sadistic murderer," Lex said, nipping me under the chin playfully.

I huffed at his insensitivity but nodded my head in agreement.

Lex looked at Rachel and me thoughtfully for a moment and animatedly declared, "I've got it, we'll go out. We'll go dancing. A night out, just the three of us." He beamed at us hopefully.

Rachel looked uneasy again, but I nudged her. "Come on, Ray. We haven't been dancing in forever. Come on, it'll be fun."

Rachel sighed like she was irritated but agreed, "Fine, I'll go. I did have other plans, but I guess I can break them."

I looked at Rachel questioningly. "What other plans?"

Before she could answer Lex shouted enthusiastically, "Fantastic! Go change." Then he added with that big, boyish smile on his face again, "Make sure it's something blatantly seductive."

Rachel and I hurried back to our room to change. Rachel chose a black silk, high-collared, Chinese style dress with slits on the outer legs and I threw on a knee-length pale pink form-fitting dress with a v-neckline. We brushed our hair and ran to the Porsche where Lex was already sitting with the motor on.

Lex took us to a little blues bar in the city with a live band playing. Not his usual taste. Usually he would have picked the biggest, loudest, most over-crowded club he could find. I was going to point that out to him, but I didn't want to give him any ideas, because after the drama of the day I really just wanted to be able to spend time with both Lex and Rachel without having to fight crowds to do so. Somehow I think Lex knew all that, for once really putting our feelings before his own, plus he probably still felt guilty for his actions of the night before and wanted to keep his show-boating to a minimum that night.

Whatever his reasons were, it was a perfect night. The band was wonderful, it got crowded but not to the point where you couldn't move, and Lex danced to almost every song with us. There was no intrigue or death, just a meaninglessly fun evening. For the first time since we'd left North Carolina I felt like a regular girl hanging out with regular friends, and best of all there was no vampire drama. We stayed at the bar past closing time, four in the morning; Lex convinced the bar manager that he wouldn't get into any trouble staying open an hour past the city ordinance time. Hopefully that was true.

Rachel and I were exhausted walking back to the car, and though all the bars had closed an hour before, throngs of people still littered the sidewalks and street. Finally, Lex decided we were walking far too slow for him and told us to just wait where we were. He left us to go get the car and pull it around, even though cars were not permitted on the street due to pedestrian traffic. Rachel sat on a bench on the sidewalk with her head in her hands, tipsy and too tired to even talk. As I watched for Lex's Porsche to come barreling onto the street he wasn't even supposed to be driving on, I noticed someone staring at us from across the street.

A man, dressed all in black.

The strange thing was he was wearing a black velvet coat over his black button-up shirt and waistcoat; as if it weren't the middle of summer. Even stranger were the style of his clothes, they seemed old-fashioned, maybe Victorian. At first I thought he was probably dressed up for some theme-club or maybe he was in a theater show, but something felt wrong. He was stunning, too stunning.

I could feel the hair on the back of my neck stand up. Though there were still hundreds of people crowding the street, the man was staring straight at me. I knew he could plainly see that I noticed him watching me, but his expression didn't change and he didn't look away. I felt like time had slowed down as I studied every detail of the man's familiar pale face. He had full black eyebrows that cast shadows over his eyes, making him seem like he had a permanent scowl, a long almost flat nose, what might be described as a roman nose, and strong angular cheek and jaw bones. His hair was so black it nearly blended in with his clothing; the pin-straight, glossy black strands spilled over his shoulders. Although everything about him seemed so dark, even from across the street I could see that he had piercing, icy blue eyes. They were so bright they very nearly looked florescent, shining their beam on me. It felt as if those cold shafts of light were boring right into me, as if he were trying to pick away at the very wall of my hidden mind.

My heart was pounding and my brain kept screaming, V*ampire! He's a vampire!*

But if he were a vampire he should have sensed Lex was near. Lex may not have been particularly old but he had been given some very old, very powerful blood, and this man, this vampire, should have sensed it and been scared to come so close. Instead the man stood calmly still; only his long black hair moved slightly from the breeze as his lips curled into a cruel, familiar smile. His eyes wouldn't let me go; they were like beacons shining from across the street, calling me to him. I felt a pull from inside my middle that made me want to go to him, but I fought it.

"Ray, I think we need to go," I said as calmly as possible, not taking my eyes off the man.

Rachel lifted her head and looked in the direction I was looking. "Who is that? He looks like a..."

"A vampire," I finished for her.

"Look, here comes Lex," Rachel said anxiously as she waved her arms above her head signaling to Lex.

Without realizing what I was doing I started walking toward the dark-haired vampire. I felt like I was dreaming, my mind was telling me to stop, but my body just kept moving forward. It was terrifying not having control over myself, and yet I felt strangely drawn to the man and almost anxious to find out what he was going to do once I reached him. I heard my own voice saying something, but I couldn't understand why I was hearing my voice because I wasn't talking. I thought it sounded as if I'd said I missed you, and then something that sounded like general. The last thing I remembered was looking into those cold blue eyes, hearing Rachel scream my name, and tires screeching to a halt.

The next time I woke up it was two days later. June twenty-ninth. I opened my eyes in a dimly lit room and felt a pair of freezing cold hands on mine. I sat up abruptly, confused, and Lex screamed my name so loud that it hurt my ears. Everyone looked up and beamed relieved smiles at me.

The first ones to my side were Mason, Rachel, and...Dallen Gray? I stared at Dallen, confused that he was there. I thought maybe this was all just a dream, but my stomach was burning so severely from hunger I knew that it all must have been real. I noticed that even Osborn was there, standing off against the wall, looking anxiously on, and giving me a look of relief as our eyes met.

Osborn still made me uncomfortable and he must have realized he was staring again, because he cleared his throat uncomfortably and when everyone turned to him he explained apologetically, "I have to be going. I'm happy to see you're better, Lillian." Then he nodded to someone in the room and walked out.

Lex finally took his hands off mine and left something there. I opened my hands and looked. Rosary beads? I laughed to myself thinking of the old myths about vampires not being able to look at crosses. I felt my chest where something cold was hung around my neck. I took it from under my shirt and saw a large silver crucifix with a ruby in its center. *Why would they give me crosses?*

Dallen sat on the end of the bed by my feet. I sat up a little to look at him.

My eyes blinked questioningly and finally I asked, "I thought you couldn't come back? I thought your work wouldn't let you?"

Dallen smiled looking around a little uneasily and answered, "My boss decided I needed more time off. Then I heard you weren't well so I..." He cleared his throat nervously, blushing as he whispered, "I had to make sure you were all right."

I blushed a little myself. "Thank you. I'm glad you came back."

Dallen seemed to check how near Lex was as he whispered, "As am I," and then loud enough for everyone to hear he explained brightly, "I look forward to reading more of your poetry."

My heart was beating a little faster than usual, but I tried to calm it by convincing myself that Dallen was just being kind because I hadn't been well. He couldn't have really returned just to see how I was doing, he had been so adamant about not being able to come back, but I decided maybe his company had really just talked him into taking more time off and he had nowhere else to go. I looked around from face to face, waiting for someone to actually explain what had happened, because I was a little foggy after being knocked out for two days, but everyone seemed to just want to stare at me dumbly with smiles on their faces.

Frustrated I blurted out, "You know I still don't know what's going on? What happened? The last thing I remember was leaving a club with Rachel and Lex."

Everyone tried to explain what happened all at the same time, and I noticed that Rachel was not among them. I hadn't even seen her leave, but for some reason she had slipped out without saying goodbye. At last Lex told them I needed rest; Lex stayed behind to explain to me what had happened. I could see him watching uncomfortably as everyone left. If I didn't know him better I would've said he looked almost anxious.

"You fainted outside the bar waiting for me to pick you and Rachel up. We're not sure why. I had a doctor, a good friend of mine, come to check you out, he said you were fine. The only thing he could think was that you drank something at the club that caused it."

I shook my head starting to remember and questioned, "What about that other vampire? It must have had something to do with him. He made me feel so strange."

Lex paced along the side of the bed. "There was no vampire, little queen. You must have imagined that." I could see he was nervously waiting to see if I accepted his answer.

If I haven't mentioned before, you've probably guessed by now; Lex is a terrible liar. You'd think someone whose very existence depended on lying would be an expert, but all you had to do was watch his mannerisms closely and it was a dead giveaway. Two hundred and twenty-three years had not made him good at looking someone in the eye and convincing them that he was telling the truth. Good thing he had a knack for charming people.

I leaned back against my pillows, watching him, in time I just sighed, "Lex, I know you're lying. What are you hiding?"

"Me, hiding, why would you...what would make you think that?"

I didn't even explain, I just looked hard at him, until finally he nodded his head in defeat. "You're right, Lilly. Rachel told me you had seen a man, you thought he was a vampire; I asked her not to say anything to anyone else, but I didn't tell her why. She was pretty scared, and has been lecturing me non-stop about the danger I put you two in and my inability to give you two a normal life and blah, blah, blah..."

I didn't like seeing Lex this unnerved, I asked shakily, "You know who he is, don't you?"

Lex sat on the side of the bed and took my hands in his. "Lilly, I admit it, I have put you in terrible danger. If I had known that he knew where we were I would've never brought you and Rachel here." Lex rubbed his forehead in agitation. "I thought you would be safer here. I thought I could protect you better here and he wouldn't be able to find you."

"What do you mean, are you talking about him knowing where the council is? And who is he?" I was getting impatient.

"His name is Dardanos. He's the one that created me, part of the reason I'm so strong is because I have his blood flowing through me. He was created by Malika, so I don't have to tell you how powerful he is, and he's very old. I'm talking before Christ old," he explained as he started wringing his hands agitatedly.

I felt a shiver. "Dardanos. I feel like I know that name."

Lex continued, "You said his name a few times and you kept mentioning someone called General. I assumed he planted his name in your mind, but I don't know who the General is. You were a bit crazy for a while there. It was like you were hypnotized or in a trance; you weren't awake but you would talk sometimes. You told me I belonged in hell and that I'm a filthy murderer. That this house and everyone in it should be burned. You said something about your family being killed." Lex paused as if he were waiting for me to react, but went on, "Then you asked for a rosary to ward off evil. You said you needed a crucifix to protect you from the evil man. I'm guessing you meant Dardanos. Lilly, he's unbelievably powerful. Look what he did to you and you were almost fifty feet away from him. I think...I think I should send you and Rachel away. Somewhere you'd be safe."

I was stunned. "Send us away? Don't you think he would follow us, don't you think we'd be safer here with you?"

Lex shook his head at a loss. "I don't know. I don't know for sure that he's after you or not. I have reason to believe he's been following you for a long time, but he may just be after me and the council." Lex stopped seeing the question on the tip of my tongue and replied, "I can't tell you why. Some of it has to do with the council and I don't have permission to share it...with anyone. I just...I don't know what to do, little queen."

Lex leaned over and hugged me, pulling back slowly. "I have to go. I haven't fed since two nights ago, and I can't risk being in a weakened state again with Dardanos so near."

"Lex, again? What have you been doing since I've been like this?"

He brushed my cheek lightly with the back of his hand. "I've been with you. I couldn't leave. Not for a second. Not when I knew it was my fault. I made a promise to keep you safe." He kissed my forehead and as he left the room he whispered, "I won't let anything happen to you, Lilly. I swear it, on my soul."

I lay back in bed thinking about this new turn of events when I noticed I was in another room. The bed had four high posts around it, and a fluffy comforter that matched the white lace and blue sheer curtains that were drawn around the bed. I remembered this room. The comforter that was laid over me was the same one I'd thrown out the window when I'd gotten so angry at Lex.

It was Lex's room. The same room that held Lex's coffin, or so I believed. Not exactly a comforting thought that by night he was sitting near me holding my hand, and by day sleeping below me out of the reach of the sun's rays. Then again would he actually allow so many people, vampires and mortals, in his room to visit me if his coffin really was there somewhere?

Maybe I'd been wrong all along about Lex's coffin being in that room. Maybe Lex let everyone believe his coffin was hidden there so that he didn't have to worry about anyone trying to go looking for it, or maybe it had been there and he moved it after my little tantrum. Still, it made me a little uneasy to have been unconscious for two days in someone's bed, not my own. Further still I felt uneasy that Lex was hiding more than just the things he told me he couldn't tell me pertaining to the council.

Although he speculated that Dardanos had shown up so close to the mansion because of some vendetta against Lex and the council, I felt an overwhelming despair that it had more to do with my arrival there. I looked around for my poetry book, longing to look at my photo of Ben. I tried imagining what he would say to me if he were actually there at that moment, but I had known him for such a short time I really couldn't remember how he spoke or what his personality was like. I found my book lying on the nightstand beside the bed, but instead of taking out the photo of Ben I found myself writing. I couldn't stop thinking about Dardanos, and the strange feelings he'd produced in me. I reread the first few lines I'd just written:

> *His face of pale moon*
>
> *With that haunting shade*
>
> *Beckoned me from afar*
>
> *And my soul obeyed*

I finally fell asleep after hours of failed attempts to get the memory of Dardanos' face out of my mind, but once asleep my dreams were filled with images of him which I found strangely enticing. I couldn't help it; no matter how frightened I was, I also felt inexplicably drawn to him. Thankfully, I was ripped from these disturbing dreams of Dardanos around three in the morning by a raving member of Lex's household staff. He was jumping up and down screaming for me to get up. His French accent was so thick and he was so agitated I couldn't make out what he was saying, and how he'd gotten into Lex's bedroom, I couldn't figure out. Finally, I told him to calm down and tell me slowly what was wrong.

"Monsieur Cavanaugh and Monsieur Rossi, Ils sont fous! They are mad! Ils sont combat á l'épée! Sword Fighting! Monsieur Rossi has been cut twice and Monsieur Cavanaugh seemed to have been stabbed! Mr. Spencer will not allow us to call la police!" the man screamed as I tried to understand through his accent.

"Mr. Spencer?" I asked groggily, not able to place the name.

After a moment I realized he meant Bradley, the high and mighty butler. I was still half asleep and not really understanding what the man was telling me. I just sat there staring at him thinking this must be part of my delusions from the past two days and was about to go back to bed when the man threw back the covers and dragged me out of bed. I noticed I was wearing a white silk nightgown that I didn't remember putting on myself. The man led me to the garden where I saw a group of people watching, and either cheering on Vann and Lex or pleading with them to stop fighting. Rachel ran to me screaming excitedly and jumping up and down telling me to stop them, and something about our moral judgment deteriorating around such ridiculous spectacles.

Dallen Gray walked up to us, told Rachel to calm down, and turned to me. "Lillian, will you please try to persuade them to stop this nonsense? They're going to expose themselves to much more than ridicule if they continue."

I looked down at the ground, not wanting to be bothered. I didn't want to be in the middle of anything anymore, and I certainly didn't want to be drug out of bed to reprimand Lex for his behavior. How had I become known as the one that could "handle" Lex and curb his conduct? I was still a teenager; I should have been the one doing stupid stuff and being told to act right, instead of being in charge of keeping Lex's eccentricities in check. I sighed as I reluctantly walked to the front of the crowd and saw Lex and Vann fighting. There were three swords covered with blood discarded on the ground.

"Stop!" I yelled, attempting to sound authoritative.

Lex and Vann stopped, smiled, waved at me, and then began fighting again.

I walked closer to them with one of the swords in hand, and said only loud enough for them to hear, "Stop. If you don't I'll lick the blood off of this sword. You know what that would do to me."

This time they stopped and walked toward me, confused by my threat.

"That is not enough blood to do anything, but make you severely ill," Lex answered smartly.

"Besides we only were having a bit of fun," Vann said.

"Well, everyone is going crazy." I gestured to the crowd. "And I got yanked out of bed by one of your employees who was ready to call the cops."

"Oh, we didn't notice." Lex shrugged calmly. "Sorry."

I shook my head disapprovingly at him and rolled my eyes. Then I grabbed the swords from Lex and Vann and was about to walk away with them when I noticed we were still surrounded by people and they were staring at me. The crowd was quiet, anxiously awaiting an explanation.

"Wasn't that a great show? Fantastic sword play! You never know what entertainment you'll get when Lex has a party. Great job, guys!" I yelled nervously and started clapping.

Vann and Lex seemed lost as to what I was talking about, but everyone else watching started clapping. I smiled at the crowd of people and gestured for one of the staff to take the swords away as I realized I was only wearing my white silk nightgown in front of dozens of strangers. No one seemed to think anything of it. Of course, I did see more than one person stumble as they walked. Thankfully I think everyone believed Vann and Lex's sparring had all been some kind of theatrical entertainment from their somewhat eccentric host. I'm sure stranger things had happened at Lex's parties.

Music started playing from dozens of small speakers placed around the garden and people were suddenly dancing around me. Dallen made his way through the crowd to where I was standing, grabbed my hand, and pulled me close.

"I hope you don't mind dancing with me? You looked like you were waiting to be asked." Dallen's smile made my heart melt.

"Actually I feel like I'm still asleep. I have no idea what is going on."

Dallen led me in a slow dance, even though the music was somewhat fast-paced. It didn't matter, nothing else seemed to exist. I was entranced by everything about him, his beautiful face, his soft yearning eyes, and the soft powdery musk clinging to his skin. He in turn studied me, smiling now and then, and then he would look away saddened by something. Finally, the music slowed to our pace and couples surrounded us.

"You are perfect, you know?" Dallen admitted as if he had hoped to find me otherwise.

I tucked my hair behind my ear and stammered uneasily, "No, I am far from perfect." Then I leaned closer to whisper in his ear, "Are you trying to make me fall in love with you?"

Dallen lent back a little, raising an eyebrow exaggeratedly. "Why, is it working?"

I giggled and teased back, "No. Not even remotely."

"I must warn you, if you show up in your nightgown you must expect men to try to make you fall in love with them," Dallen purred with his beautiful accent.

I smirked sourly at him. "Hey, I was yanked out of bed unexpectedly by a crazed French-speaking servant. I really didn't have time to dress for the occasion."

Dallen laughed and squeezed me tighter to his body. I liked the way he laughed, and smiled, and looked at me, and spoke to me, and held me, and it made me wonder if, perhaps, I would fall in love with him after all. It seemed like such an easy thing, to fall in love with Dallen. It was strange, though, that he'd shown up just after Malika had put Rachel and me on a probationary period to decide if we wanted to become vampires or not. He was the perfect alternative; he was soft and gentle, obviously intelligent yet so humble and simple, he was beautiful and engaging, and for some reason he took an earnest interest in me. It almost felt like a test. As if someone knew I was trying to decide whether I wanted The Immortal Fate or not, and decided to present me with a perfect mortal man to delay or confuse my decision. I decided I was just not used to the attention from a seemingly normal man; it was a new experience for me to actually be attracted to someone that was attracted to me as well...and was...well, human.

The party was winding down, and I was now beyond exhausted by all of the unplanned dancing, but I also felt a little exhilarated by Dallen's attentions. It was getting close to daybreak and the vampires had to start retiring; the mortals followed the lead of their host and departed.

After all of the people left, Lex showed me to my new room.

"What's wrong with my old room?" I asked, confused.

Lex pursed his lips as if he didn't want to have to be the one to tell me. "It seems Rachel is in need of some personal space."

I scrunched my eyebrows confused. "Personal space? I don't under-"

Lex cut me off, "Apparently she's met someone and feels that it might be inconvenient to have a roommate at this time. I don't know, she doesn't confide anything to me anymore, but I think she wants more alone time. Anyway this will be your room. I believe the only other person in this wing is Dallen. He's right next door," Lex said pointing to the door just beyond my room.

I said goodnight to Lex and entered the room. It had the same four-poster bed as the first room I shared with Rachel, only everything in this room was a dark, rich crimson. There was a balcony like the one in the other room as well, only not quite as large

I suddenly realized I hadn't talked to Rachel since I had awoken from my two day slumber. Unless, of course, you counted when she had run up to me screaming like a crazy person. I was trying to remember who she had been dancing with. I recalled glimpsing her dancing with a man with exceedingly short brown hair. They were dancing very close, but Rachel looked strange. It was almost like she was disgusted with everything around her; as if she were seeing everything in a new light, and she didn't much like it. I saw the man she was dancing with hold her face so she would look at him, and he whispered something in her ear. She had smiled and if I had to guess I'd say she gave the man a look of absolute worship.

He must have been the one that Lex was talking about, the one Rachel had met. How in the world had she met someone, confined to the mansion as we were? Apparently a lot can happen while you're knocked out for two days; an evil vampire was out to destroy Lex, Dallen Gray had mysteriously returned, I had gotten kicked out of my own room, and Rachel had somehow fallen in love.

I suddenly realized who Rachel had been dancing with and it did not make me feel all warm and fuzzy inside. Now I remembered noticing Dallen glance at Rachel and the man and as I turned to see what he was looking at I saw Osborn Hune returning a severe look of distaste, whether directed at Dallen or myself I wasn't sure. At the time, I was so focused on being with Dallen it didn't even hit me that I had seen Osborn.

How could Rachel be in love with Osborn? I had only spoken with the man a few times but I certainly did not like the impressions he left, and maybe it was just my imagination but I felt like he was always watching me. I supposed I'd have to find out what had happened from

Rachel tomorrow, but right then I needed sleep.

Being put into a two day coma by a diabolical vampire really took a lot of a girl.

A NIGHT IN THE UN-LIFE...

The knock at the door distracted Lillian from her book. She got up from the desk, grabbed the oval pendant she'd placed next to her laptop, slipped the chain over her head, and moved to open the door.

"Oh, hello, Ash, how are you?"

The artist ran his fingers through his shoulder-length brown hair nervously. "Fine, Lilly. I'm very sorry to bother you, but there's a man down stairs with a very big package for you. So I thought instead of letting some sleazy old man you don't know bother you, I would." He smiled broadly realizing how silly he had sounded.

"So you're going to be the sleazy man that bothers me?" Lillian laughed lightly at his nervousness.

Ash looked shyly at the floor. "Now you know why I paint. I don't exactly have a way with words."

"Well, painting is a form of expression. So you speak through your paintings. Though, since I've never seen any, I can't say how well you speak," Lillian said trying to hint her curiosity to him.

"I guess you'll never know then," Ash teased.

Lillian walked past him down the stairs. "I don't see why you're so secretive about it." She opened the front door in the hall as Ash walked down the stairs to her side. "Unless you're really awful."

Ash smiled at the jab, and countered, "No, I'm just going by your motto: People can't hate you if they don't know you."

Lillian turned around while signing her name as the receiver of the large package that was sitting on the sidewalk in front of the door. "That's not my motto. When ever did I say that?"

"You didn't. I just assumed it was, because, well, in the two months that you've lived here this is the most you've ever said to me. So I convinced myself that the only reason you never really talked to me before was because it went against your personal rules for human contact. Either that or you're scared of me," Ash said playfully raising his eyebrows.

"Well, Ash, I'm afraid you're wrong on both counts. I really only have one personal rule for human contact, and I won't tell you what it is because it's my little secret. And don't flatter yourself into thinking that I'm scared to talk to you. The only reason I never talked to you that much before was either I thought you were too busy painting or I was too busy writing." Lillian handed the signing sheet back to the man outside the door. "Could you please bring that up for me?"

"Sure lady," The man grunted unhappily.

"Ash, I wish I weren't so pressed for time but I promised myself I would at least finish two more chapters of my book tonight. I'm sorry, but I really need to work."

"I understand. I have to finish some work too before I go bankrupt." Ash paused a moment giving Lillian a strange stare and then asked hesitantly, "I bought this poetry book a few weeks ago by a Lillian Gray, did you write that? It was called *Immortal Dreams*, but I couldn't find a picture connected with the author so I wasn't sure if it was you or not?"

Lillian smiled bashfully, knowing that Ash had most likely searched her name looking for information about her. "Yes, that was me. Poetry was always my first love, novel writing is very new to me, but not everyone takes to poetry the way they take to a story so I thought I'd try it out."

"Well, I can't say that I'm an avid reader of poetry, but I did very much enjoy your poems. Some of them were very sad, hopeless even, but they certainly kept me interested. Anyway I guess I should go. I know you're busy." Ash turned to leave but stopped and looked back at Lillian, finally summoning the nerve to ask her, "Would you like to go out sometime? I mean I know you probably have better things to do, but I think I would hate myself if I never had the courage to at least ask." Ash held his breath waiting for the answer.

Lillian could hear the pounding of his heart and see the miniscule dots of sweat forming on his skin. She couldn't help but smile at his anxiousness as she answered, "Sure. How about tomorrow night?"

"Wonderful!" Ash exclaimed, and Lillian thought she actually heard his heart skip a beat.

"But now I really have to get back to my book."

"Of course, of course. Tomorrow night, then." Ash jumped wildly down the stairs. When he was half way down he turned around and threw his arms out. "You… are an angel!" Then he continued dancing down the stairs into his studio.

Lillian thanked the delivery man for lugging the large, heavy box upstairs for her. After escorting him back out of the apartment Lillian stood looking at the large box filled with wood for the custom coffin she was going to build. She thought about opening the box, but instead sat down at her desk to continue writing.

Now where was I? Lillian thought to herself, thumbing the pendant hanging at her neck.

"Ahhh, yes. Dallen….."

ಬ7ଔ

I fell into the plush, dreamy bed ready to sleep peacefully, but it was not to be. After I turned the light out and pulled the covers over myself I heard a noise. I opened my eyes to inspect the origin of the noise when a shadowy figure darted from behind the massive dresser to the closet and closed the door softy. My heart began to race like it was trying to beat out of my chest. I wanted to pull the covers over my head so that whatever it was couldn't get me, but instead I pretended that I hadn't seen it. I swung my feet over the side of the bed and yawned.

"Why does Dallen have to make so much noise?" I asked out loud as I walked out of the room trying to convince the monster in my closet I hadn't seen him.

As soon as I exited my room I bolted to the right, straight into Dallen's room, frightened that whatever was in my room may chase after me.

"Dallen," I whispered urgently into the darkness. "Dallen, are you here?"

As I waited for a reply it dawned on me that Dallen might not even be in his room, but then I heard a sniffle followed by Dallen's voice sounding confused, "Yes. Lillian? Is that you?"

Finding a light switch on the wall I flicked it on. Dallen sat up abruptly in bed, pulling the covers up to his waist so all I could see was his bare chest and arms. He looked amazing not wearing his usual stuffy dress shirt and pants, and his hair was beautifully tussled instead of his severe, clean-cut side part. I stared at him for a moment, feeling embarrassed by the feelings that his half-clothed form was producing, but then I remembered how frightened I was.

I tried not to let his appearance affect my already shaky composure as I explained, "Dallen, there's someone in my room. They were watching me. I'm really scared. After I got in bed, they ran into my closet, and I don't think they realized I saw them. I think they're still in there."

He threw back the covers, and I think my breathe actually caught in my throat as he got out of bed, but I saw that he was at least wearing gray pajama pants. I could feel my cheeks reddening for what I had thought I'd see when he stood up. Dallen looked at me slyly and smiled. I wondered if he had read my mind, and felt even more embarrassed.

He put his robe on and placed his hand protectively on my arm. "Don't worry, I'll go look. Wait here," he said walking out of the room.

I sat down on the right side of the bed, and waited as Dallen left to inspect my room. A moment after he had left I thought, perhaps, I shouldn't have let him go. What if the intruder had a weapon, or worse, what if the intruder was a vampire. I could have just sent Dallen to his death. I was startled by a noise that sounded like it came from just outside Dallen's balcony doors, but before I could work up the courage to go check Dallen was back. I looked at him anxiously for an answer.

"Whoever was in your room must have climbed down from the balcony. All I saw was someone running across the yard, looking back at your window. I couldn't see what he looked like, it was too dark," he explained, though, strangely he wouldn't meet my eyes.

I shivered and drew my knees up to my chin, pulling my long nightgown down over my feet. "Why would anyone sneak into my room? It doesn't make sense; I don't have anything worth taking. Who would know that was my room, anyway? I didn't even know it was my room until about fifteen minutes ago when Lex broke the news to me that I was switching rooms."

"Indeed, how would anyone know that was your room, I didn't even know, and that is probably just it," Dallen reasoned, "this intruder most likely wasn't after you. For all we know it could have been some drunken guest from the party looking for valuables in an empty room. You know how negligent Lex is with his guest list; any manner of people could be in the mansion during one of his parties."

I nodded my head, feeling a little better. "Whatever the reason, I certainly don't want to sleep in that room. At least not tonight." I pursed my lips and laughed nervously. "I don't think I'm going to be able to sleep at all tonight, no matter where I sleep."

"You can sleep here if you like," Dallen offered softly. "I won't let anything harm you. At least you'll be able to relax knowing someone is right beside you, and I promise to be a complete gentleman," Dallen promised holding up his right hand.

I wanted to say no, because I wasn't sure I'd be able to sleep in the same bed as a man that I couldn't look at without blushing, but I also felt rattled. After what had happened with Dardanos just nights before and then an intruder sneaking about in my room, I was starting to feel something like a target. So many things seemed to be swirling closer and closer to me, and it was scaring me. In the end I was just too scared to spend the night alone, and so I agreed.

I got under the covers beneath where I sat and scooted my body as far to the right as I could without falling off the bed. Dallen turned out the light and crawled under the covers on the far left side of the bed. I was actually starting to doze off when I heard Dallen sniffle a few times and then his body shook as if he were trying not to cry. It was impossible to ignore the sound of his muffled sobs, which seemed to be getting ever so slightly louder, and go back to sleep. I touched him on the shoulder and asked him what was wrong.

Dallen rolled over onto his back and whispered, "Do you remember last week when I told you my brother died?"

"Yes," I whispered uncomfortably, regretting I'd said anything.

Of course I was too young at the time to know that when a man is crying in bed the best thing to do is roll over and pretend to be sleeping. There are only two reasons a man ever cries in bed with a woman: either he's trying to gain her sympathy and in so doing gain something else from her or he is very, very guilty of something. Like I said I was too young and inexperienced to know better, I truly felt concern for his feelings, and I thought it might help if he talked about what was wrong.

"I lied to you. I didn't want to bother you with the horrid truth. My life has always presented me with some misery and I didn't want to bring you into it." He paused a moment as if collecting his thoughts, and then whispered sadly, "I honestly didn't think I'd see you ever again, and I didn't want to burden you with the tragedies in my life."

My heart sank in sympathy and I lost a little of my discomfort as I thought about the tragedies in my own life. "I've known my share of misery as well. I know how hard it is to keep things inside, so people don't see how troubled you are. You can tell me, I promise it won't change my feelings for you." I felt my cheeks getting hot again and quickly corrected, "I mean it won't affect our friendship."

Dallen pulled my hand to his lips. "Lillian, I do consider you a friend. More than a friend, really. I should have known any woman that can handle living with a vampire could handle my tragedies." He let out a sigh. "I told you my brother had died a year ago but that was a lie, he didn't die until just a little over a month before I met you."

"That isn't such a bad lie," I tried soothing. "I can understand why you wouldn't want to tell a stranger that your brother had just died, it was probably easier to deal with the pain to pretend it had happened longer ago."

"No, no, that's not it," Dallen interrupted. "It's the circumstances surrounding his death, and...and it has to do with my wife."

I muttered in surprise, "Your wife? You're married?"

"Not anymore," he replied sadly and continued, "About a year ago my brother had gone missing, we thought maybe he had gotten into drugs, he had started acting strange before his disappearance. I had to go away for work for a few days, hoping that my brother would just show up with some crazy story about going off on some solitary camping trip, but my wife called me every day to tell me there had been no news. When I got back from my trip I pulled in the driveway and noticed the front door wide open. I ran for the door, knowing something was not right, but before I even got to the front step I heard gunshots. When I entered the house I saw my wife dead on the floor. My brother was just standing over her with a gun in his hand, staring at her as if he couldn't figure out what had happened, but when he saw me he seemed to snap awake and realized what he had done and he ran. He'd been on the run up until about two months ago. When the police found him there was a stand-off...he was shot. They said he died straight off...no suffering."

I could feel warm tears slowly tracing down my cheeks. For the first time in my life I actually thought maybe what I'd gone through hadn't been so bad. Maybe there were worse things than seeing your uncle kill himself, than being despised by your parents, than being treated like an outcast for your whole life, than being attacked by an out-of-control vampire, or worse than being thrust into a dark, decadent world of death and deception from which I may not be able to ever leave...even if I should want to.

I was shocked by Dallen's story, but managed to say, "Oh, Dallen, I'm so sorry. You didn't have to tell me. I'm sure you must think I'm so nosy. I had no idea."

"I don't think you're nosy at all. You're very kind," he said turning over on his side to look at me. "I'm sorry that I upset you. I should have warned you again. I guess I'm not very good with people. I never know what to say or how to behave when I'm alone with someone. I am sorry I didn't tell you the truth from the beginning. I felt ashamed to share so much with a stranger, but I don't want to keep things from you any longer." Dallen reached over wiping my tears away with his thumbs.

"You don't owe me any explanations, Dallen. Death is difficult to deal with, especially when it involves people we love," I said simply, feeling confused about how Dallen had seemed, yet again, to not want to talk about what was bothering him, but then spilled the entire story as if he had actually just been waiting for an opportunity to tell me.

"I just want you to know that I trust you," Dallen whispered back, "You are one of the only people I do trust. I think it may be because you remind me of my wife. You're so understanding and...lovely. I'm sure I don't have to tell you that you are beautiful...and unbelievably charming. After spending just one afternoon with you, I don't think I could have stayed away. Even if you had never been ill, I would have had to come back to see you. You seem to have this effect on me; you put me at ease like I have never felt before."

I didn't know what to say to that. Dallen had just told me about his brother's and wife's deaths and now it seemed like he was trying to seduce me. I was unbelievably attracted to him, but there was this little voice telling me something didn't quite fit. Again, I wondered if my feelings of suspicion were more to do with my lack of experience with the opposite sex than actual leery behavior on Dallen's part.

I tossed off, "That's just because you don't know me very well. Trust me, Dallen, there is nothing easy about me. I'm moody, I make rash decisions, I make jokes in uncomfortable situations, and I'm completely useless."

"I don't think you're useless." He sat up, leaning on his elbow to face me. "I could find use for you. I could kiss you right now, if I thought you wouldn't be angry with me," he said in a low serious whisper.

I was surprised by his request, but decided it was probably part of his grieving process. Everyone deals with things differently right? Maybe he needed to feel some human contact, feel like he belonged in the world, or maybe he was just too enticing for me to refuse and I was making excuses to myself.

"I wouldn't be angry," I whispered back slowly, not sure if that was the right thing to say.

Suddenly I felt his hand slip under my hip and his other up my back to cradle my head. He pulled me forward and pressed his mouth firmly against mine, lapping at my tongue with his. When I realized what was going on I put my arms around him and kissed back forcefully feeling my hunger for passion rising. I liked the way his body felt pressed close to mine.

Of course I had kissed boys before, but this was different. This was serious. This was leading to something more. This was the first time as a woman that I had kissed a man. Not to mention that we were in bed, in the dark, half-clothed. I didn't want it to stop no matter how much my brain tried reasoning with me, but in the end the decision to stop was made for me.

Suddenly the door had slammed open, and the light was on.

There in the doorway stood Lex.

Dallen and I both stopped dead, so to speak, and looked at him waiting for his reaction.

"What the hell were you two doing?" Lex demanded.

"Frankly, it's none of your business," I said sitting up, caught completely off-guard by Lex's over-protective attention.

"I think it is. You live in my home. Anything you do is my business. Now get your ass out of this room, Lillian!" Lex shouted.

"No!" I screamed back.

Lex stomped over to the bed and grabbed my arm, dragging me out of the room.

"That hurts! Let me go!" I screamed, not believing that Lex was actually behaving that way.

"Let her go!" Dallen screamed as he made to get out of bed.

"Sit down!" Lex ordered Dallen.

Dallen sat on the bed. Anger flooding his face. Lex practically threw me into the wall across from the room.

"Stay!" he said pointing to me.

"Yes, master," I said sarcastically.

Lex walked back into the room to reprimand Dallen, "This is my home, Dallen, and *YOU* are *MY* guest! I cannot believe you would act so disrespectfully to me! I don't want you touching her, ever! Do you know how old she is?"

Dallen put his hand to his head. "She's nineteen, Lex, not exactly a child! She can make her own decisions, and I never planned for this to happen, it's just......."

"She reminds you of Christine," Lex spat.

Dallen hesitated as if that wasn't what he'd meant, but instead simply answered, "She reminds me of my wife."

Lex shook his head. "You're such a sentimental idiot. Let me tell you something; Lillian is no Christine. I only spoke with your wife a few times, but I read her thoughts and I know you must have as well. She wasn't true to you. As a matter of fact her thoughts told me she resented your marriage. She wanted to be free to fool around with whomever she chose. Which she did, as I'm sure you already know. So don't you dare say that Lillian reminds you of Christine. I'll tell you something else that you probably don't know. She actually told me that she wanted The Immortal Fate; she asked if I might turn her. Your own wife...she was planning on leaving you a long time before she died." Then he walked out of the room slamming the door.

"Now. What were you doing?" Lex asked looking at me authoritatively.

I smiled slyly. "Wouldn't you like to know."

"I don't want you near him," Lex said, pointing to the door.

"Excuse me? Are you trying to tell me what I can and cannot do? You're not my father."

"Well thank God for small favors. The point is I want you to stay away from him, and all the rest of my friends for that matter," Lex stated, walking away down the hall.

I burst out laughing, almost falling on the floor. Lex turned around, watched me, and then walked back toward me.

"What are you laughing at?" he asked, folding his arms moodily.

"You," I said still laughing.

"Why?" he asked with a puzzled look on his face. "Did I do something funny?"

"You're jealous of me," I declared.

He looked down at me and scrunched his eyebrows in mystification. "What?"

"You're jealous because your friends like me better. They think I'm so sweet and kind and understanding. They love me. They think I'm an angel, even when I flip out and start tearing everything up. Your friends would rather be with me than with you," I said, laughing uncontrollably.

Lex pointed his finger in my face. "That is not why." Then he softened and said calmly, "I have told you, I made a promise to keep you safe, and I intend to do that. I won't have you throwing your virginity away on some lonely, and older I might add, broken man, who is only pining away for his dead wife."

My face was aflame as I shouted back, "My virginity is none of your business! No one ever told you to keep me from ever having sex. Don't you think that might be an experience I'd like to have at least once before I choose to become a vampire...or end up murdered by some ancient immortal out for revenge against you?" I folded my arms, exhausted, and slid down the wall to sit.

Lex looked at me all choked up, he didn't say anything, just shook his head at a loss, and walked away. I sat on the floor, my back against the wall and cried softly, for how long I can't say.

When I awoke the next morning, my entire body aching I might add, I was still in the hall. I must have fallen asleep there, and my body was not thanking me for that. I got up and noticed that Dallen's door was open just slightly, but when I pushed the door open I could see that he had gone. I couldn't understand why he had just left me in the hall; he must have heard me crying just across the hall from his door. Why hadn't he even checked to see if I was all right? Maybe Lex had really scared him, or maybe he just didn't care about me as much as he had tried to make me believe.

I was trying to come up with a million different reasons for why Dallen hadn't rescued me from an uncomfortable night's sleep on the hallway floor as I went into my room to get dressed. The first thing I saw as I entered was my clothing haphazardly piled inside a suitcase that was lying open on the bed. I checked the dresser and the closet, but all of my clothes were gone. All that was left was whatever was in the suitcase. I searched through the messy pile and found an ivory, satin-lined chiffon dress that came just past my knees that didn't seem to have gotten too wrinkled. I threw it over my head sliding my arms through the thin straps and adjusting the empire waist so that the bead-work was straight. I looked back at the suitcase of clothes, fuming over Lex's absurd reaction to finding me with Dallen.

Typical. Lex took the time to move my clothes but left me sleeping on the floor in the hall. The fact that he had actually moved all of my things because of what he saw Dallen and me doing was infuriating. I was old enough to make my own decisions about what I wanted to do and with whom; Lex was behaving like a jealous child. I couldn't understand his need to have control over me, he'd never behaved like that before, but now it seemed he had this plan set in his mind for me and he was determined to have his way. Even at the risk of going against my wishes.

I ran out of the room and down the hall screaming for Lex although it was still day. I ran to my old room where Rachel still resided. I ran down the hall closet and into my old dressing room. I pushed the sun symbol at the top of the mirror and yanked the mirror open. I ran down the long set of stairs as fast as I could, flicking the lights on as I went. I don't know what made me think to go down there. I really just wanted to vent to Rachel about Lex, and I knew she really wasn't comfortable in the secret room, so it didn't even make sense to look for her there, but something was drawing me down there. Maybe I was just so angry with Lex that I wanted to look at the coffins he had never told us about. Maybe

I needed to look at something else that made me angry at him so that when I finally saw him I would explode, and he would have no choice but to surrender and tell me I was right.

As I was getting closer to the bottom of the stairs I heard voices echoing through the open room. When I got to the bottom I saw a television on. I hesitated a moment not sure who would ever sit down there and watch television. It wasn't exactly cozy. The television was placed in front of the two coffins as if they were recliners. One coffin was closed, the other was open and I could see a shadow of a person moving in the open coffin. I walked up to the open coffin, and there was Rachel watching television.

"Ray, what are you doing?" I asked loudly so she would hear me over the television, my voice echoing slightly in the large space.

She turned her head and frowned. "He'd kill you if he knew you were down here."

"Who's he?" I was confused about why she would even be in the room, let alone who wouldn't want me there.

"Lex."

"Lex?" I asked walking to the other side of Rachel to better see her face. "Where exactly is Lex?" I questioned her suspiciously.

Her eyes flickered to the left where the lid of her coffin blocked her direct gaze to the coffin next to her.

"I don't know where he is," Rachel answered somewhat angrily, as if she were being forced to do something she didn't want to. "He doesn't want us to know where he sleeps. You know that. Anyway none of this matters. Everything we've been through and whatever plans Lex has. You know we probably won't be here much longer."

"What?" I didn't understand what Rachel was talking about, but she had been more and more withdrawn lately, and I felt like she was not only pulling away from Lex and this lifestyle but from me as well.

Rachel turned to me with a hard look in her eyes and then just sighed, "Nothing. I've just got a lot on my mind."

I looked around the room for a moment, lost for what to say to her, and noticed a glass of wine on the bar next to an open bottle.

"Whose wine?" I asked trying to change the subject as I walked to the bar to inspect the bottle of wine next to the glass and a folding bottle opener.

"Oh, I forgot that was there. I think Osborn poured it for me earlier. He brought me that bottle as a going away present. I was so upset he was leaving I forgot all about the wine. Did Lex tell you about Osborn?" Rachel's voice took on an excited tone as she talked about Osborn.

I absently picked up the folding wine bottle opener, turning it in my hands as I spoke. "He told me that you had met someone, and needed space. I assumed when I saw you two dancing last night that was who Lex was referring to."

Rachel's voice took on a superior tone, "Well, I would have told you about him, but...you were busy."

"I was basically unconscious for two days," I said defensively.

"Osborn and I have been talking since the first day we met. I was supposed to go out with him the night that you and Lex dragged me to that blues bar in the city," Rachel answered as if I should have known these things.

Apparently being in a coma didn't carry as much weight for an excuse as it used to. I decided to leave things at that. Rachel was, for some reason, annoyed with me and I couldn't say anything to change that right then. Without thinking I picked up the wine that was sitting on the bar, gulped it down, and walked behind Rachel's coffin stopping to inspect the other one beside her. I was fairly certain Lex was inside it. I could feel my heart pounding. Rachel couldn't see me over her open coffin lid; I could just take a quick peek and no one would ever know.

I was curious. Curious to see Lex in his daily slumber. Would he look the same? Would he wake up? What was it like to be a vampire and be completely vulnerable? I opened the coffin and jumped back startled.

"Lillian, where are you?" Rachel questioned loudly, making sounds as if she were moving in her coffin to better see where I was.

I slipped around her coffin so that I was standing directly behind her. "I'm right here."

She turned her head to look up at me. "Oh, I didn't see you there."

"I'm just going to go upstairs and look for Dallen. I'll see you later," I said, walking back to the other coffin.

I looked into the coffin and saw Lex. A statue cradled in the purple velvet lined coffin. He looked so harsh. He looked like a corpse untouched by time, a man made of gleaming marble with no imperfection...and no life. I leaned over the coffin to try and hear his breathing, not completely convinced he was actually still alive. I didn't know at that time that a vampire's body completely shuts down during their deep, daylight sleep, even if they had just fed, every function of their body stops. I dared to lean just a little closer, getting a light scent of strawberry coming off of him, when Lex's hand shot up to my neck.

He hadn't even flinched. I was gasping for air struggling with him, but Rachel couldn't hear me over the roar of the television. I felt the blood rushing to my head, I was getting dizzy, and I could feel my neck being crushed under Lex's grasp. I still had the bottle opener in my hand. I didn't want to hurt him, but I didn't want to die either. I stabbed the corkscrew into Lex' arm repeatedly. His blood splattered wildly from the wound. I tried to cover my face with my free hand to protect myself from ingesting any of his vampiric blood, though so little probably wouldn't have affected me. His grip weakened and finally I was able to wrestle his hand from my throat. I quietly placed his arm back into the blood splattered coffin and closed the lid.

I tiptoed up the stairs with blood splattered on my dress, in my hair, and on my hands. I started crying when I got to the hall of clothes, seeing the blood covering me, but I still continued walking. When I entered the bedroom I saw Osborn sitting on Rachel's bed looking out the open balcony doors. He seemed to be smirking about something and swinging his leg happily over the side of the bed, as if he were waiting for good news that he was already sure was coming to him. When I closed the closet door he turned around. I looked him right in the eyes and to my surprise I saw genuine concern there. I remembered thinking it was so strange the tender look he gave me.

"Lillian, not you," he said, rushing toward me as my body fell to the floor and everything went black.

I awoke from the sting of a sharp slap across my face. I opened my eyes to see Lex, glaring down at me angrily, and yet it looked as though he'd been crying.

"What in hell ya doin'!" Mason yelled. He was trying to get at Lex, but Vann was holding him back.

Another voice from somewhere in the room said softly, "Please, don't hurt her. You know it wasn't really her fault."

Mason threatened in his thick Southern accent, "I'll kill ya if ya touch 'er again!"

"Mason, my patience is only so strong, and it is quickly running out for you," Lex said in uncharacteristic cruelty.

"Lex, let the ragazzo be. The boy, he is young, and full of spirit," Vann said simply.

"Stop talkin' 'bout me like I'm a kid !" Mason spat, defending himself. "Why ya hittin' 'er?"

"Lillian, would you like to tell them what you did? No? I didn't think you would. Osborn, why don't you leave us. Go talk to Rachel or something," Lex said, looking over in the shadows of the room.

"Of course," came a voice out of the dark corner.

I forced myself to show some gratitude, though, I still didn't like him. "Thank you, Osborn, for helping me."

He stepped into the light of the bedside lamp, a surprised smile spreading over his lips as he nodded. "I just wanted to make sure...I'm glad you're all right. I was...worried."

He looked exactly the same as that first day we'd met him: severely short brown hair, too many muscles in my opinion (but some girls found that appealing), and a cool calculating look on his face. His eyes flickered momentarily to me and again I saw the same look of concern he'd given me before I'd fainted. Although he didn't seem pleased with Lex's demand, Osborn left the room as he had been instructed to do.

"May I at least sit by 'er?" Mason asked, motioning to the bed.

"Do what you please with her. Kill her if you wish," Lex answered dramatically, pacing with his hand to his head.

Mason gritted his teeth and narrowed his eyes as he passed Lex to sit on the edge of the bed and hold my hand.

"Last night I found her in bed…with Dallen…"

I looked at him wide eyed. "You're still on about that! I was scared!"

"Oh I'm sorry did the boogeyman scare you?" Lex mocked.

"No, for your information there was a man in my closet! I didn't want to sleep alone and especially not in my room. I didn't think anything would happen, but one thing led to another-"

"As I was saying I found them in bed practically in the act of…" Lex seemed unable to say it.

"We were just kissing! And it was none of your business anyway!" I protested. "I am nineteen years old-"

"I got mad nether the less. I didn't want her sleeping next door to him so after she fell asleep in the hall I moved her things to another room. I was about to take the last suitcase, but I noticed the sun pouring in the windows. So I panicked and went to sleep in one of the coffins below her old room. Rachel and Osborn were in the bedroom..."

"I bet you didn't freak out on them," I interrupted.

Lex continued, ignoring me, "Osborn convinced Rachel to stay in the safe-room with me while I slept to make sure no one came down there."

I broke in again, confused, "Wait, Osborn wanted Rachel to stay down in the safe-room with you, while you slept, and with only one way out?"

Lex huffed in annoyance, "Yes, apparently he was concerned for my safety."

"But not for Rachel's, apparently," I countered suspiciously.

"Anyway, I asked Rachel specifically not to let Lillian down there. Then Lillian shows up and when Rachel isn't looking she opens my coffin." He stopped and looked at me dramatically, and then went on. "She must have gotten too close to me and I almost crushed her neck, which would have served her right. Trying to get free, I suppose, she stabbed my arm here." He pulled his sleeve up to show an almost completely healed scar. He turned to me. "You're lucky I didn't kill you. Did you think I wouldn't notice all of the blood and the wound?"

"Yeah, yeah, yeah, I know I was very bad," I said distractedly. "So Osborn asked Rachel to stay locked in an underground room next to a coffin with an unconscious vampire in it?"

"Wait, ya mean blood got all ov'r everythin'?" Mason asked with concern looking at me.

I tried to get his attention. "That's not the point-"

"Yes, of course it got all over," Lex answered over me. "But like Lillian said that's not the point. The point is she opened my coffin while I slept *and* she stabbed me *and* she could have gotten killed."

"No, that's not what I meant," I again tried explaining.

Mason anxiously questioned Lex, "What if she swallowed some?"

"When Osborn found her there was no blood on her face. Her dress was covered with it and her hands. She probably covered her face," Lex answered annoyed.

Mason and Vann fell silent, looking first at each other and then at me.

"Doesn't anyone else find it strange-" I began.

"Exactly!" Lex looked angrily at Mason and Vann. "You're missing the big picture here. She can't just go snooping around my coffin or whatever coffin I'm sleeping in. That is against our laws...remember? If the council finds out about this they will demand she be punished. Now I have to keep them from finding out, and if they do I'll have to protect her. Plus, I certainly can't keep my promise of keeping her safe if I inadvertently kill her in my sleep."

I replied annoyed, "But Rachel was sitting right next to your coffin, and you let her and Osborn know where..." I stopped, feeling peculiar suddenly.

I started taking short raspy breaths that caused an almost painful sensation near my heart. The three of them stared at me in frigid silence. My eyes felt heavy and hard to keep open, and my whole body was cold. I was shivering violently. Lex and Vann came to the bedside to look at me.

"Lillian, are you alright?" Lex asked with genuine concern.

"I...I gotta go. Everything...everything is spinning." I felt like I was going to be sick.

"Oh, Lillian. God forgive me. She's dying," Lex said stunned.

I looked at him feeling dizzy and queasy. "I'm not dying. I just don't feel well. If I'm going to be sick I'd rather not do it in front of everyone ...again."

Vann turned to Lex. "Il tuo sangue, it is your blood, Lex. That is the only thing that could be wrong with her."

I started to get up. "I have to go."

"No, Lillian, lie down. Giovanni, I need to talk to you, outside," Lex said sternly.

"Mason, stay with her," Vann directed, pointing to me and then walking out of the room after Lex.

Mason took me in his arms. "Lillian, did ya drink 'is blood? Any of it?"

"No, I...I cov...covered my...face," I struggled to answer.

I could hear hushed voices just outside the door and then Vann saying angrily, "No, Lex, you cannot! The council won't allow it!"

"Did ya do anythin' before that, that coulda caused this?" Mason asked as he turned my face toward his. "Anythin' at all?"

I heard Lex's voice, now loud, and heartbroken, "I have to, Giovanni. I can't lose her."

I tried to remember every little thing I had done that morning. Anything that I could have ingested that would make me sick. "I had a glass of wine, but wine has never made me feel like this before."

"Lillian, ya look so pale." Mason touched my face sadly.

Realization struck me and I knew I had to try to warn Lex. I tried to jump out of bed, but Mason pushed me back down.

"Lillian, lay down, sugar. Ya' sick."

I tried once more to get up as I argued, "You don't understand. I have to find Lex. I have to tell him. I think it was……"

Mason moved to catch me as I blacked-out yet again, but this time it wasn't from some ancient, evil vampire messing with my mind.

J.M. Merillo

I managed to utter my last thought, "...poison."

❧8☙

This time it was the piercing scream of a man that woke me. It was certainly better than being slapped in the face, but still disturbing to wake up to.

"Damn you!" Lex shouted vehemently at the floor. "How dare you threaten me!"

Lex made a move toward a person that must have been on the floor out of sight. I saw the person's head pop up.

Dallen?

"Lex? Dallen?" I whispered, confused.

Lex stopped what he was doing or rather what he was about to do, caught off guard by my interruption for a moment. I could see his brain working to come up with an explanation before I even asked what he was doing. I just stared at him, waiting.

"Lilly." He smiled, calming down, relief spreading across his face.

"What's going on?" My look of puzzlement at Dallen ignited Lex's fury again.

He looked at Dallen. "Get out of here! I think it would be in your best interest to leave my home," Lex growled, and then he turned to me smiling as he came to sit at the bedside. "Now, little queen, how are you feeling?" he asked, smoothing back my hair as if nothing had happened.

"I suppose…I'm fine...but...what's going on?" I turned my eyes questioningly toward the door Dallen had just walked out of, shaken by the scene I'd woken up to.

"Oh, Lilly, you would understand if you had heard what he said," Lex replied, averting his eyes slightly.

"Are you sure it had nothing to do with what happened the other night...the night before last night? It was the night before last, wasn't it?

Please tell me I haven't been unconscious for days again," I muttered half to myself. Then addressing Lex I asked halfheartedly, "That had nothing to do with you being jealous, right?"

"Jealous, please," Lex scoffed, "Whenever have I acted jealous?"

I looked up at him with raised eyebrows.

"Lillian, please. I would never act out of jealousy. I always do things for a good reason."

"Oh, really? How about never telling me about my uncle, or about Dardanos for that matter, or physically throwing me out of Dallen's room, or slapping me in the face, or leaving me to sleep on the floor in the hallway? What were your reasons for all of that?" I quipped.

"Well...you see...about the hallway, I was going to carry you to your new room, but the sun...do we really have to talk about this right now?" Lex pouted, obviously at loss for an explanation. "The point is if you had heard what Dallen said you'd understand why I was so angry. He told me it would be just as well if you...died. He said you did nothing but cause trouble...and seduce every man you come into contact with. He said you were manipulative ...and immoral...and as heartless as a vampire. I think that last part was directed at me. So I got angry, I threatened him, but I was just so furious because...I love you. I don't know how or why, but I love you, and I can't stand to hear anyone say horrible things like that about you."

My eyes actually misted up as I sat up and hugged him. We held each other, like two normal people sharing an affectionate moment. It was strange to see Lex so serious and so tender. Something had changed in him, he seemed worried and even more protective than ever. I thought about Dallen and why he would have said what he had and why Lex seemed to be hiding something. I lay back in bed and sighed looking away as I felt Lex's strong hand gently envelop mine.

"Lex, would you do something for me? Even if you really didn't want to?"

Lex hesitated, "Probably."

"Will you let Dallen back in so that I can talk to him?"

"But, Lilly-" Lex started to protest.

"I need to talk to him, Lex. I just can't believe he could say such awful things. That doesn't seem like him." I looked up pleadingly at Lex. "I thought he was falling in love with me. I know you don't want to hear that, but I was starting to think that maybe I might be falling in love with him too. He made me believe he had feelings for me. Why would he lie to me like that? I need to talk to him."

Lex just kissed my hand and grudgingly answered, "Of course." Then left the room.

I looked around the room and noticed that once again I was in Lex's room. I still couldn't understand how Lex could allow so many people, mortals and vampires, to enter the room that hid his coffin. Firstly, because such things were supposed to be against his own council's rules, and secondly because it's very dangerous for even one other to have access to a vampire's safe-room, let alone a dozen. Not necessarily because the person (or people in Lex's case) that had access would actually try to harm him, but because should any other vampire want that information it would be as easy as reading that person's mind or threatening to kill them. Either I was wrong and Lex's coffin wasn't in the room, or he was even more reckless than I believed him to be.

I heard a bang at the door and looked over to see Dallen stumbling in backwards, and Lex strolling in casually behind him as if he'd *accidentally* tossed Dallen into the room.

"Lex, I'd like to talk to Dallen alone," I said as gently as I could. "Please."

Lex's jaw dropped. "You're sending me out of the room. What if he tries to-"

"Lex, just wait in the hall," I demanded in annoyance. I wanted to talk to Dallen without Lex's threatening glares deterring him from being completely honest with me.

"All right," Lex finally agreed leaving the room and closing the door behind him.

"Dallen, I don't understand what is going on. Wasn't it you that wanted to kiss me?" I asked sadly.

"Yes," he answered, looking confused.

"And wasn't it you who told me I could sleep in your room?"

Dallen looked at me completely mystified. "Yes, but what does that have to do with anything?"

I countered, "It has to do with you accusing me of being some kind of wanton seductress and saying that it would be perfectly fine if I had died." I paused, distressed. "What did I do wrong? I thought you cared about me. Why would you tell Lex I was better off dead?"

"Lillian, I never said or thought anything along those lines about you, and I do care about you very much. I came to visit you and when I walked in Lex was standing over you about to drink from you. I told him to get away from you, that he couldn't turn you, especially while you lay there helpless. I told him he was heartless and a coward, and that I would not allow him to make you a vampire. He pushed me to the floor and was advancing upon me when you woke." Dallen gave a sigh, "I would never say anything so terrible about you; I would never do anything to hurt you. I'm in love with you," Dallen explained wearily, as if admitting he was in love with me was the biggest burden of his life.

Strangely, my own feelings seemed the same. I should have been over-joyed to hear the words I love you from a man that I felt I was falling in love with, but instead I felt like a great weight had been laid on me. I looked at him feeling the urge to tell him that I loved him too, but too strong was my dread that our feelings for each other were only going to make things more difficult.

Just then the door banged open. Lex came thundering into the room headed straight for Dallen.

"Liar!" Lex had his arms outstretched toward Dallen.

I jumped between the two and put my hands on Lex's chest, stopping him momentarily. "Dallen go!" I urged.

Dallen ran hurriedly from the room before he could even register the thought that he was yet again leaving me alone with Lex. Before Lex had an opportunity to follow after him I closed the door and stood in front of it.

"Lex, you lied to me," I reprimanded halfheartedly, "why? And try the truth this time."

He turned away from me and put his hand to his head. "You know

126

damn well why! Oh, Lilly, I was scared. I was so scared." He looked at me apprehensively. "We weren't sure if you were going to make it, and I felt so helpless. It was driving me crazy, the thought of losing you. I've never felt that way about anyone before. Well, once I did, and I lost her. That's all I could think, looking at you lying there, and remembering her, and I couldn't bare the thought of losing you. I panicked; I had to try to save you. Then I saw you waking up and I knew I couldn't tell you the truth. You might have stabbed me with a corkscrew, but I didn't want you to know what I had almost done. I know that you're still not even sure that you want The Immortal Fate, and I nearly took that choice from you."

"Lex, first of all, you know the whole corkscrew thing was just because you grabbed me in your sleep and I couldn't breathe. I happened to have the bottle opener in my hand. I know I shouldn't have opened the coffin, but ever since Malika decided we should take the next year to decide if we even want to be turned I've been more curious about what it means to be a vampire; that's all. We've been through so much in the past few months; did you really think I would get upset at you trying to save me from death?"

"I guess not. But I was more worried that Dallen would tell you differently." Lex smiled up at me. "He doesn't approve of immortality you know. He told me once that I was selfish for accepting it. I know that he thinks very highly of you and he doesn't want you to…be cheated out of life."

"I wish everyone would stop trying to protect me all the time," I said irritatedly, "and Dallen needs to lighten up a little. In the end it is my decision, and whatever I decide he needs to accept."

All of a sudden Dallen was pounding on the door, apparently just realizing his error in judgment of leaving me locked in a room with Lex. I had momentarily forgotten that Dallen had just been in the room, and was probably imagining Lex would follow through with his plan to turn me now that we were alone.

"Lex! Don't you dare touch her! I will kill you if you touch her!"

"Lilly," Lex whispered excitedly, "I suddenly have a brilliant plan to help Dallen get over his...seriousness."

I guessed, "You want to play a trick on him?"

"Oh yeah," Lex said smiling deviously. "You lay in bed like your unconscious, like I just drained you, and I'll pretend I haven't turned you yet. I can even bite my lip to make it look like I spilled a little blood as I drank. I can be quite messy sometimes." Lex looked like a kid that had just found a bike under the Christmas tree.

I bit my lip and shook my head at his ridiculous excitement. "And then what? You want me to jump up and yell boo?"

Lex nodded his head deliriously. "Something like that. Wait for him to sit on the bed and then grab him. It will be hysterical."

I didn't want to play a trick on Dallen, especially since he had been looking out for my best interest, but sometimes it was hard to not give into Lex. His excitement was infectious and it didn't help that he happened to have the most hypnotizing multicolored blue eyes that he had learned to pout perfectly when he really wanted something.

Lex must have seen my hesitation and added, "You know, Dallen let you sleep in the hallway too. He could have woken you up or carried you back to bed, but he didn't."

"Ugghhh, fine," I agreed, thinking that maybe Dallen did deserve to be tricked just a little.

Lex went to the door to let Dallen in, making sure I was ready before he opened it.

Dallen threw the door open and pushed past Lex. "Where is she?!"

"It's done, Dallen. There's nothing you can do, unless you want to let her die," Lex said, gesturing to the bed dramatically.

I stole a peek and saw Dallen looking at Lex in disbelief seeing the blood on his lips and my body lying limply in the bed.

"You drank from her? Is she dead?" Dallen sounded on the verge of tears.

"She isn't dead yet. If I don't give her my blood she will die."

I could hear Dallen approaching the bed and felt as he sat close to where I was lying. He turned to Lex just as I happened to steal another glance and saw Lex trying his best not to laugh.

Dallen ordered sullenly, "Do it then, if it will-"

"Dallen!" I shouted as loud as I could, grabbing his arm.

Dallen screamed at the top of his lungs, not exactly in a manly way, and jumped off the bed. He nearly tripped over his own feet trying to get away. Lex and I were literally rolling on the bed with laughter.

Dallen got so angry he stomped his foot like a furious child. "Very funny! See if I ever try to save you again!" He walked out arms folded.

"Oh, come on, Dallen, it was just a joke," I called after him, sprinting into the hall.

"Did you see his face?" Lex still couldn't stop laughing.

"I can imagine." I smirked.

"You scared the hell out of him. It was perfect," Lex gushed, impersonating Dallen's surprised face.

We started laughing again, Lex's arm around my waist as he ushered me out of his room and down the hallway.

Lex, between his giggles, managed to ask, "Do you think he'll forgive you for this?"

"Of course," I said slyly, "he loves me."

A moment later, though I was glad to be laughing with Lex again, I realized something felt like it was missing. Joking around and being goofy with Lex made me think of Rachel. It was strange that she hadn't been there when I woke; on the other hand she hadn't exactly reacted as if she were concerned when Dardanos had knocked me unconscious for two days. Maybe she was mad at me, again, for being the center of attention.

"Where is Rachel?" I asked sadly.

"Rachel's around somewhere. She doesn't spend much time with me anymore, and when she does she spends the whole time lecturing me on everything that is wrong with me. She's probably off with Osborn again. They make a cute couple, don't you think?" Lex said the last sarcastically.

"A cute couple?" I asked, raising my eyebrows. "I don't know. I can't put my finger on it, but there's something about Osborn, like he's putting on a show. I don't trust him. I get this weird feeling that he's using Rachel."

"I guess you don't like him then?" Lex smirked.

"I don't really know him well enough, I suppose, but he makes me feel uncomfortable whenever he's around. I get this strange feeling like he's staring at me all the time. I don't know, I guess he just comes off as a creepy military guy to me."

Lex corrected, "Well, he isn't a military guy, and he was the one that looked after you when you passed out after stabbing me. He was really worried about you. Maybe you're just judging him by how he looks."

I had been so sure about that; he had struck me as having some kind of military background since the moment he'd spoken to Rachel and me. Also, I was surprised to hear that he had taken care of me after I'd fainted. Why wouldn't he have gotten Rachel or even tried to find Dallen? It had always seemed like he was trying to avoid being in my company for too long, yet he'd taken care of me after I'd fainted? I felt a small shudder at the idea of being alone and unconscious in Osborn's care, and was even more curious about him and his behavior.

Snapping out of my uncomfortable thoughts, I added, "Well, he behaves like he's on a mission or something."

"He is, in a way," Lex muttered absently, then as if trying to cover his slip he added, "You know, a mission of love."

I rolled my eyes knowing that Lex would never seriously say something so corny and argued, "I think he's hiding something, and I think you know something that you're not sharing. I can never tell what he's thinking or why he behaves so strangely, and you are no help at all."

"You know, now that you mention it I've never been able to read his thoughts." Lex seemed to genuinely stop and contemplate this idea. "I mean of course there are some people who purposely put up mind blocks, and there are people that vampires simply cannot penetrate. But it's odd that he just happens to be one of those few. I never thought about it before."

"That is strange," I said pensively.

"Well, I wouldn't say anything about it to Rachel. She won't hear anything bad about Osborn. He is perfect in her eyes," Lex warned, leading me down another hallway.

"Maybe her eyes aren't open when she's with him."

Lex opened a door to a bedroom. "Maybe," he admitted, shrugging his shoulders. "This will be your new room. There are fresh towels in the bathroom, your clothes in the closet, and if you should need anything just ring the front desk."

"Ha, ha. Great! Another room. Soon you'll be building me my own guest house, because you're going to run out of rooms to move me into," I replied sarcastically. "Anyway, shouldn't you be getting your beauty sleep soon?"

"Yeah, I guess I should go." He walked out the door, but peeked back in. "Little queen, you know I wouldn't trade you for anyone else on earth," he said sweetly and then added, "Even if you did stab me with a corkscrew."

"I told you..." I began, but Lex had already left, so instead I just said, "Thanks," and then fell back into my new bed, passed almost immediately into sleep, and dreamed.

I dreamed about something that I hadn't even thought about since we'd arrived at the mansion.

Home.

At least the place I had inhabited before Lex had brought me to the mansion; it had never really felt like home.

Rachel was in my dream, knocking on my window to get me up so we could go jogging. We jogged past a house I didn't know, but Rachel seemed to know the man that stood in front of it, and stopped to talk with him. I kept jogging because I didn't see her stop, and she didn't try to stop me. She didn't care that she left me alone. She only cared about talking to this man. As I kept on jogging I looked back and saw the man laughing at Rachel like he was making fun of her. Rachel looked heartbroken but listened to the man like a child being scolded. They finally turned to look at me and at that moment I was hit by a car. They didn't even warn me or move when I got hit. The woman driving the car got out and started screaming at Rachel and the man to help, but Rachel just wanted to talk to the man. I remember thinking she would rather let me die than leave his side for one minute.

The dream continued in an operating room. Rachel and the man were sitting at the end of my bed talking. I could now see the man more clearly; Osborn was staring back at me like he was in charge of watching me. He got up from his seat next to Rachel and began stroking my face as if he were trying to mesmerize every detail. I looked to my left and saw a silver tray of knives. I started asking why I was there. They wouldn't answer me so I started screaming at them. Osborn started to bend toward me as if he were going to kiss me, but before he did Rachel jumped up, grabbed a knife off the tray, and stabbed me. My eyes immediately opened as if I had been startled awake.

"How horrible," came a familiar voice. "But I guess it serves you right for what you did to me last night."

My eyes searched the room to see Dallen leaning against the wall arms folded.

"Can you please not do that?" I asked.

"Do what?" he asked innocently.

"Read my thoughts. Especially when I'm sleeping, it's kind of creepy. Anyway last night was just a joke. Call it payback for leaving me to sleep on a cold hard floor all night. I couldn't resist." I smiled sweetly at him.

"And I couldn't resist reading your thoughts. Tantalizing stuff there."

"Oh, is that so? Hmm, well I have been told that I am unbelievably charming. I suppose it must go for when I'm asleep as well. So are we friends today or were you bribed to come here?" I asked half jokingly, eyebrows raised.

Dallen let a small laugh escape his lips before saying matter-of-factly, "Yes, we're friends today, and as your friend I have a favor to ask. Lex has been behaving strangely the past few days, I know you've been ill and probably haven't noticed, but I believe, as do some of the others, that he is up to something. Osborn, that strange one, he's in on it too. I don't think it could be anything good. God only knows it must be at least remotely bad for Lex to be keeping it a secret."

"Why are you telling me this?" I asked suspiciously.

"I know you've had some uncertain feelings about Osborn, but I'm worried that he and Lex may be planning something, and it just seems like an unlikely partnership. Can you ask Lex what all this secrecy is about? Maybe do a little investigating, just to be safe."

"Yeah, I'll ask him. Even though it sounds pretty silly. I mean maybe he and Osborn are...bonding," I joked.

"Bonding, Lillian, be serious. Lex doesn't even bond with you, and he loves you."

I smiled. "Lex was asking me what I thought about Osborn this morning. I know they don't normally spend time together, but I think Lex has known Osborn for quite a long time. I'm sure it's nothing, but if it will make you feel better I'll try to find out why he's had such an interest in Osborn lately. Will that do?"

"Thank you, it will."

I yawned and looked at the clock on the table beside me, it was nearly five o'clock. "Well, I think it's about time I got up and got dressed."

"I'll let you do that. By the way I'm going out this evening," Dallen said, running his hands through his hair, which he had suspiciously not parted that day.

"Coward. You just don't want to be here when I talk to Lex," I teased.

"That's not even remotely close to why I'm going out. I am not scared of Lex. Especially with you here. He usually knows better than to challenge you."

Dallen came over to the bed, bent down, kissed me on the cheek, and walked out of the room. It was done very sweetly, but I'll admit at the time my heart beat a bit faster thinking he was going to take me in his arms again. I sat in bed daydreaming for a moment about three nights ago, but I soon shook off the distracting thought, got up and threw on a tank top and shorts, and went for a long stroll through the gardens. I had remembered to bring my poetry book, and so ended up sitting on the bench across from my favorite statue, looking at the photo of my uncle. I wasn't sure why, but I felt especially sad that he wasn't there at that moment. There was nothing particularly special about that day, but Ben's absence seemed to be overpowering. I thought I might just sit there until it was dark, feeling lonely, but wanting to be alone. In the end, though, it was just too hot. Even with the lovely breeze that swept through that spot, the humidity was causing uncomfortable amounts of sweat to pour down my face.

I went back to my new room to take a shower and cool off before Lex showed up to drag me on some adventure. I put on a black and white strapless form-fitting dress and my black suede heels with the ankle straps. As I was brushing my hair I saw a shadow pass the mirror.

"Lex, is that you?" I turned around and saw Lex leaning against the door, legs crossed.

"Have you seen Dallen?" he asked, smiling suspiciously.

"He was just in here about two hours ago. He went out. He had to take care of some business or something like that."

Lex laughed to himself. "What did he say about your little joke last night?"

"He forgives me. Of course."

"Of course," Lex said with pity.

"Lex, I've noticed you and Osborn spending a lot of time together. Is there any particular reason?" I asked a little too quickly.

"Well, I guess you could say we're...ummm...bonding. He's an old friend." He shrugged. "Jealous?"

I looked at him and laughed. "Extremely."

"When you get hungry just go down in the banquet hall. I'll have someone waiting to fix you something. I'm going out for dinner."

"Have fun."

"I will," he said, giving me a strange smile before walking out.

So Lex is up to something, obviously. Now I need to find out what. Vann! He might know something. Now how do I find out where Vann is?

"You ask the butler," I said to myself, running out of the room. "Bradley! Bradley!" I ran to the main stairs. "Bradley!"

"Yes, Miss? You bellowed?" Bradley appeared in the main hall at the bottom of the stairs.

"Can you get a hold of Vann for me?" I asked and then corrected,

"Giovanni?"

"Before I answer that will you tell me this: Are you an escaped mental patient?" he asked completely serious.

"No. Why would you ask...? Oh. I...umm wasn't myself that night I threatened you. I had just found out how my uncle died and I was really upset." I added, "I'm really sorry."

"Well, then I do know how you can "get a hold of" Mr. Rossi," he said, making quotation marks with his fingers.

"Will you call him, please, and ask him to come over right away?"

"Do I look like your slave?" he looked at me sternly.

I gave him a hard stare. "Gee, I don't know, I guess I could be crazy, but I was under the impression that you work here?"

Bradley huffed, "I'll call him."

"Tell him I'll be in the garden just outside the banquet hall," I said, walking past Bradley and into the banquet hall to eat.

As I was getting up from the spacious and lonely banquet table Bradley came in. "Miss, Mr. Rossi will be here any minute, if he isn't here already. I called him half an hour ago. I thought you were in the garden, I couldn't find you," Bradley said with annoyance.

"That's where I'm going right now." I walked outside and into the garden.

As I sat on a bench I looked out at the night sky. It was so perfect, the amazing multitudes of stars twinkling, and the moon completely round and close enough to touch. It felt like a strange kind of night, like there was something in the air. I hoped it was a good kind of something, but the way things had been going I didn't think it could be.

How could anything evil happen under a sky like this?

"Why do you think such curious things, uccellino?" came the purr of a comforting voice.

"Vann. You know I don't like being called that. It's so-"

He answered before I could say it, "I know, childish. But it is how you will always seem to me. A sweet little dove, my little bird." He smiled warmly.

"I'm glad you came. I wanted to ask you something that's been bothering me. Do you know anything about Lex and Osborn being up to something? They've-"

"I come to see you and you want to talk about Lex. Mi hai abbandonato, you have forsaken me, and fallen in love with him?" he asked playfully.

I gave him a hard look. "Vann, be serious and listen! They've been spending a lot of time together, and Lex made me believe yesterday that he had suspicions about Osborn."

"Well, maybe...maybe they are...bonding, and what is wrong with Osborn?"

Absently I said, "Yeah, Lex said they were bonding."

"You know he is not being truthful then." Vann came and sat next to me, grinning.

"Of course I know he's lying. I just want to know why, and I don't think he even likes Osborn. Even if he hasn't said so I know the whole Rachel-Osborn thing irks him, or maybe there's some dark secret to why Lex is friends with Osborn. I just can't figure it out. Maybe he's planning something horrible. Something is going on and I plan on getting to the bottom of it," I announced, slapping my hands down on my legs resolutely.

Vann looked at me and then exploded into laughter. I couldn't think of why he would be laughing at me, but before I could ask he grabbed my hand.

"It...is...horrible," he said between laughs as he led me into the house.

I tried to pull away, but before I knew what was happening a room full of people yelled surprise.

I was astounded. Actually, I was so astounded I just stood there in a stupor staring at them, trying to figure out why they were yelling at me.

"Lilly," Lex whispered in my ear, "it's your birthday."

I smiled, feeling a little ridiculous. "I knew that."

Actually I hadn't. It was July 2nd and it had never even occurred to me that it was my birthday that whole day. I had known something felt different that day, but the thought of it being my birthday never crossed my mind. I wanted to be happy, but I felt strange looking at all those smiling faces that had surprised me. They had probably known for days that it was my birthday, and I had only found out moments ago. Was I starting to go mad, as Vann had warned can happen when I first arrived, from living among vampires? Was I losing touch with reality? It scared me a little to think that I might actually be in the early stages of insanity.

People I didn't even know were coming up and talking to me, obviously mortal regulars of Lex's parties. There was a live band and people dancing. All I could do was stand there taking everything in. People walked by and said happy birthday to me, but I was just too stunned. I attempted to smile gratefully, but I have a feeling I looked somewhat manic instead.

Suddenly Lex got up where the band was. As they finished the song he said something to them and took the microphone.

"Thank you everyone for coming. Let's hear it for my little queen! Please join me in singing to my darling Lilly!" Then he gestured toward a door where a cake was being brought out.

Dallen came in carrying the huge five layer cake along with the help of Vann. They put it on a table and someone grabbed my hand and pulled me toward the table as everyone began singing.

When I looked up the first faces I saw were Lex, Dallen, Rachel, and Vann. They were smiling at me, except for Rachel, who looked down as if she were avoiding making eye contact with me. Directly behind her stood Osborn. He was smiling at me with such confusing tenderness I wasn't sure if he was simply showing polite mirth because it was my birthday, or if the look he gave me was the reason Rachel wouldn't look me in the eye. I tried to shake off the thought and instead focused on everyone else.

After the singing stopped Dallen put his arm around me and whispered in my ear, "You have to make a wish."

I stopped and looked around the table at all their faces. "I don't know what to wish for. I have everything I ever wanted right here."

"How disgustingly sweet. Well, then, blow the candles out and wish for world peace," Lex said exasperatedly.

"I know what I'll wish for," I said as I blew the candles out.

Lex grinned. "Thank God. The whole cake was about to go up in flames."

The band started playing again and I started serving cake, which most of the attendees couldn't even eat. Lex kissed me full on the lips, leaving behind that familiar scent of strawberries, before dashing away to be admired by a group of mortal women begging him to dance with them.

"Lillian, come dance with me," Dallen demanded, pulling me away from my cake cutting duties, to the dance floor.

We danced all night, Lex showing everyone up with his seemingly coordinated routines. Osborn even danced a little with Rachel, but I think he was trying to stay away from someone. There was one point where I actually thought Osborn was going to ask me to dance, but Dallen magically appeared and whisked me away. Osborn did actually find me later, sitting by myself, having a drink, and resting my feet.

Rachel, for some reason, had decided to ask Dallen to dance with her. I hoped she was making an attempt to show she was still my friend, and wanted to get to know Dallen because I was interested in him. While the two of them danced Osborn came and sat down at the table with me. I wasn't sure what to say so I just smiled.

"Birthdays seem to agree with you," he said softly.

I laughed, not understanding his meaning. "What do you mean?"

He leaned closer and admitted, sadly, "I've never seen you look so beautiful."

I nervously took a swig from my wine glass, trying to think of something to say to change the subject. "I...ummm...wanted to thank you again for helping me the other day. Lex told me that you took care of me until he woke up."

There was a pained look in his eyes, none of that fake swagger he seemed to always exhibit. "I was so worried. I thought," he paused, composing himself, as if he had been about to say something he shouldn't have. "Well, I suppose I thought what everyone thought. That you'd swallowed vampire blood. I don't think I could bare it if you had."

I was about to ask why, but was interrupted by the approach of Rachel and Dallen.

Rachel seemed to glare at me for a moment before saying in a bored tone, "Happy Birthday, Lillian. Osborn, are you ready, I'm tired from all the work I did today."

Osborn got up, half smiling at me, and walked off with Rachel trailing behind. I watched her follow Osborn out of the room, feeling sad and angry. Sad that Rachel was so blind that she couldn't see that Osborn wanted nothing to do with her, and angry that Osborn was so obviously flirting with me and must be using Rachel for some reason.

"Did you have a nice chat?" Dallen asked snickering, as he knew my dislike for Osborn.

I just shook my head and uttered, "No, not at all."

At about two thirty in the morning everyone started leaving and the band was packing up, but Lex had one more surprise before the night ended. I had completely forgotten about our bet, but while there were still some thirty people milling about Lex got on stage with the microphone, on his knees, and begged my forgiveness. It was, of course, done dramatically and mostly showed off Lex's ability to use complex wording, but I won't bore you with the details.

Although I found it completely hilarious to see Lex groveling, no matter how absurd he made it sound, I was more excited about the other half of our deal. "You know this means you're buying me a car, right?"

Lex threw his hands up in defeat. "Of course. That's your real birthday present. As soon as you decide what you want, I will get it for you."

I threw my arms around him. "Thank you, Lex. This was the best birthday I've ever had. I really mean that. I think the last real birthday party I had was when Ben was still alive." As I said it I realized that had probably been why I felt Ben's absence so keenly that day, even if I hadn't remembered it was my birthday, I still remembered the feeling of sharing special memories with the only person I'd ever felt attached to.

"Even though I should get all the credit," Lex said superiorly,

139

placing his hand over the center of his chest, he admitted, "I didn't put this together all by myself. Rachel helped decorate, Dallen got the cake, and Giovanni got the band. Oh and of course we threw in a little conspiracy to keep your mind off of your birthday."

I laughed to myself. "Yes, and I've been worrying all day, and I guess that's why Dallen left earlier?"

"Yes, I had to pick up your cake. So, how does it feel to be twenty?" Dallen took my hand.

"Oh kind of like starting a new life. This is the first birthday in a long time that I didn't have to celebrate by myself. It almost doesn't feel like my birthday at all, I've gotten used to it not being a special day, and this was...just wonderful."

"What was your wish for?" Vann asked with a broad smile.

"Maybe I'll tell you one day," I said walking away. "but for now..." I turned back toward them. "...it's a secret."

I went to my most recently issued room, threw my dress on the floor, and went to sleep in my strapless slip. This time not even a noisy ghost ducking into the closet would wake me. Especially because I couldn't just run into Dallen's arms this time. As I was dozing off I was still troubled with suspicions about Osborn. I knew they had used my dislike for him to distract me, but there really were some peculiarities I couldn't get out of my head.

My mind was flooded with random thoughts. I just couldn't shake the image of the way Osborn had scowled at Dallen earlier in the night and Dallen had given him a familiar, haughty look back, as if they had had an argument. I had never even seen them speak to each other, and as far as I knew they weren't friends. Maybe I had just imagined it, or maybe it had something to do with me. I was still troubled by the affectionate way Osborn had spoken to me, did he have feelings for me? If only Dallen and Rachel hadn't walked up when they had I might have been able to get a better idea of why Osborn had spoken the way he had. Maybe he was just showing concern because I was Rachel's best friend. Maybe he really did have feelings for Rachel and only took an interest in me for Rachel's sake, to protect her from losing someone she loved. If only I could read people's thoughts like some vampires...and like Dallen for that matter. *How strange that I had never found it odd that Dallen can read thoughts.*

Why did I always think of these things just before sleep? I would just ask Dallen why Osborn looked at him the way he had. It was ludicrous to try and figure these things out when you were exhausted.

A NIGHT IN THE UN-LIFE...

Lillian rose from the coffin she had constructed with the wood that had arrived the evening before. She had built it to look like a bench seat, should anyone ever get into her safe-room. Her safe-room was actually a darkroom that had been created by the previous owner, apparently a photographer. She had added a security lock on the revolving door of the darkroom that could only be opened with a code.

As she gently closed the hinged lid of the coffin she remembered the date with Ash she had agreed to the night before.

Why did I tell Ash I would go out with him? Lillian asked herself stepping out of the coffin and heading to her bedroom down the hall.

She went to her closet to look for something to wear as she was still wearing the black lace corset and panties she had worn the night before. Lillian had been too lazy to change as the sun was near rising that morning and had just thrown off her dress and jumped into her coffin.

Her cat Merlin was meowing for food in that demanding way that let Lillian know she had to stop whatever she was doing and meet his demands immediately, or else!

Lillian opened a can of cat food and put it on a small china plate. "Here you go, Merlin."

Lillian went back to her closet to find something to wear, and before she knew it Merlin came sauntering back in to see what she was up to. She had been standing there staring into the open closet for ten minutes.

"Oh, Merlin, look at me. I'm nervous to go on a date...with a mortal! I kill mortals to survive and I'm nervous to go on a date with one."

Merlin looked up from the spot he had chosen on the king-size bed that only he slept on and tilted his head to the side.

Lillian sighed, "I know, I know, I'm being silly. I'm acting like a love sick school girl. Still...it's been a long time since I've been around someone that accepted me." She absently played with the pendant hanging from her neck.

Merlin rolled onto his back and covered his eyes with his paws.

"So he doesn't know what I am." Lillian picked Merlin up and turned his face to hers. "At least so far he isn't scared of me. It's been five years since I even saw another vampire and that included all of a polite nod from thirty feet away. Don't get me wrong, you're great company, Merlin, but a girl needs more companionship than a cat."

Lillian put Merlin down as he meowed.

"I know you need more companionship than me. I told you as soon as I finish my book I'll get you a cute little girlfriend."

Lillian pulled a sleeveless green velvet dress from the closet. "How about this, Merlin?" she asked holding the dress up to her body.

Merlin decided to leave the room at that moment.

"You're right, green velvet is too 'I'm ready for my Christmas picture'."

Lillian stopped and considered that maybe this was a bad idea. Maybe she should just cancel. Ash would understand that she had too much work to do.

Suddenly there was a knock on the door. Lillian, still trying to decide how to tell Ash she was going to have to cancel their date, opened her front door forgetting she was still only wearing a corset and underwear.

Ash was unexpectedly standing on the other side of the door. He opened his mouth like he was going to say something, but all that came out was "Uuuhhh..."

Lillian still unaware of the show she was putting on smiled pleasantly. "Ash, you're early. I didn't think you would be here until later. I'm not ready yet."

Ash gulped anxiously. "I can see that." Ash paused looking Lillian up and down slowly as he continued, "I just remembered I never asked if you wanted to go anywhere in par...tic...u...lar."

Lillian followed Ash's gaze down and finally realized why he was acting so distracted.

Lillian put her hand over her eyes. "Oh, my God!" She bit her lip and looked back at Ash. "Excuse me," she said, holding up her pointer finger, "one minute."

Lillian closed the door flustered. She rested her head against the door trying to shake off her embarrassment. She found a cotton robe to throw on and went back to the door.

Lillian smiled nervously at Ash. "I'm sorry, Ash, I was up late writing. I'm a little out of it right now. I don't usually answer my door half-naked."

Ash exhaled a little laugh. "No, don't be sorry. I was actual worried that you were expecting someone else coming to the door like that. What I came to bother you about, was to see if you might be up for swing dancing? I know this lounge that has it going on tonight and it's really easy. I mean, I can show you-"

"That sounds wonderful," Lillian interrupted, "I haven't been swing dancing in years."

"Great!" Ash replied a little eagerly. "I'll come back to pick you up in a couple hours, if that sounds okay, nine o'clock?"

Lillian just shook her head yes and smiled again. As soon as the door was closed she raced back to her closet. Now that she knew where she was going it would be much easier to pick something out to wear. She grabbed a rockabilly style dress she had bought years ago and never worn. It was black with white polka dots, had a tight bodice, a full circle skirt, and tied around the neck. Lillian found the matching black and white T-strap swing shoes she had bought to go with the dress in the very back of the closet, still in the box. She hurried to the bathroom, pulled her strawberry blonde hair into a tight ponytail, applied some make-up, and made sure to apply the shiniest red lipstick she had.

Lillian looked at the clock. That had taken her all of ten minutes. Three hours until nine o'clock. Plenty of time to finish chapter nine before Ash came back to get her.

ଛ**9**ଓ

As I woke up the next morning, well we'll call it before noon, Dallen was walking into my room.

"Oh, good you're up," he said sitting down in a chair next to my bed. "How would you like to play tennis with me today? That is when you're actually awake."

I yawned, "I'd love to. Just give me another hour to wake up."

"Do you want breakfast, coffee, tea, anything?" Dallen asked.

"Am I really up early enough for breakfast?" I asked in mock astonishment.

"I know, the wonders of life. Isn't it amazing? I think you almost look different in the morning light. Almost sweeter." He looked at me thoughtfully. "As if that face could look any sweeter."

"Nice save, Romeo. So, what do you have up your sleeve?" I asked.

"What on Earth do you mean? Isn't it a beautiful day?" He turned to look out the window.

"Yes, Dallen, it's a beautiful day. What I meant was, what are you hiding? Why are you so happy?"

"Lillian, I hate to tell you this, but people are usually happy. Now get up! Come on out of bed! Time to get dressed." He stood up and yanked the covers off of the bed.

"Oh, I don't want to get up right now. It's too early. Besides it's unhealthy to be that happy in the morning, Dallen." I pulled the covers back on.

"It is no longer morning so get up. Let's go, Lillian, you are going to spend some time out of doors in the sunshine today," Dallen commanded as he grabbed my hand and pulled me out of bed.

Dallen practically pushed me into my walk-in closet to find something to wear. I had no choice but to obey and get dressed. I walked down one side of the closet pretending I was actually looking for an outfit, but mostly I was still trying to wake up. I could feel Dallen watching me, I assumed to make sure that I didn't just make a mad dash back to my bed, so I grabbed the first thing that caught my eye to prove that I was really planning on getting dressed.

"How about this?" I said, turning around to show him a ridiculous jumpsuit, then noticed he was staring at me with a strange look on his face.

Dallen stood statue still, his eyes fixed on my body, and his lips slightly parted. My heart was pounding the way it had the night he had kissed me in his bed. I looked down at myself, feeling a little uneasy. I realized I was wearing only the form-fitting black strapless slip that I had been too lazy to change out of the night before.

"I don't normally sleep in things like this. I'll just put a robe on." I reached for a robe on a hanger behind him but he caught my arm.

He looked straight in my eyes and whispered resolutely, "You should start sleeping in things like that."

Finally he let my arm go. I didn't know what to do. I thought, *if I move he might grab me, and I know if he grabs me I won't be able to control myself. Perhaps if I stand still he'll just leave me alone.*

Dallen took the robe from behind him, never taking his eyes off of me. "If you don't trust me you can put the robe on." Perhaps reading my mind, he held the robe out to me.

I hesitated a moment, because I didn't want him to think I didn't trust him. At last I decided it would be best to take the robe. I extended my hand to take the robe, but Dallen shook his head playfully.

"Turn around, I'll help you."

I turned around reluctantly, feeling anxious.

Dallen held the robe up to my shoulders as if to help me into it, and then let it fall soundlessly to the floor. I tried to turn around but he

146

held my shoulders tightly.

My heart pounded with my fervid breathing as I felt his breath on my ear while he cooed softly, "Lillian, I cannot stand not to touch you anymore. I have to feel the softness of your skin, if for but a moment."

I could feel myself ready to fall into his arms. He slid his hand down the side of my body and put his arm around my waist. He held my throat with his other hand and kissed my neck. I felt tears roll down my face, though, I didn't feel threatened by him. I felt complete love, or what I thought was love anyway. Dallen must have felt my tears fall onto his hand. He turned me around and looked in my eyes.

He held my face and said gently, "Maybe this is wrong. I shouldn't do this to you. Please forgive me. I don't know what came over me. Lillian, I love you, and I don't want to hurt you or upset you. I shouldn't have been so bold without your permission."

His lips slid to my cheek and I knew he was going to leave. As he pulled his lips from my cheek they hovered just for a moment past my lips. I plunged forward. Forcing my lips against his. Hoping this would persuade him to stay.

Dallen's arms locked around my waist and I felt him pulling me back, out of the closet, and toward the bed. I didn't try to hold back any longer. I let him pull me gently along, toward my bed. I tried in vain to rip his button-up shirt off, but all I could manage was to get it half-way unbuttoned. I put my hand inside his shirt feeling his solid chest, now beating fiercely with passion. Right before he was about to fall into the bed he stopped and turned me around.

Then faster than I could imagine he picked me up, still kissing my lips, moving to my throat, then to my breasts, and threw me onto the bed. Dallen looked at me smiling while he tore his own shirt off. He stepped closer to the bed unbuckling his smooth black belt. I crawled to the edge of the bed on my knees and threw my arms around him, putting my head against his chest, hearing the beautiful throb of his heart.

I couldn't move from that spot. I stayed kneeling on the bed with my head on his chest. Dallen didn't move. He didn't say a word; he just threw his arms around me protectively. At the moment that I felt him put his arms around me, comforting me, and felt his lips touch the top of my head, I knew I had lost him. I knew at that moment he was going to protect me, even it meant protecting me from himself. I couldn't bare to look at him for fear of that truth, but I couldn't let him go either.

"I know, I know," were the only words that escaped lightly from his lips.

He pulled away from me and soothingly made me lie down. I felt like dying right there in that bed. I was ashamed that I had pushed him to make love to me...when I wasn't even ready for it. I had spent so much of my teen years pining for Lex and Vann, I never explored physical love. The feelings were too new...and confusing, especially with everything else that was happening. I was just too inexperienced and now I had acted so foolish with Dallen; he would probably never want me again. Maybe he knew what I was thinking. Maybe he had read my mind, because he didn't leave me to brood in silence. The lonely, judgmental silence.

He sank into the bed beside me and put his arms around me. He had said he loved me, but I had made him second guess being my lover. I wished I could explain to him, but it would sound ridiculous. A twenty year old girl, who had seen death (more than once), fallen in love (yes more than once also), and was completely surrounded by blood-thirsty vampires; yet I was scared of sex.

I left it at that. I didn't tell him. If it was going to happen it would, if not...who knows maybe I would be turned before I ever found out what sex was like. I just knew that moment could not be changed right then. There was nothing to be said. I tried to sleep to escape my shame at trying to make Dallen be someone that I wasn't ready for him to be.

When I woke up I almost forgot my shameful behavior. I rolled over and I realized something was missing. Then it came to me…

Dallen.

He was no longer lying beside me.

The whole embarrassing event came back to me. I rolled myself out of bed bracing myself for whatever lecturing I would surely get from Lex, as he probably knew what had happened, or had almost happened. I threw a robe on and drug myself downstairs.

"Well, sleeping beauty, you've finally awoken," Lex said teasingly.

"Lex, I'm really not in the mood for your shit today. Everything's gone to hell," I said wretchedly.

Lex looked at me baffled. "I'm guessing you got up on the wrong side of the bed this evening?"

"Then you don't know?" I asked.

Lex shook his head. "Know what? That your supply of Midol ran out?"

I ignored his joke. "Didn't you talk to Dallen today?"

"Dallen? No, he left before I rose. Why?"

Just then Vann walked in from the other end of the house. "Ciao, Lillian, how are you?"

I looked at him and sighed.

"That good? I am not interrupting a fight am I?" Vann turned to Lex.

Lex shrugged his shoulders. "I was just having a polite conversation, but I get the feeling more went on today than I'm being told."

Vann thought for a moment. "Lillian, are you all right? You are not incinta, pregnant, or anything are you?" he asked the last question absurdly.

I sat down on the bottom stair and started crying. I couldn't stop myself from doing it. How could I explain something so silly as being afraid of sex with two vampires; they would laugh at me and point out the many other things that I should be scared of besides that. Vann and Lex came and sat down beside me.

"Mi dispiace, I'm sorry, Lillian, I did not mean to upset you. Please, tell us what is wrong," Vann said gently.

Lex put his arm around me and asked loudly, "Are you pregnant?! I knew this would happen! I told you, Giovanni, I should have kicked Dallen out when I had the chance!"

"No! No, I'm not pregnant. It's nothing like that." I almost laughed, but instead tried to explain through my sobs, "I...this morning...I just almost..."

The door opened and Dallen walked in. I got up and ran to him.

He put his arms around me and whispered in my ear, "I'm sorry, Lillian. I am so sorry."

I looked up into his eyes. "Why did you leave me? I thought you left for good, because of me, because of what happened."

Lex stood up, bewildered. "Dallen, maybe you can figure out what's wrong with her. She burst into tears for no reason."

I looked from Lex to Dallen nervously. I didn't know how Lex would react if he found out the real reason I was upset so I just stood there dumbly, waiting for someone else to say something.

Vann came toward me, took my hands in his, and spoke to Dallen. "Dallen, Lex and I, we have business tonight. You will look after Lillian while we are out?"

I could see Dallen was trying to conceal our secret from Lex and Vann's prying mind probing. "Of course, I will look after her."

Although Lex could see there was some secret between Dallen and me, he, thank god, could not read either of our thoughts to discover the truth. Instead he took Dallen to the side to speak to him in private before he and Vann left.

Dallen turned around sullenly. He looked at me for a moment as if he were about to say something important, but instead walked away with a sigh.

I sat back down on the stairs to collect myself. I reasoned that Dallen was trying to stay away from me because he didn't want to push me again. The more I thought about it the more angry I became. I thought I was in love with Dallen and I thought he loved me. It was silly for us to try to stay away from each other when what we really wanted was to be together. I went to look for him and try to explain my behavior to him; that it wasn't his fault; I should have just told him I was scared from the beginning. I decided to first look in his room.

I went to push Dallen's door open, but stopped myself, realizing someone else was in his room speaking with him. It was a male voice. I pressed my ear to the door to try to hear better.

"You've gotten too close, Gray. OPTS will terminate you from this assignment when they hear what you've done. You know that she is part of our objective."

I could hear Dallen's cool reply, "I was simply using any means to find the truth."

The other man seemed impatient. "I think you were acting on your emotions. Plus, if he finds out you've been toying with the girl, he'll be furious. I've seen the way you look at her, Gray, I can't say that I blame you, but I assure you if it goes any further I will have to report you to The General. Do you think he's going to like the idea of her having feelings for you? No. You've already exposed Lex to OPTS. Why not close the case at that and let better qualified members discontinue this nest? Before you do something that you won't be able to come back from." The man's voice seemed familiar, but I couldn't put it to a face, the voice was whispering too low.

I could hear Dallen clear his voice over-dramatically, and then there was an uneasy silence. After five minutes of silence I decided to knock and then quickly entered Dallen's room. I pushed the door open to see Dallen lying cross-legged on his bed staring at the door, as if he had been waiting for me. There wasn't another soul in the room.

"I'm sorry, Dallen, did I interrupt you?" I asked, glancing around the room.

Dallen swung his legs over the edge of the bed. "No, no. Why would you think that?"

"I thought I heard someone talking with you." I stopped seeing Dallen's balcony door ajar.

Dallen tried to cover. "Oh you probably just heard me mumbling to myself. I have a tendency to do that when I have a lot on my mind"

I walked over to the balcony doors throwing them open and stepping out onto the balcony.

As I looked out across the lawn I could see a man running. The image reminded me of the night a man had been hiding in my room. I walked back into Dallen's room closing the doors.

I knew Dallen was trying to read my mind. I wasn't sure if he was able to actually read any of my thoughts, because he wasn't trying to explain away any of the horrible thoughts I was having. He was just standing beside his bed impassively awaiting my questions.

"Dallen, what is going on? Why is there a man sneaking out of your room? Why have you been hiding things from me? What does OPTS mean?" I was overwhelmed. "What girl have you been toying with? Is it me? Can I even trust you anymore?"

Dallen came toward me and wound his arms around me comfortably. "You can trust me, Lillian. I told you I would never let anything hurt you. I'll tell you everything when the time comes. For now, just know that I am doing what is right."

I tried to pull away from his embrace, but only managed to turn my head away from him, mumbling, "What is right?"

Dallen brushed the hair off of my face and turned it back toward his. "This is right," he said, plunging his lips against mine.

I wanted to protest, to demand he tell me the truth, but again I was completely under his spell. I couldn't help kissing him back and I didn't stop him as he untied my robe and slipped it off my shoulders.

I pulled away from his demanding kisses, confused. "Dallen, are you sure this is right? Before you didn't want…"

He pushed back my hair with his hands and held my face. "I want you, Lillian. Before I was scared I would hurt you, but I have always wanted you." His lips were close enough to taste in their seductive whisper.

Dallen ran his hand down my neck to my breasts, caressing them, patiently.

"Dallen, please, tell me what's going on? Just tell me what you want with me?" I whispered heavily, trying to remember why I was resisting.

"Lillian, I …" he paused, looking into my eyes with the same hunger I'd seen in a vampire about to feed. "I want to make love to you. Since the moment I met you I've wanted you, even against my own will. I need to have you."

Dallen gently removed my slip, pushing me away slightly to behold my blushing body. He hesitated for a moment but then took off his shirt, watching me with a determined look in his eyes. I felt awkward and

152

uneasy standing there so exposed.

"Are you all right, Lillian? I don't want to force you into anything. I do want you, but your happiness is more important to me." Dallen ran his fingers through his lightly tussled hair.

I looked down, trying to control my discomfort. "I do want you, Dallen. It's just..." I shut my eyes tight, biting my lip in embarrassment. "For all my talk...I'm still scared."

Dallen looked at me, curiosity sketched on his face, he scrunched his eyebrows questioningly.

I smiled bashfully, and said low, "I've never done this before." I looked up into his eyes. "I don't want to disappoint you."

He moved toward me, each movement quickening my heart, and slid both hands below my ears, pulling my face close to his. "Don't you know you could never disappoint me? You have already given me more pleasure than any other woman in my whole life." He focused on my lips, running his thumb across them.

I was so intoxicated by his touch that I hadn't really heard what he said. When I thought about the last thing he had said I was disturbed by the thought of his murdered wife. "What about Chris...?"

Suddenly his lips were covering mine, forcing my mind to stop turning. Dallen swept me up in his arms, dropping me into his bed. He undid his pants and let them drop to the floor, leaving only his black silk boxers to cover his desire. I lay back on the pillow, feeling my own hunger growing for him as he neared. My lips trembled anxiously and my chest heaved. He crawled onto the bed by my feet, on all-fours like a starving lion advancing on its wounded prey. He hovered over me, his mouth lapping at mine. I closed my eyes as he ran his hand up the inner part of my leg.

He stopped massaging my inner thigh, and looked up at me. I was so disturbed by the ceasing of pleasure I opened my eyes to see Dallen staring at me as if he had some secret surprise. His body rose over mine as he moved to kiss my throat.

Dallen looked at me enlivened, and said half serious, "You're in trouble now."

I couldn't help but giggle. "What could you do to me?"

He grinned, shrewdly. "I'll show you." Then he stood by the bed and removed his silk boxers, exposing his nude form.

He moved gently across the bed and over my body. His lips locked to mine, and his hand circling my nipples, luring me onward.

He pushed back my hair, purring in my ear, "Tell me you want me."

I put my mouth to his ear and said, "I want you, now."

He moved between my legs and slid gently in. My first impulse was to scream in agony, though it wasn't exactly agony I felt. It was a kind of wonderful pain. Dallen pushed himself inside me even as I half struggled. I let out a moan of absolute surrender.

Between his breathy kisses he managed to ask, "How do you feel?"

All I could manage was to say his name.

Dallen smiled warmly and covered me with kisses as he poured in and out of me. He never failed to focus completely on my pleasure, caressing me, kissing me, loving my entire body.

Afterward Dallen started to pull away. I put my arms around him and whispered in his ear, "Just stay for a little while."

He lifted his head to look in my eyes and saw the tears running down my face. "Oh, Lillian, did I hurt you? I'm sorry." He gently kissed at the streams.

"You didn't hurt me. I don't know why I'm crying, but that certainly was the most amazing thing I've ever felt." I laid back in utter pleasure.

"Lillian, I love you." Dallen fell back against the pillow, and declared as if he were surprised by his discovery, "No matter the danger, I really do love you."

Dallen rolled his body toward me and threw his arm around my waist, and nuzzled his mouth against my neck. I didn't know what he'd meant by that, but I was too tired to ask.

I could hear the tinkle of champagne glasses.

"Congratulations to the newlyweds! May they live in everlasting joy and never want for blood!" Lex raised his glass to the room of guests.

"And may they never hide things from one another as Dallen did in the past!" Vann said, raising his glass.

Everyone looked at me smiling and raised their glasses. "Hooray!"

Dallen looked at me raising his glass and smiling like a joyous fool.

I grabbed Dallen by the shoulders. "What is going on? Why is everyone acting so ridiculous?"

Dallen smiled broadly and took both of my hands, "Honey, they're celebrating our engagement, just as we are. They're as happy as we are. Especially with the little package on the way," he said the last while rubbing my stomach.

I pushed his hand away. "What are you talking about engagement?! And what little package?!"

Dallen leaned in close, "Darling, you agreed to marry me after you found out you were pregnant with my child, don't you remember? All of our vampire friends are here to celebrate our baby's birth."

I looked at him short of breath. "Why would they want to celebrate our baby's birth?"

Dallen laughed as did everyone around him. "Why, sweetheart, everyone is celebrating because we promised to sacrifice our child to the vampires."

I backed away looking at them in disbelief. "No! No! You're not going to have my child! No!"

"Nooooo!" I screamed, sitting up straight in bed.

Dallen put his hand to my head. "It's all right, Lillian, it was just a dream. It wasn't real."

I caught my breath and looked at him. "You saw it, didn't you? You know what I dreamed?"

Dallen said soothingly, "Yes, I saw. It wasn't real. You are not pregnant. Even if you were, no vampire would feed on your child." Then he added earnestly, "I swear it."

His last remark gave me pause. Why did he seem so grave?

Dallen took my hand in his, rolling my fingers through his own. "I told you I wouldn't let anything hurt you and I meant it. No matter what happens in the next few days I will protect you from any harm, because for better or for worse I am in love with you."

Ah, so we're back to keeping secrets. I shook my head, exasperated. "You're in love with me? Then why are you hiding things from me? Why won't you tell me the truth? You don't love me, you're just using me! Why are you really here?! I bet you never even had a wife. I don't know what to believe. Your name probably isn't even Dallen."

"Lillian, you're just upset from your dream. I am not hiding anything from-"

I threw my hand over his mouth. "Shhh. I hear Lex. He's in the main hall."

Dallen pulled my hand off of his mouth. "Lillian, are you mad?! The main hall is too far from my room. There is no way you could hear him."

"You're the expert, Dallen, can't you read his mind. He is here and now he's walking up the stairs."

Dallen became silent, lowering his head, trying to concentrate.

"Dallen, he's coming down the hall," I warned.

Finally Dallen looked at me in alarm. "He's at the door."

The door was opening. I could feel Lex there. His heart pounding from the blood he had recently taken, and worried for some unknown reason.

"Lex?" I questioned before he entered the room.

The door swung open revealing Lex's unnerved form in the light of the corridor. He didn't ask for an explanation, he just stood there with the light at his back.

In confusion I asked again, "Lex, is that you?"

A long pause followed during which all I felt was Dallen's hand squeezing my own.

I couldn't stand the unbearable silence. "Lex, what's the matter? Is something wrong? Did something happen?"

Lex stepped into the room reluctantly, first switching the light on. He walked mournfully toward the bed. His expression was so vacant my thoughts were filled with uncanny thoughts.

I sat up letting the covers fall, exposing my bare breasts. "Lex, you're scaring me, what is it? Please tell me...please....." I felt my voice about to fail me.

Lex just kept walking slowly and calmly. He stopped just before the bed. I could see him contemplating his own thoughts, sorting out what he was going to say.

"You are...both in danger. The council has decided one of you must die." Lex pulled a gold dagger from his sleeve.

I looked from Dallen to Lex shaking my head. This was wrong. This was not Lex. He would never do such a thing. I looked back to Dallen; his face was turned down as in guilt.

"What is going on? Lex, why does the council want us dead? Dallen, what is going on? You know something don't you?"

Lex looked directly into my eyes. "I've decided it will be......" He raised the dagger with inhuman speed, but I knew where he meant to aim it. "...Dallen!"

I plunged in front of Dallen before Lex even finished saying his name. The dagger dove straight through my neck, in one side and out the other. I was still alive but I couldn't breathe, I was choking. My eyes found Lex and I waited for him to react.

"Oh my God," Lex said plainly, looking at Dallen.

Lex pulled the dagger out and looked back at me. I knew he would save me. He wouldn't let me die, but he didn't move. I made a mumbling noise to bring his attention back to me and snap him out of his disbelief.

He looked at me and cocked his head in annoyance. Then Lex said slowly, "Too bad you didn't die...but someone has to pay!"

With the last word he raised the dagger and brought it vigorously down piercing through my heart. My weakest part apparently.

"Lex!...Lex!..." it was my voice screaming. "Don't kill me!"

Someone was shaking me. "Lillian! Lillian! Wake up! Wake up!"

I was yanked upright in bed.

"Where am I?" My eyes searched the half darkness trying to focus.

Dallen's bedroom. I turned to see Dallen sitting next to me his arms holding me up.

Dallen pulled my body toward him. "It's all right, Lillian, it was just a dream. It wasn't real."

I put my hand out, laying it flat on his chest to steady myself. "You saw it didn't you? You saw what I dreamed? All of it?" My mouth quivered.

"No, I was asleep. Your scream woke me. But trust me Lex is not going to kill you. Even if he wanted to, he couldn't. No vampire is going to hurt you," his voice was resolute, as though he knew the future.

I suddenly had an uneasy feeling of déjà vu. I let my hand slide away from Dallen's chest. He caught my hand in his and pulled it to his lips to kiss my fingertips.

"Lillian, I promised you I wouldn't let anything harm you and I mean to keep that promise. I don't know what is going to happen in the next few days, but I will protect you no matter what." He stopped, and I saw his head drop while he played with my fingers. "You know it's quite against my own will, but I do love you. With all of my heart."

"Love?" I said it half to myself because I remembered these words, and I knew my lines, and I knew how it would end but I continued, "Why won't you tell me why you're really here? Why won't you tell me the truth? Don't tell me you love me. Did you even have a wife named Christine? Or a wife at all for that matter? Who are you?"

My eyes were tearing up as I felt an overwhelming sense of doom.

Dallen sighed lightly, "Lillian, you're just upset from your dream. I'm not lying to you or hiding any-" I put my hand gingerly over his mouth to stop him.

"Lex is home. He just came in the door. He's in..." I took a deep breath remembering my dream. "He's in the main hall and I know it's impossible for me to know that. The hall is really far away. Right? By now he's already up the stairs and coming down this hall. Try to read his mind, you'll see."

Dallen's face dropped. "He's at the door. How did you..."Dallen asked, looking at me in puzzlement.

The door opened slowly, but I knew who it was. There was no need to ask. I called his name anyway. "Lex? Lex, I know it's you. What happened? What did the council say?"

I felt Dallen's hand shoot across the bed to mine, squeezing to reassure himself of his own strength.

Lex stepped in, turned the light on, and without looking up drug his feet across the floor until he stood on my side of the bed. As I reached out to grab his hand the sheet fell, but I succeeded in catching it before revealing my naked upper half.

"Lex, please tell me." I pulled him toward me and forced him to sit on the edge of the bed. I put both of my hands on either side of his cheeks and turned his eyes to mine. "Lex, I'll understand. Whatever they said. Tell me."

I felt tapping on my shoulder. "Umm…Lillian, I think maybe this isn't the best time or place."

I turned to Dallen and was surprised to see he was clutching the blanket protectively. He made a gesture at himself as if to say "in case you've forgotten I'm still naked."

I just waved him silent. I was more worried about my dream being true, and if it was this was going to end badly. I had to change things somehow. I turned back to Lex.

He muttered, "He's dead."

I shook my head in confusion. He wasn't supposed to say that.

I asked with curiosity, "Who's dead?"

Lex looked up, tears splashing down his face.

Dallen finally decided to join the conversation. "Lex, you're not going to kill me, are you?"

I smiled at Lex and he even snickered a little. "No, Dallen, I'm not going kill you. I don't know why you would think that. Well," Lex said as he looked at Dallen and I wrapped in the covers, "I know why you would think that, but I realize I can't stop what you two feel for each other. Anyway, have I ever been able to tell Lillian what she can or cannot do?" he said it with such melancholy in his voice. I thought perhaps that was why he was acting so strange; that he had finally come to realize he couldn't control me and expect me to love him for it.

I smiled tenderly and threw my arms around him.

I didn't expect the news he whispered in my ear as I squeezed him. "It's Mason…"

I pushed him back shaking my head in disbelief, pursing my mouth to stop the sobs. "No! No…no. Mason." I grew calm, taking deep breaths. "Lex, what about Mason?" I let my eyes fall waiting for him to tell me why he had said Mason's name, waiting for him to tell me Mason was not dead.

"Oh, dear God," Dallen's voice managed to exude with breathy reluctance.

His arms slid to crisscross my chest, hands cradling both my shoulders; I felt his heart racing against my back.

I closed my eyes.

I knew, without Lex's answer.

I knew, because Dallen knew.

Because Dallen had read Lex's unguarded, dreary thoughts.

More to answer my own question than to ask a question, I said aloud, "Mason is dead."

"Yes," was all Lex said before leaving the room silently.

Dallen and I stayed in our embrace for most of the morning. I, because I couldn't bring myself to move. Dallen, well, I really didn't know what Dallen was thinking or feeling. When I look back now I can guess what was going through his mind, but I never did ask him. At the time I thought, naively, that it was out of love that he stayed with me. I know now that he was starting to question how he felt about something that he had given his faith, his devotion, and his entire life to. In case you're wondering that thing was not me, but I like to still think that he partly stayed because of love.

I didn't sleep at all that morning or the whole rest of the day for that matter. I couldn't. I needed answers. Lex hadn't even told us how Mason died. Lex had barely been able to even tell us Mason was dead, let alone give any details. I still couldn't believe it, it didn't feel real. I had all these questions running through my mind and no way to find the answers. On top of that I still couldn't get out of my head Dallen's secrecy and his absolute assurance that no vampire would ever harm me. As if he knew something was going to happen, perhaps happen to those I cared about.

But mostly I thought about Mason.

Beautiful, sweet Mason. Even as a vampire he'd been harmless. He loved the world and everything in it. He cherished humans, animals, vampires, and everything strange and unknown to him in the world. I knew he wasn't as strong as most of the others, and maybe that was part of his pleasant demeanor. He was still so caught up in being alive, even though I guess technically he wasn't. Mason saw it all as some great plan. God knew what he was doing, that was what Mason would say with his charming southern accent.

I imagined what he would say to me at that moment, *Don't cry for me, sugar. It was meant, thas all. Fate, ya know.*

He was probably one of the few vampires most deserving of life, and it was taken from him. Don't worry, Mason, I won't cry; not for too long anyway. This story is for you Mason, I'll never forget you, and I will always treasure the little time we had.

A NIGHT IN THE UN-LIFE...

Lillian let another tear fall gently down her cheek as she sat rereading the last page.

"Dear Mason," she sighed aloud wiping at her eyes, "I do miss you."

The knock at the door brought her back from her memories. She glanced once more at her laptop and then pulled herself reluctantly away to compose herself before answering the door.

"Hello, Mason-" she stopped, catching herself, "I'm sorry, Ash. I was right in the middle of my book. I get a little wrapped up in it sometimes."

He looked at her seriously. "It must be sad."

"Why do you say that?"

Ash brushed his finger over Lillian's cheek. "You look like you've been crying."

Lillian touched her face, embarrassed. "I probably look awful, and now you won't want to take me anywhere."

"Actually, just the opposite. You look beautiful, and nothing would make me happier than to get you out of this apartment and away from your work to spend the evening getting to know you better." Ash walked into the apartment and turned to Lillian as he added, "By the way I'm dying to hear about this book of yours."

"Not the best choice of words," Lillian said as she gestured for Ash to take a seat. "Just give me a minute and I'll be ready to go."

As Lillian was making herself look a little more presentable in the bathroom mirror Ash decided to take a peek at her obsession. He leaned over the laptop skimming the page that was still pulled up.

"Vampires?" Ash whispered to himself.

Lillian heard him say something, but hadn't been concentrating enough to hear. "What was that?"

Ash straightened up and called toward the bathroom, "Oh nothing, I was just taking a look at your book. I hope that's all right. Since it is the excuse you always use to get rid of me, I've been really curious to see it."

Lillian hurried from the bathroom, trying to sound polite as she said, "I'd rather no one saw it until it's completely done. Call it a writer's eccentricity, but I don't want to jinx it by letting anyone see it until it's perfect." She gently shut the laptop from Ash's prying eyes, feeling a little awkward.

Finally Ash broke the uneasy silence. "I see your main character is named Lillian. Is she like you?"

"Quite a bit. I would say she is nearly exactly like me, but younger...and much more naïve."

"Darn," Ash said, snapping his fingers dramatically, "and I thought I would get lucky with a naïve girl."

"Nobody said you were going to get lucky at all," Lillian said flatly, raising an eyebrow.

Ash blushed slightly, not realizing how he had worded his playful remark. "I didn't mean..." he stammered, shaking his head, "I was just joking."

Lillian laughed. "I know. I'm teasing you. I know you didn't mean it that way. I was just trying to be funny. I'm not very good at this as you can see. I haven't dated...much." Then she added, "But I really did mean the part about you not getting-"

Ash cut her off raising his hands as if in defeat, "Okay, I get it. You have rules, that's fine." Then he smiled warmly and asked Lillian in his most playfully serious tone, "So are you ready to tear yourself away from your book and Lillian and...what was the other one...Mason?"

Lillian looked down at the floor and thought a moment as if this were a crucial decision she was making.

"Leave my book..." She stole a glance at her laptop. "For now."

Ash thought she was just teasing him again with her seriousness, but as Lillian led Ash out the door she lingered on those days following Mason's death.

It still felt odd to repeat those words, even if just in her mind, *Mason's death*. She couldn't help reciting the beginning of the next chapter in her head as she walked down the stairwell and out into the night. With Ash and on a date. Probably only the third actual date she'd ever been on in her life; mortal or immortal.

೮೦10೦ಃ

I felt cold all over every time I repeated the words in my head:
Mason is dead.

I was in shock. How could this have happened? He was immortal,
and yet, just like that he was gone. I didn't even know how he had died,
but I felt guilty, as if it were somehow my fault. All of the things that had
happened since we'd arrived: Lex's bizarre need to keep me safe, Rachel's
sudden personality change, Dallen's suspicious behavior, and the
emergence of a powerful, evil vampire hell bent on some kind of revenge;
it all seemed connected, and it all felt like my fault.

I sat in Dallen's bed three days straight with nothing but thoughts
of Mason, and how I would avenge his death, should I ever discover who
it was that had killed him. Was it this Dardanos that Lex had described?
Was that why Lex had been hiding things? Had he been worried
something like this was going to happen? If so, he never mentioned his
fears to me. He had been disturbed by Dardanos's appearance, especially
so close to the mansion, but Lex had never spoken to me about it again
after the night I'd woken in his bed. Had someone else gone after Mason?
I couldn't think who would ever want Mason dead or why, but then I
really hadn't known Mason that well. All of the time I'd spent with him
before I'd moved into the mansion had been with Vann present, and I'm
sure I don't have to remind you of the blind adoration I'd had for Vann.
Although we'd become much closer since I relinquished my childish
feelings for Vann, I knew there was a lot I didn't know about Mason, but I
did know that he was one of the sweetest, kindest beings I'd ever met.

I stayed in Dallen's room, lying in bed. Dallen seemed to give up
his room to my whims, but he rarely came to visit me. I'm not sure what
he did exactly, but he would tell me he had to go out and I wouldn't see
him all day. It didn't matter to me that Dallen wasn't there, or rather I

should say I didn't think on it enough for it to matter. Only when he did come to see me was I aware that he hadn't been there the whole time.

"Lillian, you need to eat," Dallen's voice woke me out of thoughts.

Without looking up at him I replied, "I know, Dallen. Just leave the food on the table, I'll eat later."

He put the food down and came to sit next to me. "Lillian, I've been leaving your food on the table. You haven't touched it. It's been almost two days since you've eaten," Dallen said anxiously.

I looked over at the table overflowing with dishes.

"Oh, I didn't even notice," I muttered

"That's what you said last time. Please eat."

"Yes, Dallen, I will."

Then he left again, whether out of frustration or because he really had somewhere he had to be, I'm not sure.

Rachel would come lie next to me, quietly for an hour here and there. Sometimes urging me to at least eat; as if that would make everything better. I did finally give in to her pushing a plate of fruit at me in bed, and picked at it to make her feel better at least. Sometimes she would clasp my hand and talk about our lives before we'd met Lex, making it sound like a fairytale, which it had never been, or at least not for me, but I knew Mason's death had only convinced her of her recent change of heart about our situation. She didn't want to live like this anymore. She never said it outright, but she would rattle on about how wonderful life had been before we'd stumbled upon vampires, and what we would be doing if we had never let Lex talk us into living with him. Then she would inevitably run out of things to say, get tired of my mood, and leave. Plus, she was spending more and more time with Osborn now, and I could tell she viewed our moments together as a chore that she was required to complete before she was allowed to go off and do what she really wanted. Once or twice I thought I even saw Osborn hovering outside the door, but he never came in, thank goodness.

Lex would come at night and whisper in my ear. Telling me how much he had loved Mason, and how much he would miss him. He reassured me that Mason had loved me and told me things that Mason had said to him about me, but he never gave me any more information about

Mason's death. I only half listened. I really didn't want anyone around me. Every time someone came to talk to me my heart would break again, and I would cry incessantly.

Then they would go, and I would be alone again, but it really wasn't any better. Sometimes I would think about Ben. Someone had brought my poetry book, and I would stare at his picture feeling the pain of losing him all over again. Sometimes I would sit and stare for hours at nothing and think of nothing until I passed out from boredom or exhaustion. I felt stuck, like my wretched feelings were a trap I couldn't escape. I didn't know how to get past those feelings, and I wasn't sure I wanted to. Was this how life as a vampire would be? Constant loss? Constant struggles to remain invisible? Love in and out of your life? Always surrounded by death?

Then on the third night I got out of bed, went to my room to shower, put on a simple loose fitting black dress, and went downstairs. I walked slowly down the marble steps dragging my bare feet, feeling the hem of my dress brushing against the tops of my feet as I walked. I could hear voices coming from the banquet hall.

"They must all be here," I said aloud to myself.

Then I heard Lex's voice eagerly call, "Lillian, we're in here!"

I really wasn't in the mood to be among the eternal council, but I knew Lex would come after me if I tried to sneak out to walk in the gardens as I had planned. I longed to sit before the Palladium statue and feel its comforting magic. It had protected the city of Troy, and I thought perhaps if I asked it, it might protect the rest us from our invisible foe. I reluctantly entered the banquet hall.

I didn't say anything; I just entered, nodded at everyone, and searched the table until I found the empty seat next to Lex. He had apparently been saving the seat for me, and must have been trying to get my attention from the moment that I had entered the room.

I felt like a doll that was just being pushed along, not caring where I was being pushed. A doll with everything in the right place on the outside but nothing on the inside. Just a stuffed thing sewn together sloppily, waiting for my seams to come undone. Maybe wanting, secretly, for someone to be there to sew me back up when I did come undone.

I slumped in the chair next to Lex, not even turning to look at him.

I thought I could just be among them and be invisible, but they wouldn't let me.

"We are all upset about Mason, Lillian. We are going to find out exactly what happened. Some just cannot accept that Mason would commit suicide," Malika explained plainly.

All at once my eyes shot wide, my mouth dropped, and I whipped my head to look at Lex. He didn't look at me, with purpose. I could see he knew I was glaring at him in bewilderment, but he pretended to not notice. Now I knew why he hadn't given me any details about Mason's death.

"When were you going to tell me?" I demanded angrily.

He finally turned to face me, his eyes blank with sadness, but he didn't speak.

Instead it was Malika that answered, "Alexander doesn't believe Mason would ever end his own life. We are taking his opinion into consideration, and intend to investigate."

"Investigate? You mean you haven't even begun to investigate? What have you been doing for the past three days? Do you even know how he supposedly...died?" I was outraged at the passiveness of Malika's words.

Lex spoke up, quietly, "Many of us have been mourning. As I believe you have been. We've been somewhat grief stricken to concentrate on looking for answers to questions we don't even know to ask." He fell back into his chair as if his little outburst had taken too much energy.

I would have felt guilty for accusing them of doing exactly what I had been doing, but I was now consumed by my second question, which had gone unanswered.

"And how did Mason supposedly die?" I asked obnoxiously.

Lex simply stated, "The sun."

I searched the faces around the table eager to find Vann, who would surely explain in more detail. I was sure he wouldn't deny me the truth, no matter how painful. I was sure he, at least would understand, and comfort me. Vann had turned Mason and surely he had been affected more so than everyone else, I knew he would be sympathetic to my reaction.

"Where's Vann?" I almost demanded.

Solemnly Tor, who usually let Malika do all the talking for him, answered, "We haven't seen or heard from Giovanni since the night we found out. When Glen told us the news about Mason, Giovanni just walked out without a word."

Lex was quick to add, "I'm sure it's just his way. Everyone mourns differently. Some need to be surrounded, some need to talk, and some..."he paused and put his hand lightly over mine, "some need to be completely alone. Without thought or memory."

I nodded guiltily. Without thought or memory. That was exactly how I'd been the past few days; selfish and cold, not wanting to feel, not wanting to even be touched. Of course I wasn't the only one in mourning, but I had shut everyone out. I'd acted as though it was something done to me, as if I was the only one in the world that ever loved Mason and the only one that would miss him properly. I felt so ashamed.

"You're not cold, little queen. You're anything but cold. I said everyone mourns differently... because it's true. It's not good or bad; it's just how you deal with it. We're all upset and on edge. If we say cruel or insensitive things to each other it's just because we're trying to deal with all of these feelings that we're not used to." Lex smiled slightly, obviously pleased with himself. *Probably because he had actually come off as insightful and unselfish for the first time in his entire life.*

Lex knotted his eyebrows in mock furry. "I can be insightful on occasion. Unselfish? You may be right, those are indeed rare moments in my life, but I think I'm rather insightful on a regular basis."

I had to laugh. "Yes, I have to say your insight astounds me almost daily."

My thoughts quickly turned back to Mason, and so they turned gloomy. My moment of amusement felt disrespectful, and I silently reprimanded myself. My darkened mood made me think back to Tor's words about Vann. *When Glen told us...Giovanni just walked out.*

"What did you mean Glen told you?" I asked.

Glen, who until now had been completely quiet, as was his way, spoke, "I found Mason's body, or rather, excuse my saying, what was left of his body."

I shook my head unsure what he meant and repeated the words questioningly, "What was left of his body?"

Glen moved a little uneasily in his seat looking around the table for someone else to explain. Everyone, who I assume all knew the story well enough to tell it, stared at him as if they too were curious to hear his response.

"Ashes. Nothing but ashes," he whispered.

My eyes filled with tears as I pictured Mason being reduced to a pile of dust. He wouldn't have done that to himself. He couldn't have. He loved life, or rather his existence. He had never even been prone to the bouts of despair that most vampires felt from time to time. It all seemed so unreal, and so unlikely. Of all the vampires on the council, perhaps save Lex, Mason was the last one I would have ever guessed to do something like kill himself. I could see that the council was shaken by what had happened to Mason. Maybe that was why they wanted to believe he'd done it to himself, because if someone had gone after Mason then the most logical conclusion would be that any one of them could be next. Was the council actually scared to even consider the idea that there might be a vampire killer out there?

I inhaled deeply to clear my voice of any quivering and turned to Lex. "Why do you think it wasn't suicide?"

"The ashes," Lex said as if that explained it all, waving his right hand dramatically in the air.

I looked at him blankly and opened my mouth but couldn't think of a response. Finally I shook my head, frustrated. "Okay, I haven't been here. I don't know what all of you have talked about in the past three days. Can you pretend I know absolutely nothing and explain in detail?" Yes, it should have gone without saying, but sometimes Lex is so wrapped up in his own world he forgets that anything else exists.

He continued, unperturbed by my irritation, "You pictured in your mind a nondescript pile of dust. That was how he was found; except for his arm. You know the one with the tattoo of the intertwined snakes. That was solid."

I had no idea where he was going with that. I raised my hands at a loss and stammered, "I…I don't…"

Lex smirked, obviously proud of his cleverness. "We don't burn into a pile of dust in the sun. This isn't the movies. Imagine when the sun has been beating down on mud in the desert, it forms a somewhat hardened surface. If you apply pressure it cracks to reveal the dust beneath, but if nothing disturbs it that surface is like a hardened shell over the ground." He paused to make sure I was following him so far. "It's the same with us. It's like our bodies are made of wet clay and when the sun hits us our mold hardens, but if you crack the outer layer then we dissolve into dust. Unless someone or something disturbs the body it would stay preserved just as it was when it was burnt in the sun. Fragile enough to be smashed by a strong human hand, but solid enough that a moderate wind wouldn't disturb it."

"But the only thing that was still intact was his arm," I said as I finally realized, "and it just happened to be the arm with the tattoo? Making it easy for us to identify him."

"Exactly," Lex said, waving his hands in triumph. "It's too coincidental. Plus his coffin was moved."

"What?!" I asked shocked, on the edge of my seat.

I felt like I had missed an entire month of my favorite TV show in which everything I needed to know had happened. Why hadn't I asked questions earlier? Why had I sulked and felt sorry for myself for so long? I should have been saying the same things Lex was saying right now. I should have been trying to figure out what had really happened, although, I never even considered that Mason had killed himself. From the start I had assumed murder.

I looked to Glen. "His coffin was moved?"

Glen was obviously uneasy not only to be the center of attention, but also to have to repeat such heartbreaking information. "His coffin had been pulled out of the hidden…" Glen stopped and looked at Malika and Tor, who shook their heads in dissension. "…out of the hidden safe-room. It was pulled all the way to the glass doors that led to the back deck."

"Is that where you found him?" I asked sadly, then realized I still didn't know where he meant. "Wait where was this? What deck?

Glen averted his eyes and explained, "At his home. Well the home he shared with Giovanni, on the beach. He was just outside the back doors that led onto a wood deck. His ashes I mean. I'm sorry, Lillian, I don't want to upset you by telling you these things."

I had never even asked Mason and Vann where they lived. They were always at Lex's mansion. I never even imagined they lived somewhere else, let alone on a beach. I was finding there was a lot I didn't know. Enough to fill a book...*oh wait*.

I smiled warmly at Glen and reassured, "I need to know. I don't want to sit useless anymore. I want to know what happened. I want to know even if it rips my heart in two. The only thing that would upset me is to not know. Is there anything else that seems strange?"

Lex chimed in, "The glass doors. They were closed."

I thought a moment. "Okay."

"Before he even opened the glass doors he would have started burning, and Mason was young, I mean as far as vampires go, and would have been more susceptible to the burning rays of the sun." Lex sighed impatiently seeing I still didn't get it, "If you were being painfully burned alive would you take the time to close the door behind you?"

I almost smiled at the sense of it. "No, I wouldn't. Why would he drag his coffin to the doors?"

Malika offered a reason, "He could have been planning on bringing it out on the deck to lie in while the sun claimed him. Many are territorial about their coffins and wish to die within them."

Lex rolled his eyes slightly but made sure Malika didn't notice. "Then why were there scratch marks on the floor from the coffin being drug across it?" He turned intently to me. "Mason could easily have lifted the coffin, over his head if he had wanted to. Why would he drag it? Why would he only walk a foot out of the door? If I were going to perish in the sun and I lived on the beach I would have gone out toward the water, onto the sand at least. Plus, he could have prepared everything before sunrise and been outside waiting for the sun to come up. Why would he wait until the sun was already up to move his coffin and go outside? Plus, being so young and not very powerful, it would have been difficult for him to even be conscious past sunrise." Lex stopped, shaking his head as if to emphasize his theory.

I didn't understand how any of the council could not agree that there were, at least, some very bizarre concurrences. It all made sense to me. Lex seemed to be right, amazingly enough, there were too many coincidences involved, and I once heard someone say that there is no such thing as coincidence. Things happen for a reason, with purpose, and in this case, to me at least, it seemed obvious. The only thing that made sense was that someone was responsible for, or involved in, Mason's death. It was too sudden, too unbelievable, too questionable.

Malika reprimanded lightly, "We cannot make such assumptions until we know more. We must speak with Giovanni and find out all that he knows before we decide that someone is at fault for Mason's death."

I understood what Malika was saying. Among vampires, the council was judge, jury, and executioner. If someone had been responsible for Mason's death and the council decided they needed to be punished...well, there was only one form of punishment for vampires. They were killed for their crimes, just as Jerrod had been for his reckless behavior. Malika was trying to make it well understood that should an investigation begin, the council was obligated to find the truth and bring those at fault to justice...their justice.

I suddenly thought of something I hadn't before, as I hadn't known Mason and Vann lived together. "Where was Vann when this happened? Wasn't he in the safe-room with Mason?"

Lex patted my shoulder a little too excitedly and gushed, "Lillian, you ask all the right questions. I never even thought of that. It's so obvious, now, it was all planned."

I looked from Lex to Glen eagerly, rubbing my now sore shoulder. "What? What didn't you think of?"

"My God," Tor muttered, "that does seem quite a coincidence."

Everyone turned respectfully toward him. Twice in one day he had now spoken, it must have been some kind of record. Even Malika looked at him with astonishment, but that might have been more because he seemed to be starting to agree with Lex than because he'd actually spoken again.

Tor raised his thoughtful eyes and explained, "Giovanni received a phone call to come to this house just before dawn. Once he arrived it was too late for him to leave. He slept here during the day in which Mason was…the day Mason…when he was…taken."

"A call? From who? Who called him? Who would call him right before sunrise, and what could they have possibly said to make him come here?" I demanded as if they had the answers and I just had to wrench them from their minds.

Lex spoke soothingly, "We don't know. There was no call from here that morning. We never found out if Vann had checked where the call came from, because he walked out before we'd gotten much information from him. Though…" Lex let out a sigh, staring at me thoughtfully.

I gulped nervously. "Though what?"

I suddenly felt uncomfortably focused on. Everyone at the table looked at me with a knowledge that I didn't have, again. Some seemed to have a strange look of accusation on their face; especially Kara, Una, and Demetrius who always seemed to agree on everything, and were in definite agreement about their dislike for me. Demetrius, especially, seemed to have curled his lips into a cruel smile, as if the information about to be revealed pleased him immensely. I decided at that moment if I could have any super power it would have been to shoot flames from my eyes, because I would have singed that stupid grin right off of Demetrius's superior-looking face. The others looked at me apprehensively, but seemed to be undecided about my involvement. Still no one spoke, but looked to me to answer some question that had not been asked.

Finally I turned anxiously to Lex, tired of feeling so left out, and demanded, "Though what?!"

"It doesn't mean anything but…" Lex bit his lip, his eyes lingering tenderly on me. "Giovanni was originally under the impression that…well...that…it was you."

I pulled back from him so firmly that my chair screeched across the floor, and yelled defensively, "What was me?!"

Lex put his hands out to try to calm me. "He thought…he was under the impression that you…after your party…that night…or really it was morning...that you had called him. He thought you were still upset about the suspicions we'd tricked you into believing about Osborn."

I shook my head in defense. "I didn't. I never called Vann. You know I didn't!"

"I know," Lex reassured.

Demetrius interrupted with his slippery tone, "But you could have.

Someone called him at quarter to six and told him to come here. It was a woman, and from what she said he was convinced it was you."

Though, I certainly did not have my wish for a super power, I could feel my eyes blazing toward Demetrius, but I calmed myself and instead turned to Lex. "What you're saying is…" I pursed my lips as I cautiously queried, "…you're saying a woman called Vann to get him out of his house so that Mason would be left alone? That someone was conspiring to murder Mason, and somehow this person knew that they could convince Vann to come here even though the sun was about to rise, just by using my name, or pretending to be me?"

That hurt a bit.

Through all of my thoughts of Mason being murdered I never imagined my own name would end up being connected to his death. Now, though, it seemed as if someone had used my relationship with Vann to get to Mason. Guilt should have been a familiar thought, but when it involved the death of a loved one. No, I couldn't even think on the guilt I was going to feel later over just having my name connected to Mason's murder, that Vann had rushed here for me and had left Mason vulnerable. Mason had only been a vampire a little over twenty years, he wasn't as strong as the others, and for a vampire in general he had few developed abilities. The truth of the matter was a mortal, if well planned out, could have killed Mason without Vann there. Now I understood why Vann had left abruptly after hearing that Mason had died. He felt he had failed to protect him. He felt guilty.

Lex affirmed my thoughts, "Yes, they used your relationship with Giovanni, his weakness for you, to persuade him to leave. It seems like it was all planned, but as to why anyone would go after Mason, I still can't understand. Unless it was just because he was a member of this council."

"Who knows who planned what, but some scheme was devised and acted on, and there are consequences for such things," Demetrius explained as he gave me a cold stare. "Very severe consequences. Perhaps someone thought they would have a better chance becoming a council member if there were more available positions." I could see both Una and Kara nodding in agreement.

"Well, I am not seeing why you are looking at her," Sylvia, the tall blonde, interjected on my behalf. "She was friend to dear, dear Mason.

She is not being a murderer." Sylvia winked at me.

Malika obviously wanted to remind everyone, "There is still no definitive evidence that Mason was indeed murdered. An investigation needs to be conducted."

"It is being true. Some have hard time living as vampire. He, maybe, was not happy," Sylvia offered in her simple way, not meaning to be offensive, but sometimes stating things too bluntly.

Lex and I both looked at each other at the same time, rolling our eyes in frustration. How could they not be convinced that one of their own had just been murdered, right under their noses I might point out, and still be considering it was suicide? There was no doubt in our minds Mason was murdered and we would find out why and by whom, without the council's help if need be. I knew Lex agreed with me, but I could also tell, though he had voiced his opinions, he had been much more conservative than was usual for him. He hadn't really put up a fight with anyone, nor had he done something outlandish like jump on the table and stomp his foot declaring the entire council blind fools. That would have been more his style, but he had been polite and had not pushed the issue too hard. He was obviously hiding something.

It could also not be overlooked that there were a few on the council, no need to name names, which actually considered me to be guilty; thinking that I was involved in some way. More likely they were just excited to be able to accuse me of some heinous act to get rid of me. I wasn't sure how far Demetrius, or his two sidekicks, would go to make it look like I was guilty, but they had certainly made it clear on more than one occasion that they found my presence there ridiculous. It was definitely in my best interest to find the truth or I could possibly end up just like Mason, condemned to death. Also, there were a few on the council that seemed to truly think that Mason had just reached the end of the line and killed himself, and in my heart I couldn't allow anyone to believe such a thing.

I should have felt disheartened to be accused of something beyond even my nightmares. I should have felt afraid that revenge, though misplaced, might take hold of one of the vampires and put me in danger. I should have felt these things but instead I felt compelled, willed by Lex's belief, to find the answers that the others were so easily dismissing. This was going to be my future after all, it's what Lex had always planned for me, and I needed to protect it. This was now my family, and when the family has a problem, everyone has a problem. On top of everything else I was afraid for Vann. If he had found something, if he had gone after whoever had done this, he could be in danger...or worse. No, I didn't want to think that. Right then the priority was finding answers.

You should know by now I would never let sorrow, guilt, or accusation get in the way of finding the truth. It's a sickness, an obsession, or it became one at least. My life seemed to have always been weighed down by burdensome lies meant to protect me, but all they had done was prolong the inevitable. The truth always seemed to find a way of presenting itself whether it was wanted or not, and I thought it was better to know the truth right away, than to wallow in uncertainties. I needed to know what really happened; no matter what the consequences.

Come disappointment, come danger, come death, but give me the truth.

ᏚᎾ11ᏟᏚ

"Lillian, darling, wake up," the whisper roused me out of a fitful sleep.

I tried to focus with my drowsy eyes, but the room was pitch black. I barely made a noise to acknowledge the voice.

The whisper came again, "Lillian, are you awake?"

This time I sat up in bed groggily, almost growling at the intruder, not caring who or what was disturbing me, "What do you want?"

A hand shot out in the dark grasping my hand easily. "I'm sorry, Lillian, I didn't want to disturb you, but I had to know if you were all right."

I should have guessed, the all too concerned voice was Dallen's. He seemed to be coming and going at all hours of the day and night, as if he were terribly busy, but I had no idea with what. As far as I knew he wasn't working, he'd told me his boss had given him a prolonged leave of absence due to the wretched circumstances surrounding his brother's and wife's deaths. I had no idea what else he could be doing with his time, unless he simply felt uncomfortable being in Lex's home after what we'd done together.

"Dallen, it's really late. It took me forever to finally fall asleep after all the crap I had to listen to tonight. I would really just love to go back to sleep before I really wake up and can't get back to sleep."

"Of course, darling." Dallen's right hand grazed my right cheek.

I thought that was his way of saying goodnight, but without warning his lips were pressed precisely and firmly against mine. It was a strange sensation to have someone unexpectedly find the exact position of my lips with their lips in the pitch darkness. I should say it was also unbelievably arousing, being kissed without warning, half-asleep and unable to see who was doing the kissing. How could I argue with desire? Even with how exhausted and weary I felt I couldn't push Dallen away. I was starting to realize that Dallen was something of a weakness for me. I had a very difficult time saying no to him, and unfortunately I think he knew that.

As I was trying to focus on Dallen's ardent kisses my thoughts instead were focused on Dallen's power over me. I still didn't know what was going on a few nights ago when I had overheard Dallen talking to someone secretly in his room. Even when I confronted him about my suspicions he pushed them aside and instead distracted me with passion. He used my own desire against me; to make me believe I could trust him.

Dallen pulled away slowly. "Lillian, you can trust me. I love you; I'm not pretending to want you. You must know that."

I pulled my knees up to my chest protectively. "I know you want me. I just haven't figured out why and to what end."

"Don't say that," came his gentle whisper. "I love you without purpose or agenda. I never planned to fall in love with you, it just happened. If anything, I tried to stay away from you because I could see that you had an effect on me. The last thing I would ever do would be to use you for my own selfish reasons. Believe me, I took a great risk in getting close to you, and for falling in love with you I may..." He didn't finish what he was going to say.

I wanted to believe him, my whole body wanted to believe him, but I had this feeling, as I so often had with Lex, that he was hiding things from me. Important things. Plus I couldn't figure out why he thought he had taken a risk, unless he meant because of Lex, but that had all passed. Even before Dallen and I had sealed the deal, so to speak, Dallen had always stood up to Lex and never hid his interest in me. So who else would be angry and possibly punish him for falling in love with me. None of it made sense, but unfortunately as I said before he was a weakness. So instead of being on my guard and pulling away from him as my instincts were telling me to, I let myself believe him. I leaned forward and embraced him wanting to think that he was really in love with me.

He must have sensed my abandonment of his guilt, because he fell to kissing my neck and moved up to my lips once again. I was resigned to accept his declaration of love as truth and let myself fall into his salacious caresses. I'll blame my bad judgment on the grieving process. I had obviously been so overwhelmed with grief I couldn't think straight. Yeah, that sounded good, it had nothing to do with my lack of willpower.

As we made love for the second time, I realized it was very different than our first experience. It felt as if we were two different people, excited by the mystery of one another, and perhaps the danger of one another. Like we had just met for the first time, but needed the other for some selfish reason. When I look back now I think Dallen must have believed this would be the last time we would ever be together, and as for me, I think I knew deep down he was lying to me and I wanted to punish him. Only my punishment was to use him, to pretend he was nothing to me but a warm body that could give me pleasure. Afterward we lay side by side without touching, as if we had just realized we were enemies and didn't know how to react. Somehow in the past few days since finding out about Mason's death, Dallen and I had become strangers.

Finally, Dallen rolled on his side to face me, though it was still too dark to see the features of his face. "How are you holding up with Mason's death?"

I winced. It didn't feel right talking about Mason's death so plainly, as if I had only lost something, not someone. Not to mention that death was not exactly a subject I was keen to discuss just after such an intimate experience that is supposed to be a focus of love and openness.

"I guess I'm doing better than I was," I answered somewhat annoyed by his question.

"Did the council make you feel any better?" Dallen asked a little too eagerly.

"They weren't here to make me feel better," I retorted. "Actually, they think I'm involved."

Dallen was outraged, "They shouldn't have believed that!"

I was confused. *Why would he say it that way?*

"Believed what?" I asked suspiciously.
"I meant, why would they believe that?" he tried to change his tone to curiosity.

He's hiding something...again.

179

I pushed the thought from my mind and said numbly, "A woman, pretending to be me, called Vann and convinced him to come here just before sunrise on the day Mason was murdered."

I could feel Dallen jerk slightly. "Murdered? I thought it was suicide. Who said it was murder? Does the council really believe he was murdered?" Dallen inquired uneasily.

Before considering Dallen's suspicious reaction I rattled off, "The council wants to write it off as suicide. I think they're worried about the possible attention they might attract trying to find the truth. Plus, like I said before, a few of them are convinced I'm involved somehow, but Lex is convinced it was murder and I have to agree with him. There are just too many things that point to murder. At least this will keep my mind off of missing him."

Dallen laid his hand across my chest possessively. "What do you mean?"

"I'm going to help Lex find Mason's killer," I declared resolutely.

"Lillian," Dallen sighed, "that sounds dangerous. If Lex wants to go on a pointless excursion to blame someone for Mason's death I think you should stay out of it. I'm sure it will come to no good. Chances are Mason was just fed up with living and Lex is going to end up killing some innocent person just to sate his vengeance."

That was a harsh sentiment. Especially from Dallen, who was usually all tact and understanding.

"Then it will be good for him to have someone else there to keep him from doing something stupid, won't it?" I retorted angrily.

Dallen let out a long breath, "Lillian, I don't want you to get involved in this."

I was taken aback by the finality in his voice. He was genuinely worried about something, and I knew it had to be more than this theory that Mason was actually murdered. He was making it very clear he didn't want me getting hurt, but he didn't seem at all worried about Lex. Shouldn't a friend be more concerned?

"Unfortunately, I am involved whether I want to be or not," I insisted. "A few members of the council gave me the distinct impression that they were willing to place the blame on me, maybe even frame me.

Do you know what the penalty for being involved in the death of one of their kind is?" I asked dramatically.

Dallen huffed and answered sarcastically, "I don't know, death?"

I tried to control my voice from breaking with fear. "Exactly, Dallen. Death. Don't you see, I need to find the answers to protect myself as much as to bring Mason some kind of justice."

I could feel Dallen's whole body tensing as he stated authoritatively, "Lillian, I do not want you to do this."

"That seems a bit presumptuous of you to think that you can give me orders just because we slept together," I stated meanly. "I believe I can make up my own mind about what I will and will not do." I could feel my cheeks burning, angry with Dallen for his reaction.

"It wasn't an order, Lillian; you know I would never presume anything of the sort. I'm just looking out for your safety, because I care about you. I don't want you to get hurt, that is all."

I felt again that he was keeping something from me. "What makes you think that I would get hurt? You know Lex would never let anything happen to me."

Dallen pulled me closer. "I know you would like to think that Lex is invincible, but there are things out there...I'm simply worried that Lex won't be able to do anything to protect you. He may not be able to protect himself, let alone you."

I felt a chill run through my body as if a snake had just slithered across my feet without warning. How would Lex not be able to protect himself? Lex was stronger than almost any other vampire on the council, excepting Malika and Tor. That was the reason he was even on the council, though he had a reputation for being absurd and outlandish at times, he was very powerful and perhaps even feared by many.

I said the first thing that came to mind, "You think there's a vampire involved that is stronger than Lex, don't you?"

Dallen was quiet for much too long, but finally decided what to say, "Mason committed suicide, Lillian. No vampire was involved...no one was involved. What I'm worried about is that Lex is going to drag you into a man-hunt for a man that doesn't exist. In the end it will either leave you more miserable than you are now or you'll end up accusing the wrong person. Lex may have a limitless vacuum for his guilt to disappear into, but I know how you are. You cling to your guilt. It's almost your security blanket, like you need it to get through every day. Only sometimes it's so bad you barely get through at all. Please don't let Lex convince you that there was some conspiracy to kill Mason. There wasn't. Lex just needs to tell himself there was so that his world will still make sense to him." Dallen paused, composing himself, and asked slowly, "So the council isn't planning on investigating at all?"

I shook my head, though it was too dark for him to see, and reluctantly answered, "No, I don't think they will. Malika kept saying they needed to, but I think that was really just to put Lex at ease. Of course for all we know Vann could be out there on his own trying to find the killer right now. I wish he had told someone where he was going."

"Giovanni thinks Mason was murdered too? Where do you think he would go?" Dallen inquired a little too harshly.

"I don't know, Dallen. I'm not even sure that's what he's doing, but if I had to guess I'd say he felt exactly the way Lex and I do. Otherwise he would probably have been here questioning why I had called him at such an hour. I know in my heart Vann is out there looking for who did this. I'm so afraid he may actually find that person. What if he isn't strong enough? What if he ends up..."

I couldn't say the word dead anymore tonight. It was enough to link the word to Mason, but if Vann was really out there I certainly didn't want to curse him by linking it to his name. Don't laugh; when you think about it, being superstitious is much more acceptable than a belief in vampires. Yet there I was living in a vampire's mansion, considering becoming a vampire, and here I am at this moment a vampire...writing about it, and there you are reading about it. It's okay, though, you can pretend it's just a story. I know the truth. Sometimes the truth is scary and people don't want to accept it; I won't hold it against you.

There was an awkward silence. I thought perhaps Dallen was just tired of talking about this and had decided to try to go to sleep, or maybe he was pretending to fall asleep so he didn't have to answer me. Seconds later I felt him sit up abruptly.

"What's wrong? Dallen?" I asked, genuinely worried I had been too harsh toward him.

As angry and frustrated as I felt I didn't really want to push him away. As much as I was convinced he was keeping things from me, I wanted him, and I wanted him to want me. He was the first thing in my life, besides Rachel, that had ever seemed good, and I didn't want to lose him. I was on the verge of tears, perhaps my sadness for Mason had caused me to say things I didn't really mean, and I had ruined everything with Dallen.

Dallen swung his legs over the side of the bed. "I have to go. There's something I forgot I had to do. Work."

"Dallen, it's three in the morning." I was worried to see him acting so strange.

He turned back toward me and put his hand gently to my cheek. "I have to pack so I can leave on the first available flight. I'll be back in a day or so."

As he pulled away I couldn't help feeling he was a completely different person. I felt like a stranger was leaving my bed. More than being upset by the thought, I was confused. What had changed? Was it something I had done or said? Was he tired of me now that he had slept with me? Was he involved somehow in Mason's...No I wouldn't even think it. Everyone mourns in different ways, right? Maybe this was just his way of dealing with all of these larger-than-life problems. Maybe he had realized he had enough of all this vampire drama; perhaps he was really leaving and never coming back. I didn't even notice as Dallen turned the light on and got dressed.

While I was lost in thought Dallen put his lips gently to mine and placed something in my hand. "I forgot to give you your birthday present. So much happened. I meant to give it to you the afternoon I came to invite you to play tennis."

He was very careful not to say the day we'd had sex or the day we'd learned Mason was dead. I opened what appeared to be a jewelry box and looked inside.

"Moonstone," I said sadly, looking at the pendant.

Of course he would know it was my favorite. I didn't remember ever telling him, but he must have noticed that I very nearly always wore moonstone earrings; a pair Ben had bought me for my fifth birthday.

"I had it handmade," Dallen explained gently as he removed it from the box and pulled it around my neck to do the clasp for me, though the chain was long enough to simply slip over my head. "It's said that moonstone is good luck for lovers. It will bring them back together and it's supposed to calm your mind, help you see more clearly."

I turned to look at him, to see if the moonstone would help me to see him more clearly, but again I felt confused. I wanted so much to trust him...and to love him, but instead I felt scared. Things seemed to be getting worse and worse and I didn't know how to stop it, yet, I felt it was because of me or that I had somehow inadvertently caused all of these events to be set into motion.

"Thank you, it's beautiful," I said finally, lifting the pendant to better see the large oval-shaped gem caught in a silver setting of spirals.

"The setting is a Celtic knot," Dallen explained as I stared down at the pendant. "The spirals represent the transition of body into soul, enlightenment, and higher consciousness. I thought it made sense, we are always in a state of transition to something better, and birthdays always seem to be a day for marking such achievements of enlightenment."

"I don't feel very enlightened. I feel like I'm in the dark." I let the moonstone fall heavily to my chest as if it were a door slamming loudly on my heart. I looked up into Dallen's blue-green eyes and managed to whisper, "It is really, very lovely, Dallen. I'll wear it...always...I promise."

Dallen put his hand over the place where the pendant had fallen. "It suits you, Lillian. I hope when you wear it you'll think of me." He stopped seeing the confusion on my face and then he added, "I love you, Lillian. Don't forget that. I'll come back for you, I promise. In a few days I'll be back. Please, wait for me. Don't do anything before I get back." Then he turned to leave.

Finally I looked up, remembering something I had been meaning to ask, "How long have you known Osborn Hune?"

Dallen stopped in his tracks and turned slowly around. The expression on his face was not confusion as I would have expected, but rather a look of unease. As if he had been waiting for me to figure something out. He stood there for a moment, his face showing the effort of trying to formulate an answer. Finally he came back and sat beside me on the bed, apparently I'd gotten his attention, but still I could see he wasn't sure what to say. He instead looked over to my bedside table where he'd placed the box my pendant had been in. I had forgotten I'd left my poetry book open as I had been writing to try to help me fall asleep. Dallen suddenly seemed transfixed as he lifted it, perusing the slanted handwriting.

"'The Flood'...is this about me?" he asked, his eyes seeming to light happily. "Lillian, this is quite good. You really do have quite a talent for poetry."

I calmly took the book from his hands, closing it, and mumbled in frustration, "It wasn't meant for you to see, it's just some silly idea of love from a silly girl. I wrote it days ago, when things were different." I shook my head and pushed, "You didn't answer me, how do you know Osborn Hune?"

Dallen took a very deep, very loud breath, and stated resolutely, "I don't know Osborn. I have, of course, seen him here and there around the mansion, but we have never spoken. All I know is that he's an old friend of Lex's."

"But..." That didn't seem right. I decided to confront him about the looks I'd seen them give each other. "At my birthday party and even that night that Lex and Vann were sword-fighting, I saw you two give each other dirty looks. As if you despised each other or had just had an argument. Not exactly the way two people who'd never spoken would glare at each other."

Dallen was looking down at the bed, but after a moment he looked up and smiled reassuringly. "I never meant to give any one a dirty look and if he had given me one most likely it was out of jealousy."

"Jealousy for what?" I asked, convinced he had just made that up.

Dallen put his palm to my cheek. "Jealousy for you. Have you noticed how he's gone after Rachel? He probably wanted you from the beginning, but settled for her."

"Rachel," I said, wondering if he'd been able to read my own suspicions from my thoughts. I argued, "No he liked Rachel from the beginning. When we first met him he barely spoke to me and flirted with Rachel the whole time." I didn't mention the uncomfortably long, tender looks he always seemed to give me.

"Maybe that's what he wants you to think now that he and Rachel are together. I'm sure that's what it is, he probably dislikes me because I got you and he didn't," Dallen said, winking at me in a very uncharacteristic way.

"But-" I began.

Dallen kissed my lips quickly and stated, "I have to go, I'm sorry, we'll talk more when I return." He walked all the way to the door before turning around to add, "Please wait until I get back before you do anything...and don't give up on me." With that he was gone.

I didn't know what to make of his comments; more disturbing were his expressions. He was obviously lying about not knowing Osborn. It was plain by his reaction, I'd caught him off guard, he never expected anyone to notice what I had. Moreover, every time I tried to ask him serious questions about what he was keeping from me he seemed to answer by complimenting me...or out-right seducing me. I may not have much experience with men but I was fairly certain I could tell when someone was using desire to change the subject, and that seemed to be exactly what Dallen was doing. I didn't know what to think about Dallen's suggestion that the glares between himself and Osborn were simply to do with jealousy. I myself had considered that Osborn had feelings for me and was hiding it behind an invented interest in Rachel, but the idea of Osborn secretly having feelings for me just seemed too ridiculous to believe. Even if I did consider that Osborn had some kind of jealousy toward Dallen over me, the fact that Dallen claimed they had never even spoken just didn't seem to fit. There had obviously been some kind of words between them, whether about me or not I don't know, but certainly Dallen was lying about never even speaking with Osborn.

The worst thing for a confused mind is a dark, empty room. There is nothing to distract your thoughts. Especially when the only thing you could possibly want would be to sleep; that becomes the one thing you can't achieve. No, sleep was impossible now. Not with the conversation with Dallen swirling in my head and the questions that his behavior raised. I was far from a comforting night of sleep, or rather morning of sleep. I opened my poetry book, turning to a blank page and began jotting down lines as I thought about Dallen's behavior.

I hoped that I was wrong about everything. How could I be so suspicious of Dallen? Maybe I was still upset over Mason. Maybe I was just looking for things to be wrong where there was nothing wrong. Maybe I was just trying to distract my mind from its grief by creating a problem where none existed. Dallen had been nothing but sweet and attentive; how could I accuse him of hiding things?

I wrote the last lines of my poem, feeling heartbroken...

But where is my love?

He's gone away from here

He never felt close,

Even when he was near

I felt the pendant around my neck, thinking of Dallen. No, it must all be a result of Mason's death and the circumstances surrounding it. Dallen would never betray me.

Would he?

A NIGHT IN THE UN-LIFE...

"You seemed to be scribbling a lot whenever we sat down, like you were preoccupied with something else. Are you sure you had a good time?" Ash asked anxiously as they walked back toward Lillian's apartment.

"Yes, I had a wonderful time!" Lillian smiled, almost triumphantly. *And I even got some work done!* "I just had some ideas for my book that I didn't want to forget."

In actuality Lillian had very nearly written the entire twelfth chapter of her book in between dancing with Ash and several other men that had asked her. She had confiscated a pen from the bartender and a huge wad of napkins from off the bar. The napkins were now stuffed erratically in her purse, completely covered with writing.

Lillian finally realized she should have asked earlier, "That didn't bother you when I danced with other guys, did it? I just really love dancing and I didn't want to be mean. It wasn't because I didn't want to dance with you."

"Are you kidding?" Ash beamed. "I felt like the luckiest guy there. Of course if you had actually shown any attention to any of those guys I would've been really upset, but I think every guy there wanted to be me, just because I was with you." He paused, obviously considering something, "Did you have a good time with me? Or would you have had a good time regardless?"

Lillian thought about the question carefully, wanting to say the right thing, but also wanting to be absolutely honest. "If I say I had a good time with you that doesn't mean that I wouldn't have had a good time without you. If I say I only had a good time because you were there that would sound as if I needed you there to have a good time and I don't want to sound needy. Because I do have fun...on my own."

Ash scrunched his eyebrows almost mockingly. "Oookaaay, let me rephrase that. Did you have a good time tonight?"

Lillian laughed. "Yes, I had a wonderful time. The fact that you were there made it all the better."

"Let me just make a mental note of this: When asking Lillian a question, make sure it is strictly a yes or no question, or she will go off on a tangent and be really confusing."

Lillian punched him lightly on the shoulder, making a concerted effort not to hurt him.

"Well I can see that you like your women simple. No complications."

Ash looked at her thoughtfully and said, "Actually, I always thought I did. I used to always end up going after beautiful girls with nothing going on upstairs, but you know the saying beauty is in the eye of the beholder? Well, as an artist, aesthetic beauty becomes boring, and I realized I needed more. I need someone that has as much beauty inside as they do outside, maybe even more so inside. It's too easy to look at something beautiful and paint it; I need to be able to see beauty beyond what is obvious to the average eye. That was why I was so taken with you to begin with. I admit, you are most likely the most amazingly beautiful thing I've ever seen, but you always exuded this knowledge that was just so captivating. I find you absolutely mesmerizing, and I think you may be the furthest thing from a simple woman that I've ever met. But I don't see you as complicated. Challenging, maybe, and definitely mysterious."

They had finally arrived at the door to the hallway that led to Ash's studio and Lillian's apartment. Lillian was blushing from Ash's comments and felt slightly awkward, having only been on two previous dates, but to her knowledge this was the moment the guy expected to kiss the girl or vice versa. She wasn't sure if she should even initiate a kiss if Ash didn't. She wasn't sure she should have let things go this far to begin with, gotten this...familiar. But what harm was there in a kiss? She ran through her mind all her experiences. Most had been with vampires while she was still a mortal and of course they had seemed beyond rapture, but most of the time they were followed by great pain. A few had been mortal, but only one of those had been serious and she still couldn't decide if it had been the greatest kiss of her life or the greatest mistake.

"Maybe both," Lillian said aloud without realizing it.

"I'm sorry?" Ash asked, grinning affectionately.

"Oh, I was just thinking of someone..." Lillian paused, not really wanting to tell Ash, so she answered him with part of the truth, "I was just thinking of one of my characters. You just made me think of him."

Ash smiled and said playfully, "He must be something else."

Lillian didn't realize she had gotten that sad look in her eyes again as she stated, "He was...I mean he is...unforgettable."

She looked up at Ash a little uneasily, thinking he might have caught her slip, but instead their eyes locked. This was it...the moment. All at once Lillian decided if it was going to happen she wanted to be in control so she lunged forward kissing Ash so abruptly he didn't even have time to react.

"I had a wonderful time. Goodnight!" Lillian half shouted, smiling as she fumbled to open the door, enter, and close it behind her in one fluid motion.

Lillian put her hand to her head as she stomped up her stairs feeling annoyed with herself for doing what she did. She enjoyed Ash's company, but now he would think she was interested in him, and she didn't know if she really was or if she was just lonely. It certainly complicated matters that if she did decide she liked him she would have to confess what she truly was, and how would he react to that? Lillian decided as she entered her apartment that she had probably saved herself a lot of headaches and heartaches by becoming a vampire.

How did normal people deal with such things? Dating was so weird!

❧12❧

The sun streaming in the window woke me. It must have been after four in the afternoon, that's the only time the sun was low enough in the sky to shine through the window and light directly in my eyes when I was in bed. I rolled over to check the clock on the bedside table.

4:51 PM.

An entire day gone, again. I couldn't even remember what day it was anymore. They all seemed to just melt into each other, and time simply didn't seem to matter anymore. It was either night or it wasn't, there was nothing else left in my world. I rolled back toward the window and extended my arm out to an empty bed.

Dallen?

Of course, he had left abruptly that morning on urgent business that he had somehow forgotten about until our conversation about Mason's death had somehow sparked his memory. I felt around my neck for the moonstone necklace he'd given me. Good luck for lovers he'd said.

Did he really think I was that naive? Was I that naive? Perhaps I had allowed him too much trust and too much desire. Maybe I shared too much with him and never followed through on my demands for explanations from him, but maybe it was time I started. It was at least time to find out a little more about Dallen. I didn't even know what he really did. He worked for a large, extremely wealthy company whose name he had never mentioned, they sent him all over the world, and he made it sound as if he did some kind of legal work for them, but I really wasn't sure. It was time to find some answers.

I walked downstairs trying to figure out a way to find out about Dallen without seeming too suspicious when I saw Rachel walking toward the front door. I put my hand to my forehead in frustration.

Through everything that had been going on I'd completely forgotten about Rachel, again. My poor Rachel, she probably thought I had abandoned her, maybe that was why she'd become so withdrawn.

"Rachel!" I shouted to her. I was so happy to see her after not seeing her for days that I forgot about my mission for the moment. I had to make sure she was okay. "Where are you going?"

Rachel turned around slowly, her face didn't light at all to see me, and she waited until I was a foot away before answering me, "I was just going for a walk."

"Would you mind if I came with you?" I asked feeling guilty for not keeping her close to me all that time. She was obviously angry. I was hoping I could explain everything to her and hopefully she would eventually forgive me.

Rachel just shrugged her shoulders indifferently. "Suit yourself."

I followed her out the front door and to the entrance of the side garden, which I had walked in many times before, but not from this point of entrance.

I bit my lip almost nervously and asked apprehensively, "So...how is everything?"

My best friend in the world and I was nervous to talk to her. I was afraid if I said the wrong thing she might get angry and just stomp away. My best friend and I felt I had to watch what I said until I could figure out exactly what she was angry at me for.

"Everything's fine, Lillian," she said sternly, without looking at me. It was a cold response, one you might make cynically under your breath. Only she had said it loud and clear for me to hear.

I felt guilty for neglecting her. I had been too selfish. I had forgotten Rachel's feelings; I had forgotten my best friend. I had dealt with everything alone, sharing nothing with her. We were all sad and hurting, but I hadn't been able to see past my own selfish feelings to let anyone in. Of course she was upset, she had loved Mason as much as I had, and I'm sure it frightened her as much as it had me to lose someone so suddenly.

"I'm sorry I didn't confide in you and that I pulled away. I didn't know how to react to everything that was happening. I just thought it would be better for everyone if I spent time alone."

Rachel laughed under her breath. "Alone? I'm amazed that you can be alone and sleep with Dallen at the same time."

"How did you know that?" I asked, shocked by her bluntness.

Rachel, of course, had known about my feelings for Dallen, but so much had happened in the past few days there hadn't been time to tell her what occurred between Dallen and me. Was that why she was upset, because I hadn't confided in her? Because someone else knew before her? On that note who would tell her anyway? It wasn't as if it would be discussed around the council table. Only Lex knew besides Dallen and me and he had seen Rachel about as much as I had.

We continued walking along the path, but I had to finally ask, "Who told you?"

Rachel opened her mouth, but paused before sneering, "Everyone knows, Lillian, it's not like you hid it very well. It must be so nice to be wanted by everyone."

That was an evasive answer. She almost seemed jealous, but that didn't make sense, because she had been positively worshiping Osborn for the past weeks and had never shown any interest in Dallen. Was she just jealous of the attention I got from Dallen that she didn't get from Osborn? I was at a loss. This wasn't going at all the way I had hoped. I had been tempted to ask Rachel, though the chance was slim, if she knew anything more than I did about Dallen, but now I wasn't sure that would be a good idea. At this point she might just say something cruel to get even with me. Best to stick to my first plan of finding out why she was angry with me.

Rachel walked nonchalantly over to a bench and sat down. I followed her slowly and was just about to sit when I realized where I was. The path had opened up and I was standing across from the statue of Pallas, her fearsome shield daring her enemies to try to intrude upon the space. This was my bench, my spot. Did Rachel know this was where I came to sit when I was feeling out of sorts or was it just a coincidence that she had happened upon that particular bench?

Looking at the bench made me think back to the day I'd first met Dallen, sitting on the bench reading his book. What a sap I was to fall for all that "I'm depressed because my brother died" crap. That had probably all been a lie too. For all I knew he probably never even had a brother...or a wife for that matter. He had probably just made it all up to get my sympathy and trust. Of course he had gotten much more than that. I had been completely taken with him from the moment I first saw him sitting on my bench. Even with the quiet whispers in my head that said something didn't seem right, he was hiding something, still I accepted everything he had said and relished the attention he gave me.

"What are you staring at?" Rachel's voice shook me out of my daydream.

I had been standing in front of the bench staring at the empty space next to her. I sat down.

"Just remembering something." I smiled sadly, but decided to change the subject, "so what have you been up to the past few days?"

Rachel folded her hands nervously. "I've just been…with Osborn."

Still Osborn? I had hoped Rachel would have been tired of him by now. She usually didn't dote on any guy for so long. I still didn't trust Osborn, even though all the suspicion surrounding him before was meant to just distract me from a surprise party. There was still something about him; I couldn't quite say what, that unsettled me. Besides my misgivings that he was only using Rachel for some purpose and that he showed me an eerie and mysterious kind of attention, he was too cool and calculating in his manner and words. He seemed to always be listening in as if making note of everything, and he had this gift of being able to be near without being noticed. Mostly I was bothered by the apparent connection between Osborn and Dallen, which Dallen was obviously trying to cover up, though even that didn't make sense. Why would Dallen and Osborn be so worried that anyone should know that they knew each other? Was there a connection that they feared others would figure out?

Finally I responded to Rachel, "So it's okay for you to spend all your time with Osborn, leaving Lex and I to the wayside, but by me spending time with Dallen I've neglected you?" I asked confused.

Rachel shook her head and answered smoothly, "I didn't say that."

I couldn't take the cryptic answers anymore. "Fine, then why are you pissed at me?"

"I never said I was pissed," Rachel stated coolly.

I raised my eyebrows at her. "You've got to be kidding. You've been treating me as if I ran over your favorite dog ever since I ran into you."

She just shrugged her shoulders. "I didn't mean to be angry toward you. I'm just angry in general at what we've done to ourselves. I've just had a lot of time to think of things, to think of our situation. What it means if we stay; what might happen if we try to leave; what sin will be on our souls and what sin is already there. This isn't a childish game anymore, Lillian. Things are happening around us, bad things, and we need to decide if we want to be part of them or if we should leave and forget all of this. I don't think we should be here anymore. We shouldn't stay…there's too much evil."

I didn't know what to say. I was a little shocked. We *had* been through a lot since we'd been there, but to hear Rachel call this evil was a bit melodramatic, especially for her. She was always the level-headed, go-with- the-flow, everything is going to be fine, kind of girl. I think she had actually found it thrilling to be around vampires, and had always secretly wanted to be turned. And what did she mean things are happening around us; did she mean Mason's death and all the questions surrounding it, or was there something else? Was she just still shaken over what had happened to Mason? Perhaps she was scared. If Mason could be killed so easily, what chance did we have?

"Rachel, you know we're not in any danger. Lex would never let anything happen to us. Not to mention Vann, and Osborn, and Dallen...even if he is keeping things from me."

Rachel turned her eyes abruptly toward me as I said the last. "What is Dallen keeping from you?"

I pursed my lips and locked my hand protectively about the moonstone around my neck. "I don't know. He's keeping something from me. I can tell by the way he looks at me, and when he says certain things, that he's lying or hiding something. Plus…" I paused because I almost didn't want Rachel to know, but I had already said more than I had wanted. "…last week he met someone in private in his room. He didn't know I was outside the door at first so I heard a little of what they said."

Rachel looked worried. "What did you hear? Do you know who he was talking with?"

I didn't want to lie to her, but her tone gave me pause. So I told her part of the truth. "Just something about Dallen being too emotional, but I don't know who the other person was. A man, I think, but I can't be absolutely sure." There, I hadn't exactly lied. I just left out that I overheard the word OPTS, and something about a girl being part of the mission, and that the man's voice had sounded familiar.

"This is what I mean, Lillian, things are going on that you don't even know about. Lex has already lied to us, I'm sure there are other things he hasn't told us, and now Dallen is hiding something. We shouldn't be here, it isn't right, what if it's already too late? What if we've condemned ourselves to hell?" Rachel paused a moment, calming herself she stated, "Osborn said he would rather I didn't stay here-"

"Osborn?" I interrupted suspiciously.

"Well Osborn and I have become very close and he's worried about me," she stammered.

I was starting to get angry now. "*What* is going on? What is Osborn telling you?"

"Osborn just doesn't like the idea of his potential future wife being surrounded by vampires. We want to start a life together, a normal life, and we can't have that if I stay here," she stated defensively.

Had I really been so wrapped up in my own thoughts to have not seen the seriousness of Osborn's and Rachel's feelings for each other? Osborn had always seemed so indifferent, sometimes even callous toward Rachel, sure he flirted, but it all seemed like a joke. Now he was ready to run away with Rachel and get married?

It has to be because of Mason, she's just upset, and is making rash decisions so she can feel more in control, right?

"What about Osborn's friendship with Lex? He's just going to forget about that? I thought they've been friends for a long time?" I asked.

Rachel answered matter-of-factly, "Osborn isn't Lex's friend. Osborn knew Lex through someone else. Someone he knew years ago. Osborn needed Lex's help with something, that's the only reason Osborn had contact with Lex in the first place, and then of course Lex invited Osborn to stay whenever he likes. You know, the way Lex does with everyone. We were so blind to think he actually cared anything for us. We weren't special to him; we were just more playthings for him to add to his collection. Osborn does important work and travels a lot, so it's convenient for him to have a place to stay when he's in town. That's the only reason he still treats Lex like a friend, because it's convenient for him."

Finally, some kind of information! It may not have been what I intended to find out, but it certainly was interesting. So Osborn had weaseled his way into the house by asking Lex for a favor, and then he coaxed his way into Rachel's trust. She almost sounded brain-washed; it was like talking to someone I'd never met before and frankly wouldn't want to talk to again. I was beginning to feel so isolated. The people that I had felt closest to were acting like complete strangers, nutty strangers at that. I hoped all of the odd behavior was due to everyone being shaken by what had happened to Mason, but in my heart I could feel there was some other underlying reason and it scared me to think that.

My head was turning with so many ideas, but I didn't want Rachel to know how suspicious I was so I kept the conversation rolling. "So have you and Osborn made plans to leave then?"

"Not exactly, but we've talked about what we want and where we would go-"

I stopped listening to Rachel gush over Osborn as I tried to memorize everything we had talked about. I needed to talk to Lex. I needed to find out what he knew and make sure that he knew what I knew. Plus, I was curious who would've introduced Lex and Osborn and what this favor was that Lex did? I glanced up past the statue of Pallas to see the lovely shade of lavender spreading across the sky that I was so hoping for. I got up and walked away without even saying goodbye to Rachel. I was pretty sure she would be relieved by my departure anyway.

"Lex, thank goodness, I was worried I might have missed you," I said as I walked toward him down the familiar hallway leading to his bedroom. I stopped a little puzzled. "Weren't you supposed to have changed rooms once I knew where you slept?"

Lex grinned delightedly. "As if I would let you scare me away from my own bedroom. What do you think I am a little baby?"

"Sometimes," I answered quickly, "but that's not what I'm here for. Can we go somewhere to talk? Somewhere we won't be interrupted or overheard."

Lex turned in an exaggerated fashion back toward his bedroom, but stopped suddenly. "This isn't a trick to get me alone in my bedroom to kill me is it," he asked in mock distrust, and then smirked adding, "or to have your way with me?"

I pushed past him haughtily. "Now you *are* acting like a baby!"

"It was just a joke," he said, catching up with me quickly.

I barged into his room flopping onto his bed. I quickly told him about the less involved details of Dallen's hasty departure first thing that morning, leaving out the gift he'd given me, and then going over the strange conversation I had had with Rachel. Once I had finished I started in with the questions, not even allowing him to comment on what I'd said. Plus, I had noticed his face twist into a sour expression at the mention of Dallen showing up in my room in the middle of the night, so I figured if I didn't give him time to think too much about that I wouldn't be bothered by his annoyingly sarcastic remarks.

"So who exactly was it that introduced you and Osborn? It had to be someone you trusted very much to do a favor for a mortal you hardly knew. Unless you really are that stupid," I said the last under my breath.

Lex gulped nervously and sighed, "I can't tell you who it was. All I can say is that it was someone I trusted absolutely; someone that trusted me without question. If he considered someone a friend then so did I. We're bound to each other and our trust is unwavering."

"Uughh," I groaned, "why all this secrecy? Can't anyone tell me the truth for once? Just come out and say this is the way it is whether you like it or not and stop trying to protect me from something potentially upsetting! Please just tell me! There are too many things I don't know right now and maybe if I had one part of the puzzle I could solve the rest."

Lex was at a loss. "See what you don't understand is-"

"I don't understand anything at the moment! I feel like I'm completely in the dark! Just tell me this one little thing. I need someone to tell me the truth. Lex, please," I pleaded softly.

Lex nodded his head, but was obviously not keen to tell me. "I don't want you to be angry, especially with me, because it wasn't my choice. I was simply helping a friend. But I don't want you to be angry at him either, because he thought he was doing the best thing for you…"

I didn't understand what Lex was talking about. "Who was it?"

Then I saw the tears in Lex's eyes and I thought for a moment maybe I didn't want to know that badly. How could a name upset him so? Who could it be that he thought I would get upset? I had a fleeting thought that I pushed out of my mind because it didn't make sense, but then Lex said the very name that had popped into my head unexpectedly.

"Ben," his voice quivered.

I shook my head. "That's not possible. Osborn couldn't have known Ben."

"He did. They were very close for a time. I even thought Ben might turn Osborn, and maybe he would have, if Osborn had stayed with him."

I shook my head again vigorously. "No, you don't understand, Lex, Osborn is too young to have known Ben. Ben died when I was five." I paused doing the math in my head. "That means Osborn would have had to been about twelve or thirteen when Ben died."

Lex gave a crooked, almost shamed smile. "That's not exactly true."

"What's not true?" I asked harshly.

"Ben didn't die when you were five," Lex admitted, looking down guiltily. "As a matter-of-fact most of what you think happened regarding your uncle isn't exactly…correct."

My jaw dropped. I felt like I was going to start crying uncontrollably. What was he saying? I remembered the day Ben died. I remembered his guilt at almost feeding on me, but something Lex had said to me before repeated in my mind. *Despite what you think you remember, Ben didn't try to hurt you…you're confusing him with someone else.* But who had I confused him with? My head was swimming with all of this new information, all of these truths that had never been revealed, and which seemed to be all connected. Had I been so wrong about everything? Had my five year old mind created a scenario to cope with some occurrence that was even worse than what I remembered?

I looked up into Lex's eyes as tears welled up. "Tell me. I should know the truth about my uncle no matter how much it hurts. You owe me that much for taking him away from me."

Lex put his hand gently on my shoulder. "You're right, you should know. I swore to keep this secret to protect not only you, but Ben. Now...as you've said...you need to know everything, perhaps then we'll be able to piece it together. I've had my suspicions for a while and should have shared it with you, but I am fairly certain that what is happening now may be directly linked to what happened when you were five years old."

"Do you mean Mason's death?" I asked tentatively.

Lex nodded and elaborated, "Yes, there's that and other things that have been happening that seem to be connected in general to what happened when you were five, and more specifically with you. We were trying so hard to protect you, but we thought there was a chance we had misunderstood what was going on. I should have known the night I met you, when I saw how much you looked like..."

"Who?" I demanded, "Who do I look like, and what does that have to do with anything?"

Lex looked at me with sad eyes, obviously not wanting to talk about it yet again, but offered, "I don't know how he knew, but he knew, even then when you were five. Ben had his suspicions, but he wasn't sure, and that's why he had to do what he did."

I shook my head overwhelmed. "I don't understand. How could Ben killing himself have anything to do with what's happening now? You're not making any sense. What possible connection could there be between what is going on now and what happened when I was five?"

ಬ13ಲ

I had never seen Lex so unnerved, so uneasy about sharing anything. He had obviously been keeping this secret a long time and the look on his face showed how apprehensive he was to reveal the truth. I could tell this hurt him to have to tell me what he was about to tell me, but I had to know. Everything had suddenly become a mystery, a tangled web of new and old lies that had to be unraveled. The thing that I had blamed my entire life's unhappiness for, now, seemed to have happened very differently than what I remembered.

Lex began hesitantly, "The first thing I am going to tell you is going to shock you because it will change what you have thought to be true for practically your entire life." Lex exhaled loudly before restating, "Ben didn't die when you were five."

I was struck by his statement yet again, but managed, "But I remember vividly being in that church when I was five and all that was left were-"

Lex said it before I could, "Ashes. I'm sure you remember our little discussion about ashes and how sunlight does not reduce us to a mere pile of them."

I put my hand to my head bringing the memory of that day back. "That doesn't make sense, though. Ben told me he was going to leave me. He told me he was going to commit suicide."

Lex shook his head, sitting on the bed facing me. "Ben said he was going to leave you and he meant exactly that. It was fake. It was all staged. It only had to look real enough to convince you."

I tried to take this all in, but so much still didn't make sense. "But I was there, in that church-"

"He didn't die in that church. He left you there. All you remember is him being there one moment and gone the next. He didn't die, he left. He disappeared. He wanted it to look as though he had gone there to die, but he was actually escaping."

This was all so unbelievable. Still not able to accept what Lex was saying, I asked sarcastically, "Okay so he didn't commit suicide and he didn't die in that church, so when did he die then?"

Lex looked uncomfortably at the door, but answered, "I shouldn't be telling you this. Any of this. Not only does it put people in danger but I swore an oath to the council elders. If Malika finds out..." Lex sighed and conceded, "Ben isn't dead, Lillian."

My heart started pounding. "He's not dead? He's alive? Ben...is alive?" I kept shaking my head unable to accept what Lex was telling me. "No, Lex, he's dead. He died when I was five. He died, I know he did. If he didn't, than why was I treated like I'd done something that had caused his death?! Why was I punished all those years like some kind of demon-child that I never was?! Why would he do that to me?!" I yelled at him, almost in hysterics, as tears streamed down my cheeks.

Lex bit his lip as if it pained him to see me so upset. "I know it's a lot to take in, but it's true. Ben is alive. I wasn't allowed to tell anyone, not even you," Lex's voice trembled, as he brushed my cheek lightly with his hand. "I'm sorry. It wasn't my secret to tell. This was all organized through the elders. Besides me, only Malika and Tor know everything. I'm sure you remember Giovanni mentioning Ben's death had been suspicious. We wanted everyone to think Ben had committed suicide, but naturally there were questions that just couldn't be answered. Starting with who had actually created Ben. We also kept that a secret."

I wiped my tears and retorted smartly, "I'm sure everyone knew you'd turned Ben. I mean we talked about it at the council meeting. No one seemed shocked when I said it."

"Lilly, I let you believe certain things at that meeting so as not to draw too much attention to all the missing pieces about Ben's death." Lex paused, looking down, and admitted, "I didn't give Ben The Immortal Fate. Everyone just assumed I did because I brought him before the council. I actually didn't even meet Ben until a week after he'd been turned."

"But...how can that be?" I asked astounded. "Then...who turned

Ben?"

Lex got up and paced in front of the bed. "What you have to understand, Lilly, is everything Ben did...he did to protect you. He was afraid you'd get hurt."

Now I was really confused. "But you said he never tried to hurt me."

"He didn't," Lex said simply. "He would never hurt you. You really don't remember everything, do you? It wasn't from himself he was trying to protect you. It was-"

I broke in, "From you? He was afraid you would hurt me? You can tell me, I won't be angry."

"Not me, I told you he trusted me completely. He was afraid the one who made him would hurt you."

I pursed my lips in thought. "But...I'm sorry, Lex, but I remembered you and I remembered Ben being afraid of you. If he was afraid of anyone it was you."

"I told you, Lillian, you don't remember things exactly." Lex put his hand to my cheek to comfort me. "You never met me when you were young. You met the one that gave Ben The Immortal Fate. I don't know why you thought it was me? Except that we both have dark hair and blue eyes we look nothing alike. I told you, I just let you believe those things at the council meeting because I couldn't correct you in front of everyone and admit to the lies we had been covering up all these years. Also, there are a few in our own council that we simply cannot trust with this information."

"Demetrius, Una, and Kara," I blurted out plainly. Sadly I murmured, "I still don't understand, I thought I had remembered everything. I don't even know what memories are real anymore."

How could this be? How had I twisted things so much in my mind to confuse Lex with someone else? Lex was right, what he was telling me disproved everything I had believed about my uncle's death my entire life. I needed to know everything. I needed to replace all of the false memories with truth, and I needed to find out how all of these past events connected to what was happening to me, to all of us, right then.

"Tell me everything," I pleaded and then added quietly, "Tell me who made Ben a vampire."

"Dardanos," Lex admitted, pausing for my reaction.

I was too appalled to respond. There it was again, that name. It made me shiver just to hear it, and it filled me with dread to think that once more Dardanos was behind my misery. The last time Dardanos had come into my life, I'd had nightmares and bizarre dreams for days. It had troubled me more so because he didn't just produce a feeling of terror or revulsion in me, but also an indescribable attraction that made me feel ashamed.

Lex continued, seeing the blank look on my face, "I know it doesn't make sense. I don't know why Dardanos made Ben; I don't even think Ben knows for sure why he made him. We had our theories at the time, and now with what's happening I think we may have been closer to the truth than we had thought. Dardanos has always been calculating and does everything for a reason. I mean he only turned me because in a time when most people followed blindly I was outspoken and brash. I didn't follow decorum and social rules, I did what I wanted and didn't care what people thought about me. He thought I was going to help him conquer the world or some such nonsense. Lilly?"Lex asked, realizing I was only half listening to his assessment of himself.

I forced myself to try and be rational. "Just tell me...everything...from the beginning. Then maybe it will make more sense."

Lex recounted, "It was something like what you remember. Except it was Dardanos who turned Ben. At that time the council was trying to keep an eye on Dardanos, without him knowing. I was kind of volunteered for the job as I had a history with Dardanos and knew something of how his mind worked. I started spending a lot of time trying to convince him that I might be keen on coming back to him and joining in whatever endeavor he was currently involved in. I was accepted by him, or at least he felt I was not a threat, and he allowed me to be among his circle. I was actually able to get close enough to him to meet your uncle. Ben confided in me almost immediately and we became friends. He had been turned against his will and I guess Dardanos asked him to do things he couldn't bring himself to do, like killing people and vampires to aid in one of his insane schemes. Dardanos was always cooking up some kind of scheme for more power, but they were always so far..." Lex stopped and cleared his throat seeing the impatient look on my face. "Anyway, I know Ben tried to stay with you and your family through all of it. He tried to lead a double life as vampire and human, but it's always too hard. I believe he even told your grandfather the truth about what had happened, and probably your parents knew or figured it out eventually. Your grandfather supported him and tried to help him lead as normal a life as he could for a time, but your parents made it hard for him and your grandfather didn't exactly have a strong will to stand up to anyone."

I interrupted, "Then why did he leave? How could he abandon us? How could he let us think he had died? How could he...leave me?"

"Because of Dardanos. I told you before he's ancient and immensely powerful. He's not as old as Malika, who created him, or Tor, but still not a vampire to trifle with. He's unbelievably cruel and doesn't think twice about using lives to play his games. One day I'll tell you a story about a girl I once knew, and how Dardanos played with her life." Lex's face was awash in uncharacteristic sadness for a moment before he continued, "Ben began to fear for your safety; he feared that Dardanos might use you to make Ben do what he wanted."

"But why? Why did he think Dardanos would do something to me?"

Lex responded, "You obviously must remember Dardanos coming to your house. You thought it was me but it must have been him. You're uncle never wanted him to come near your family, but Dardanos did because he knew it made Ben uncomfortable...and loyal." Lex stopped, gazing at me purposefully. "For some reason I don't know, well I do know now, but at that time I don't know how Dardanos could have known-"

"Lex, you're rambling. Just spit it out," I commanded in frustration.

Lex stated simply, "Dardanos took a liking to you. He became preoccupied with you. If someone did try to hurt you it had probably been Dardanos. As for what I know, Ben told me that Dardanos kept trying to convince him to kidnap you and the three of you would flee together."

I put my hand up to stop Lex a moment. "But how would Ben pretending to die keep me safe? Wouldn't that just leave me one less vampire-uncle to protect me?"

"Ben was convinced that Dardanos was simply trying to play with his emotions. Dardanos knew how much you meant to Ben. He knew if he had you, he had Ben completely. He thought, and I agreed at the time, that you were just a means to keep control over Ben, or perhaps to keep Ben with him. You see Dardanos had experience with a fledgling that didn't exactly do what he wanted and decided to venture into the world on his own," Lex explained proudly.

Lex continued, "So Ben made the decision that the best thing to do for you and your family would be for him to leave, but the only way to ensure Dardanos wouldn't hound your family trying to find him, he had to die. He came to me and told me his plan, and although it killed him to involve you he wanted to be able to say goodbye to you, and you were still so young he didn't think you would understand. Once you told your family all you knew they could only come to one conclusion already knowing what he was, and if Dardanos did ever return he would have an eye witness to corroborate what had happened. Even if he tried to read your mind, your five year old brain truly believed what you had seen and that would have convinced Dardanos it was true, Ben was dead. That was why it was so important to make it look real for you; you were the perfect witness, because you didn't know it was all just a show. I do believe Dardanos did actually return to your house once more and I believe he spoke to you. Whatever you said to him must have been enough for him to relinquish his ideas for you, at least for a time. Do you remember what you said?"

I was concentrating so hard on listening that I didn't realize at first that he had asked me a question. "No, I don't even remember talking to him." Then I snapped back suddenly. "Where did Ben go after that?"

"I brought him here to stay with me for awhile. I was still in the process of getting this place built, so it wasn't exactly like I had many visitors dropping by, and of course this wasn't the meeting house for the council yet. Dardanos never knew we had been friends so I knew he wouldn't come looking for him here even if he did discover where I was. Ben stayed with me for a few years, until Malika and Tor both agreed that it was too risky for Ben to be so near the council, even though he was technically our thirteenth member; someone was bound to find out he was still alive or worse Dardanos would find out and we'd all be in danger. I know he spent most of his years traveling Europe, trying to keep under the radar, so to speak. I probably saw him at least once every two years. I can't tell you where he is now. It's not my secret to tell."

206

I laughed suddenly. "So that's why you just happened to be there that night I ran into Vann and Jerrod? And why you brought us here?"

Lex smiled warmly. "Actually I've been following you since you were five, little queen. Ben wanted me to keep an eye on you if he couldn't. I saved you that night in the alley because I made a promise to Ben that I would protect you as best I could, even if I had to face Dardanos himself. Ben even looked in on you when he could, but he was hesitant to draw attention to you by his presence. You don't know how he wanted to be able to walk up to you and hug you. As for bringing you here...I have to confess I persuaded him it was for the best. Ben was against the idea, but I convinced him that there were very specific reasons to hide you before you turned twenty. Not to mention that despite everything, I really, truly, fell in love with you. I didn't tell Ben that, but I suppose you could say I brought you here selfishly. I wanted you close. I wanted to make sure I could protect you at a moment's notice. Ben, of course, would agree to anything that involved keeping you safe." Lex almost looked embarrassed by his declaration, a rare emotion for him, which only proved he truly meant everything he'd said.

Now the tears were falling without control. Ben had lived and he had protected me. He had loved me enough to abandon everyone he loved and everything he knew to keep me safe. He was the reason Lex came for me. The reason I was probably still alive myself. Most amazing, he was out there somewhere in the world, alive, and maybe thinking about me.

"What about Osborn?" I asked wiping at my tears, trying to collect myself and focus my mind.

Lex thought a moment. "Osborn he met on his travels. I'm not exactly sure where, somewhere in Europe, but they apparently traveled together for awhile. I really don't know too much about Osborn, and Ben's relationship with him, but he brought him here a few times which could only mean he trusted him."

"So what was it that you did for Osborn? This so-called favor?" I asked.

"Oh, that. Well it had to do with Dardanos again. Ben sent Osborn here because he was afraid he had endangered him. He felt so guilty, especially having already put you through so much danger; he couldn't bare the thought of involving anyone else that he cared for. He thought that Dardanos had discovered he was still alive and knew where he was and that he was traveling with Osborn. Ben was afraid that, like with you, Dardanos would go after Osborn, knowing that your uncle would do anything he wanted to protect an innocent mortal. Osborn eventually came to me asking that I help him find where Dardanos was and kill him, to protect both himself and Ben. I wanted to, trust me, but I refused him. I was too afraid of putting you at risk should anything happen to me. Osborn said that he would do it himself, if I could help him now and then with money and a place to stay and any information I might come across. I agreed. I wouldn't hear from him for months then he would show up here asking to stay a couple days, tell me what he'd found out and where he thought Dardanos was, and I would tell him any information I'd come across, and then he'd leave again for months. I never questioned what he was doing or where he was going. I always assumed he was doing what he had set out to do. I never had suspicions about him, but mostly I think I was indulging in an unlikely hope that he really would track Dardanos down and kill him, solving all of our problems. It was a very convenient proposition for me, I took no risk by helping him from time to time and in return I could lose an enemy that has plagued me since he created me.

"Then I brought you and Rachel here. That was no coincidence either. It wasn't for the reason Giovanni had said, that I was waiting until you'd turned eighteen as our laws don't permit us to turn anyone younger. Obviously, if that was the case I would have sent for you the moment you had turned eighteen and not waited until you were almost twenty. The reason I brought you and Rachel at that particular time was that I had heard rumors Dardanos had been seen in our region, the region our council resides over, and I have this feeling that you turning twenty has more to do with Dardanos showing up then that he found where the council is. I thought the best way to protect you would be to bring you here."

"And now Dardanos is here," I said simply, trying to think why Lex would think my turning twenty would be significant to Dardanos.

"So it would seem." Lex nodded his head gravely. "Oddly, he has never been seen in this area and no hint or rumor of him has ever been heard...until you came here."

"And he wants revenge on you?" I asked a little too hopefully.

Lex cleared his throat uncomfortably. "Unfortunately, I'm beginning to think that Dardanos wasn't using you to get to your uncle, but that he was using Ben to get to you."

"What?" I asked bewildered. "What do you mean to get to me? That doesn't make any sense, why would Dardanos care anything about me?"

Lex gave me a sad look, as if he'd already seen my future and it didn't look good. I wanted to be happy about the news that my uncle was actually alive, but here was Lex raining on my parade and telling me something even more unbelievable.

He answered slowly, almost theatrically, "I have a theory; based on what I've been told and what has recently happened, not to mention your uncanny resemblance to-" Lex paused and instead explained, "I think all of this, going back to when Ben was made a vampire up to what happened to Mason, is actually all to do with you, and who Dardanos *thinks* you may be."

A NIGHT IN THE UN-LIFE...

"All to do with you," Lillian uttered dismally.

She glanced over at the clock.

"Ugh, no wonder I can't see straight."

The sun had been up for nearly an hour. Lillian inspected her thick, layered velvet curtains. Not even a menacing glow was sneaking through. That's why she hadn't noticed the time.

After twenty years as a vampire and having shared some very old, very powerful blood, it was now possible for Lillian to stay awake past sunrise. As long as she was protected from coming into contact with sunlight, that is. She could usually make it about two hours past sunrise before her vampiric blood inevitably forced her into a state of unconsciousness. She could make it maybe five minutes before passing out in direct sunlight, and questionably about thirty minutes before the direct sunlight reduced her body to a hardened shell of ash. Though, that was just Lillian's guess. She had never really tested how long she could last in sunlight.

Lillian thought back to that first week in the city when she had come very close to testing her limits. When Ash had saved her. She had decided to travel outside the city proper to explore and hunt. She was about twenty minutes from her apartment when she realized the sky was growing dangerously light. Only a mistake a very young vampire would ever make. Lillian made it a block from her apartment by the time the sun was rising above the horizon. She actually made it all the way to the front of her building before she started to feel the unmistakable pull of everything in her body and mind completely shutting down on her. A few steps from the front door she hurled herself forward, crashing through the glass door and fainting in the hallway in front of Ash's studio door.

Ash had fallen asleep in his studio, as he did most nights that he spent painting. The loud crash woke him and he went to check the hall to see what had happened.

When he saw Lillian, passed out on the cold floor, surrounded by broken glass, he thought she had gotten herself absurdly drunk and had passed out in a stupor. Ash decided to rescue her from waking up embarrassed in the hall and carried her up twenty three steps to her apartment. He tried the door and luckily it wasn't locked. Once inside Ash laid Lillian on the couch, taking care to put a pillow under her head, closing the curtains so the light wouldn't bother her, and pulling a waste basket over to the couch, just in case.

All this Lillian knew because Ash had been sure to tell her every detail of how he had rescued her. What he didn't tell her, though, was that he had sat on the couch beside her for almost two hours, watching her sleep, memorizing every detail of her.

When she had introduced herself to him earlier that evening Ash had been completely taken with her, and now, even after her strange behavior, he thought she was the most beautiful thing to ever cross his path.

Lillian snapped out of her daydream and looked back at the laptop. "Enough for now," she said dreamily, "time for bed."

She clicked save, closed the laptop, and walked to the back of her apartment where the darkroom was located. She slid aside a picture frame on the wall with an old photo of Rachel and herself that hid a small numbered keypad. She entered her code and the door to the darkroom slid open to reveal a black revolving door that kept all light from entering the room beyond. Once inside the room Lillian re-entered her code to send the door revolving to close the outer entrance and open the portal into the darkroom itself. She walked to the opposite side of the room where she had built her custom coffin against the wall. The coffin looked like a wide bench seat pushed up against the back wall, but inside it was well cushioned, with what looked like a pillow at one end, the whole thing was lined with purple velvet, and Lillian had even added three dead-bolt locks on the inside of the lid. None of this would keep another vampire out, but it at least protected her from mortals, and she assumed that she stayed up later and probably woke up earlier than most vampires anyway. Her consumption of multiple ancient bloods allowed her the ability to stay awake just a little past sunset and wake just a little before sunrise, unlike most vampires that had to wait for the spell of complete darkness to release them from their coma-like sleep. So really her only worry was some stupid mortal looking for valuables stumbling upon her safe-room...or the hunters finding her. She tried not to think about them, though, because if they found her nothing would keep them out.

Lillian climbed into her specially designed coffin hoping she would pass immediately into a deep dreamless sleep, but instead images of Dardanos danced in her mind. She waited for the pull of unconsciousness to come and shut the memories out. When she did slip restlessly into her coma it was not without dreams and not without memories. Sometimes sleep was worse than waking memories. At least one can try to ignore memories, but ignoring visions in your sleep was an entirely different matter.

&14෯

"Oh great, the most evil creature walking this earth, and he wants to be my friend," I stated sarcastically.

Lex gave me a stern look, not unlike the look I usually gave him when he was being ridiculous.

"Lilly, I think he wants to be more than your friend. I have been too naïve, and ignored all the clues that I already had. Based on what Dardanos said to Ben when you were five, he must have had plans for you all this time. Somehow he knew even when you were only five," Lex mumbled the last part to himself. "Plus I find it extremely coincidental that Dardanos basically disappeared from view all this time, just to show up unexpectedly, not fifty feet from you, just before your twentieth birthday."

Lex's theory seemed far-fetched to me, not to mention cryptic, as there were still things he was leaving out. I countered, "What about the time he went after Ben and Osborn?" Thinking that would prove that it was Ben Dardanos was after, not me.

"He didn't actually go after Ben and Osborn," Lex answered. "Neither one of them actually saw Dardanos. Ben had just heard rumors from other vampires and didn't want to drag Osborn into it. I think Ben was just being over-protective because of what he had had to do to protect you."

"But-"I began before being shushed.

Lex looked at me, eyes wide, and put his finger to his mouth. He started moving dramatically toward the door as if he were going to surprise someone on the other side of it. Instead he pressed his ear to the door, listening. Finally he stood up and put his hand up as if to say it was okay. Perhaps my panic-stricken eyes told him it would be nice if he explained what was going on.

He decided to whisper across the room to me, "Someone's coming, that's all. Whoever it is, we cannot discuss what we've just talked about in front of them."

I swallowed hard but shook my head in agreement. *Who would come looking for Lex in his bedroom? Wasn't I the only one that stooped to that level?* I was so fidgety I could feel the bed shaking beneath me. As far as I knew no other vampire would dare to intrude on Lex's sanctuary, the room that housed his safe-room and coffin, without being expressly invited by him.

At last Lex gave me a look as if to say *this is it!* He pulled the door open so forcefully he actually took it completely off the hinges. He quickly jumped back taking a stance that either meant he was ready to use the unhinged door as a weapon or he was posing for a very strange statue of himself; I imagine it would have been called something like "Take your best shot, for some reason there's a door in my hand."

"Vann!" I screamed, jumping up from the bed, and throwing my arms around him. "We were so worried."

Though we had previously discovered we did not in fact feel passionate love for one another I couldn't help but kiss Vann full on the mouth. He certainly didn't fight me, returning my kiss before acknowledging Lex was even in the room.

Lex promptly dropped the door as if he had no idea how it had even gotten into his hands. "Giovanni, it's good to see you," he said relieved.

For the first time since I'd known them Lex and Vann embraced.

As Vann pulled away he gave us both grave looks. He said simply, "I do not have good news."

"Well I think we're pretty used to bad news. Go ahead, try your best," I quipped lightly, hoping his bad news was something like 'sorry guys couldn't find anything.'

We were not that lucky.

Vann cleared his throat uncomfortably. "First I want you to know, Lillian, I did not leave because of you, I was not angry with you."

I must have had a blank look on my face because finally Lex explained, "He means about the woman that called him the morning of Mason's death. The woman claiming to be you."

Vann smiled warmly at me. "I knew it could not be you, but I thought...I thought maybe someone would harm you. That was why I came. It was so strange a phone call, it worried me. I never, for un momento, thought you had been involved. I just want you to know that. I left because I had to look for myself. To see if there was something that Glen missed. In my search I stumbled upon someone non possibile, and I can read from your mind you already know he is vivo, alive. Ben is here, he is in the city."

"He's here?!" I yelled before yet again being shushed by Lex.

Vann stated almost impressed, "All these years you kept it segreto. I could not believe it. You, of all people, kept such a secret."

Lex put his finger to his lips to silence Vann, but smiled conceitedly to himself. Lex then lent out the doorway to his bedroom, pulling the hidden outer door closed, propped the door he'd ripped from its hinges against the frame as best he could, and fished what looked like a car remote on a key-chain out of his pocket. I couldn't see exactly what he was doing but he was pushing multiple buttons. Suddenly his entire bed, black marble base and all, began rising as if being pushed from underneath. He gestured frantically for us to go in. I followed behind Vann who stepped down as he got to the edge of where the bed used to be. I looked down to see stairs circling around the center pillar that had raised the bed.

Of course, a secret room beneath his own, why was I surprised?

It looked similar to the room he had built beneath mine and Rachel's old room, except of course only one set of stairs, and the stairs wound completely around the center pillar all the way to the bottom. The underside of the raised bed, pillar, walls, and floor all looked like black marble with small splashes of white throughout. It was very beautiful, but cold and dark. It reminded me too much of a mausoleum, besides that it wasn't a free-standing building, I suppose it kind of was one.

The room itself was vast and uncluttered. The walls and floor were that same black granite as the stairway. The only furniture was a white leather sectional couch and a white marble coffee table set back in front of what I assumed was a television, although I'd never seen one that large in anyone's home. Lex explained at the time it was a 45-inch rear projection TV with some kind of plexiglass shield that improved the picture. He was very excited to explain all of the amazing features which led me to believe that it had cost him a whole lot of money, and was probably something few, if anyone, had. Of course Lex's coffin, which seemed to also be made of white marble, was there as well, tucked near the back wall.

"What no gold coffin?" I asked jokingly.

Lex played at being serious, "You know, I may like to show off a bit, but when it comes to my own private room, where no one is allowed, I just like to be comfortable."

"Hmmm, yes, I could see how being surrounded by marble and

leather could put you right at ease," I mocked.

Even Vann who'd been so stern this whole time seemed impressed. "I cannot believe this is where you sleep. All I have is a small, segreto door in my wall leading to a room just big enough for my coffin."

Lex plopped comfortably onto the couch, putting his feet up on the marble table. "That, my friend, is the sacrifice you make living on the beach. No basements."

I wanted to argue that, technically, basements were not normal for any area of Florida, but the idea would be lost on Lex who was used to being able to buy anything deemed impossible for the majority of human kind.

Vann joined Lex on the couch and I sat in front of them on the marble table.

Hey, if Lex could prop his dirty shoes on the marble table then I could rest my bottom, uncomfortably I might add, on it.

I wanted to be able to look at both of them face to face. I always felt that people gave things away in their facial expressions and I wanted to make sure I wasn't missing anything.

Vann started slowly, probably worried I would be upset, "I found a ticket, an aeroplano ticket, in my home. It was the only thing I found that seemed out of place, that I could follow. I know Mason did not buy it. He would never leave without telling me." Vann stopped composing himself. Evidently just talking about Mason still choked him up. "The volo, flight, was to London Gatwick Airport..."Vann looked at me purposefully. "In England."

I felt the implication of what he was implying, but stammered, "What are you saying?"

"I am saying it is quite the coincidenza that I found an aeroplano ticket in my home days after Mason was killed, and that ticket goes to England, and we just happen to know someone who is English and has been taking a lot of trips lately."

I looked to Lex, who just had his hand over his mouth as if he too didn't want to believe what Vann was saying.

I shook my head. "Dallen? You think Dallen did this?"

"Non so, I don't know," Vann said, throwing his hands up in frustration. "I just think it is...molto sospettoso, suspicious."

"Wasn't there a name on the ticket?" Lex finally chimed in.

Vann sighed, realizing he hadn't explained correctly. "It was not an actual ticket; it was more like a receipt. It looked as if it had been copied from the originale confirmation and pasted onto a blank page on the computer with some of the informazioni missing. I had to call the airline to find where it went. They said it was a gift card purchase for flight from Tampa to Gatwick, but it never was redeemed and the purchaser came up blank. She said either the name was accidentally erased or it was an anonymous gift."

"I just don't think we should jump to any conclusions. I mean there are any number of way-ward European travelers that have been in and out of this house over the past months," I said defensively, looking pointedly at Lex.

He got the hint and decided to finally chime in, "Yes, yes, I know I allow too many mortals to get too close. And you're right it could literally have been any one of about a hundred people who'd been here and perhaps found out more than they should have. But let's not be naïve either, we should at least consider the idea."

I knew the naïve comment was directed at me, trust me I had already been feeling that way for quite a while, but I couldn't accept that Dallen would be capable of such a betrayal. It was one thing to think that he had played with my emotions and used me; it was quite another to think he had purposefully and systematically committed murder.

I decided this was not a time to seem emotionally weak and agreed, "Yes, I suppose we should at least consider it possible." I was very proud of my diplomatic response and urged Vann to continue. "Now what about Ben?"

"Ahh, I was getting to that," he said, pointing to me. "I was entertaining the thought of using the ticket myself and flying-"

"On an airplane?!" Lex cut in shocked.

Vann looked at him annoyed. "Si, on an aeroplano. Not all of us have the ability to fly, Lex."

"Give it another century, I'm sure you'll get it," Lex encouraged, completely oblivious to Vann's impatient tone.

Vann just sighed and let it go. "As I was trying to say, I was in a little squallido bar in the city, I was trying to figure out what my next move would be and considered flying...*on aeroplano,*" he said, directing the last comment at Lex. "I suddenly felt the presence of another vampire in the bar. I searched the entire bar until I realized he had been sitting behind me on a chair in the corner the whole time. He must have been watching me since I'd entered the bar, deciding if it was sicuro, safe, to approach me or not. I have to admit when I realized who he was I almost smothered him in an embrace. I never knew Ben that well, but with everything that has been happening it was so wonderful to see someone that I had thought was morti, dead.

"Of course, I thought of you as well, Lillian. How happy you would be to find that not only had Lex not been responsabile for Ben's death, but that he is actually alive and so close. He told me everything, about the cover up of his death and how he disappeared to protect you.

"I told him as much as I could about you and what's been happening. By the way he has a few choice words for you, Lex. He also told me who he believes orchestrated Mason's death."

I nodded my head and absently muttered, "Dardanos."

"What?!" Vann and Lex exclaimed together, caught off guard.

"It only makes sense you were going to say Dardanos after talking to Ben. Plus we know Dardanos is in the area," I said as I noticed Lex shaking his head discouragingly.

Vann looked from Lex to me, confused. "What do you mean you know he is in the area?"

"I saw him," I confessed. "That night that I supposedly fainted in the city, well, he had done something to me. All I remember is feeling like I was being pulled toward him and then I blacked out. Lex told me about Dardanos when I finally came out of it a few days later, but he didn't want anyone-"

Lex interrupted, "I didn't want to cause a panic, plus it would have eventually brought up questions about Ben, and unfortunately I'm not even sure we can trust everyone on the council. I know now, despite my worries, I should have shared this information, it may have saved..."

Lex couldn't even say it, but clearly he had considered that by not warning everyone about Dardanos, he had in fact failed to keep those in danger on their guard. Like he was about to say, it may have saved Mason's life. Then again from what Lex had told me about Dardanos, maybe there was no escape if Dardanos wanted you dead. I couldn't be mad at Lex for keeping the secret about Dardanos. For one thing a few members of the council actually thought I was somehow involved in Mason's death; if they knew some creepy, powerful vampire had singled me out I'm pretty sure that would not have made things look any better for me.

I decided to try to redirect their focus to the mystery of Mason's death. "But if it was Dardanos he must have a mortal helping him. Otherwise how could Mason have been brought out into the daylight, and if you tell me this guy can walk around during the day I am going to freak out."

Lex laughed lightly and assured me, "No he can't walk around during the day. Sunlight probably wouldn't kill him though, just hurt him. I assume he has the same abilities I do and probably some I don't even know about. My abilities are only so advanced because he made me, and once, Malika shared her blood with me. Let me tell you, that following morning after receiving Malika's blood I felt invincible, but I wasn't. I survived an entire day of sunlight, well, it didn't feel like surviving, but I mended in time. It was like having every single bone in your body broken, slowly, every time you moved; like being pricked with a needle, continuously, on every little inch of your skin; like being put into a full body cast to recover, only the body cast was your skin. It was like-"

I felt my stomach turning in disgust as I interrupted, "Oookaay...we get the idea! Put me down for no sun tanning if I ever become a vampire."

Lex replied, "I just want you to know what we're dealing with, if I could survive that so can he, and maybe more. That aside I do think you're right about him having mortal help. Dardanos could have pulled Mason out into the sunlight, but I doubt he would've risked the weakness he would have had to endure, for perhaps months, before he recovered. Even if he could heal faster than I can, it couldn't be immediate, it would still be days maybe even weeks in which he'd be vulnerable. If I know anything about Dardanos, I know that he doesn't like to feel vulnerable; he doesn't like not having complete control. No, I'm sure he had help and it must have been from a mortal or mortals."

Vann who had been a focused listener this entire time, made a little grunting noise. "Perhaps you would like to know what Ben and I found in England, then?"

"You went?" I asked trying to figure out in my head how logistically they had managed such a thing.

I'm sure it was possible for a vampire to leave Florida at night, be on a plane for nine hours during the night, arrive in England at night, even considering the time change, and still have time to find a safe place to sleep before the sun rose. I was sure it must have been possible, but my head hurt trying to figure it out.

Vann noticed my perplexed expression and responded, "We flew."

"I know, you already said that. I just can't for the life of me figure out how," I stated annoyed.

Lex pointed at Vann and reasoned, "Ben can fly. I forgot about that, of course, that's how he's been able to travel so easily all this time."

"Yes, Ben took me. This is where things get bad," Vann said.

I had to laugh. "Bad. You mean things weren't bad with a super evil vampire out to destroy us all?"

Vann had no smile, he offered gravely, "Not when the super evil vampire has an army behind him."

Now I was completely lost. This guy, Dardanos, had unimaginable vampire powers, mortals doing his bidding, and now he had an army. I looked from Vann to Lex waiting for one of them to throw confetti at me and yell 'Gotcha!'

They didn't, and this was apparently no joke. Best of all, Dardanos has had a thing for me since I was five. Wonderful! What else could happen?

Vann continued, "We went to the area that the airline ticket was for, Gatwick, West Sussex. After we asked around a bit and heard some strange stories we end up in a village called Cuckfield."

I perked up, "Wait...did you say Cuckfield? In England?"

"Yes, in England, that was where we went," he answered, looking at me somewhat irritated, but then thought better of it and asked, "Why? You have heard of it?"

I looked at them thoughtfully for a moment. I really didn't want to admit that yet again I knew something, from Dallen's own lips no less, which I could have shared earlier.

I decided to tell them part of the truth. "I just thought that Cuckfield was in Georgia."

Lex caught on to my uneasiness. "Who told you that? Dallen?"

I was about to answer but Vann decided to cut me off. "It seems there is some kind of...anti-vampirism cult in Cuckfield. On the outside they proclaim to be a school, for the furthering of scienza sperimentale, experimental scientific research, but we were able to find out they secretly go by another name."

I was on the edge of my seat, well the table to be exact, but Vann didn't go on. I asked, "What was it? Have you heard of it?"

Vann shook his head. "I had never heard the name, but every vampire has heard the stories of such a group." He glanced at Lex uneasily, and said in a hushed voice, "They call themselves The Order for the Pursuit and Termination of Strigoi."

I put my hand to my mouth as I gasped, "Oh my god, OPTS." I

shook my head, angry at myself.

"Cosa?" Vann asked.

I answered reluctantly, "They go by OPTS...and you were right, Dallen must be involved. The day I met him he slipped and told me he had to return to work in Cuckfield. When I asked where it was he told me Georgia. I didn't think anything of it at the time. I had just met him and he told me he was leaving and never coming back. I had no reason to think he was lying to me or really any reason to care as I thought I'd never see him again. I'm sorry."

Lex pulled me forward and hugged me. When he let me go he held my face so close our noses almost touched. "Lillian, as much as I've scolded you about Dallen, you aren't to blame. There are things in this world which not even vampires are immune to, love being one of those things. I understand sometimes you just can't help who you fall in love with."

Vann finally interrupted, "That is molto bella, Lex, but I still don't understand how Lillian knows the cult is called OPTS, or why she has suddenly decided that Dallen is involved." He paused and glared at me, more harshly than I would have thought him capable. "How could you know these things and not tell anyone? Was he really so importante to you that you protect him and lie to us? What else have you kept from us?"

∞15∞

I decided it was time to tell them a few things I had been keeping to myself. I hadn't meant to keep things from anyone, I simply thought I was being paranoid, or that it really only had to do with me. When I considered all the little clues I'd had, I realized how silly I'd been for not telling at least Lex everything. I felt ashamed, and yes, guilty, again. I too could have given some warning to those I loved that something secretive, something potentially dangerous was going on around us, but as Vann had pointed out I let myself protect Dallen. Even when I didn't believe a word he was telling me I convinced myself that the lies he told were about getting me into bed and nothing more.

I pursed my lips to keep from crying outright and struggled to tell them as much as I could remember. "I overheard Dallen talking to someone, a man I think, in his room, and they said something about OPTS. The other man said something like you've already told them about Lex why not let them send in a....." I tried to remember, but so much had happened since then I couldn't remember. I shook my head annoyed. "Oh I can't remember exactly, but something about discontinuing the nest and getting too close to the girl and someone will be mad because she's part of the mission. I tried to confront Dallen about it, but he..."

Lex leaned toward me anticipating what I was going to say, but when I didn't finish he offered gently, "But he seduced you instead."

Vann looked from me to Lex and realized, "Ahh, so that is why you have been so protettivo of Dallen's innocence. He took your verginità and you feel you owe him something in return."

"No, that isn't why," I said defensively, wrapping my hand absently around the pendant at my neck. "One thing has nothing to do with the other. I didn't feel I owed him anything, I guess I let him distract me from my suspicions. I just...I just...I had an idea in my head of who I wanted him to be, when he lied to me or became cryptic I ignored his behavior, because I imagined him to be perfect in my mind and thought I was the problem. I'm sorry; I should have told you about this sooner!

There were just too many things going on and I didn't really put everything together, because I was so distracted by my feelings for Dallen. There were other things, too. Dallen told me stories about his wife and brother and then changed the story, and he would never tell me anything particular about his work. One night I saw a man hiding in my closet and Dallen went to check and said the man had climbed down the balcony and was running away across the lawn, and the night I'd heard Dallen talking to someone in his room I also saw someone running across the lawn. He denied any kind of relationship with Osborn even though I'd seen them glare at each other more than once and got the distinct feeling they'd quarreled over something, and don't even get me started about Osborn because everything about him is suspicious. Let's see...oh, Dallen was really uncomfortable when I told him we believed Mason had been murdered and had not committed suicide as was supposed by everyone else, and he slipped and said something to the effect that the council wasn't supposed to have believed that I had really called Vann that morning. Oh and there was the poison, too." I felt like a wave unloading onto the shore, everything had just spilled out.

"The Poison?" Vann asked confused. "What poison?"

Honestly, I had forgotten all about the incident in which I thought I had been poisoned until then. There had been too many things happening, one right after the other, that I never actually had the time to reconsider the idea of being poisoned, but when I looked at Lex's face I could see that he had known about it. He had found something out, and again, had not shared it with me. I looked at him hard until he realized I'd seen the look on his face.

He just sighed, "Yes, I knew. I never brought it up because...I was afraid you had done it to yourself. I was afraid you were having trouble coping with living here and all of the things you were seeing. I had my doctor friend come look at you and he took a sample of your blood to test. When he told me you'd ingested Belladonna, most likely along with alcohol, I was afraid you'd done it on purpose, and I decided to not mention it if you had no memory of it when you woke. The doctor said most likely you'd have trouble with your memory because of the Belladonna."

I didn't know if I should have felt relieved to know that I had been poisoned with a drug that probably affected much of my behavior in the following days afterward or if I should have been angry that Lex never told me the truth.

"I didn't try to poison myself, Lex. I drank from a glass of red wine that must have had Belladonna in it. I tried to tell Mason that I thought I'd been poisoned, but he must not have understood what I said," I stated defensively.

Vann had been listening quietly, his finger tapping his lips in thought.

"Curious. Who do you think would leave a glass of vino laced with Belladonna sitting out so carelessly?" Vann finally asked.

Lex chimed in, "Some people do think Belladonna has medicinal properties."

"But mixed with vino?" Vann answered incredulously. "Lillian is lucky she did not die from such a mixture."

Before I could even think about what I was saying I blurted out, "Rachel said the wine was from Osborn and she thought Osborn poured the glass for-"

"Osborn?" Lex asked.

I could see from their expressions we'd all hit upon the same thought, and it completely had us stumped, or at least it had Lex and me stumped. Vann almost seemed like he was reaffirming a theory he had come up with a long time ago. Was Osborn involved too somehow? And if so, how was he connected? I suppose my frustration was evident, because finally Vann lightly touched my knee to get my attention.

He smiled reassuringly, but it soon faded as he remarked, "Let me tell you what Ben and I found in England. Perhaps it will bring some of the pieces of this puzzle together.

"Where was I? Ahh, we started at the airport, London-Gatwick. We were not sure where to go from there, so we decided to head to London where another coven of The Council of the Eternal is located, the Quarto Ordine, Fourth Order. We were able to convince them we were only there to find answers; as you may have noticed some vampires are suspicious of strangers." Vann paused, looking directly at Lex with his eyebrows raised.

Lex missed Vann's jab at him and quipped, "You should have told them you knew me, I'm sure you wouldn't have had any problems."

"We did," Vann answered bitterly. "By the way, their elder, Kane, accidentally shattered a glass he was holding when we mentioned your name, but in the end we were able to convince them that we meant no harm and were sent by Malika and Tor themselves. Those names actually had some pull.

"We told them about Mason and our suspicions about who killed him, we told them what we knew of Dardanos, and how we had been led to England. I know you are not going to like this, Lillian, but I also mentioned Dallen. I did explain at that point we did not know who was involved, but I thought there might be a chance one of them might have heard his name."

I could feel my cheeks burning, but I bit back my dispute. After all, I'd been wrong all this time about Dallen. Who was I to be angry at Vann for offering up Dallen as a target for some band of English vampires to take their revenge on. I feverishly rubbed the moonstone pendant, it's supposed to reunite lovers, wasn't that what Dallen had said? I secretly prayed he was safe, even if he had lied to me. *Sometimes you just can't help who you fall in love with.*

I looked down trying to hide my anxiety for Dallen's safety. "And...had they heard of him?"

"No," Vann answered simply, "but they had heard of Osborn. They call him the last Hunyadi."

I scrunched my eyebrows quizzically. "Osborn? So he is English?"

Lex asked confused, "Hunyadi, now why does that sound familiar?"

Vann nodded his head and explained, "I felt like such a fool for not connecting it before, and Ben, poor Ben was heartbroken."

"What connection?" Lex questioned, still at a loss.

"Osborn Hune. He comes from the line of Hunyadi. The name had changed, been shortened over the centuries, but is still traceable back to its origin. It was there in front of us the whole time, if we had just taken time to find out who we were allowing into our confidence and into our safe-house," Vann reprimanded, but Lex seemed to ignore his remark and merely looked at him puzzled.

I was so lost, and looking at Lex it was obvious he too didn't understand what Vann was trying to say. I queried, "Hunyadi is Osborn's family name? What does that have to do with anything?"

Suddenly Lex whipped his head around to face Vann. "Oh my god! You don't mean Hunyadi as in Laszlo Hunyadi, as in Corvin Castle, the vampire hell?"

I stared at the two of them, glaring sternly from one to the other. Vann again just nodded his head.

I felt like slapping them both, but contented myself with yelling instead, "What?! Who is Laszlo Hunyadi?! What does any of this have to do with a Castle?! And since when is there a hell just for vampires?!" I was seriously starting to re-think this idea about accepting The Immortal Fate, especially if there was going to be a special hell waiting for me when I finally did die.

Lex laid back into the couch, putting his hand to his head, evidently shocked. He didn't even try to answer any of my questions.

Vann finally continued responding, "Laszlo Hunyadi was the son of John Hunyadi, a celebrated general and nobleman from Romania in uhhh... 1400's. John Hunyadi started building Corvin Castle some time around 1430 for suo famiglia, his family, but it wasn't finished until after his death. He was supposed to be a brilliant general, but he made enemies early in his career, most importantly Count Ulrich of Celje. John Hunyadi became, they call it Regent of Hungary in 1445, while the King was in captivity, which of course makes Ulrich hate him even more, he was jealous and wanted power himself. To Ulrich's credit or perhaps to his conspiring, Ulrich was able to negotiate the release of the King and used his distant relationship as the King's cousin to secure himself as the succeeding Regent of Hungary after John Hunyadi's death.

"The traditional successor should have been John Hunyadi's eldest son, Lazslo, but one cannot go against a king's decree. As you may guess John Hunyadi's eldest son, Laszlo, was not very happy about these turn of events and then his father suffered a sudden, unexplainable death. Laszlo had suspicions that Ulrich had in fact had a hand in his father's death in order to speed his rise to Regent."

I interrupted frustrated, "Wait, what does any of this have to do with Osborn? So what he's distantly related to Romanian nobility?"

Vann sighed, but replied patiently, "You will comprendere when I get to the end. Now in history books it was written that Laszlo Hunyadi tricked the King and Ulrich to come visit him in his castle, at the time they called it Hunyadi Castle. Laszlo separates the King and Ulrich in order to seek his revenge on Ulrich. The King is taken to tour the castle and Ulrich is taken to have his head removed and burned. Now in history books it is said The King only pretends to agree with Laszlo's need for vengeance and makes him Regent, but soon after sets up his own trap in which he supposedly has Laszlo decapitato, beheaded, I believe that was in 1457."

This time it was Lex interjecting, "But Laszlo was never beheaded. That was just a rumor that somehow made it into history."

"Esattamente," Vann continued. "Also, Laszlo was never out to seek revenge for not being named Regent after his father. He was ridding the Kingdom of a threat to Christianity and...vampires."

"Whoa!" I exclaimed, not sure I was understanding this correctly. "Are you saying that...that Osborn is distantly related to some medieval vampire hunter?"

Vann touched his finger to his lips thoughtfully and answered plainly, "Osborn is quite literally a direct descendant of Laszlo Hunyadi, rumored to be the most successful vampire hunter in history. Laszlo Hunyadi's blood was passed from male child to male child all the way down to Osborn. After destroying Ulrich, the King actually put grandi quantità of wealth at Laszlo's disposal in order to continue his quest to rid the kingdom of vampires. Laszlo used the money to finish building Corvin Castle, which became his headquarters for the beginning of OPTS, as you called it."

"He even imprisoned Vlad III in Corvin Castle for a time, you know...Dracula, but ultimately he was released," Lex added, proud he could actually add something to the conversation. "There were rumors among older vampires that Vlad had actually been a vampire hunter. I suppose it makes sense that he probably joined Laszlo's organization after being released. Ironic isn't it, the man most identifiable as a vampire and he had most likely been hunting them in real life."

Vann nodded his head in agreement but continued with his narrative, "Well the Hunyadi's eventually had to relocate their operation. During the 1600s the Ottoman Empire was expanding further into what is now Romania and had control over who ruled within the kingdoms. The Sultan basically appointed whoever paid him a superiore bribe. With Muslim Turks gaining more and more power, any one or any organizzazione associated with Christianity were either stamped out completely or heavily taxed. The Sultan had no interest in ridding the land of vampires and taxed Corvin Castle excessively for being owned by a Christian. Laszlo's descendant, I believe his name was Toma Hunyadi, decided it was time to leave Romania and settled on the village of Cuckfield. He purchased a large manor house there in 1691, but The Order dwindled over the next two hundred years until it was only kept going by the male descendants of Hunyadi. They no longer had followers at their disposal. Then in the early 1800s a brother and sister took over together, but for some reason the brother gave up his family inheritance and the male line was broken. That is the line that Osborn is descended from, but the sister continued The Order with her husband, and then with her sons.

"All this we had learned from the London council. They have been taking it upon themselves to keep an eye on this secret order. After Ben told them how he had come into contact with Osborn in the first place, they were able to fill in the gaps of how he became associato with OPTS. At some point, maybe a year or two before Osborn ran into Ben, Osborn had found out about his link to the Romanian Hunyadi's and traveled to Romania to find out more about his ascendenza, ancestry. Whatever he found led him back to England and straight to The Order, which up until 1887 had been run by a direct discendente of Laszlo Hunyadi. Of course, we can only speculate that they shared informazioni with him and most likely trained him. From what the London council has learned, once a member of The Order, or OPTS as you call it, completes their training they are sent out to prove themselves. They are basically shoved out the door and told to try to find a vampire on their own and once they do they are to bring whatever informazioni they discover back to OPTS before being instructed further.

"It was per caso, by chance, that Ben was the vampire Osborn stumbled upon. He convinced Ben that he was just a poor soul that had endured some tragedy that had forced him to give up on a normal life to just try to survive in the world."

"Gee, that sounds familiar," I stated sarcastically, referring to the stories Dallen had fed me.

Vann just gave me a weak smile and went on, "Osborn and Ben became very close and traveled for nearly a year together before Osborn supposedly returned to OPTS with his findings. When the General, which is what they refer to their leader as, heard his report on Ben he decided to not give the order for him to kill Ben, but to further investigate. Unfortunately for the General, rumors were starting to spread about him being seen and it was making a lot of vampires nervous, and eventually Ben also heard the rumors."

"Wait," I stopped him, scared to ask my question. "You don't mean Dardanos?" I gave Lex a troubled look, remembering Lex telling me that I had mentioned someone called General.

Vann nodded gravely. "Yes, Dardanos has been heading OPTS since 1887. He apparently acquired the property after the owners, a Lord and Lady Sergison and their only son, all died mysteriously. There were no other living relatives, besides the Hune line that had cut itself off from the Sergisons, and somehow Dardanos was able to prove that he was a distant relative and thereby inherited the entire estate. How he proved this we do not know, because he is in no way related to the Hunyadis, Hunes, or Sergisons. From then on he continued the Hunyadi's family mission of hunting vampires, and he runs The Order like it is literally his own personal army of God."

"Damn!" Lex muttered, "I always thought those stories about a secret vampire hunting group were just made up to scare new vampires."

Vann pursed his lips sympathetically. "I felt the same way when I found out, but there is more."

"What more could there possibly be?" I inquired a little too loudly.

"The reason they did not go after Ben," Vann began slowly, "was because they had found out about the council, The Seventh Council. Our council."

Lex just nodded his head as if he wasn't surprised. "I'm sure that was why Osborn ended up coming here. He probably convinced Ben he was scared of Dardanos and needed to be sent away somewhere he'd be safe. It even gave him a reason to come and go when he wanted, because he had convinced me he was going after Dardanos."

Vann confirmed, "Esattamente, once Osborn returned to OPTS with the informazioni Ben was sharing with him, Dardanos was more interested in going after the council, thirteen vampires in one fell swoop. He was probably never really interested in Ben anyway." Vann glanced briefly at me.

There it was again. That reminder that Dardanos had some plan for me. That Dardanos had been waiting for me since I was five years old for some dread purpose. Did he want me to join this Order, had he always planned for me to become one of their hunters? I didn't think so; he seemed to have plenty of mortals readily volunteering to help him. Why would he wait all this time for me? Maybe he knew that Ben hadn't really died and he just wanted me to lead him to Ben or perhaps he knew that Lex had intervened and had been watching me hoping I'd eventually lead him to Lex?

Lex must have noticed the concerned look on my face. "Little queen, none of this is your fault. Trust me, Dardanos has been looking for a reason to kill me practically since the day he made me and as for the council, he would try to destroy anyone connected to Malika. Of course, Malika is much too strong for him, so the next best thing would be for him to kill every living thing around her. I think he has mommy issues," Lex tried to joke.

I did crack a smile, but only for a moment. "So where does all this leave us?"

Vann ticked off our major liabilities on his fingers as he said, "We have the last living descendant of the greatest living vampire hunter after us, we have forte incredibilmente, unbelievably strong, vampire after us, and they both are backed by a literal army of hundreds maybe even thousands of well trained, ready to die for their cause vampire hunters, oh and they know our location, have already proved they can kill one of us, and now you tell me that Dardanos was seen not an hour from here just weeks ago. Whatever is their plan, it will obviously be put into play any day now."

I couldn't stop myself from blurting out, "What about Dallen?"

"You have issues," Lex said in annoyance.

Vann, trying to be more sensitive stated, "I don't know. He must be connected somehow, but no one has heard of him, so whether he is connected to OPTS-" Vann paused and shrugged. "We can only assume based on what you heard from his own lips. I am sorry, uccellino, but he may very well be our enemy. If he has any connection at all to Dardanos he is your enemy as well."

Lex put his hand on my cheek, comfortingly, and softened his tone, "I'm sorry. I know you had fallen in love with him, which was partly my fault for even allowing him to stay here and allowing the two of you to spend so much time together. I don't mean to be cruel, but he could be planning to kill us all and we need to be ready for that, and we need to think about what will need to be done."

I put my head down, trying to hide the tears starting to pool in my eyes. Lex was basically telling me that Dallen may have to die to protect us all. Perhaps even to protect me. Though, now I remembered all those times Dallen had assured me that I would be safe, that he would protect me, that he would come back for me. Of course. He knew something was coming and he had been trying to hint to me.

"Nothing should happen for at least a few days," I said sadly, again absently thumbing the moonstone necklace.

"How do you know?" Vann asked, though I think he already suspected my answer.

"Dallen," I volunteered. "I can't be absolutely sure, but I think he was trying to warn me that something bad was about to happen and he didn't want me getting put in the middle of it. He told me to wait for him...that he would be back in a few days for me. He must think nothing will happen until then, or until after then."

I waited for one of them to yell at me for once again not offering up all the information I possessed, but instead they just looked off into opposite directions as if trying to calculate what they were going to do next.

"Ben should be here domani sera, tomorrow evening, at the latest," Vann mumbled absently.

"Good," Lex perked up, "We'll call the council. We'll be ready for whatever they plan."

I smiled weakly at Lex's attempt at being positive and the thought of finally seeing my uncle. I wanted to be excited to see him, but I had no energy for excitement after what Vann had told us. I looked from Vann to Lex happy, at least, to have them there with me when I realized we were yet again missing someone. We had neglected to include Rachel in our discussion. What was she going to say when she found out about Osborn? She'd probably be more protective and heartbroken than I'd been about Dallen. She'd probably lecture Lex incessantly about his choice of friends and blame him for putting us in so much danger.

"We need to tell Rachel. She needs to know about Osborn. Poor Rachel, she'll be devastated when she finds out," I said, secretly happy that I had a reason to pull Rachel away from Osborn.

Vann cleared his throat uncomfortably. "There is more bad news. You are not going to like it, perhaps even less than what you have already heard."

"Really, Giovanni, couldn't you have just listed all the bad news up front and then told us the details. What else could there be?" Lex asked smartly.

Vann uttered mournfully, "It's Rachel."

Rachel!

"Oh my God, is she okay? What happened? What did he do to her?!" I demanded. I felt on the verge of tears. "Please, please just tell me she isn't dead."

"She isn't dead," Vann stated gravely, as if there could be something worse.

Lex became interested in the conversation, "What is it, Giovanni? What's wrong with her?"

Suddenly I had a horrible thought. "She ran away with him didn't she? She kept saying that Osborn didn't want her to stay here, she said they wanted to start a family together, that they were thinking about running away together."

"No, uccellino, she did not run away with Osborn. I wish I did not have to be the one to tell either of you this but..."Vann was obviously struggling with the news he was trying to impart.

Lex again tried joking, "Well then, did she kill him? Because that would at least solve one of our problems."

Vann just ignored Lex and looked at me, uttering compassionately, "She has been given The Immortal Fate."

I was so unprepared for the statement I didn't understand who he meant. "Who has been given The Immortal Fate?"

"Rachel," Vann spoke calmly, "I do not know who did it. I saw her when I arrived here. I tried to talk to her but she ran the opposite way. I was more concerned telling you both what I had found out in England to go after her."

Lex was at a loss, "Who would...why would anyone...how could she? I don't understand. She's been lecturing me for weeks about the evils of being a vampire, obviously fed to her by Osborn, and she's been telling Lillian that she and Osborn were planning to start a normal life together. Why would she allow someone to turn her? Who would she even go to besides me?"

"Maybe it was not her choice," Vann offered.

I was too shocked to speak. Lex was right, Rachel had been so against becoming a vampire ever since she and Osborn started dating, why would she suddenly change her mind? And like Lex said, who would she even ask to make her a vampire if not Lex? Vann's words were ringing in my ears, *maybe it was not her choice.* Who would force Rachel to become a vampire against her own will, and why?

I stood up abruptly. Without thinking what I was doing I started heading determinately for the stairs.

"Where are you going?!" Lex called after me.

"I need to see her!" I yelled back, not even turning to look at them, "I have to see for myself!"

A NIGHT IN THE UN-LIFE...

"Lillian?"

Lillian snapped out of her daze and whipped her head toward the door, ready to attack whatever intruder had dared disturb her. Seeing the concerned face staring back at her, she quickly steadied her beastly gaze, and tried to hide the bearing of her fangs.

Ash hadn't seemed to have noticed anything strange in Lillian's reaction. "I didn't mean to startle you. I've been knocking for a few minutes now and I could hear you typing...the door was unlocked."

Lillian rose from her desk and put on her best "silly me" smile. "I'm sorry, Ash, I told you I get really caught up in my book. I completely forgot about our date. Let me just go freshen up."

Lillian walked back to her bedroom, chastising herself for forgetting that she'd agreed to go on a second date with Ash. He was taking her to see a jazz band one of his friends played piano for. She still wasn't sure if it was a good idea to be spending so much time with Ash. After all she was only here to write her book, and after that...she wasn't sure, maybe she would start looking for the others again. Forming an attachment to Ash would just complicate matters. Unless she decided to turn him, to give him The Immortal Fate.

"No, I won't," Lillian stated to her reflection as she decided whether the black corset, tight jeans, and knee-high boots looked all right.

"Is this Rachel?" Ash's voice rang from the hallway.

Lillian quickly dashed out of the bedroom to find Ash standing directly in front of the picture of Rachel and herself hanging on the wall just to the right of the entrance to her safe-room.

When Ash saw the look on Lillian's face he explained, "I didn't mean to snoop. I was just looking for the bathroom, and I saw the picture hanging here."

Without taking her eyes off the picture Lillian asked sadly, "How do you know who Rachel is?"

Ash cleared his throat uncomfortably. "I...ummm...I took a look at your book. I thought from your previous explanations that maybe all your character's are based on real people, and the last thing you wrote just happened to be about Rachel. It was just a guess."

Since writing her book, Lillian had been feeling as though she were reliving everything as she wrote about it. One of the downsides of being a vampire...emotions seem to be harder to control and much more vivid when they hit. Lillian took a deep breath and approached the picture, staring at Rachel with anguish. The picture was from one of the early days they'd spent at Lex's mansion, laughing and joking, and Rachel's face glowing with happiness.

Absently Lillian declared, "Rachel was my best friend."

"Was?" Ash asked tentatively.

Lillian put her hand on Ash's shoulder and smiled warmly. "We had better get going. I'm sorry I wasn't ready when you got here. My mind just wanders so much these days."

Ash looked keenly at Lillian, as if he'd just noticed she had changed her clothes, and stated, "You have every right to make a mere mortal like me wait for you."

Lillian was startled and asked uneasily, "What do you mean *a mere mortal*?"

"I mean...a goddess doesn't have to apologize, and if I were an ancient Greek I would worship you, not Aphrodite." His eyes showed complete sincerity as he made his profession.

Lillian laughed a little at herself for thinking that Ash had actually realized she was a vampire and was trying to hint it to her. "Well, goddesses are meant for pedestals and I am meant to see a jazz band."

Ash smiled and grabbed Lillian's hand. "Then I am your man."

Later that night, as Ash walked Lillian hopefully to the door leading into the adjoined hallway to his studio and Lillian's stairway, Lillian suddenly realized she still knew nothing of Ash's art.

"So second date and all," Lillian said slyly, "maybe tonight would be a good night to show me your paintings."

Ash seemed apprehensive and stammered, "I don't think that's a good idea." Then he corrected himself saying, "It's just...right now I have a lot of unfinished projects...it just looks like a mess. When I get it somewhat decent looking, I promise, I will show you. It's just really hard to let anyone see my paintings before they've reached their full potential and I wouldn't want you second guessing my process."

His response reminded Lillian of her own excuses for not allowing

Ash to see her book. It made her excessively curious about what he was doing in his studio. Perhaps he was hiding some dark secret, just like she was. Maybe he wasn't a painter at all, but some kind of drug dealer or smuggler and the studio was just a front. Lillian looked at Ash with his determined yet nervous approach to the door, and laughed at the idea of him doing something so dangerous.

Lillian could feel the moment coming, when they would say there uncomfortable goodbyes, and one of them would have to make the first move. Again, Lillian decided she would initiate the kiss with Ash, keeping control of the situation, but Ash had other plans. He side-stepped in front of her, and put his hand behind her head holding her still as he dove into her lips. Lillian found the kiss exciting and much more passionate than their first. Unfortunately kissing Ash just made Lillian think of Dallen, and thinking of Dallen made Lillian's heart ache to the point she thought her heart might actually explode.

When Ash finally pulled slightly away, he rested his forehead against Lillian's. "I know I shouldn't ask, but if you let me come upstairs I will worship you...in every way."

Lillian hesitated. No one had ever given her so much power over themselves, and in so little time. She toyed with the idea of seeing what sex was like as a vampire, but she worried she didn't have the discipline to not reveal what she truly was during such a passionate act. Lillian had never gotten close enough to anyone before for sex to even be an issue, and she decided it would be a shame if she accidentally ripped Ash's throat out during the throws of erotic passion.

"Ash, I can't," she lied, "It's not that I don't want to...but I have a deadline." Lillian added, "Plus, what would you think of me, if I invited you upstairs after only two dates? What kind of girl would do that?"

Ash cupped her face in his hands. "I could never think anything but that you are the most radiant creature I have ever seen." He kissed her lightly and whispered, "I'm sorry I asked. I will wait for you. Forever, if I have to." Then he kissed her once more before turning to go.

"Be careful what you say," Lillian said under her breath.

Climbing the steps to her apartment Lillian couldn't help but think that things were definitely getting too heated between her and Ash, but she was determined to push that aside for now and write. Then she remembered where she'd left off writing.

"Rachel. My poor Rachel," Lillian sighed as she entered her apartment and headed straight for her laptop.

꧁16꧂

As I reached the first turn in the staircase I realized I couldn't get out of the safe-room. Apparently, I had failed to notice the pillar moving back into place and sealing us within the safe-room. I turned to go back down and saw Lex standing at the bottom of the stairs ready to punch a code into the keypad I hadn't noticed on the pillar.

"Why don't I come with you? Or Giovanni?" Lex asked anxiously.

I shook my head. "I'll be alright, Lex. I need to talk to Rachel alone."

Lex answered by putting the code into the keypad, raising the staircase and pillar so that I could continue my assent.

"Lillian, just remember, if Rachel really is a vampire, you can't be sure how she'll react to anything you say. Newborn vampires can't always control themselves, especially if she hasn't fed yet. Please, be careful," Lex pleaded.

"I will be." I added, "If I'm not back within the hour, it might be a good idea to come look for me."

"Lillian!" Lex yelled to stop me. "Here, take this." He took the key-chain I'd seen him use earlier out of his pocket and threw it to me. "The code is 54559 and then press the sun symbol. So you can get back in."

I smiled reassuringly and turned, sprinting up the black marble stairs.

Unfortunately, I had no clue where to look for Rachel so I decided to start with the room we'd shared, though I was fairly certain she'd moved out of that room by now. As I suspected the room looked vacant, very few clothes were left hanging in the closet and none of Rachel's things were in the dresser or the bathroom. Just to be sure I checked the safe-room below, but, thankfully, she wasn't there either. I had been hesitant to even check the room as it offered only one way out and was completely sound proof. Not an ideal location to have a difficult discussion with a potentially volatile new vampire.

Next I went to my most recent room, not because I thought Rachel would be there, but because I felt I needed to freshen up. I quickly wiped down my entire body with a washcloth, brushed my now waist-length hair, and added a little perfume so I had the feeling of being clean and fresh at least. I slipped my arms through the spaghetti straps of a simple, tight-fitting black dress that went down to my ankles and had slits up both sides to the knee. Before I left the room I grabbed my poetry book, slipping a picture of Rachel and I in between the pages. I needed something to remind me of the Rachel that had come to the mansion with me, the Rachel that I loved like a sister.

I ran through the rest of the house trying to figure out where Rachel would go. She must have known that Vann had seen her and knew what she was. Undoubtedly, she knew he would tell everyone, and how did she expect us to react? I decided she had probably just meant to sneak back into the house to retrieve her things and to leave without being noticed. That was probably why she'd run the other way when Vann saw her; she must have assumed we would all be hurt, if not downright angry. That was it. I would most likely never see her again.

I again found myself placing my hand over the place where the moonstone pendant fell against my chest. I wished so much that Dallen were there; the Dallen that I had thought I'd fallen in love with. The Dallen that seemed to want so much to just be with me...and nothing more. I thought back to that first day I'd met Dallen, to the way he had tried so hard to charm me, and how he'd tried so hard to gain my sympathy. I thought all the way back to the day Rachel and I had awoken in our beautiful new room, amazed to actually be so lucky to live among such splendor. I thought back to the anguish and misunderstandings we'd experienced in those first few days; I was actually nostalgic to have nothing but the uncertainties of love and memories to be my biggest ordeals. How had everything gotten so tangled?

Eventually I found myself wandering back to my favorite spot in the garden. I seemed to always end up there when I needed to think, and somehow looking at the tragic image of Pallas, immortalized by her closest friend, I never felt exactly alone. Pallas, who had been loved and lost by a mere accident, and whose statue had gone on to protect the Trojans for so long, until she had been stolen, causing the city to fall. This time it seemed that the statue itself had been calling to me, for there sat

Rachel on the bench staring at my beloved Palladium.

Something had obviously drawn her there as well.

I didn't run to her, nor did I even make the slightest noise to alert her of my presence. I was overwhelmed and bewildered staring at her. It obviously still looked like Rachel, but if I tilted my head just slightly it wasn't her. Her skin had taken on a moderately paler tone, not unnaturally pale, just pale enough to make her already bright blue eyes seem almost electric. The most disturbing feature, though, was her hair. Rachel had always had long, beautiful, wavy brown hair. Now it seemed to be a living thing itself. It seemed to not only move with the breeze but against it as well, reminding me of those anime cartoons where the character's hair seemed to be continuously caught up in the wind, snaking and turning every which way but never coming to rest. Added to all that was the fact that her hair had taken on a sheen that would make any model jealous; it almost seemed to be made of small luminous fibers.

Even her attire was completely different. No longer was she dressed like a prudish business woman, but was clothed so strangely that she looked as though she belonged at a Neo-Victorian masquerade. She was wearing a brown suede corset with what I thought was something like a Victorian-style brown traveling skirt, slight bustle in the back and straight hem to the ground; she even seemed to be wearing black Victorian-style boots. At her neck was a black choker with black chains looping down and a black cameo at the center of the chains. I also noticed she was wearing a ring I'd never seen before, a grayish colored stone with a bright glint in its center.

From head to toe Rachel seemed radiant, that is, if you didn't notice her expression.

She was obviously troubled, and it showed on her face. Her mouth was drawn down so severely I thought for a moment she might erupt in anger, but after watching her for a few moments I realized it seemed more like complete despair than anger. I was getting close to tears just looking at her. The way she stared at my dear statue I feared I might have to stop her from doing it harm. I wondered if perhaps she were thinking of the last time she'd sat there, as a mortal, and talked with me. I wondered if she had thought of me at all in whatever decisions she had made.

"Lillian," Rachel's cool voice lilted.

I didn't move, I didn't answer, uncertain how long she'd known I was standing there. I felt like an intruder upon her space, and I was still dumbstruck by not only her appearance but the idea of her having accepted The Immortal Fate.

Rachel turned her head slowly in my direction and said smoothly, "Lillian, come sit with me."

I walked cautiously toward the bench, trying to decide if Rachel seemed dangerous or not. I decided she looked more heartbroken than dangerous and sat beside her.

I wasn't sure how to even begin a conversation with her. *So, you're a vampire! Gee, that must be super!*

Thankfully Rachel broke the silence, "You should leave."

I looked at her quizzically and stated annoyed, "You're the one that asked me to sit."

"I meant from this house," she declared, turning to me with those glowing eyes, "there will be nothing but ruin in the end."

I didn't quite know how to respond to that so I decided to steer the conversation to the obvious issue at hand. "What happened to you?" I asked carefully.

"It doesn't matter. Just know that it isn't safe here," Rachel replied coolly as she made a move to rise from the bench.

Though I knew it probably wasn't the best idea I put my hand on her shoulder to keep her seated. She turned to me, surprised, and I half expected her to shove me away or perhaps lunge at my throat. Instead she just fixed me with an emotionless stare that showed she cared for little at this point, even being pushed around by a trivial mortal like myself. I couldn't understand her, she behaved as if she despised what she was, yet she had allowed someone to turn her. Then I remembered something that might get her talking.

I questioned, "I thought that you and Osborn had plans...a future? Weren't the two of you talking about starting a family?"

She sighed as if we'd already been over this before, even though we hadn't. "Things have changed. Osborn finds me repulsive. There is no hope for the life I thought I wanted now."

"Rachel, please, tell me what's happened. Why did you let someone turn you if you wanted to be with Osborn?" I pleaded.

Rachel let her eyes fall guiltily to the ground. "I didn't let anyone turn me. I let myself believe lies that led me directly to the devil."

I was so frustrated with Rachel. Not only had her appearance and mood changed, but her way of speaking was so different, as if she were rehearsing for a part in a play. She was evidently trying to avoid telling me the whole truth, but I couldn't understand why she'd returned if not to tell at least me what had happened to her.

Rachel turned to me, placing her hands on my shoulders, and said earnestly, "You must leave. No matter what happens, no matter what you find out, please, leave here. I don't want you to suffer the same fate."

Now I understood.

Rachel hadn't come back to retrieve her things or to tell anyone that she'd been turned. She had come back to warn me of something. She was genuinely scared for my safety and was trying to protect me by persuading me to leave. It now made sense that she'd come to this spot to sit, she knew it was my favorite spot when I was troubled, and she probably had wanted to avoid running into anyone else.

"Who did this to you?" I asked in anguish.

Rachel let go of my shoulders and drew back. "I can't tell you. All I can say is that you are in danger here. You need to leave and...find a way to disappear. Convince Dallen if you can, leave with him." She paused seeing that the mention of Dallen's name had made me uncomfortable. She grabbed my hand gently. "Whatever he has told you or not told you, forget about it, he loves you, I know he does. I also know he would do anything to protect you. Tell him it is the only way and leave. If you want any chance at happiness you'll forgive Dallen and go away with him, far away, and forget about all of this."

I was so confused by Rachel's words. She'd always seemed annoyed at my relationship with Dallen, jealous even, now she was sticking up for his behavior and telling me to run away with him. I reasoned it probably had more to do with her feelings for Osborn than a change of heart about Dallen. I was beginning to think that Osborn had done something to make her mad or perhaps just lost interest in her and out of anger Rachel had asked a vampire to turn her to get even with him.

"Ray," I began steadily, "What happened with you and Osborn? How could you have done this to him? I thought you two were going to leave and get married and start a family?"

"I didn't do this to him...I did it for him," Rachel answered dryly.

That didn't make sense. Rachel had told me that Osborn didn't even like Rachel living under the same roof as a vampire, not to mention that if he was planning to have children with her he obviously would not want her to become a vampire.

I shook my head at a loss and stated, "I don't understand."

Rachel said simply, "You don't need to understand, you just need to leave. While you still can."

"But," I pressed, "What about the ring you're wearing? Isn't it an engagement ring?"

Rachel glanced down uneasily at the ring on her left hand as if she'd forgotten she still had it on. "It's a promise ring," she stated coldly.

"So you and Osborn are still together then?" I asked gently, making a move to lift her hand so I could better see the ring, but she just pulled away. "It's very beautiful. What is it?"

"You should know," she spat somewhat meanly, "It's moonstone and it's not from Osborn."

"Oh, I've never seen moonstone that looked like that," I said softly, "but I thought you said it was a promise ring. Who else would you promise yourself to, if not Osborn?"

Rachel huffed loudly, but explained, "I can't tell you who it's from, and it's black moonstone. I thought perhaps you would have remembered it because it was significant to you once, but then, maybe you're not who everyone thinks you are. *And...*my promise is not to marry anyone. The ring is a symbol of my promise to be loyal."

This time I didn't stop Rachel as she rose from the bench. I was still trying to figure out everything Rachel had just told me...and not told me. When I realized Rachel was no longer sitting next to me I looked up, and saw her walking away soundlessly.

I stood, still troubled, and yelled, "Tell me who it was! Who made you a vampire?!"

Rachel turned reluctantly, I could see her face was set in stone, but in the end she decided to tell me, "He may kill me just for telling you, but if it will convince you that you must leave then I will tell you." She paused resolving herself to answer me despite the consequences she may face. "He turned me because he thought it would make it easier to get to you. He thought it would make you more willing to go with him."

"Who?" I asked quietly this time, almost hoping Rachel would change her mind and not tell me out of fear of being punished if she did so, because I already had an idea of who she meant.

"Dardanos," she said gravely, and turned to go.

For the first time ever in my acquaintance with vampires I witnessed one take off in flight. Rachel had taken one step, crouched slightly, and shot into the air so quickly I lost sight of her within seconds. I wasn't sure what was more disturbing; that Rachel had the ability to fly within days of being turned into a vampire or that she had somehow gotten herself mixed up with Dardanos, who perhaps had forcibly turned her into a vampire. What had she said? *He thought it would make it easier to get to you.* I felt a shiver run down my spine.

As completely horrified as I was about Rachel I knew I had to get back to Lex and Vann and tell them everything. Well, maybe I would leave out the part about Rachel's shiny new "promise" ring. I didn't want anyone to think Rachel was beyond saving, because I couldn't accept that my best friend in the whole world was now on our enemy's side. I looked up at the sky. Still no hint of morning glow, but it must have been getting late...or early for all you mortal types. I ran breathlessly back to Lex's bedroom, praying that they were still there.

As I ran into the room knocking the already broken door onto the floor I saw Vann emerging from the subterranean staircase. Our eyes locked for a moment and I could see that Vann was relieved to see me. Obviously my hour was up and he was the search party.

Vann just nodded his head knowingly. "You found her."

Though I knew I would have to repeat everything again for Lex's sake I couldn't contain my agitation and spilled the entire conversation between Rachel and me to Vann, excluding the ring, of course.

Vann tapped thoughtfully on his lips. "So she has gone to his side."

"No! She would never...and he must have forced her to become a vampire or had Osborn convince her to let him turn her," I objected.

"Still, he turned her to get at you and now we can be assolutamente certo that Osborn is working with Dardanos. It must have been his plan from the beginning, to get to Rachel first, to convince you to go along quietly, so to speak." Vann stopped and looked at me grievously. "Unfortunately, we must now assume Rachel is also helping Dardanos, whether out of loyalty or fear, and that makes her un nemico, an enemy."

I nodded in acknowledgment, holding back my tears. I'd already been told once today that someone I cared about was to be considered an enemy and treated as such, now I was being told again. I knew what that meant; if it came down to it and a choice needed to be made both Dallen and Rachel may have to die to protect the rest of us. I could feel my heart breaking when Vann lightly touched my arm.

"Come with me. I have something to show you," he said gently, smiling.

He gestured for me to follow him back down the stairs. As we walked I knew I would have to repeat everything I'd just told Vann to Lex, and Lex would probably tell me the same thing. Rachel is now our enemy. When I reached the bottom of the stairs I didn't even lift my head, but walked solemnly back toward the white leather sectional couch.

"Lillian?" An unfamiliar voice asked shakily.

I looked up, confused that Vann and Lex had let someone else into the room. At first I didn't understand who I was looking at, but finally my brain shouted at me, *He's alive! He's alive!*

Of course I should have recognized him immediately, after all, he hadn't changed one bit in fifteen years. He was a few inches taller than me, with straight blonde hair that fell just below his shoulders, bright green eyes, a trim but slightly muscular physique, and though his face had a soft oval shape his chin came to a slight rounded point. With his slim fitting t-shirt and black leather pants he looked like he belonged in a rock band, but he certainly made a cool looking vampire.

"Ben? Uncle Ben?" I too sounded shaky, though in my defense up until a few hours ago I'd thought Ben was dead.

He was standing beside Lex beaming. I suppose he wasn't sure how I would react to anything he did so he looked uncomfortably at Lex who just nodded warmly. Before I knew what was happening Ben had rushed toward me and caught me in a warm blanketed embrace. This time I didn't even try to stop the tears; I let them fall freely, as I clung to my beloved uncle. When he pulled away from me I could see the streams cascading down his cheeks as well; he had loved me all this time.

"Uncle Ben..." I began not sure what I wanted to tell him first.

Instead he led me to the couch and gently pulled me to sit down. "There is something I need to tell you," came his soft melodic voice. "I know you've been through a lot these past months, well, I should say you've been through a lot in the last fifteen years, but there is something that I swore I would tell you should we ever be reunited. Now seems as good a time as any as we may be facing some very dangerous times ahead."

"My God!" Lex interrupted loudly.

Ben and I turned to see Lex with his hand over his mouth. Apparently Vann had begun the arduous task of telling Lex about Rachel. I turned back to Ben and gestured for him to continue.

Ben put his fist to his mouth and made a noise like he was clearing his throat. "Lillian, I'm not your uncle."

I wished someone would have taken a picture of me at that moment because I'm sure the look on my face was priceless. I retorted,

"What do you mean? All this time...how could you not be...why would everyone tell me you were my uncle?"

"Because that's what we wanted them to think," he answered calmly.

"Who's we?"

Ben put his hand over mine protectively and said, "Your mother and I."

I thought I knew where he was going with this, but I was too shocked to say anything.

"Honey, I'm your father," he explained soothingly, knitting his eyebrows in sympathy. "I had an affair with your mother just a year after she married my brother. We found out that you were mine, but I agreed to let my brother think you were his. No one ever knew, but it certainly annoyed my brother the way you seemed to cling to me even as a baby. After I left, your mother decided to tell him the truth for some reason and that is the reason you were treated the way you were. It was because of me, not because of anything you did."

I didn't have to turn around to know that Lex and Vann had stopped talking and were listening to every word Ben was saying. Somehow it felt...right. As if somewhere deep down inside I had always known Ben was my father. Now it made so much sense to me, the way I had always compared my appearance with his, the way I'd always felt comfort looking at an old wrinkled photo. I think I had actually wished it with all my heart, even when I thought him to be dead. He had been a better father to me in death than the man I'd always thought was my father.

"I'm sorry," Ben told me anguished. "I always wanted you, but I also loved your mother...and my brother, and I didn't want my blunderings to punish us all. I never was very grounded and I truly thought they could give you a better life together than I could. The drinking and recklessness didn't start until about a year after you were born. I don't know what happened to them, but something in them just fell apart, and at that point I didn't know how to come back from the lie."

I plunged forward, hugging him in earnest, and replied, "You were always my father. Even when I didn't know it and if you never told me that you were my blood father I would still have looked at you as such. No father could ever make the sacrifices you've made for me," I paused, getting weepy eyed again, "and no daughter could ever be as grateful as I am."

There was a long pause in which I could hear Lex and Vann shifting uneasily behind me.

Naturally it was Lex that broke the silence. "Ben I think it's time you also told your daughter about Dardanos. Everything. She needs to know."

I turned and looked cautiously at Lex. "I'm not going to like this am I?"

He shook his head as he walked around to sit on the other side of Ben.

"It has to do with what Dardanos said to you after I had left. He visited you one last time before he disappeared. I can't be absolutely positive what he said to you, but I have an idea from what your mother was able to hear. Do you remember anything about that conversation?" Ben asked.

My heart was beating in anticipation of more bad news. "No, I don't really remember Dardanos. I'm sure Lex probably told you I actually thought he was the one that I used to see with you."

Ben stated, "I believe Dardanos actually singled me out because he had met you once and whatever you said to him made him believe you were important. All these years I've been gone I've spent a lot of my time investigating Dardanos's past. I was only able to go back so far, as he is quite old, but one name kept recurring in connection with him."

I interrupted, "You mean OPTS?"

Surprisingly Ben shook his head and said, "No, I just found out all the details about OPTS with Vann a few days ago. I had only ever heard rumors about Dardanos being some kind of leader of a vampire-hunting army, but I never knew where they were or what they were called. It certainly was a recurring story that I heard but no one had enough information for me to know for certain if it were true. No, the name I mean was that of a woman." Ben paused looking hard at me, studying my reaction as if I should recognize who he was talking about when he continued, "Her name was Elizabeth Cranford."

I replied confused, "Okay, so who was she, his girlfriend or something?"

"Yes, as a matter of fact she was. He made her a vampire some time in the mid to late 1800s," Ben said.

Lex softly uttered, "It has been a long time since I've heard that name. Lizzy Cranford." Lex shook his head sadly, and then noticing that I was staring at him quizzically he added, "You know, Lillian, you actually look quite a bit like her, if I'm remembering her correctly."

I looked suspiciously at Lex, because he had, on more than one occasion, made references to me looking like someone, and always seemed to find a way to not tell me who. I suspected that he had been thinking of this same woman, but for some reason didn't want to admit it. From the few slips he'd made it was obvious he had been much closer to this woman than he was letting on. Lex looked away quickly, obviously feeling a bit guilty about his silence thus far on the subject.

I didn't understand the woman's connection, but I was interested to know more about another of Dardanos's vampire children. "So where is she now?"

Lex, surprisingly, was the one that answered, "Well, she's dead. She died just a few years after Dardanos gave her The Immortal Fate. I think it was 1886 or sometime close to that. The following year is when Giovanni said Dardanos took over OPTS. Maybe her death had something to do with that." Lex bit his lip, trying to decide how much to reveal and finally admitted, "Lizzy Cranford is tied up with the reason Dardanos wants revenge on Malika...and on me."

"So what does she have to do with me?" I asked turning to Ben for more forthright information.

"The first time you met Dardanos was not after I'd been turned by him," Ben said flatly. "We ran into him at a street fair in North Carolina. I accidentally bumped into his shoulder as I was walking, carrying you in my arms, and when I turned to apologize to him you said something like *always charging ahead, ay, General?* I thought you were just being a silly four year old but he looked like he'd seen a ghost. He just stared at you, said you had the loveliest green eyes, and then walked away looking back at us like he was spooked."

I just shrugged my shoulders. "Okay so what did it mean? Why would he be spooked?"

Lex again interrupted Ben's explanation, "That's what she always called him! Lizzy Cranford I mean. It was her pet name for Dardanos. Of course, how could I forget, she always called him General."

I glared at Lex, sure it hadn't just slipped his mind, after we'd already had the name General brought up twice in reference to Dardanos. If I hadn't been so interested in finding out what they were talking about I would have screamed at him for hiding something like that. I turned my head to look at each of them, still not understanding what it was they were inferring, and each of them in turn seemed to be examining me as if I were a very interesting specimen to be put under their microscope.

Ben took my hand again and said softly, "Honey, I believe, and I could be wrong, but I believe Dardanos thinks that you are the reincarnation of Elizabeth Cranford. The love of his immortal life."

"Okay, I didn't think I could get any more freaked out by this guy. Thank you for that," I said sarcastically. "So what you're telling me is this guy has been following me for the last fifteen years because he thinks I'm his dead girlfriend come back to life and he's just biding his time before he comes to get me?"

"Basically," Lex answered, oblivious to the sarcasm in my voice.

Ben glared at Lex and turned back to me to explain, "There's more. I found out from your grandfather a few months after I had left that Dardanos had visited you once more-"

"You talked to Grandpa?" I asked surprised.

"Yes, he swore he'd never tell anyone, but from time to time I would meet him somewhere just to make sure you were all safe. He told me that your mother allowed Dardanos to see you, alone. This was a few days after I'd disappeared, when you were all still living with Grandpa. Your mother listened at the door while Dardanos spoke to you and later told your grandfather because she was frightened. Dardanos had come back to make a deal with you."

"A deal? What kind of deal?" I asked.

Ben seemed to have thought I would remember. Eventually he replied, "He promised he would leave the family alone and never bother any of them, including you, if you promised to go away with him when you turned twenty. You agreed."

I could feel my mouth falling open in shock. All I could say was, "I didn't know."

Ben put his arms around me comfortingly. "Of course you didn't. You were only five."

"Well, it's safe to assume that Dardanos must actually believe Lilly is Lizzy or he wouldn't have waited all these years," Lex added.

I pulled away from Ben's embrace and looked to Lex. "But why would he wait all this time? Why didn't he just kidnap me when I was five?"

Lex scrunched his eyebrows and finally reasoned, "If I remember right Lizzy was twenty when he turned her, and he probably feared that one of his acquaintances might harm you before he was able to turn you. That's probably why he didn't take you as a child; he wanted to recreate a lifetime similar to Lizzy's for you."

I put my hand to my head exhausted by the night's excitements. I'd learned too many things in just a few hours, and it all seemed so unreal. Just sitting next to Ben seemed like a dream. Then I thought back to Rachel. Poor Rachel had gotten caught up in a tangled web that had been spun fifteen years ago. No matter what Vann or Lex said I couldn't completely abandon hope that Rachel was still my friend, that she was still true to me no matter what Dardanos had done to her. I wondered if she knew about Dardanos's obsession with Elizabeth Cranford and his belief that I was her in my past life. Was that what she had been hinting about with the black moonstone ring? Perhaps Elizabeth Cranford had been fond of black moonstone and Rachel had expected it to spark a memory in me. Rachel obviously knew that all this had to do with Dardanos wanting me, but had she been trying to protect me by trying to convince me to leave, or did she resent me for being the object of Dardanos's desire?

I put my head in my hands trying to put pressure on the pain that I could feel creeping into my brain when Lex crouched in front of me and put his hands on either side of my face.

"Don't worry, little queen, we won't let him take you," Lex declared firmly.

I looked up and tried to smile reassuringly. "I know, Lex. I'm just worried that Rachel was right. That he will come here and destroy everything...and everyone. I worry that I am putting all of you in danger, just because some ancient demon-vampire guy has a crush on me."

❧17☙

Ben couldn't stop himself from snickering, "Lex said you were funny."

"Oh, yes, I'm completely hilarious, especially when I'm scared out of my mind," I replied half jokingly.

Vann, who'd been silent for so long chimed in, "I am sorry to interrupt, but it is getting to be that time."

My heart started to flutter anxiously. I hadn't even thought what I would do while they were tucked away secure in their safe-rooms. I was trying to consider where I might hide during the day while they were incapacitated when Lex brushed the back of his hand against my cheek to get my attention.

He soothed, "Lilly, you can sleep here, on the couch. I have multiple safe-rooms hidden off of this one; one does get tired of sleeping in the same luxuriously comfortable coffin and must change it up from time to time. Ben and Vann will be sleeping down here as well, in one of my extra rooms. You will be completely safe down here and you need sleep."

I certainly didn't need to be told. I was already fighting to keep my eyelids from shutting and the comfort of knowing I now had a place to sleep without worrying who might come after me relaxed me to exhaustion. Ben hugged me one last time before choosing one of Lex's "extra bedrooms" to sleep in and Vann kissed my cheek gently before also retiring. I was left with Lex.

"Here's your key-chain, I guess I didn't need it after all," I said as I handed Lex back the key-chain that opened his safe-room.

Lex took the key-chain, placing it back in his pocket, and smiled sadly at me. "I'm sorry about Rachel, truly," Lex said softly. "I wondered why Osborn had gotten attached to her so quickly and why she'd changed so abruptly. It must have been his plan from the beginning...or Dardanos's plan. I just don't understand-"

"Lex," I interjected sadly, "I don't believe she's completely lost to us. I can't. Maybe she was brainwashed or Dardanos did something to her mind like he did to me."

"He sent you into a coma for two days; Rachel changed her entire ideology of life. That's not the same thing. You can't make someone believe something unless there is already some doubt in their mind. No, Rachel made conscious decisions that led her to where she is."

I had known that I was going to hear this from Lex, but I was still horrified. "This is Rachel we're talking about, not some random bimbo that wandered into our lives and back out in search of greener pastures. She was...miserable...when I saw her. Lex, she probably was forced into becoming a vampire and doesn't know where to go because...she probably feels no one would accept her as Dardanos's progeny."

Lex put his hands on my shoulders lovingly and responded, "I know how you feel about Rachel and I do hope in my heart, or what I have left of a heart, that you're right and she'll prove she hasn't abandoned us. Try not to think about it anymore. Get some sleep. We'll figure everything out, I promise."

Then he kissed my lips so forcefully I forgot entirely about sleep and kissed him back with sensual abandon, tasting the sweet strawberry aroma that always seemed to hover around Lex's lips. My troubled mind wanted to be lost in the excitement of passion. I ran my fingers through his hair and thought how different it was kissing him than Dallen. Lex, of course, didn't feel the same excitement I did from physical contact; his excitement was more from the close proximity of fresh blood. Still he seemed genuinely aroused by our exchange and ran his hands playfully around my neck and across the tops of my breasts.

After a few minutes Lex pulled back reluctantly and gave me a devilish smile before telling me, "I love you, little queen. I hope your daydreams about me are thoroughly shocking."

I laughed, trying to calm my raging lust, and joked, "They always are. That's why I never tell you about them. I wouldn't want you getting more full of yourself than you already are."

"I knew it," he whispered dramatically before climbing into his massive white marble coffin.

I sat on the couch not sure if I even wanted to sleep, though my body definitely did. I picked up my poetry book from where I'd laid it on the marble coffee table and began scribbling down lines to calm myself.
I have sunk

Into the depths
Where my mind has receded
Too numbed by the nothingness
Too cooled for the warmth
      -of an easy love

Finally, my eyes burning to close, I decided to check the time. Finding no clocks in the cavernous room I turned on the huge television to find a news channel that displayed the time.

6:35 AM.

Lex must have been minutes away from falling into utter unconsciousness when we'd had our goodnight kiss. I told myself that was probably the reason Lex had pulled away abruptly from our little play of intimacy, and not because he had thought we'd gone too far. I turned the large chandelier, which illuminated the entire room, off by a switch on the wall. I then turned the television off and lay down on the couch just to see how it felt. There was absolutely no way I was going to be able to get any sleep, my head was just buzzing with too many things to relax, and leather wasn't exactly the most comfortable fabric to sleep on.

I was thoroughly and irrevocably wrong. It must have taken less than two minutes before I passed out, dead to the world, I believe the expression is.

I woke up to pitch blackness, a little confused about where I was. I started walking toward the wall where I thought the light switch was when I bumped my shin into the marble coffee table. Then it all came back to me. I wasn't in my room; I was in Lex's safe-room, with three vampires sleeping within a few dozen feet of where I'd just been lying. I tried to make it to the wall by the stairs from memory, it did help that Lex hadn't cluttered the room with very many furnishings, but still it felt like it was taking much too long to reach the wall. At last, after groping around for more than five minutes I found the light switches. Looking at the staircase I realized I had no way of getting out of the room without either a pass code for the keypad on the pillar or the key-chain that I had given back to Lex and was now in his pocket.

I longed to take a shower and change. Maybe even brush my hair and put perfume on. I felt so dirty, and groggy, and I knew a shower would help me feel refreshed at least. Plus, when I realized I couldn't get out of the room I felt an unexplainable need to get out, like I was being held prisoner, even though I wasn't, but a small wave of panic spread over me.

I walked over to the keypad near the stairs, but realized I had forgotten the code. So much had happened the night before I never committed the numbers to memory. I knew it started with a five and there were more fives, but I couldn't force myself to remember. I stood there, staring at the little numbers on the keypad, trying to think of some logical way to figure out the numbers. As I stared at the keypad I thought of the numbers on a telephone, how every number stood for letters of the alphabet. I pictured the letters the way they would appear on a phone keypad; five, would be L. I thought it was too easy, but I guessed the next digits would be four, five, five, and nine. Lex had used my name as his code, the numbers stood for L I L L Y. I punched the code followed by the sun symbol into the keypad on the pillar, thinking that should open the hidden stairway under his bed.

Nothing happened.

I tried twice more with the same result. I knew I was right about the numbers, they were the numbers Lex had told me, but he must have had a different code for the keypad on the pillar. My only choice, if I wanted to get out of the safe-room any time before nightfall, was to get the key-chain Lex had in his pocket, in his coffin.

I turned and looked at Lex's coffin wearily. "I can do this," I assured myself.

All I had to do was open the coffin, quickly shove my hand into Lex's pants pocket to retrieve the key-chain, and close the lid again. I thought back to the last time I'd opened Lex's coffin, just out of curiosity, and I imagined I could still feel that iron grip around my neck. I put my hand to my throat protectively as I stared at the menacing coffin and felt the moonstone pendant Dallen had given me hanging there. As I clutched the pendant I suddenly felt it was very important that I get out of that room as soon as I could. I made up my mind to try.

I put my hands gingerly under the lip of the lid of the coffin and took a few deep breaths before throwing it open and jumping back a foot. No movement. Lex lay there like last time, a perfect statue, not even his hair was moved out of place from the force of the lid being open. I looked at his pocket, planning my assault, when I realized I didn't even know what pocket the key-chain was in. I certainly did not want to have to be groping around in his pants...twice! Even if his body didn't automatically react to my close proximity and grab me, I'd never hear the end of it from him, especially with the goodnight kiss we'd shared.

After considering how to go forward I decided the best chance I had was to try his right pocket as he was right handed. The only problem with that was that the way in which he was lying in his coffin I would have to reach across him to get to his right hand pants pocket. I held my breath and plunged my hand across him as quickly as I could, watching his face for any sign of movement, went into his pocket, and pulled out everything I could get my hands around. I thought I saw his finger twitch, but I slammed the coffin lid down immediately not waiting to see if I was right or not.

I opened my hand and was relieved to find that the key-chain was among the things I'd grabbed, along with a set of keys, a small compact mirror, and strawberry chap-stick. *No wonder he always smelled like strawberry.*

The key-chain had numbers one through nine and a golden sun with sixteen points. The sun was the same symbol on the mirrors in the changing rooms of the bedroom Rachel and I had shared. I wasn't sure what it meant, but I assumed Lex thought it was funny to use a sun symbol to denote a vampire's resting place.

I grabbed my poetry book, pointed the key-chain sensor at the the pillar, and punched in the numbers followed by the sun symbol. I smiled to myself, relieved as the staircase opened, and dashed up the stairs.

I went back to my most recent room after I took a much needed detour to the nearest little girl's room, if you get my meaning. Before I even opened the door to my room I felt someone was already in there, but I went in anyway. There was Dallen, going through my dresser as if looking for something. I let the door bang loudly against the wall and waited for Dallen to notice me.

He turned, startled, but when he saw it was me, he looked as if he were about to cry. "Thank God your still here," he said rushing to embrace me.

I pushed him away as hard as I could. "You lied to me! You've been using me all this time!"

Dallen just sat down on the bed, which was basically where he'd landed anyway from the force of my push, and licked his lips nervously. "Yes, I lied to you. But I never used you. Every intimate thing that happened between us was real and...I am in love with you," he said earnestly.

I clutched my hands into fists. I wanted so much to hate him, to blame him for everything that had gone wrong, and maybe even to punch him square in his all too handsome face just because I thought it might make me feel better. Instead I looked into his soft aqua-colored eyes and saw not only shame and regret...but love and concern. I turned and closed the door, locking it behind me. I sat beside Dallen, looking at him without a word, giving him the chance to explain himself.

Dallen hung his head in guilt and explained, "I don't know how much you know so I'll start at the very beginning. I'm sure you've discovered what OPTS is at this point, but I want to explain to you how I got involved with them. Maybe, then, you won't think of me so harshly."

"We'll see," I stated imperiously, trying to give him my most criticizing look.

Dallen swallowed nervously and recounted, "I was in my second year at The University of Sussex, studying Philosophy and English when a few people started taking notice of my unusual ability. I never exactly told anyone that I could sometimes pick what people were thinking out of their heads but a few teachers seemed to notice. I don't know exactly who, but someone gave my name to a special school situated in Cuckfield. It was by all outward appearances a school for the scientific investigation of unexplainable and paranormal phenomenon."

"OPTS," I interrupted, "Yes, I know all that."

Without raising his head to look at me he answered, "Yes, but at the time I didn't know what they really were. They accepted me to study and they really did do a lot of scientific research. It was all very interesting. Then, and I now have suspicions that they were involved in this, I found out my brother had been attacked. They brought him to the school and explained to me that he'd been attacked by a vampire and that they would have to keep him for observation to make sure he hadn't been turned. I thought that they were insane at first; I was very nearly ready to break my brother out, and get as far away from the school as I could, but then a few nights later my brother escaped somehow on his own. They tried to convince me that we needed to go after him, he was a threat to anyone he came into contact with, and they told me what they really were. An order of vampire hunters. I think I might have actually laughed at them; to convince me they assembled a group of trained hunters and took me to look for my brother. The first place they suggested we look was my flat, just outside of town. He was there when we..." Dallen stopped, trying to compose himself.

"Did they kill him?" I asked softly.

Dallen shook his head sadly. "No. When I unlocked the door, the hunters burst in behind me, but it was too late. My fiancé, Fran, he...he had sucked her dry. When he saw us he leaped through the window. It was only the second story, but he was too fast for us. After that they convinced me to become a hunter myself." Dallen finally looked up and pleaded, "You must understand how I felt. A vampire had not only taken my brother away from me but had killed the woman I loved. Fran and I were to be married in a year. I was angry for a long time and OPTS used that anger to drive me."

I didn't want to be taken in by lies, but this time it felt like he was telling the truth. Then I remembered something else he had told me.

"What about Christine? You said you had a wife named Christine and she died," I demanded.

Dallen clasped his hands and replied, "That wasn't entirely false. Christine was actually my partner at OPTS. We had stumbled upon Lex while trying to find another vampire and somehow got invited to a huge party he was throwing in New York City. When we reported back to OPTS they reassigned us to follow Lex for two years. I assume they were hoping Lex would eventually lead us to the council. Christine and I were instructed to keep up the act of being married, which of course made it difficult to keep a professional relationship when in such close proximity all the time, but I can honestly say we were not in love with each other. Christine was certainly beautiful and charismatic, but she was also loud and bossy at times and mostly she forgot about our mission and spent her time trying to gain the attention of every man within sight."

"So where is she now?" I asked tentatively.

"I was actually mostly telling you the truth about Christine," he replied sadly.

I scrunched my eyebrows. "You mean your brother did kill Christine? I thought the hunters went after him."

"The hunters did go after him but they never found him. Eventually my brother ended up mixed up with Lex's crowd, though I doubt he and Lex ever actually met. He showed up at a party Christine and I were attending. He didn't see me, but I knew if he did see me he would give us away as hunters for OPTS. Christine and I decided to trail him and call in back-up when we found where he rested. The problem was Christine seemed to think she could take him on alone and went after him on her own without telling me. She was dead by time we got there and my brother had disappeared again."

I still wasn't sure if I should believe any of what he was telling me, but it seemed to make more sense than the lies he'd told me before. "So what about your brother? Is he still out there somewhere?"

Dallen shook his head and I could see tears falling down from his eyes. "No he isn't out there. Christine was killed a little over a year ago. Though I wasn't in love with Christine she was the closest I'd come to a relationship since Fran, and her death brought back all the feelings of loss I had for Fran. I was so angry I left my assignment and went after my brother. It took me six months but I finally found him."

"You...killed...your brother?" I gasped.

Dallen broke down completely and laid his head on my lap as he convulsed in sobs. Though still shaking uncontrollably Dallen managed, "I was so angry. First Fran and then Christine. Plus OPTS basically brainwashed me to despise vampires. I did kill him. I waited until the sun rose and I set fire to his coffin." He paused and sat up to look me in the eyes. "I even stayed and watched until nothing was left. Since I've been here, and especially since I met you, I've been so confused about everything. I started to think that maybe OPTS had orchestrated my brother becoming a vampire just to bait me, and the fact that he actually escaped OPTS, no vampire has ever escaped the underground prisons there. I don't know what to believe anymore. They could even be responsible for setting my brother on my fiancé. She was the only thing keeping me from giving my entire life to OPTS. When I told you that you reminded me of my wife, I meant her not Christine. Fran was my world and when she was taken all I had left was OPTS, but I don't know how I can possibly work for them now.

"Then, of course, there's General D. How could I possibly go on killing vampires when I'm taking orders from a vampire?"

"You mean Dardanos?" I asked numbly.

Dallen seemed surprised. "You've heard of him? Yes, he runs OPTS, but it makes no sense the radical fervor he preaches about the evils of vampires in the world, and yet he is one. Even Osborn, who takes orders like a good little soldier, sometimes questions the General's motives."

"There's something I have to tell you about Dardanos," I said softly.

I decided to tell Dallen everything, going back to Ben's faked death up to my most recent discovery of Dardanos's dead lover Elizabeth Cranford, who died less than a year before Dardanos took over OPTS. I also told him the bizarre theory that Dardanos believed I was actually the reincarnated Lizzy Cranford, and that many of the events plaguing us at present were part of Dardanos's scheme to get Lizzy Cranford back. In other words he was coming for me.

Dallen hung his head and whispered, "I know."

I was a little surprised by that. "What do you mean you know? You knew and you never told me?!"

Dallen put his hand to my cheek and explained patiently, "I knew that he wanted you. That's all. We'd been instructed, I mean Osborn and me, to stay away from you, but to also try to protect you. We were to make sure you didn't receive The Immortal Fate and protect you from any danger, but we weren't supposed to get close to you. Osborn threatened me many times to relinquish my intimacy with you, but he never did tell the General. I think he was afraid General D might actually kill me for disobeying him. If what you say is true and General D thinks you're this Lizzy Cranford then he very well might have killed me if he knew what went on between us, and he might yet. That's why I came back so soon. I need to get you out of here."

"Dallen, I can't just leave! No matter what danger I'm in, I've brought this on everyone. I can't run away and just hope that Dardanos leaves everyone alone. I won't leave them. I'll fight him myself if I have to. You don't understand, Dallen, this is my family and I've put them in terrible danger."

"I understand, Lillian, that you never felt like you had a real family," Dallen said harshly, "but we're talking about vampires here! They're killers, not innocent victims!"

I countered hotly, "My father is a vampire and I will not let him die after he spent the last fifteen years protecting me!"

"Your father?" Dallen asked confused.

"Yes, my father. Ben. He's actually my father. I just found out last night. I can't leave him, not after I just got him back. Anyway, we plan on being ready for Dardanos when he comes."

Dallen pursed his lips nervously. "You may not have time. That's what I've been trying to tell you. He wasn't supposed to make his move for another week, but he was tipped off that you knew something and he could attack any day. That's why I came back two days early. As soon as I got back to OPTS Rachel told me she'd seen you and what you talked about. Unfortunately she still has a soft spot for Osborn-"

"Yeah, I know how that is," I said sarcastically.

Dallen smiled a little to himself and continued, "Well, she also told him about your encounter and as Osborn is basically the General's lap dog he ran and told him everything. When I stumbled upon Osborn himself, he told me we were mobilizing and our ETA was no later than two days from then. I didn't wait around to find anything else out. I just turned around and got back on a plane...to get to you before it was too late."

"My mind is made up. I won't leave, and it would probably be a good idea if you weren't here when Lex and Vann woke. No matter how you may feel now, you betrayed them, all of them, and they do not take betrayal lightly," I declared.

Dallen clasped both my hands in his and replied feebly, "I know. I'm as good as dead if any of them ever see me again...but how can I possibly leave you?" He looked down at the necklace hanging around my neck and smiled. "You're still wearing it."

"Yes," I answered almost ashamed. "Oh, Dallen, I don't know what to think or feel, but you've always been my weakness. No matter what happens I think I will always love you, even if I try not to. That is why, for my sake, you will go and leave me and OPTS and all of this behind you." I paused and held the moonstone in my hand looking at it thoughtfully. "Who knows maybe you're right, maybe the moonstone reunites lovers, and maybe it will again."

Dallen seemed confused as he kissed my cheek slowly and got up, but agreed, "I'll go for now, but I won't promise to never see you again." He turned to go and as he went he muttered, "In another life, perhaps, we'd have been terribly happy."

I sighed and said to myself, "In another life I was Lizzy Cranford."

I lay back on my bed, contemplating how much more comfortable it was then Lex's leather couch, and longing for Dallen. Though I didn't mean to, I let my eyes shut momentarily to daydream about Dallen's body lying next to mine, which was all it took for me to pass peacefully into slumber.

I don't remember everything that I dreamed, but I do remember what I was dreaming just before I awoke. I saw teeth and fingernails ripping something apart in half darkness and Dardanos's smiling blood-drenched face looming up over me. It felt so real I threw my hands out in front of me and woke myself screaming. My heart was beating out of my chest, but it had just been a dream. I looked over toward the balcony and realized something didn't seem quite right. Then it hit me.

"Damn! It's already dark!" I was again speaking to myself.

I ran to the bathroom and showered quickly. We might all be facing our death soon, but I certainly didn't need to smell like I'd already faced mine. I couldn't even remember the last time I'd taken a shower. Had it been two days ago or a week; that thought made me feel a little embarrassed to have been so close to Dallen earlier. I still chose to wear black and decided on a Roman style dress with an empire waist of gold cord crisscrossing around my waist and tying just above my hips. My hair had gotten too long to do anything with, unless I had another hour to spare which I did not, so the brush was all it got.

I didn't bother to check my appearance in the mirror as I was eager to get back to Lex, Vann, and Ben; assuming they were still where I left them. As I walked toward my bedroom door I noticed something hanging on it. A piece of paper. Lex had found me sleeping in my bed and left me a note. I sat down and read the note over quickly. Basically Lex didn't want to disturb me I looked so peaceful, blah, blah, blah. Something about not being able to keep my hands off him, which I won't bore you with. They went out to hunt and would be back soon. The council had been notified and were probably on their way if not already there. Lex suggested I wait in the banquet hall where the council meets.

That sounded fine by me. I had suddenly realized I was starving and hoped I would be able to get something to eat before everyone showed up. I found myself unable to remember when I had last eaten or even what I had last eaten. I was fantasizing about the gluttonous meal I would ask the kitchen staff to prepare for me, but my fantasy was squashed by the sound of quiet voices. I walked into the banquet hall and everyone was already assembled. Well, almost everyone.

Lex rushed to me and caught me unexpectedly in his arms as if I'd been missing for days. I felt a strange foreboding as I stood there, perplexed, letting him smother me. As soon as I felt tears rolling onto my bare shoulder I pushed him back, scared of what he would tell me.

"What happened?" I demanded.

Lex looked at me and wept harder. He couldn't even tell me. I searched the table and was relieved to see Ben sitting there, tears falling sparsely from his reddened eyes. Finally it was Malika who came to me and ushered both Lex and me into seats. Malika sat me to the right of herself and held my hand over the table.

When she didn't speak, it was Tor, who seldom speaks, that fixed me with his kind eyes and explained in a hushed voice, "Giovanni is dead."

I didn't cry. I looked from face to face, around the table, until I came back to Tor. I could see it in everyone's eyes; it was true. I decided I was still dreaming and I would wake up any moment on Lex's white leather couch, having never seen Dallen, having never fallen asleep in my bed, and having never heard the words: Giovanni is dead.

I knew I must be dreaming because I was still so calm. "What about Demetrius, Una, and Kara?" I asked, having noticed my three least favorite council members were also missing.

This time Malika answered, "We don't know. We can only hope that they've been detained for some reason, but in light of what we are dealing with I don't think we can deny the possibility that they too may be dead."

Finally Ben, who somehow must have understood my reluctance to believe any of this was real, came over and knelt in front of me. He explained gently, "Honey, Giovanni is dead. He was found with scratches all over his body as if he'd been bitten and clawed at. He was completely drained of blood."

My heart sank as I remembered my dream of teeth and nails; bitten and clawed at Ben had said. I felt the flood building in my heart, but instead I disputed, "But that couldn't kill him. He would just heal. He couldn't die just from losing blood!"

"Actually he can...and he did," Ben insisted gently, "Some vampires can die from being drained of blood, but only by a very powerful vampire. It takes a great will to drain another vampire to death. I've only ever heard of it happening to very young, very weak vampires; which of course Giovanni was neither of those things. Dardanos is just so incredibly strong."

I stood up numbly and stated as calmly as I could, "I'll be back. I need a moment...to...to...I need to be alone."

I didn't wait for them to excuse me. I ran. I ran as quickly as I could straight to the Palladium statue. When I stopped short just in front of the statue I found myself doubling over on the ground trying to vomit, but after not eating for over a day there was nothing left in my stomach. I knelt there on the ground, clutching my sides, angry at myself and the others. We were letting Dardanos pick us off one at a time instead of going after him. I raised my eyes to the statue of Pallas to ask her help, to ask that she at least protect those of us that were left, but instead I looked into emptiness. The statue was gone. I wasn't sure if it meant anything, but if felt like it had been stolen on purpose, just as the Greeks had done to the Trojans just before they attacked them and destroyed their city. I lay down on the paved path and wept loudly. I wanted to scream, I wanted to hit something, destroy something, but all I could muster were pitiful wails of sorrow.

Again a voice inside my head was berating me; this was my fault! If I'd never come to the mansion, if I'd never wanted this life with Lex, Mason would still be alive...Rachel wouldn't have been turned by Dardanos...Vann would still be alive. Dardanos hadn't wanted them; they were just in the way of him getting his prize. Everything that had happened was the unfortunate result of my strange comment to Dardanos in a chance meeting when I was four years old.

Now Vann, my love, my first love, was gone...forever. The man that had taught me to swing dance, the man that had forced Lex to make contact with me before he'd planned to, the man that had spent countless summer nights patiently listening to my childish thoughts, and the man that finally confessed his love to me; though not the love I'd originally hoped for. More than anything he had helped me to accept the concept that things didn't always turn out the way you might plan, and I learned a valuable lesson about the many different kinds of love out there. Some people come into your life like a storm, some come in quietly, and others build a home in your heart when you aren't even looking. This story is for you Vann, I will always remember your gentle patience with me and the beauty you put into everything you said. I will always be your uccellino, your little bird.

A NIGHT IN THE UN-LIFE...

Lillian felt a presence behind her as she walked hand in hand with Ash at the downtown street festival. She glanced behind her and noticed a vampire watching her. If she were alone she would try to make contact with the stranger, but as she had Ash by her side she couldn't risk his safety. She bared her fangs slightly and sent out a warning message with her mind.

I am far more powerful than you, do not provoke me!

The vampire lowered his eyes and darted in the opposite direction. Though she took no pride in being a bully, Lillian smiled confidently to herself, knowing there were few things, even other vampires, that could harm her. She had tasted some of the oldest vampiric blood and as a result she had acquired abilities and powers that most vampires only dreamed of. The best part was she never even had to prove herself, she just made a threat, and other vampires backed off.

"Everything okay?" Ash asked, smiling contently at her.

Lillian nodded her head. "Yeah, I just thought I saw someone I knew, but I was wrong."

Lillian watched Ash, smiling to herself, as he pointed out other artists selling their paintings. He seemed to know, or know of, every painter, musician, and craft artist they saw. He had stories about them all, especially the painters, and what they were doing wrong. Listening to his animated narrative about other painters made Lillian, yet again, curious about Ash's paintings.

"You know I might have a better opinion about these painters if I had something to compare them to," Lillian said slyly. "Perhaps, if I had ever seen your paintings, I might be able to agree with how amateur these paintings are in comparison."

Ash pursed his lips nervously and stammered, "Well, I really don't have anything ready to look at right now." He paused seeing the disappointment on Lillian's face. "I really do paint, and I think I 'm quite good, but I'm just not ready to show you yet. Kind of like how you're not ready to show me your book."

Lillian had to admit that did seem fair, except that Ash had sneaked a few peaks at her book, and he at least knew what her book was about. She knew absolutely nothing about his paintings, and it suddenly bothered her beyond words. Ash claimed he was a painter, it was what he did, who he was, and yet he didn't share it. Not even with her. Lillian decided he was hiding something, and she was going to find out what.

While Lillian was lost in thought about how to go about finding out Ash's secret, Ash had turned to the side to purchase a necklace from a vendor they had stopped in front of. He took Lillian's hand and began walking again, waiting for the right moment to give her the memento. Lillian seemed distant at the moment and Ash decided he would wait for her dark mood to pass before giving her the necklace.

He had been noticing the more time he spent with Lillian that she was prone to daydreaming, like she forgot where she was and whom she was with, and just entered another world. Then she would be back and smiling as if nothing out of the ordinary had happened. Ash knew, under normal circumstances, he would be annoyed with someone who seemed to fade in and out of reality, but with Lillian it just added to her mystery. Ash could tell she'd been through something traumatic, and he was perfectly willing to wait around for Lillian to confide in him.

As Ash, yet again, walked Lillian to her apartment he decided to give her the necklace he'd bought. Just before they reached the doorway he pulled the little wad of tissue paper it was wrapped in out of his pocket. Lillian turned to say goodnight, but stopped seeing Ash unwrapping something.

"I got you a little something. I figured after five dates it was time I bought you a present." He held his open hand out for Lillian to see the necklace.

Lillian's heart stopped. She didn't make a move to take it, but just stared.

Ash was confused and explained, "I just figured moonstones were your favorite, because I always see you wearing moonstone earrings and that one necklace." Ash stopped and closed his eyes in realization. "Of course, you could also be wearing that necklace all the time because it reminds you of someone."

Lillian picked up the delicate little necklace from Ash's hand. "Moonstones are my favorite. It's beautiful, thank you." Lillian lent in and gently kissed Ash on the lips.

Ash smiled weakly and asked, "So will I see you tomorrow night?"

"Of course," Lillian said warmly, and bent toward him again for a proper goodnight kiss.

❧18❧

I lay on the flagstone paved path in the garden, staring up at the star-scattered sky, letting the rain of sorrow gush from my eyes. I imagined that if Vann had seen me like that he would reprimand me and make me get up off the dirty ground. He'd probably brush the debris from the back of my dress and gently kiss the lines of tears on my face. He would tell me we needed a plan, we needed to do something, not lay around feeling sorry for ourselves. I was so wrapped up in imagining Vann was there that I didn't even notice Ben walking up soundlessly.

He picked me up off the ground easily, and consoled, "Honey, now's not the time for mourning. We need to be strong and figure out what we're going to do. One day we'll give Giovanni the thoughts and tears he deserves, but for now we need to lock them away."

I didn't answer him, but I thought to myself that Vann must have whispered in my father's ear, because it sounded exactly like something he would say. I just lay my head against Ben's chest and let him carry me back to the banquet hall, as if I were just a little girl being rescued from a bad dream. He set me down just outside the door.

Ben clipped me under the chin and asked warmly, "Are you ready?"

I nodded my head and entered the room. I paused a moment to take stock of who was left. We were now down to seven council members, Ben, and me. I shook my head sadly and took my place at the table next to Malika. They were already in deep discussion. Evidently Lex was recounting everything we'd learned over the past days to the council. He was, at that moment, telling them about Rachel.

"Just because Dardanos turned her doesn't necessarily mean she's on his side," I interjected defensively.

"But she went back to him, Lillian," Glen answered softly. "What else should we think?"

I felt my cheeks burning, though Glen had not meant the comment meanly. Before I exploded in a cruel torrent aimed at Glen, who was only pointing out the obvious, Malika placed her hand consolingly over mine.

Malika let her voice boom through the room, "No one is suggesting that they would attack Rachel. We must wait and see what she has chosen. I give you my word that no one, and I mean no one," she commanded, looking around the room, "will touch Rachel unless she gives us a clear sign of her allegiance to Dardanos." Malika drew her hand from mine and turned to Lex. "Now, Alexander, please continue."

"That was about it. Well I suppose I should explain why Dardanos wants Lillian," Lex sighed looking apologetically at me, as if to say I'm sorry we have to go through this again. "Apparently when Lillian was four she and Ben bumped into Dardanos, literally, and Lillian called him a nickname that only one other person ever called him. Elizabeth Cranford."

Glen interrupted with a quizzical look on his face, "Wait, Elizabeth...you mean Lizzy Cranford? Isn't she the one that you and Dardanos fought-"

Lex cut him off before he could finish, "The point is Dardanos believes that Lillian is the reincarnation of Lizzy Cranford and plans on coming for her."

This time it was the sing-song voice of Sylvia that joined in, "I apologize, Lillian, but if...he wants *you*...why not let him take you? If it would save us...the rest of us?"

I was so lost in trying to figure out where Sylvia came from listening to her rough but melodic accent, I really hadn't heard her suggestion of offering me up on a platter to Dardanos. Lex obviously had heard her and was not at all happy with the idea.

"Aren't you supposed to be descended from Vikings?!" He admonished, "What kind of strategy is that? Just give him what he wants to save our own hides?! I'm sorry but I am no coward and I am certainly not going to let him take Lillian! You're living in a dream world if you think that will appease him. Dardanos would take Lillian and set his vampire-hunting dogs on the rest of us anyway!"

Ahhh, Vikings. She must be Scandinavian. I wasn't shocked or even concerned with Sylvia's comment, because like Glen, she had just said the most obvious answer to our problems. I also knew she hadn't suggested it out of viciousness; Sylvia just had a habit of saying any random thing that popped into her head.

Sylvia shook her white-blonde hair in distress. "Oh no, I did not mean we should do that. I...I just do not know what to think. This is all so strange."

Malika announced, "Alexander, rest assured we will not be offering Lillian up to Dardanos. As you may well remember he has more scores to settle than to just take Lillian away."

Although the others gave each other blank looks, I remembered Lex telling me that Dardanos wanted revenge on Malika and it seemed it might have something to do with Elizabeth Cranford. I sat there, dazed, listening to their plans. Malika was sending Sylvia, who also possessed the ability to fly, to get help from nearby councils. It seemed there were at least five orders of The Council of The Eternal in the U.S. alone. They were to meet at the mansion tomorrow evening, where Malika was going to try to convince them to join us in our assault on Dardanos.

Lex had finally convinced Malika and Tor that the time for waiting for Dardanos to make his move had passed. We needed to bring the fight to his door. We were going to England to invade OPTS and put an end to the secret society of vampire hunters.

"We'll have to find a safe place for Lillian," Ben stated.

I was shocked and sputtered, "What?! Wait, you're not going to take me? I should be going."

Lex snickered but added seriously, "Little queen, you truly have the heart of a lion, but it's too dangerous. Especially for a mortal."

"Then turn me," I replied matter-of-factly, not even thinking about what I was saying.

I could see by the big boyish grin on Lex's face that he was completely delighted by my idea, but Ben was not of the same mind.

"No, she will not be turned," he said flatly, looking first at Lex and then to Malika.

"Ben," I began softly.

"No, I won't let you," Ben huffed, "I just got you back."

I tried another tactic. "Father," I addressed him firmly but sweetly, "It may be my only chance. I'm not strong enough to stand up to vampire hunters or Dardanos, but I could at least have a fighting chance if I were a vampire. What if something happens to all of you and I'm left in hiding alone. I can't stay in hiding forever, and eventually Dardanos would come for me anyway. At least as a vampire I have a chance to protect myself."

I could see that my use of the word father had tugged at his emotions. He may have been a vampire but he was also my blood, and he'd been absent from my life for far too long. He had a lot of making up to do, and I could tell saying no to me made him feel guilty. I hoped that meant he would give in and allow me to have The Immortal Fate. Most girls ask their fathers for a pony or a car, all I was asking for was eternal life, how could he say no?

I wasn't even sure I wanted to be a vampire, but if it meant I could walk up to Dardanos and potentially have the strength to slap him without it seeming completely ridiculous, I just might accept immortality. Yeah, you could say I was still fuming over Vann and Mason, to make a decision about eternal life based on the slim chance I might get to inflict about two seconds worth of pain on someone I hated.

Malika broke the silence. "I think this is something we should all consider. Let us give it until tomorrow evening. Alexander, Ben, Lillian...immortality as a vampire is not to be taken lightly. Think on it and we shall make the decision tomorrow whether to allow Lillian to become one of us. Among other things it wouldn't hurt for us to have one more fighting on our side, and she does have a point about protecting herself. For now let us adjourn and prepare for the coming of the other councils. Sylvia, do not fail, convince them to come here, even if you have to lie. I will persuade them to join us once I have them face to face. Until tomorrow evening. Be safe, be vigilant."

With that Malika and Tor stood and walked nobly from the room. I waited until everyone else had left to talk to Ben and Lex.

"I have something to tell you both. Please don't be angry," I entreated softly.

I told them of my encounter with Dallen. Yes, everything. They already knew that I wasn't proud of my affection for Dallen, but they would've known I was hiding something if I didn't tell them absolutely everything. Lex lifted the moonstone off my chest and proclaimed it charming in that annoyingly jealous tone of his. I knew I would have to be careful how often I caressed my keepsake now that Lex knew who'd given it to me. I also told them about my ominous dream. Though I hadn't seen much, it certainly unnerved me to think that I might have dreamed of Vann's death.

It was Ben that seemed truly affected by my confession. "I'm sorry, Honey." He stroked my hair and expressed sadly, "You've had to endure so much pain and sadness in your short life. If I had done my part as your father I would have claimed you and perhaps we could have left to start a new life, and perhaps we would have never bumped into Dardanos."

I just smiled at his concern and replied reassuringly, "Some people believe that there are no accidents, everything that has happened in my life has led me to this moment, and no matter what you or I do to try to stop it, fate will fulfill itself."

"That may well be, but you are still not coming," Ben answered sternly. "I don't want to lose you...again."

Lex added just as sternly, "Not to mention that, dangling the object of his desire in front of his face may not be the best tactic for dealing with Dardanos. I agree with your father. It is too dangerous and if Dardanos does get a hold of you it will all be for nothing. Also, I certainly don't want to lose you either." Lex gave me a bashful smile.

I was very touched by their concern and love, but I also felt I was being cheated out of the serious consideration they were supposed to be giving to the thought of turning me the following night. It seemed they had already made up their minds.

"That isn't fair. I have felt as much loss from Dardanos's deeds as anyone. Not to mention that, no matter what you say, I am the reason all of these things have happened. I think I deserve to face him and I think it's almost my obligation, in light of the circumstances, to at least be there with all of you! Plus, if you're right and he means to turn me the way he turned Lizzy when she was twenty, then I think it would at least piss Dardanos off to no end that someone else had already done it and may even deter him from his plan," I lectured hotly.

Lex just patted my cheek like I was the cutest thing he'd ever seen and replied, "We'll talk about it more tomorrow. Right now I need to give instructions to my staff. I'm having all mortals vacate the premises by tomorrow morning. I don't know what to expect from these other councils and I certainly don't want to be responsible for killing off perfectly good help."

I shook my head annoyed at his change of subject which, apparently, Lex took as my being offended by his comment about his household staff.

He kissed my cheek and quipped, "Don't worry, Lilly, I'm going to give them a very generous send off. I know you get mad when I take such things as human life lightly, but I really do care, way, way, way, deep down somewhere inside for the mortals around me."

Ben also said his goodbyes. He was going out to scour for contacts that he had made in the area over the past fifteen years. He was going to try to convince them, as well, to help us. Ben explained that was how he'd been able to stay under the radar all these years. He had bonded with many other outcasts and loners to gain information and stay one step ahead of Dardanos and any other vampire that might be dangerous to him. I hugged him not wanting to let him go, but he assured me that he had spent all these years learning how not to be seen. He would return to me, safely. That was a promise.

I desperately hoped he always kept his promises.

Finally, with nothing left to do, I decided it was time to oblige my stomach with food. I went to the kitchen where I found the kitchen staff sitting around playing cards, waiting for their orders. When I entered they stood as if they'd been caught stealing, but I just smiled and gestured for them to continue their game. I raided the refrigerator which was surprisingly well stocked for a man that never ate. Although I wanted to gorge myself on absolutely every edible item, I knew that after barely eating for two days any substantial meal would probably make me sick. Instead I satisfied myself with a simple sandwich and a glass of white wine. I decided to take the remainder of the bottle of wine to my room; possibly it would help me to sleep.

It did.

Too well.

I awoke to my door slamming open and yells of, "There in the bed!"

Before I knew what was happening a sort of fabric bag was yanked over my head and I was lifted out of my bed. While I struggled in my unseeable assailant's arms, my hands and feet were bound by at least two others. I screamed as loud as my lungs would allow, but I knew that it was day and no vampire could come to my rescue, and most of the staff had already left the night before. I had seen at least four dozen of them carrying their things out before the wine had sent me off to dreamland, and any that had lingered probably left earlier that morning. Still I tried desperately to free myself, but all I managed was getting myself dropped on the hard wood floor three times.

The third time I was dropped my kidnapper kicked me in the ribs and shouted, "I'm going to beat the shit out of her!"

I heard another voice, one that sounded like it was in charge, say, "No you will not! You will follow your orders or you will answer to General D!"

My God, they were hunters!

They had attacked a whole day earlier than Dallen had said. As my kidnapper picked me up, once more I made another effort of screaming, hoping any vampires within earshot would hear me, but I knew even if they could hear me they would be completely defenseless if found during daylight hours. I tried with every fiber of my being to send out a silent message to Lex and Ben, whether it worked I never found out.

Suddenly I heard car doors, dozens of voices, and scuffling feet across what I assumed was the pebbled driveway. Again I struggled vigorously and managed to get myself dropped, this time, on the stone-covered ground. Without thinking I took off at a run and plowed right into someone causing both myself and him to tumble down.

I tried once more to struggle to my feet but was pulled back down as I heard my annoyed carrier announce, "This is ridiculous! She needs to be taken out!"

The next thing I knew I was being held from behind as someone removed my head covering, momentarily blinding me in the afternoon sun, and shoved a wet rag into my face.

I opened my eyes groggily, trying to shake off the mild thudding in my head. My first thought was to struggle and try to free myself from these people that had stormed the mansion and taken me prisoner, but I was confused. My hands and feet were no longer bound and I was lying in bed.

"Uhhhh, these dreams are getting more and more real," I huffed to myself, annoyed.

Then I realized I was not in *my* bed. I was in *a* bed, but it certainly was not my own. The room was too dark for me to make anything out, but it definitely didn't seem like any room in Lex's mansion. I sat up, which I found quite difficult from the tightly bound material covering my upper body. My head still felt a little cloudy, but finally I recognized the garment to be a corset. I hadn't been wearing a corset when I had fallen asleep, had I? I got out of bed, stumbled off a step, and found a light switch after bumping into several pieces of furniture. The light switch illuminated several gold wall sconces revealing a richly decorated oval room.

I walked over to one of the over-sized mirrors and found that I was indeed wearing a corset, black and white brocade, with a long black taffeta skirt similar to the one I'd seen Rachel wearing the last time I had talked to her. That did not put my mind at ease about my current situation.

The room was certainly not one I had ever seen before. The entire room was awash in gold, and a deep, lush, royal purple. Every piece of furniture was covered in silk and cut velvet of the same colors. Even the floor shone like gold, though it was actually a smooth polished wood. There was a small fireplace, settees and armchairs littered about, two large mirrors, a very feminine looking vanity, and an ornate writing desk. The bed, which I had stumbled off of, was raised by a foot-high platform which was also covered in purple velvet.

I tried the two doors leading out of the room, one was hidden behind a decorative gold curtain, but both were locked. I decided to try the window. It was definitely too high to jump, at least eighty feet to the ground, and there was nothing to hold on to in order to climb down. Looking out the window still left me wondering where I was. There was a huge stretch of nothing but rolling green hills with patches of densely packed trees as far as the eye could see and in the distance, taunting me with their recognizable yet inscrutable presence, were traces of misty mountains.

"I know this place," I announced to myself just as the door clicked open.

"You should," a deep, familiar voice said behind me. "Your childhood home is not thirty minutes from here."

I turned and for a moment I was taken aback by the ineffable, dark beauty of the man standing before me. I stared transfixed at his statuesque frame and clean-cut features. Even his eyes startled me, though I had seen them before. Those cold, sapphires had cost me my consciousness for two days. He was again dressed in a Neo-Victorian fashion; his gray suit had the classic old styling but with a modern fit. I assumed it was a style he'd taken a liking to because of its affiliation with Elizabeth Cranford's time.

"Dardanos," I whispered with displeasure.

He smiled, almost lovingly, at me and took slow steps toward me, as if he had all the time in the world. I found myself not exactly scared, but exhilarated. My heart was beating in vexing anticipation. I decided to prove to myself that the passionate feelings I had when I looked at Dardanos were a result of my pure loathing for him, not a curious attraction. I walked quickly up to him and slapped his face as hard as my tender hand could manage. He didn't stop me, and in the end all I achieved was a stinging sensation in my right hand, and an amused look on his face.

"I had planned to do that once I was a vampire, but unfortunately your men came for me before I could manage to get myself turned," I reproofed, irritatedly.

"Just as it should be, my dear Elizabeth," he explained as he reached out to stroke my face.

I pulled away uneasily. "I'm not Elizabeth Cranford. I know I supposedly look like her, but it's just a coincidence."

"There are no coincidences," Dardanos's deep, rich voice hummed.

I had just said basically the same thing to Ben, but I wasn't going to let that stop me from disagreeing with Dardanos. "You're wrong. I don't know anything about Elizabeth Cranford, don't you think I would have some memory of her? Or of you for that matter?"

Dardanos smiled sheepishly and responded, "You will. Soon. That's why everything had to happen in just the right way. I couldn't let you be given The Immortal Fate by someone else, I turned Elizabeth, and I will turn you. Do you think it mere coincidence that I bought this chateau and you just happened to live twenty miles away? Do you think it coincidence that I stumbled upon you in a crowd of thousands of people when you were four? Do you think it coincidence that you just happened to call me by the name only Elizabeth ever called me by? Do you think it coincidence that you look exactly like Elizabeth, excepting only your hair is much lighter? Do you think it coincidence that the man that came to protect you just happens to be my greatest rival? Do you think it mere coincidence that your dearest friend in the world happens to look remarkably like Elizabeth's older sister, Emma? Do you think it a coincidence that turning Emma made it much easier to convince Elizabeth to accept The Immortal Fate, just as I had turned Rachel for the same purpose?"

I was a little stunned by his last comments concerning Rachel. It made me think back to the portrait that had hung in our room. The one that looked so seemingly authentic, in which both Rachel and I looked slightly different than in reality. Of course, Lex must have known Elizabeth Cranford much better than he had ever let on and kept the portrait all those years. The portrait was most likely of Elizabeth and her sister Emma, not of Rachel and me as we had assumed when we'd looked at the familiar faces staring back at us.

I had to give it to Dardanos, that certainly was a lot of coincidences.

What was I thinking? I had to stop looking into those intoxicating eyes of his, stop thinking how sensual his mouth looked as he spoke, and stop imagining being wrapped in his arms with his lips at my neck. I shook my head trying to clear my mind. He was evil, he was the enemy! I wondered if perhaps he was planting those things in my head, but hadn't Vann said the ideas had to already be there to influence someone? Were my feelings being sparked by some remembrance inside of me of being Elizabeth Cranford? That would certainly be easier to accept than that I simply couldn't control my desire for a man that I loathed.

Before I had time to react Dardanos cupped my face in his hands and looked into my eyes. "Elizabeth, you will remember who you are. Once you've been given my blood, you will remember." He paused and rested his forehead against mine. "I have loved you all this time. I have waited patiently for you to reach your twentieth year, but we won't have to wait any longer. Tonight I will have you once more."

With that he pressed his lips gently, almost nervously, against mine. My mind was silently reprimanding me for not being stronger, but I allowed his kiss. I'll even admit I enjoyed it a little, but only a little...really. Then I realized his last words and pushed him away.

"What do you mean have me?" I questioned in a troubled tone.

Dardanos ran his fingers through my hair, presumably comparing it to Elizabeth's, and answered distractedly, "I will give you The Immortal Fate tonight. You will be mine forever, as you always should have been. My love, my beauty."

I wanted to scream at him that he was completely insane but just at that moment there was a knock on the door. After being told to enter, a man, who I assumed was a hunter, whispered in Dardanos's ear and left after receiving only a nod.

Dardanos turned back to me and explained in anguish, "I must go. There are things I must attend to. I almost forgot, I have something for you," Dardanos expressed in amusement, smiling strangely as he pulled something from inside his coat. "I believe this is yours."

He handed me my poetry book, but I didn't understand why anyone would have thought it important enough to take or why he thought it was amusing that he had it in his possession. I took it and flipped it open, making sure he hadn't ripped pages out or taken my photos of Ben or of Rachel and me. Everything looked the way it should have. Maybe he was just a fan of poetry.

Dardanos must have noticed my look of confusion and explained, "Osborn was very thorough in the raid on the mansion and decided to bring that along as well. I must say I found it very interesting. Needless to say I will have to have a talk with one of my hunters over his abundant appearance in your poems, but I did rather enjoy the one you wrote about me," he taunted, smiling slyly. "I will be back for you tonight. You have given me purpose these past fifteen years, but the wait has been worth it to see you standing before me once again. I have never stopped loving you and after tonight you will give me life again." Before leaving he took one last euphoric look at me.

Well, I thought to myself, *my ego will be completely ruined after this. No man will ever be able to reach my expectations when it comes to compliments from now on.*

How was I to react to this display of tenderness and affection? I had expected threats and physical assaults from Dardanos, not decades of pent up yearnings lavished on me. I had imagined this dark, evil man, ready to rip any one's throat out for disrespecting him, instead he had actually looked lovingly at me when I had slapped him.

I knew I had to find a way out before he got back. I tried the door just on the off chance he was so deluded in thinking I was Elizabeth that he hadn't locked it, but no such luck. Evidently he loved me beyond death, but he did not trust me as of yet. I decided to give the window some more thought. I looked out at what I now knew was a part of the Blue Ridge Mountains in the distance and longed for the ability to fly, which was basically the only way I would be escaping out the window. I thought about jumping, a fleeting thought mind you, to escape being turned by Dardanos and to diminish his triumph. I decided that even if I could do such a thing, which I couldn't, it wouldn't have proved anything or helped anyone else.

While I was busy daydreaming, gazing at the distant mountains, there was a light knock on the door followed by someone entering. My heart thudded, anticipating Dardanos had returned already, but when I turned it was just another of the hunters carrying a tray of food. He set it on the writing desk and poured out a glass of dark, burgundy colored wine from the bottle on the tray. Without a word he left and I heard the click of the lock after the door had closed.

I looked at the food on the plate. It looked and smelled absolutely delicious. I wasn't sure, but by the looks of it I guessed it was probably duck or pheasant with some kind of leafy greens and stuffing. As hungry as I was, I ignored the food, laid my book down on the desk and grabbed greedily at the glass of wine, and once again situated myself at the window. I suppose if I were going to kill myself I might as well get good and besotted first.

I never got the chance. Before I had even finished the glass of wine I tottered over to the bed and crumpled into it. I knew this feeling because I had felt it once before. The wine had been laced with something and I was utterly under its power. Perhaps, Dardanos had been planning to kill me all along. Perhaps, I was the object of his revenge on Lex, and nothing more. So much for never-ending love and devotion, one simple dose of poison and Dardanos was getting rid of me.

I felt lips pressed securely against mine. I wasn't sure if I was dreaming, but everything was dark and my head felt hazy like in a dream. I found myself pushing back forcefully with my own lips as my body felt warmly aroused. I felt myself being pulled up and suddenly I was liberated from my corset and long skirt. My eyes still wouldn't obey me and open, but I felt hands caressing me and lips touching me wetly. Suddenly I felt the moist tug of a mouth at my breast and I moaned in rapture. I felt the familiar pain of anticipation between my thighs and squirmed with longing. My mouth was being covered again but this time a forceful, sensuous tongue was licking at mine. I opened my eyes languidly, and though it was quite dark, I recognized the eyes staring back at me.

Icy blue eyes, like looking into frost-covered arctic waters. I tried to tell myself that it really was just a dream, but I knew the truth. Instead of pushing him away or screaming as I should have, I pulled him closer. He licked at me and touched me in ways that I thought would end me, but he didn't stop. Finally he conquered me, thrusting himself inside of me with such ease and want, it made me wonder momentarily how I had believed vampires incapable of such deeds, but only momentarily. His hair fell lushly around me as he pulsed rhythmically in and out of me. Just when I thought I could feel nothing more erotic he tongued playfully at my neck and then plunged indulgently into the vein of life blood there. It was just as passionate and arousing as the attentive piercing he was doing below.

I felt that I would again pass into unconsciousness, this time from his deep kiss, then Dardanos pulled slightly away. I heard my breath catch in surprise at his sudden withdrawal from both my neck and between my legs.

"You must drink from me, my darling one," he uttered gently.

He pulled me tenderly up to sit and lightly pressed my lips to his chest. Before I knew exactly what he meant for me to do I found myself licking wantonly at a cool, metallic liquid that seemed to be seeping from his chest.

In that moment I felt intoxicated in a way I had never been before. I saw images which I assumed were from Dardanos's past. I even saw Elizabeth Cranford, who I did indeed look exactly like, only that she had dark crimson hair. I felt Dardanos telling me he loved me, not aloud, but through the blood. There was darkness and light as if they were tangible objects, and voices, so many voices, I couldn't tell if they were speaking or singing. Through all of it Dardanos was beckoning me back; *my love*, as he whispered I was to him. Too soon it was over; Dardanos tugged me gently away from himself and lay me back down on the bed. I felt his lips once more on mine, and his hand cupping my face lovingly.

"You are mine now, forever," was the last thing he said before slipping a ring onto my left ring finger and leaving the room.

ဆ**19** beta

When I at last opened my eyes they were met with the agonizing sting of afternoon sunlight. I sat up abruptly, remembering the night before. It must have all been a dream or I wouldn't be awake in the day. Then I looked down and saw that I was completely naked. I jumped out of bed, again stumbling off the wretched platform, and gazed at myself in the mirror.

"My God," I whispered, putting my hand over my mouth.

There were indeed bite marks on my neck, though they looked as if they had healed some, and there was a small trickle of dried blood running down to my left breast. I certainly looked paler, but I also hadn't eaten much or seen daylight in days. Then I noticed my eyes. They had always been abnormally bright green, but now they looked as if there were a flickering candle behind them. They seemed to swirl and swim with so many hues of emerald, like a kaleidoscope, I found myself transfixed looking at them.

Even my hair seemed different; it didn't have that glorious sheen Rachel's hair had had, but it did look as if I'd spent hours putting every single pin-straight piece into place, though in actuality I'd just rolled out of bed after quite an exuberant night. I noticed my moonstone necklace lying just below the mirror on the fireplace mantel. I hadn't even noticed it had been removed from around my neck. I grabbed it up, guiltily thinking about what I'd done the night before, and hung the necklace once more at my throat. As I let go of the chain I noticed the glint of a ring on my left hand, remembering Dardanos had slipped something onto my ring finger just before he had left.

My heart sank as I looked down at the ring circling my left hand ring finger. After my run in with Rachel I now knew what a black moonstone looked like, otherwise I would have had no idea what kind of gem I was looking at. The ring Rachel had worn looked like a pebble compared to what I was wearing. The massive, luminous silvery-gray stone was in a Victorian-style oval setting of silver consisting of three layers of intricate filigree designs, each layer set a little lower than the last, making the moonstone much higher than the outer layer of the ring. The outer layer was a mix of silver spirals and what looked like small, round, black diamonds. The ring was so large it very nearly went from knuckle to knuckle.

Looking at the ring I wondered if it had actually belonged to Elizabeth, or if Dardanos had simply had one made that looked like one he had given her. It also made me wonder if I was going to end up having the same fate as Elizabeth, caught in the middle of Lex and Dardanos and ending up dead. I thought I remembered Lex saying something like that; there had been an argument and Elizabeth was killed accidentally? How would everyone even react when they found out Dardanos had turned me? Were they going to shun me and consider me the enemy just as they had Rachel? It was too much to worry about at the moment, my first priority was to try to find a way out, then I could figure out whether to take the chance of going back to Lex's mansion or not.

I turned to the open window, venturing yet again to see if the drop was as hopeless as I'd thought the night before, but I was struck by a sudden draining weakness. I didn't understand what was happening. If Dardanos had turned me into a vampire why wasn't I burning alive in the sunlight? The sunlight was definitely affecting me, but it should have killed me. Maybe he hadn't turned me, or hadn't finished turning me. I decided to test it and walked to the window. As soon as the full glare of the sun's rays hit my body I collapsed onto the floor. I didn't lose consciousness, but I felt unbelievably powerless. I wasn't sure if I'd even be able to stand without help.

Then I heard the doorknob to the room shaking as if someone were struggling with the lock. I was too frail to even feel embarrassed that I was nude and lying futilely on the floor. Dardanos's hunters would never do anything to me that would infuriate their general, so I had nothing to worry about on that front. Still, as an unwilling captive, it was maddening to be found in such a vulnerable state. I would probably get picked up and carried back to bed like an insolent child, followed by a reprimand of how I should know better than to do such things.

Instead I received the shock of my life.

When the door finally opened it was not a hunter that entered.

"Dallen?" I whimpered sadly.

As soon as he saw me lying on the floor he rushed to me, huddling down to take me in his arms.

He held me tightly and cried, "I'm too late. Oh, God, I'm too late."

I tried to reassure him, "I'm okay, Dallen, I just feel faint. I didn't eat last night, and I think Dardanos may have drugged me."

Finally he released me from his embrace and put his hands to my cheeks. "Darling, you're a vampire."

I think I actually laughed. "Dallen, if I were a vampire the sun would have burned me to death."

"You haven't completed the transformation. Once those bites heal completely, you will burn in the sun," he explained before once again taking me in his arms. "That's why we need to get you out of here, now, before you're unable to move about in the day."

Without a word Dallen lifted me up and placed me lovingly on the bed. He dressed me without ceremony in the corset and long skirt which had been tossed on the floor next to the bed. He found a pair of shin high black Victorian lace-up boots that had also been lying somewhere on the floor. I still felt weak but forced myself to stand.

"My God, you're beautiful," Dallen exclaimed as he kissed me briskly on the lips. "Can you walk?"

"I don't know. I'll try," I answered. "My book, don't forget..." I said pointing to the desk where I'd laid my poetry book the night before.

Dallen grabbed my book and I could see he registered the thought that Dardanos had obviously read its contents, and he seemed to close his eyes momentarily as if accepting the consequences. He then opened the door, slowly extended his head out to make sure it was empty before half pulling me out behind him into the hallway. I can't even tell you how we escaped, it happened so fast, and I had to be half carried much of the way. I remembered entering another bedroom on the same floor my room had been on, then suddenly we were in a library, and just down the hall from there we exited out of a small side door which led us outside. Dallen led me to a car parked, somewhat conspicuously I thought, on the lawn. It was all I could do to try to stay conscious as he dragged me toward the car. Once inside I let my head lull against the headrest, trying to keep my eyes from closing.

"We're going to make it. Lillian, it's okay, you can close your eyes. We're off the estate."

Before I completely faded I turned to Dallen and reached clumsily for his hand. "You came for me," I whispered in awe.

He smiled tenderly and proclaimed, "Of course. I'll always come for you. My life is nothing without you."

I could feel that I didn't have very long before the marks left by Dardanos were completely healed. Dallen was already driving much faster than he should have been, and he warned me that we might have to stop until the sun went down. I knew what he was saying; if I turned while we were still in the car, during daylight, I would start to burn, and he may not be able to get me to shelter in time. On the other hand if we had to stop we would be wasting valuable time to get back to the mansion before the councils left for their assault on Dardanos. I hoped we weren't too late; the councils should have met the night before, and I worried that they may have put their plan into action immediately. I needed to be there when they confronted Dardanos, and I needed to prove, if only to myself, that the only emotion connecting Dardanos and me was hatred.

I probably shouldn't tell you, because I don't know what you will think of me, but I didn't take Dardanos's ring off my finger and hurl it out the window of the moving car as might seem appropriate after all of the things he'd done. Instead I soundlessly slipped the ring off of my left hand and put it on my right hand ring finger, and that is where the ring sits to this day. I have no explanation for why I can't get rid of it, or why I feel compelled to wear it always. I like to tell myself that it is a reminder of what I must do, the ring cannot leave my finger until Dardanos has left this Earth. I tell myself that it is a penance I must pay, wearing the ring of my enemy, until I destroy him, and earn the right to remove it.

As we drove I opened my book up to a blank page, trying to keep my mind off of the fear that any moment my skin was going to start sizzling. I stared at the black moonstone and thought about all of the things Dardanos had said to me the night before. Well, really he had said them to Elizabeth, and barely acknowledged that I had any mind or soul of my own. It made me feel empty to think that I was wanted because I looked like someone, and not for any reason that had to do with who I was. I wrote my agitation...
He will worship
And he will try his charms
To push me back

And let her take hold
Anything for her
He would give
Anything for her

We made it back to the mansion at 11:00 PM. The marks on my throat had only just healed entirely two hours earlier, giving us no reason to stop, but what we found when we arrived stopped my heart. Well, technically it had been the vampiric blood that had stopped my heart, but if my heart had still been beating what we found would have stopped it...dead. I knew my transformation was complete because I no longer felt weak or dazed, but staring at the mansion I wanted to crumble to the ground and never get back up.

The mansion, or rather what was left of it, was charred in untidy heaps of smoldering rubble. I could still make out the foundation, but nothing more. The entire house seemed to have collapsed upon itself, leaving not one wall or frame standing, and there were still random piles of ember visible among the wreckage. Even the gardens had been scorched clean. It was obvious; no one had come to put the blaze out, no firefighters, no police, no media. Whatever had happened had been kept secret.

Dallen, who'd kept a respectful silence this whole time must have read my mind and informed, "Some hunters have the ability to influence people's thoughts, not control them or brainwash them, but make suggestions that weak-minded people are very willing to accept. They probably convinced someone in charge that there was a controlled fire being set and there was no need for anyone to check it out. We've used that excuse before."

I just nodded my head as tears rolled down my face.

"What's the good of being immortal if everyone is dead?" I asked listlessly.

"They are not all dead," came a stiff-accented female voice.

I whirled around, caught off guard, trying to see where the voice had come from. Suddenly, out of the shadows of the rubble came Sylvia, her long white-blonde hair billowing behind her. I was so relieved to see her I ran to her, much to her surprise, and swept her up in a warm embrace. Sylvia pulled me back slightly, putting her hands on my face, and looking into my eyes she gave me a sad smile.

She told me in a very tender tone, "I know we have not been...best of friends, but I always wish best for you," Sylvia paused and asked uneasily, "He did this to you?"

I nodded my head and admitted, "Yes, Dardanos turned me." I lowered my head in guilt as I remembered the lustful night I'd shared with Dardanos in which I willingly allowed him to turn me. I hoped Dallen wasn't probing my mind at that moment.

Sylvia again hugged me briefly before reassuring me, "It does not matter who turned you, just who is the side you will be on." Then for the first time she took notice of Dallen and I feared I would have to test my powers by protecting him from Sylvia, but instead she just raised her chin in his direction and declared, "And your man, he is rescuing you? I think we know who is the side he is on."

I turned and smiled proudly at Dallen, realizing for the first time that his actions had proved not only his loyalty to me, but his betrayal to Dardanos. Whether he had wanted to demonstrate it or not he was now a traitor in Dardanos's eyes. As fearful as I was for his safety, I couldn't help feeling astounded by the steady faithfulness he'd shown me and the inexplicable risk he'd taken in recovering me from Dardanos's clutches. I turned back toward the mansion and took in the scene of wretched waste and destruction.

"Who is still alive?" I asked sadly, bracing myself for the worst, and saying a silent prayer that at least Lex and Ben were not among the casualties.

Sylvia seemed confused at first then replied, "But no one has died. We still do not know of Una, Kara, and Demetrius and must assume they are no more, but fire did not kill here...no one."

I wanted to scream for joy but I had to make sure I understood Sylvia correctly. "I don't understand, how could anyone make it out of that alive?" I asked, gesturing to the ruins.

Sylvia explained, "The fire was set day before today. We assume you were taken same day fire is being set. Your Alexander, he suggest all council should sleep here that last night of meeting, I do not think you were in room when we talked of it." She paused seeing the look of shock on my face and giggled. "Your Alexander, he is genius sometimes. All safe-rooms in his house are able to withstand fire. Worst problem we had was digging out of rubble, but all rooms below ground were perfect fine."

"So Ben and Lex?" I asked excitedly, still not wanting to give myself false hope.

"They are fine," Sylvia answered warmly.

I closed my eyes thankfully and then asked, "Where are they?"

She replied, "I wait here until four and then I join them." She paused seeing my look of disappointment. "They go to England last night. They should start assault this night. I stay to see if last council that never showed makes it, but Malika did not seem surprised when they did not show last night. Still, I wait, just in case."

"They're really going after him?" I asked.

Finally Dallen was stirred to join the conversation, "Wait, they're going after General D?"

I turned and scolded him lightly, "You can't call him that anymore. He is no longer your general, but yes, that was the plan. I had been trying to convince Ben and Lex to let me become a vampire so I might fight as well. It seems I, at least, have one thing to thank Dardanos for. He has made me a somewhat worthy enemy."

"It's suicide!" Dallen exclaimed. "This is my fault! I should have stayed, I should have talked to Lex, I should have told them everything I knew!"

I put my hand on his shoulder to calm him. "Dallen, a life spent in fear is no life at all. Even if the council hadn't decided to go after Dardanos, I would've had to, alone. Everyone has been trying to protect me, but the truth is I'm the only one that can end this *thing* between Dardanos and me. If I ever want any kind of life that is worth living I have to confront Dardanos at some point. You have done more than I could ever have imagined and I won't ask you to do more than you have, but I must go. I have to face him again. Whether you come with me or not, whether you want me to or not, I am going," I lectured, knowing he would put up the same arguments Lex and Ben had.

I could see Dallen desperately wanted to argue against my decision, but instead he lowered his eyes and conceded, "What shall we do?"

I tried to bite back my triumphant smile as I turned back to Sylvia and suggested, "I don't think you should wait until four in the morning for this other council. Let's go to them. We'll all go and find out once and for all if they are going to help us. If not, we'll leave immediately for England."

"One problem being I cannot carry two people and fly, maybe one but not two," Sylvia answered discouragingly. "How can we do that in one night if not to fly? Driving will take too long and the airplanes, they take too long."

I had decided on this plan without first being sure I would be able to do what I needed to do in order for my plan to work. So without explaining myself I took a deep, shaky breath, crouched down slightly as I'd seen Rachel do, and pushed with all my might off of the ground.

I had put way too much effort into my first attempt at flying and shot well above the clouds in seconds. I had no idea how to control what I was doing, but spent the next few minutes trying out different positions to get a better feel for how to maneuver. It was glorious! I never thought in my wildest dreams I would do anything even close to that. I'd always thought sky divers were out of their minds, and here I was whooshing through tangible air. I had no fear, my body seemed to know exactly what to do, and somehow I knew that even if I fell from this height it would barely hurt, let alone kill me. That knowledge alone exhilarated me in a way that I had never known in my life. The feeling of not being afraid of something I had never done, it was gone, and it was wonderful after a life of fearing so many things. Finally I set myself, gracefully I'd like to think, back on the ground in exactly the same spot I'd taken off from.

Dallen was staring at me as if I'd just defied everything he'd ever known in his life. I found his look of amazement amusing as I knew he must have studied and maybe even witnessed many vampire abilities while with OPTS, yet he seemed to be speechless.

Sylvia laughed lightly and admitted, "Well, that is solving that. Amazing, I never see new born vampire fly in first month of being turned."

So that was why Dallen was staring. Of course, he would know all the little ins and outs of being a vampire as a trained hunter; it must have been rare to possess such powers and abilities so soon after being turned.

"I saw Rachel do it, just a few days after Dardanos had turned her. I just assumed I would be able to do it as well," I explained shyly to Dallen, worried I had shocked him to repulsion as Rachel had mentioned Osborn had felt when she'd been turned.

Instead of giving me a disgusted look or ridiculing me, Dallen walked up to me, put his hands behind my head, and pulled me into a vigorous kiss. I accidentally pricked the edge of his tongue with my newly acquired teeth, but he either didn't notice or didn't care. For a split second the tiny drops of blood that found their way down my throat ignited a vision. It wasn't a vision from Dallen's past or any deep dark secret that he'd kept from me, it was an image of us, exactly as we were, locked together in a passionate kiss. For that second nothing else existed, only us, and it seemed that second lasted years.

Eventually Dallen pulled away, still holding his hands behind my head, and declared, "You...are amazing!"

Sylvia cleared her throat and suggested, "We should be leaving. I will carry your man, you will have hard enough time to be carrying yourself."

Dallen and I just nodded. Sylvia turned Dallen to face her and put his arms around her neck, then she wound her own arms around his waist. I worried that Sylvia might not take Dallen's safety as seriously as I would, but like she said I would have a hard enough time on my own. I wasn't even sure how far I would be able to fly. After all, I'd only been a vampire for just over three hours; there must have been limits to what I could do.

"Ready?" Sylvia asked.

I again took a deep breath and replied, "As ready as I'm going to be. Don't worry about me, just go, I'll follow."

Thirty minutes later we were touching down just outside of a large city. I could see water off to one side and even mountains in the distance. I had thought the city we'd seen off in the distance to our right as we'd continued north was New York, but after seeing the quiet, small town charm of the village we'd entered I wasn't sure.

It was Dallen who spoke, chattering his teeth and rubbing his arms to get warm, "Where are we? Was that New York City we passed?"

"Yes, that was New York. This town is being Tarrytown. We are...mmm...twenty five miles outside the City," Sylvia answered.

I felt so foolish for not considering how uncomfortable it would be for Dallen to fly. As a vampire I no longer felt discomfort from the sting of the wind or the cold, but Dallen looked as if he'd just been rescued from a fall into a frozen lake. I started rubbing his arms and chest to help him revive some warmth.

"I'm so sorry. Are you alright?" I asked as I tried desperately to warm him with my cool, bloodless body.

He smiled appreciatively, stating, "Of course, I'll be fine. I should have known better. I am supposed to be an expert on all things vampire. I'll have to find something warmer for the trip across the Atlantic."

We followed Sylvia on foot to a huge Tudor-style mansion. In all honesty I felt a little uneasy just walking up, uninvited, to the headquarters of an unknown council. Sylvia didn't stop to explain anything to us so I assumed everything was fine and she would have warned us if there was something to be warned about. Dallen, though not saying a word, took my hand nervously. He also was not used to being thrown into a situation without being prepared. Sylvia rang the doorbell and left us to wait in uncomfortable silence.

A young man dressed in what looked like black velvet, obviously a vampire, opened the door and sneered at Sylvia, "You again? Come in then, I'll take you to Vasile." He pronounced it as Vah-see- lay. When he saw Dallen and me he put his hand up to stop Sylvia from entering. "Who are they? Why have you brought a mortal among us?"

Apparently not all councils were as lax as The Seventh Council, perhaps because they didn't have to put up with Lex as one of their members. I hadn't even considered that bringing a mortal among unfamiliar vampires would be a problem. Obviously, I had a lot to learn. Instead of leaving the talking to Sylvia, whom they trusted, though clearly didn't respect, I pushed forward and got a little too aggressive with the door man.

"My name is Lillian Thorne. I am the daughter of Ben Thorne, vampire child of Dardanos, and intimate friend of Malika, Tor, and Lex Cavanaugh. Who the hell are you?!" I exclaimed a bit too loudly.

The door man was taken aback by my outburst and changed to a more hesitant tone. "We don't allow mortals in our safe-house," he said almost apologetically.

I raised my eyebrows and pressed, "Well, it seems tonight you'll be making an exception. Be so kind as to tell Vasile that we are here and that *I* would like to speak to him. It's urgent, in case you were wondering."

The young man didn't argue, but opened the door for us to enter. He left us for a moment standing in the hall, presumably to announce us to Vasile, and returned gesturing for us to follow him. The dark, old-style home was much too silent and dim for my taste; I was used to Lex's mansion where everything was illuminated and there was always some kind of noise, day and night. This place reminded me of exactly what movies portrayed vampire lairs to look like: dark, creepy, eerily quiet, flickering candle light, and all too serious and elegantly dressed inhabitants. Although I guess I shouldn't have mocked, showing up with my lecture on who I was, and still dressed in my corset and Victorian-style traveling skirt. I certainly looked the part of a romantically dark, supernatural, movie starlet.

The door man led us into what I will refer to as the throne room. I believe I heard someone at some point call it the great hall, but I hardly think that appellation gave it justice. It was a vast, spacious room with vaulted ceilings; very nearly as massive as the main hall in which Lex had many of his outlandish parties. There was no table to which the members of the council sat, unfortunately the council was not present, but instead the room held what looked like short pews, able to accommodate perhaps three or four people each. The pews were situated into four rows, two on each side of the room, and looked as if they numbered close to thirty. All councils were to have a maximum number of thirteen members including the elders, so obviously the extra seating space was either for special functions or a whim of the elder.

I say the elder, because unlike The Seventh Council, this council only had one, Vasile. Perched at the head of the dozens of pews was a single chair, hence why I called it the throne room. The chair seemed to be made of a dark ebony wood and had a regally high back with ornate points on either side. The plush red velvet cushion covering the chair was occupied by a middle aged man with piercing eyes.

He was the first vampire I'd ever seen that was past the age of forty. He must have been between fifty and fifty-five when he'd been turned . He had short black hair that had already started to gray on the sides before he'd been turned and though he certainly looked young for his age, unlike most vampires I'd seen, he had a few well etched wrinkles at the sides of his mouth and around his eyes. Still, if I'd seen him and not known he was a vampire, I would have considered him a very handsome man.

"I hear from my attendant, that you think yourself very important, Miss," Vasile boomed condescendingly.

I noted that his man, the attendant, seemed embarrassed by the comment, and hung his head. Perhaps he noticed the way I turned toward him and glared angrily, as Vasile made the comment. I found it strange, though, to see a vampire, obviously older than I, cower at my stare. Was he scared of the names I had mentioned, all too proudly, when I had introduced myself? Had I really become that much more assertive now that I was a vampire?

I walked boldly forward and addressed Vasile without fear, but certainly with more respect than he had decided to show us. "Sir, I understand that you know nothing about me and that I have entered your house without an invitation, but we are facing a crucible, a turn of events that could affect every immortal. All I ask is that you listen to my plea with impartial ears."

Vasile seemed surprised by my words and was lost in thought before assenting, "Very well, I will hear what you have to say."

I took another step forward, ready to let loose a torrent of words that would surely sway him to our cause, when I felt my feet falter. It was not out of fear, but out of weakness that my body was not obeying me. I again tried to take a step closer to Vasile when I fell ungraciously to the floor. I didn't know what was happening, I'd felt like I'd been pushing myself this whole time, but I didn't think vampires felt fatigue so I had ignored the sensations, reasoning that it must have been because I'd just received The Immortal Fate. I didn't have any kind of warning that I was going to eventually lose my strength altogether, it was so sudden. I was half sitting on the floor with the palms of my hands holding me up for support, trying desperately to figure out what was wrong with me.

Dallen rushed to me, crouching down, and putting his hand on my back protectively. "Lillian, are you all right?"

I suddenly felt an uncontrollable urge to lunge at him. Though I didn't, I did feel my mouth open involuntarily as I bared my fangs, and swept my open mouth through the air that still held his scent. I closed my eyes momentarily, as I imagined I could taste Dallen in the very air that he had disturbed by moving so close to me. I was so ashamed of my inability to control myself that I cupped my hand over my mouth and pushed Dallen, a little too forcefully, away.

"When was the last time you fed, my dear?" came the now attentive voice of Vasile.

I looked up, everything swimming before my eyes and answered lethargically, "Never."

At last Sylvia made her presence known, I'd almost forgotten she was there, and explained, "My Lord, she only just receive the fate last night and finally turn but four hour ago. She does not know of feeding I think."

Vasile looked down on me with renewed interest. "Only four hours as a vampire and already acting like a queen. So, my dear, are you certain that you are ready to face Dardanos? Your maker...and your lover?"

I looked up at him, feeling my mortal fears returning. I felt like a child being lectured, and all I could do was hang my head in shame. "He is not my lover," I desperately contradicted.

Vasile seemed to smile to himself, as if he had read things from my mind which he knew I didn't want him to know. He stated frankly, "I know who he thinks you are. I know what he has sacrificed to get you back, and I know what he is willing to risk to have you...forever. So, my question is, are you ready to face a will greater than any other on Earth, one that will not cease until it has possessed its prize? Are you ready to face demons that you don't even know exist yet and ignore them to complete your task? Can you ignore the past, in order to forge a new future and destroy the man that may very well have influenced your very life to be what it is?

With all the will I possessed I forced my head to turn toward Vasile as I uttered defiantly, "I have no choice. If I have any love for those that have died, if I have any hope for happiness, then I must go after Dardanos. I must destroy him, no matter what I find out, no matter what the price, no matter what happens to me in the end. I must either fight him...or give in to him."

A NIGHT IN THE UN-LIFE...

Lillian tried to push the image of Dardanos from her mind, but those glacial eyes wouldn't leave her. She still had dreams about Dardanos. Sometimes she wondered if he were somehow putting the images in her mind, because they seemed to always consist of him declaring his love for her. Sometimes she actually played with the idea of calling out to him, trying to find him, just to be with another of her kind, but then she would think of all the lives he destroyed and the happiness he had stolen from her.

No, Dardanos was the enemy, and eventually she knew she would have to face him. After everything he'd done and the ends to which he would go to possess her, Lillian knew her only choice was to destroy him. Unfortunately, from time to time the memory of Dardanos's lips on her body and the feel of his solid form pressed against her crept into her mind, and in her loneliness she sometimes allowed the memories to linger. Later she always felt guilty for allowing herself to feel anything other than pure hatred for the man that had taken her whole life from her.

Lillian closed the laptop, not wanting to even see the name Dardanos any more that night. She knew that her day sleep would be inundated by Dardanos's face. She was not looking forward to slipping into unconsciousness that morning and reliving any intimate moments with her enemy, but she did still have a good three hours before sunrise to fill her time with not thinking about Dardanos.

"What to do? What to do?" Lillian quizzed the ceiling as she tapped her hands on her knees.

Suddenly the events of earlier that night replayed in her head. She turned her eyes down to her desk and picked up the moonstone necklace Ash had given her. She hadn't put it on. It didn't seem right to take off the necklace Dallen had given her in exchange for the one Ash had just bought. Deep down Lillian still held out hope that Dallen had been right about moonstone bringing lovers back together. She hoped it would bring him back to her...if he was still alive. Lillian looked down at the moonstone on the desk again.

"Maybe it's time to find out what he does in that studio," Lillian stated mischievously.

Lillian tip-toed down the stairs from her apartment, listening carefully for any sound to indicate Ash was in his studio. She was sure he wasn't inside, but couldn't decide how she would get in. She was fairly certain he wasn't the type to invest in a security system, but there was a dead-bolt lock.

Lillian sighed, "I'll just have to break it."

Lillian had hoped she would be able to sneak into Ash's studio undetected, but there was just no way around a dead-bolt. She would have to use her unnatural strength to push the door in, and that would unfortunately damage the door jam and frame. He would know someone broke into the studio, and would most likely call the police.

Lillian stared at the door, uncertain if she should risk exposing herself by committing a crime, but her senses were telling her she needed to get into that studio. "He's hiding something. I know it," she reassured herself.

Lillian put her hand over the dead-bolt and placed her shoulder against the door as she gently nudged her body against it. That was all it took for the dead-bolt to rip through the door jam and the door frame on the other side, allowing the door itself to swing easily open.

At first Lillian was unsure where she should start looking, but once her eyes focused in the room dimly lit by the street lights peeking slightly through the blinds she actually gasped in disbelief. The studio was filled to overflowing with finished paintings. Lillian walked the perimeter of the studio, taking in each painting, trying to estimate how many there were. Fifty? More?

Lillian spun in a circle in shock and muttered, "There all of...me."

"Now you know why I didn't want you to see my paintings," came the disappointed voice of Ash behind her.

Lillian turned toward the open door to see Ash standing there watching her. Lillian glanced back at the paintings, recognizing some of the moments Ash had caught of her. One showed her walking on the opposite side of the street, her coat pulled tightly around her. One showed her in mid twirl, obviously from the night they went swing dancing. One was of her lying passed out peacefully on her couch. Many were merely close-ups of her face in different lighting, different colors, from different angles, and even different painting styles. Then Lillian noticed one painting, very nearly finished, still on the easel.

Lillian as a goddess on a pedestal, her strawberry blond hair blowing up and out, a dagger in one hand and a flower in the other, and in the background many hues and shades of gray like billowing smoke.

Ash noticed Lillian staring at the painting and explained, "This is how I see you. More beautiful than any mortal could possibly be, but dangerous...and yet somehow tender, caught in some indiscernible darkness."

Lillian opened her mouth to say something, but didn't know what to say. Ash had caught her perfectly. Her eyes actually filled with tears staring at the painting done by a man that wanted nothing more than to be near her.

"There's something I have to tell you, Ash," Lillian said somberly.

Ash swallowed, hoping Lillian was going to reveal her troubled past and not lecture him on being a creepy stalker-type. "Anything. Tell me."

Lillian turned to look at Ash with concern and said sadly, "I don't have time to explain everything right now. Please, believe me, it will take time what I have to tell you." Lillian sighed, "You probably won't even believe me. Promise me, tomorrow night."

Ash nodded his head nervously. "When?"

Lillian thought a moment about what she really meant to tell Ash, and decided her best bet was to be somewhere he wouldn't feel threatened. "Let's meet somewhere. The diner on the corner? Midnight?"

"You want to meet somewhere?" Ash asked curiously.

Lillian pursed her lips. "I think it will be better...for you. Just promise me."

"Okay, I promise. I will meet you at the diner at midnight."

Lillian kissed Ash on the cheek. "I have to prepare for what I'm going to tell you."

Then she walked out of the studio, leaving Ash standing there confused. She went straight to her apartment, plopping down at her desk, and opening her laptop.

"I guess I'll have to finish this tonight."

Lillian had decided she would finish her book that night, and give it to Ash to read the following night when they met at the diner. Hopefully he would take her seriously, but no matter what happened at least her book would be done, and her time there wouldn't have been wasted.

"Let's see, where was I? Ah, yes, Vasile and the Great Hall."

ཀྵ20ཀྵ

My strength had completely seeped out of me and I lay on the floor of The Throne Room not even able to force myself to rise. As embarrassed as I was by this show of weakness, I was also certain that this would be the end of me. Why had I been so ignorant to not think of feeding? Sure I'd never done it, but I'd seen it before, and I knew it was the one intrinsic drawback of being an immortal.

I could hear voices around me. Apparently Dallen and Sylvia were talking heatedly with Vasile about something. I couldn't focus on the sound; I couldn't even open my eyes, or maybe they were open and I just couldn't see.

Suddenly I felt a strong, cool hand lift me from under the back of my neck. I heard whispering in my ear, but it seemed so far away I couldn't really understand what it was saying; it was soothing and made me forget how scared I felt at being so weak. Then, abruptly, I saw the bright daylight of blood in my vision. Instead of darkness clouding my eyes, I was plunged into a vivid trance of bright red blooms unfolding. I felt no pain, though I knew someone was drawing the blood out of my neck. It was not an erotic feeling as I'd had with Dardanos, but more of a calming, dream-like feeling.

"Drink, my dear," I heard Vasile coaxing.

"But, My Lord, you have never allowed another to drink from you," came the voice of the young man who had escorted us in. He obviously didn't approve of his elder allowing an outsider to partake of his ancient blood.

I opened my eyes and found that my mouth was clamped tightly upon Vasile's wrist. I was still on the floor in front of the throne, but now Vasile was kneeling in front of me forcing his life blood into me by way of his gashed wrist. There were so many visions flooding my head, like a slide-show on fast forward, that I couldn't distinguish what any of them were. I knew they were visions from Vasile's past, and just from the sheer number of endlessly streaming scenes, it was obvious this guy had been around a long, long time. His blood tasted so different from Dardanos's, not like cool melted metal, but more like liquid earth; a sort of thick, rich soil flowing out of him. Even as visions passed before my mind's eye of Vasile's life I was able to simultaneously see what was in front of me, and it was dazzling, literally. Everything from the walls and floor, to the furniture, and to the others watching us in silence seemed to emit a strange sparkle, as if I'd gotten many colors of glitter blown into my eyes.

Before I had time to really enjoy the hypnotic images in front of me Vasile pushed my shoulder lightly to disconnect me from his wrist, and ended up sending me sliding backward across the floor a few feet. I felt a momentary pang of disappointment that it was over, but then felt a little embarrassed to have been shown such extraordinary attention from a complete stranger, and one who just happens to be perhaps one of the most powerful vampires in existence.

"I apologize, my dear, sometimes I don't know my own strength," Vasile said as he turned to sit upon his throne once more. "I know why you are here, but there was a reason we did not show in Florida. My council and I will not be joining you, nor will any of our people."

I pulled myself up to stand giving more effort than I needed. My body had a kind of weightlessness to it, I almost felt if I'd put more effort into getting up I would have floated off the ground.

Steadying myself I entreated, "Sir, I don't know what you've been told, but if Dardanos isn't stopped he will eventually come after your council with his trained hunters, and then all the vampires residing within your region. This is an opportunity for us all to band together and attack him in force."

Vasile smiled affectionately at me and confided, "I understand why you feel you must go after him." Vasile stopped, stealing a sly glance at the black moonstone on my right hand. "If I knew someone was coming for me, I would want to make the first move as well, but I have others to think of. You do not understand the power he possesses."

"You're afraid of him?" I asked, disappointed.

Vasile's face became hard as he jumped to his feet. "I am afraid of nothing, my girl! I am older than you can imagine, even older than your own elders, and it is quite possible that I will never die; for I know of nothing that can kill me!" He seemed to calm himself before walking down the steps to where I stood, explaining tenderly, "I must think of my coven...my council and those we govern. Should I bring them into such a fight many would perish. It is my responsibility to protect them, just as it is theirs to protect me. I am sorry, but I won't gamble with their lives. I have already given you what you need to defeat Dardanos."

"What do you mean?" I questioned timidly.

He raised his hand toward me showing a now faded scar on his wrist. "My blood. It is different for everyone, the power it gives, the time it takes for the power to mature, but rest assured you will now face Dardanos as very nearly his equal. I suggest you feed again before you face Dardanos and his minions. Remember, blood is strength, blood is power. I wish you luck, my dear, and I do hope we shall meet again under better circumstances. Good Evening," he uttered nodding his head to us, walking out of the room, and leaving us with his attendant.

The young man led us back to the front door silently, stealing jealous glances at me. I assumed he was still angry that Vasile had shared his powerful blood with me, and obviously had never even shared it with his own council members. I didn't feel any more powerful after drinking from Vasile, but like he said it was different for everyone; what powers you develop and how long it takes for such things to develop. I would have felt more prepared to battle Dardanos if Vasile, at least, had agreed to fight with us, but I had to take what I could and hope for the best.

Just before I walked out the door the attendant grabbed my arm. "You have been shown unheard of favoritism. Do not pay him back by mentioning us or what has happened here to Dardanos." With that he let go of my arm, never looking me in the eye, and hurriedly started closing the door before I had completely walked out.

It was obvious Vasile was a very strict, very fear-inspiring elder. His attendant treated him more like a king than merely the head of his council. Then, here I am just showing up on his doorstep in the middle of the night, a stranger and fledgling vampire, treating him with as much respect as any authority figure, but not the god-like reverence the young man showed, and I basically received the crown-jewel of gifts for a vampire from this most-elevated leader. Yeah, that would probably piss me off a little too, so I really couldn't hold it against the guy. At least the trip wasn't a complete waste of time, or at least, I hoped it hadn't been. Until I actually tested my abilities I had no idea if sharing Vasile's blood had actually increased my chances of surviving against Dardanos.

"Well, that was being a waste of our time!" Sylvia exclaimed in annoyance.

Dallen said in awe, "Actually, that was unbelievable. I never knew there were any vampires older than Malika or Tor. Furthermore, receiving the gift of blood, of ancient blood, you really have a fighting chance now,

Lillian. Who knows what you'll be capable of now."

I nodded stoically, unable to be excited about acquiring abilities that I would need to fight for my own life, because I had no other choice, unless I gave into Dardanos. I tried not to think about it. What mattered now was getting to England to help those that had gone earlier. I hoped we wouldn't be too late.

"Plus," Dallen added wryly, "They had a wide assortment of fur lined coats to choose from in the foyer." He held up a shin-length, leather jacket lined with black fur, smiling triumphantly.

I couldn't help but laugh. "All right, bad-ass, put your leather jacket on and let's get this non-stop to England underway."

I had worried that flying across the Atlantic would be far too much for me, but as I discovered it was not nearly as long of a trip as I'd thought, and my encounter with Vasile seemed to have given me boundless energy. I didn't seem able to tire myself, even as I shot through the air faster than Sylvia could keep up, and then doubled back to where she still held steady with Dallen in her arms. I didn't have the confidence to admit that I had gained more power and stamina, with the ease with which I was maneuvering and at such high speeds I should have offered to take Dallen from Sylvia. I didn't trust myself, though, and as a result we were unable to go at a faster pace.

We made our descent onto a sandy beach on the edge of a village called Braunton, arriving just over two hours from the time we'd left. We were unsure which direction Cuckfield was and how far, so we stopped at a hotel situated just above the beach, Saunton Sands Hotel, to get ourselves back on track. Dallen tried pointing out that he knew where we were going, but I then proceeded to point out that it's one thing to know the general direction, but as we were flying hundreds if not thousands of miles in the air, general directions become a bit obscure. We left the hotel with explanations, maps, and a promised discount should we ever decide to return to the hotel for some leisurely time. I told them as soon as I learned how not to burst into flames in the sun I would surely return, but I don't think they got my joke.

Our destination was almost directly East of Braunton, so we just had to try to stay on a straight course. It wasn't so easy, we ended up descending three more times to get our bearings and redirect our path. Finally, nearly forty-five minutes later we landed just West of Cuckfield. It was nearing 4:30 AM, thankfully the sun didn't rise until 7:00 AM, giving us a little more time then we'd expected before we would have to find shelter.

Dallen suggested we should enter the grounds from the West through a wooded area; allowing us to approach the great manor house of OPTS from the rear instead of having to enter down a long tree-lined road from the front, which would afford us no cover. After crossing over what looked like a large pond we came upon the back corner of the house, but before we had even descended from our flight across the water we could hear commotion. There was nothing visible from where we stood; it seemed whatever was happening was confined to within the walls of the manor house or the very front lawn.

"I am not liking of all this silence," Sylvia commented as she was visibly trying to listen for any clue that our allies were inside.

Dallen turned to me and asked earnestly, "Can you hear anything?"

I forgot that as a vampire I may possess new abilities and blurted out, "I don't know, Dallen, perhaps my super-sonic hearing isn't working today."

As soon as I said it I felt foolish and waited for Dallen to point out my ignorance, but instead he explained, "With every ability you must learn to focus. Just try to shut everything else out and only pay attention to the sounds around you, and then will yourself to hear what you want."

It sounded idiotic, had anyone else told me that I would've thought they were purposely trying to make me look stupid, but as it was Dallen I took him seriously and tried. I closed my eyes, because as silly as I felt I didn't need to be looking at Dallen and Sylvia watching me. I tried focusing on just listening and found I was able to hear many more sounds than I'd realized I had been hearing this whole time. There were shouts and gunshots and screams, but I didn't let my mind focus on any of that. I desperately tried to focus my thoughts on Ben, I needed to know if he was alive.

I heard Ben's voice amongst a cacophony of other sounds, "Glen is gone! Lex, he's gone, there's nothing more we can do for him!"

I must have grimaced as I was listening as Sylvia asked with dread, "What is it? They are being dead, are they not?"

I lost my focus and opened my eyes. "Glen is dead. I heard Ben speaking to Lex." I paused pursing my lips to keep from crying and offered sadly, "At least we know Ben and Lex are still alive. There must be more alive because I could hear a lot of voices and screaming in the background."

"We had better get in there. There's an entrance on the South side of the house that not many know about. Hopefully we'll be able to sneak in there," Dallen said in a hushed voice, obviously not eager about having to break into OPTS, now as their enemy.

Before we even made it to the South wall I heard a scream from behind me. I whirled around to see Sylvia lying on the ground clutching at her side.

"I am being shot with something!" she yelled to me in obvious pain.

I looked around for some source of the bullet that had hit Sylvia, but saw nothing. I didn't understand what had happened; a mere bullet shouldn't have caused Sylvia more than an annoying sting. I ran back to her, puzzled as to why she seemed to be in so much pain. As I bent down to try to get her on her feet I felt something snapped around my neck. It felt like some kind of metal collar and as soon as it touched my skin my neck began to burn, but it was a cold burn, like having a block of ice wrapped around my neck. I started feeling dizzy as if I had been drugged, and yes, I do know how that feels. My body felt like jello and my eyes were fighting to focus. Suddenly Sylvia and I were surrounded by people in black military-style clothing.

"Dallen?" I tried to inquire.

I heard his voice from far away as he pleaded, "It's Iridium, Lillian! I'm sorry I didn't think to tell you! It's a weapon, I thought it was still in the experimental stage! I had no idea they were using it!"

I watched as Sylvia was being tied up with what looked like a long metal chain, like a chain used for necklaces, but it was too long to be a necklace. As soon as the chain touched her skin Sylvia seemed to become listless and weak. Her head seemed to loll back and forth on the ground as if she too were feeling the effects of a mood-depressing drug.

My head was foggy, but I managed to ask Dallen lethargically, "What are you talking about?"

It wasn't Dallen that answered me, but the man that was standing just behind me, obviously making sure I didn't get away, "It's like silver to a werewolf. We've found something just as useful as fire to kill you monsters." He tapped the heavy collar around my neck and scoffed, "It's also pretty good at sapping your strength. I am sorry, Lillian, that things had to turn out this way. You should have listened to Rachel, and gotten away before you became...contaminated."

I knew the voice. "Osborn?" I asked simply.

Osborn bent down to look me in the eyes and said in a hushed voice, "It is a shame such a pretty thing being turned into a monster." He brushed the hair back from my face. "Even now, I could almost look past that. I see why he's so fascinated with you." Osborn cleared his throat uncomfortably and explained, "Lucky for you General D wants you alive, your friends won't be so lucky."

Without another word he jumped up and gave a signal to the hunters surrounding Sylvia. They pointed what looked like normal handguns at her incapacitated body and riddled her with bullets. I didn't understand what they thought to accomplish because even the weakest vampire would just heal from such an assault. To my utter horror, her body seemed to not be able to regenerate fast enough, and parts of her body were actually turning gray, becoming ash, and falling away. I watched in revulsion as Sylvia was reduced to an outline of gray-white powder.

"She was supposed to have been spared, Osborn," I heard another familiar male voice say.

I struggled to turn around and was shocked to see standing there Demetrius, Kara, and Una. At first I felt relief to see that they were still alive, but then I realized why they were still alive. They had obviously gone over to Dardanos's side, perhaps they had been on his side for a long time.

"I received different orders," Osborn scoffed, obviously annoyed at having his orders questioned, especially by a vampire.

He walked over and sprayed some kind of fluid, probably gas or lighter fluid, over Sylvia's ashes and tossed a match. "Just in case," he said smirking at me, as the ground where Sylvia's ashes had been now erupted in flames. "We're pretty sure that amount of Iridium is lethal to vampires, but can't be too careful."

Out of the corner of my eye I could see Demetrius clenching his fists. Apparently, he cared for Osborn about as much as I did. I hoped that meant he was going to lose control and attack Osborn. I honestly would have shaken his hand afterward, slippery traitor that he was, but no such luck. Una and Kara whispered something in Demetrius's ear and he seemed to calm.

Kara turned her obnoxious head toward me and sneered, "What

about her? She is one of them. She'll turn on us the first chance she gets."

Osborn turned rigidly to face her and said sternly, "That is not your concern. General D wants her alive, and while I am in command that is the way she will stay." Then he focused on me. "Don't think that means I won't deliver you to him a little worse for wear if you give me any trouble." Osborn paused a moment and added in a shaky whisper, "I have no problem hurting you, you're a monster, and my job is to kill monsters." I thought I actually saw tears forming in his eyes, but he turned away too quickly. If I didn't know any better I would have guessed Osborn was trying to convince himself, more than he was trying to convince me, of his utter repulsion for me.

I decided this must all have been a dream. Maybe I hadn't really been turned by Dardanos, heck, maybe I had never even left my house in Wilmington, NC two months ago. It just could not be possible that this metal, this Iridium, could kill vampires and no one had known about it. The collar around my neck felt like it was getting heavier, or perhaps I was just getting weaker, making it harder to bear the weight. I turned my head to see Dallen, blood dripping from his nose and mouth, being forced to stand with his hands bound behind his back. Then things went hazy; I don't think I actually blacked out, but it seemed as if my brain was unable to process anything that was going on around me.

I opened my eyes in a dimly lit room. It was another richly decorated room, but it didn't hold the scale or extravagant grandeur of the room I'd been held captive in North Carolina. For a moment I had thought perhaps that was where I was, but then I remembered Dallen and Sylvia and our quest to find the OPTS home base in Cuckfield, England. I tried desperately to rise from the chair I was seated in, then realized something was wrapped around me. I looked down to see a thin metal cord, almost like a long, dark silver necklace chain, wrapped around myself and the chair. I struggled to get out of it, but nothing happened, I felt like a child trying to move a house. It seemed as though I had no strength to even put any effort into escaping. I looked down at the chain again, remembering what Osborn had said. They had discovered some metal that weakened vampires and in large enough quantities entered into the blood system...kills them.

I looked around the room and noticed someone sitting in a chair on the opposite side slumped over. Dallen was unconscious, his head drooping forward heavily, and he had obviously taken much more of a beating than I'd seen him get before I had become incoherent. I could smell the blood coming off of him...and it made me want to lunge across the room at him. I remembered what Vasile had told me just before we left his coven, feed before facing Dardanos. I had not paid any attention. Now I was sitting tied to a chair, imagining Dallen's blood rushing down my throat, and not even considering that were I not tied up I would probably have sucked him dry.

"Lillian, look at me," Dallen's dry voice mumbled across the room. "You have to fight your hunger. You need to focus."

I looked at him and wanted to cry. First because his face was dripping with blood and I was longing for it, I could very nearly taste it in the air, and second because he had evidently been beaten to the point of unconsciousness.

"Dallen, I'm so weak, I can't focus on anything," I explained halfheartedly.

Dallen coughed roughly and said, "It's the Iridium, they discovered a way to meld it with another metal and create weapons. I heard them talking about it when they were wrapping you up. They call it Necro-Aim, I assume from the Greek nekros aima, meaning dead blood." He paused swallowing hard as if it were difficult for him to speak for long. "If I understand correctly once the Iridium enters a vampire's bloodstream it reacts with the blood causing it to fast-freeze, in essence killing the blood. If enough of it enters the bloodstream all at once the resulting energy caused by the reaction of the Iridium turning the blood cold actually creates so much energy that the blood explodes and combustion occurs within the body."

"Like being lit on fire from inside?" I asked nervously.

Dallen nodded his head. "The reason you feel so weak is that the chain touching your skin is actually very slowly killing any blood flowing through your body. Remember what Vasile said?"

I said grudgingly, "Blood is strength, blood is power."

"Exactly. The best way to sap a vampire's power is to affect the blood. I think that chain is just meant to hold you, a way for them to incapacitate a vampire. I don't think it can kill you, but it could possibly make you weak enough to black out and be completely vulnerable," Dallen replied. "I had heard rumors about this stuff a few months ago, but no one thought it possible. Obviously, they didn't trust me enough to share their discovery of the Necro-Aim. I guess Dardanos listened to Osborn more than I thought."

I still felt like this must all be a dream and had dozens of questions to ask Dallen, but before I was able to ask even one the door swung open and Dardanos entered, an imperious smirk upon his face.

"Take him away," Dardanos commanded the hunters, nodding his head disgustedly at Dallen, "and leave us. I wish to speak to Elizabeth alone."

When they had left the room, I sneered at Dardanos, "Stop calling me that. I am not Elizabeth. I've already told you I have no memories of her, or you, or whatever life the two of you shared together."

Dardanos strode slowly to where I was tied and stooped to look me in the eyes, as if checking to see if Elizabeth were there. "It doesn't matter what you remember, I explained already it will all come back to you in time. If you had just stayed with me, instead of running off with some mortal, your memory might already have come back. I am sorry that we had to be reunited in this manner, my love, but it was necessary to get you away from your...companion. You will see, in time, your memory will return, and together we will be unstoppable." As he spoke he tried to effortlessly remove the Necro-Aim, though I could see it burned his fingers as he touched it, he made a show of being unaffected by it.

"You're wrong, Dardanos. I am not Elizabeth...and I don't love you," I said in my strongest, cruelest voice, "I hate you. You have taken everything that has ever been important to me."

For a moment his face showed concern, but then he smiled warmly. "Elizabeth, you just don't understand what we could achieve together. Once your memories return you will remember your devotion to me and the cruel death you endured at the hands of the very people you think are your friends. You will see, that it is I that will love and protect you, not your traitorous Alexander or even your unfaithful Dallen." He turned his back to me and began walking back toward the door. "Let us see what your mortal lover has to say, shall we?" he asked condescendingly as he left the room.

"No! Leave him alone!" I screamed to an empty room in vain.

My heart began beating fiercely as I realized he was going to question Dallen, or more likely accuse Dallen of unforgivable acts, which could only possibly end one way. Dallen had not only proved himself Dardanos's enemy, but had basically robbed Dardanos of the love he had so coveted, because, let's face it, I was implicitly in love with Dallen, and

Dardanos must have sensed it or perhaps seen it in my thoughts. If vampires were able to read thoughts the way Dallen had described he could, that it was easier and more clear when in a state of heightened sensitivity, than Dardanos had most likely learned my feelings for Dallen from my own thoughts. I'm sure during our embarrassingly intimate evening together, Dardanos had been able to see certain things that had occurred between Dallen and me. I was also sure Dardanos did not particularly like knowing that his would-be love had been in bed with another man. Dallen would most assuredly be dead once Dardanos was through "talking" to him.

Then I was struck by sudden clarity and freedom of movement. My head felt as though it had cleared, no more dizziness or fogginess, and I was able to move my arms and legs. It took me a moment to realize what was going on as I found my new found freedom to be strange.

Dardanos had removed the Necro-Aim binding. I had watched him do it, and didn't even consider what was happening. He had, openly, removed my restraints, as he once again explained how I would return to him. Well, how Elizabeth would return to him anyway. In my anger for his blind delusions and in my fear for Dallen's safety I had been unaware that I had been released from the terrible cold-burn of the Necro-Aim.

I no longer felt debilitating weakness, I could move, I could stand. If I wanted I could have jumped out of the window and flew away.

I stood staring at the unopened window, considering the idea of escaping. I could just open the window, take to the sky, and leave all this behind. I wasn't strong enough to save anyone, let alone everyone, but I could save myself. It took only a moment's thought and I knew I couldn't do it. No matter what fear entered my heart I couldn't abandon Ben, Lex, Dallen, or even any of the other vampires that had risked their lives to battle our common enemy. I couldn't live in the world knowing that I had just let them all die without even trying. I had to do something.

I still was unsure of what I was capable of, but I knew I had to at least try. Dallen was in the most immediate danger so that had to be my priority, but I found myself puzzled as to why Dardanos had even released me from the torturous chains I'd been bound in. Did he realize what he had been doing? Perhaps he had meant to bind me once more before he'd left the room. Did he believe that I just wasn't strong enough to stop him, and therefore not a threat? Or, did he still, naively, believe I would do nothing to stop him because I was his long lost love Elizabeth Cranford, who would do anything for him?

I smiled deviously to myself, *he had a rude awakening coming to him!*

❧21❧

As I crossed the room to the door, I stumbled slightly over a lump of material on the floor. Checking to see what I had tripped over I found the leather jacket Dallen had taken from Vasile's safe-house tossed in a pile near where he'd been tied up. I picked the jacket up remembering I had handed Dallen my poetry book to tuck into the protected inside pockets, because I had been forced to shove the book down the back of my corset when we'd left Lex's mansion and that was not exactly an ideal location. It wasn't so much that it was uncomfortable, because such things didn't really bother vampires, but it was more that it felt restrictive. I was already clothed in a very restrictive garment, adding a hardback journal to the already tight clothing made it worse. With no other option, unless I wanted to leave my beloved book behind, I once again slid the book into the tight confines of the back of my corset.

Putting my ear to the door, I closed my eyes, and listened carefully for any sign of the enemy. I focused my mind on the sounds emitting from the hallway just outside. When I was sure there was no movement, or guard for that matter, I willed myself to focus on Dallen. I could hear him speaking heatedly as if he were in the next room, though I knew he wasn't that close. I figured he had to be on the same floor and perhaps at most three rooms away.

I opened the door to the room I had been kept in and poked my head out slowly to make sure my assessment had been accurate. It was eerily quiet in the hall, but I reasoned that almost all the hunters were probably busy fighting vampires on the floors below. I heard a shrill scream from the left and pinpointed the sound to be emitting from the opposite side of the hall two rooms down. I rushed nervously to the door, ready to break it down. I stopped short in front of the door, deciding barging in may not be the best course of action. Instead I listened.

"How could I have known why you didn't want us near her?" came Dallen's strained voice.

"You should have followed your orders!" Osborn yelled

authoritatively.

"Osborn, there is no need to yell. The boy is dying...slowly. He will have his punishment and I will have my satisfaction," Dardanos said calmly. "You can now serve my purpose and perhaps make up for this disloyalty."

"How? By dying?" Dallen asked sarcastically.

Dardanos answered coolly, "Oh, you don't have to do anything. My darling love is very hunger. She has yet to feed properly. I'm sure once I let her loose in here, with your blood already dripping most invitingly, she will have no will power to stop herself from consuming you. So you see I get my revenge from your death by your own lover, and my dear Elizabeth will feel more compelled to stay with me once she realizes what she has done to someone she thought she loved."

I had forgotten the feeling of powerlessness I'd felt when I'd seen blood falling tantalizingly down Dallen's face. I now knew why Dardanos had freed me, he knew the temptation for blood would be too great for me to stay away from Dallen. How could I possibly help him if I couldn't control my blood lust? I felt helpless, if I barged in there now I would most likely attack Dallen, and do exactly what Dardanos wanted of me. I thought I could smell Dallen's blood from the hall; my insides felt like they were clawing at me to give in, to drain him of the sweet, flowery perfume flowing out of him at that very moment. As I battled myself trying to make up my mind what I would do I was suddenly struck by the slight gurgling noise coming from the room. It was the sound of blood drowning in a person's throat; the sound of someone dying. Whatever Dardanos had done, Dallen was dying, and probably had a few minutes at best. I had to try to save him.

I walked into the room casually as if I'd been invited and pronounced greedily, "I smelt blood coming from this room. I feel so weak...I need to feed." I put all my effort into not looking at Dallen, as the very closeness of his blood was making my body pulsate in anticipation.

Dardanos smiled adoringly at me and explained with great satisfaction, "You see, Dallen, I could not even keep her out of the room. She came of her own free will...to consume you." Dardanos gave a quick nod to Osborn and two hunters also in the room, signaling them to leave. He then lent close to Dallen running his finger through a line of Dallen's blood and licking it teasingly. "It really is a shame you know. A talent such as yours doesn't come along very often. You could have become very important to OPTS, if you hadn't dipped your pen in the inkwell, so to speak," Dardanos chided.

As hard as it was for me to stay focused on not diving at Dallen and luxuriating in the pleasure of his blood, I did feel a little surge of annoyance at having my nether regions compared to a container for black writing liquid. I was so consumed with visualizing my insides actually being filled with evil, black fluid that I hadn't heard Dardanos's question directed at me. I looked at him confused and realized he had just said something to me.

Dardanos brushed my cheek, obviously chalking my inattention up to extreme hunger, and asked again, "Shall I show you what you must do or do you want to try yourself?"

There it was, the opening I needed. I replied weakly, "I would like to try myself, but-" I paused pretending to be embarrassed. "I don't want you to watch. I don't want to disappoint you, General," I said the last as sweetly as I could muster.

I thought Dardanos would pee himself, that is if his body still had such a function. He wrapped his arms around me approvingly. "You could never disappoint me."

Wanna bet?

I put on my best pout and explained meekly, "It's just that I want to figure it out for myself and I'm afraid you'll find me barbaric in my learning."

Dardanos studied my eyes suspiciously for a moment. "Elizabeth?"

I shook my head lightly. "I still don't have any memories of her...or me, I guess, but since I've come back to you I've started to have this feeling...that this is where I'm meant to be. I think you're right, in time I'll start to remember. I should have listened to you from the beginning. I'm sorry."

Were those tears in his eyes? Dardanos cupped my face in his hands and kissed me as if a great burden had been lifted off of him. "My love, of course, whatever you wish. I'll wait just outside the door if you need me." With that he left, almost with a slight skip to his walk.

I was so proud of my performance, I'd certainly improved since my unimpressive show at the diner, that I almost forgot about Dallen. I think he was hoping I'd forgotten about him; apparently my performance had fooled him as well. I turned around to look at him and try to figure out exactly what I was going to do, and I could see the fear in his eyes. I could also see a great gaping wound on the left side of his neck, as if

Dardanos had gone to drink from him but instead used his teeth to rip at Dallen's throat. That would certainly explain the shrill scream I'd heard

"Lillian, please, you can't do this," Dallen pleaded halfheartedly, "please, you'll just be doing what he wants. You can't really believe this is where you belong."

I felt complete anguish for him, but I couldn't reassure him. Dardanos would surely be listening. I also was putting all my effort into resisting the temptation of the blatantly accessible drink now drenching Dallen's clothes, while trying to formulate an escape plan. I moved slowly toward Dallen, noticing the window behind him. That would be the easiest escape. That is, if I were able firstly to carry someone while flying, and secondly not be overwhelmed by the closeness of all that blood. Dallen had visible tears in his eyes and I decided I could risk at least giving him a sign I wasn't planning on attacking him. I winked my eye and put my finger to my mouth to signal him to be quiet. I untied him, turning my face away, and holding my breath hoping that might help me to keep control. I pushed open the windows and took Dallen in my arms, not even explaining what I meant to do, and jumped through the open window.

I discovered almost immediately I wasn't going to be able to carry Dallen far. I was still weakened from the Necro-Aim and from not feeding, and I could feel my insides again fighting me to gorge on Dallen's blood. I could see a monstrous bonfire had been set on the front lawn just thirty or so feet from the manor house. I decided setting down on the ground was not the best idea. So instead I went up. As I struggled to make it to the roof I smelled the rancid odor of burning flesh. With a shudder I realized what the bonfire was for.

The hunters were burning vampires.

I tumbled onto the roof, exhausted, and very hungry. Unfortunately, I was so weak Dallen rolled out of my embrace and landed hard a few feet away. I lay there for a moment trying to collect myself, knowing that I had to do something before Dardanos realized what I'd done and came looking for us. As I lay there I heard arguing and found that we were not the only ones on the roof. There, arguing dangerously close to the short wall at the edge of the roof, were Osborn and Rachel.

"You think I could ever love you?! You disgust me!" Osborn sneered at Rachel."

Rachel pleaded weakly, "But everything I've done, I've done for you. I told you everything I knew, I kept your secrets, I even became a vampire because you asked me to."

Osborn laughed cruelly, "Are you really that naïve? You were part of the plan from the beginning. I chose you to get closer to Lex and Lillian. You really think I had feelings for you, that's so precious, but trust me, you were nothing but a way for me to get what I wanted. I should thank you, you have done an excellent job, but like I said before I don't associate with monsters."

I waited to see Rachel's reaction. I hoped she was going to attack Osborn and suck him dry, and then I would be able to convince her to escape with Dallen and me. Instead she stood there looking like she was going to erupt into sobs. I decided I was going to have to do something before Osborn noticed us and perhaps tried to use Rachel against me. I started to slowly stand when Rachel started edging closer to Osborn. I waited, thinking this might be the moment she was going to make her move.

"Please, Osborn, I love you. Please don't turn me away," Rachel said, reaching out her hands toward Osborn's hands.

As Rachel locked her fingers through his I noticed too late the look of sheer disgust spreading across Osborn's face. I leaped to my feet and started to sprint toward them just as Osborn yanked Rachel to the edge.

"Because you've been such a good little pet I will help you. I'm going to release your tortured soul," Osborn whispered, and quicker than I could get there he shoved Rachel over the side of the roof.

I was so in shock I forgot all about Osborn and ran to the wall peering over the edge in hopes of seeing Rachel flying out of harm's way. Instead I saw what looked like a metal collar, like the one that had been put on me earlier, around her neck. Her body was limp, plummeting down like an anchor into the bonfire below. I stared into the flames, not able to believe what had just happened, but I could still see her body lying motionless within the huge blaze.

Rachel was gone.

I felt cold all over, and not just because I had no fresh blood flowing through my veins. I hadn't helped her. What did I think was going to happen? I knew that Osborn had used her, she knew for that matter, and that he had never had real feelings for Rachel. What did I think would be the outcome of an argument between a vampire and a vampire hunter hovering dangerously close to the edge of a building just above a bonfire set to kill vampires? My eyes stung with absent tears, without blood in my body I was unable to produce actual tears, but I felt them deep inside, in my non-beating heart.

Rachel was dead, my best friend, the first person to ever truly accept me, and it was my fault. I had drug her into this life, surrounded by danger, and I had failed to intervene in an argument that was obviously doomed to end badly.

This story is for you, Rachel. I'm so sorry for what I've done to you, for my neglect and for my fear of losing you. Had I not been so scared that I would lose you forever, if I had confronted you about Osborn and your change of behavior, perhaps I wouldn't have lost you forever. You were always there to raise my spirits and my confidence, and I am sure I would not be who I am without your influence. Whether I really was Elizabeth Cranford in a past life or you were Emma Cranford, you will always be my sister. A part of me has died with you.

I was still looking fixedly down at the bonfire when I felt an unbearable burning in my side. I fell feebly onto my knees, clutching at my right side. Dazed, I looked up and saw Osborn staring sadly down at me. I checked my side to see what little blood I still had slowly trickling out of a small wound. He had shot me with a Necro-Aim bullet. I could feel exactly where the bullet was inside of me and I could feel my body working hard to eject it from my insides, but unfortunately without any blood to fuel my body's natural healing reactions it seemed to be too much effort for me to achieve. I knew it wouldn't kill me, I had, thankfully, drunk from two very powerful vampires. I was fairly certain it would take a whole lot of Necro-Aim to kill me, if it could at all. Of course Osborn's desire had not been to kill me, but to render me weak enough to overpower. Most likely so he could triumphantly return me to his master and prove his superiority.

"Burns like hell, I know, I'm sorry for that," Osborn stated genuinely. "It really is too bad Dardanos has his heart set on you. I never really believed you were Elizabeth, but he wouldn't let it go. You were always an obsession of his. Not that I don't see why," he said as he ran his fingers through my hair, giving me a longing look. "I thought, perhaps, I would find a way to prevent Dardanos from achieving his aim. I've made it a little hobby, you see, to help beauties such as yourself, either avoid being turned or releasing their souls once they have been. You know, I feel it's my duty to try to rid this world of evil, my family has been doing it for centuries. It really tears my heart out to see beautiful, innocent girls, like you, turned into such disgusting demons. I know it may seem cruel, but in the end I really do enjoy torturing beautiful women that have been turned into evil monsters. After all it isn't like they have a soul anymore, so there really is no harm in having a little fun with the lovely empty shell of what they once were."

I felt a sting as he said that vampires had no soul. Was that true? I hadn't felt that I'd lost my soul. I still felt there was some ineffable spirit that resided within me. How could I even exist without a soul? It couldn't be true, it must have just been what hunters were taught. It certainly would make murdering vampires easier to handle if one thought they were nothing but evil wraiths roaming the Earth in search of blood.

I turned to him lethargically and managed to say, "What's wrong, Osborn, you can't find a woman that's into psychopaths? The only women that will let you touch them have to be tied up?"

The smile vanished from his face and he slapped me across the cheek. It didn't hurt of course, unless you count my pride, but I certainly felt it more than I would have if I hadn't been so weakened from the Necro-Aim. I let my head loll out of dizzying starvation, but Osborn must have taken that as a sign that I was in pain and knelt down next to me.

"See what you made me do?" Osborn said woefully. "I don't want to hurt you, Lillian, I never have. I've only ever wanted to save you from this fate."

Then, he held my head on either side, looking into my eyes, and I worried he was going to do something unthinkable and disturbing to my eyes, but instead he did something unthinkable and disturbing to my lips.

He kissed me.

I don't know what would have been worse, somehow I wished he had gouged my eyeballs out instead of kissing me. My eyes would always heal, my memory of that moment, not so much. I desperately wanted to bite his disgusting tongue as he shoved it in my mouth, but unfortunately the sicko had a Necro-Aim tongue guard, and my body was naturally trying to avoid it. Osborn did his best to make sure his tongue touched every inch of my mouth, and my only consolation was that it was not his actual tongue touching my mouth but a piece of burning metal which weakened me further and left me feeling like I was juggling a red-hot coal in my mouth.

Osborn pulled away and grabbed the back of my hair roughly, becoming angry once more, he teased, "How was that, sweetheart? I'm sorry, are you lost for words? Yeah, that happens sometimes." He ran his finger around my jawline. "You can't even imagine the things I would like to do to you."

Suddenly Osborn held up his gun and pointed it straight at my face. Though, I knew it wouldn't kill me, I did not want to feel the inevitable burning pain from the Necro-Aim, especially not at close range in my face. Surprisingly Osborn lifted the gun over my shoulder and shot behind me. I turned in a daze to see Dallen stumble backward a few feet, clutching his shoulder, before falling to the ground.

"Dallen," I whimpered.

I had forgotten all about him, lying on the other side of the roof, half dead. I turned back to Osborn and with what little strength I had I threw myself at him and raked my fingernails across his chest. I managed to draw a little blood, which made it even harder to focus, and in my moment of imagining lapping up that blood, Osborn kicked me back. He held the gun up, aiming at my midsection, when the door leading to the roof banged open. I glanced up to see Malika stopping short, taking in the scene, and a look of panic spreading across her face. Before I could turn back to Osborn I heard the shots. He emptied the remaining four Necro-Aim bullets into my stomach and chest.

I don't know if it was because Dallen had explained how the Necro-Aim worked, but it literally felt like there were tiny explosions going off inside of me. I looked at my skin in horror; it had turned a strange shade of gray. My eyes felt heavy, as if they were going to close and perhaps never open again. I fell straight forward and waited for my body to burn up from the inside and turn to ash on the outside. I waited, but it didn't happen.

"Oh my god, Lillian, I didn't mean to, I'm sorry," Osborn murmured through sobs, "I never wanted to hurt you. I lost control. You don't understand...you don't understand what they do to us. I'm so screwed up, I've become nothing more than a murderer, but I fell in- "

Osborn's voice trailed off. I lifted my head to see Malika lifting him off his feet with one hand.

"Malika," I strained.

She turned to me surprised, still holding Osborn aloft.

"My God, he did turn you," Malika uttered sadly.

All I could manage to say was, "Blood."

Malika understood. She pushed Osborn down on his knees in front of me and tore cruelly at his neck with her nails. I used Osborn's body as support to pull myself up to that lovely fount that was already turning my vision red.

Just before I sank my teeth in I whispered, "I still have a soul."

A girl couldn't have asked for a better, more rewarding first feeding. Not only did I get practically hand fed by one of the most powerful vampires alive, but I got to drain an evil, sadistic enemy of his life blood. To say it was satisfying would be putting it mildly. I couldn't care less about the visions I saw while ingesting his blood. I had already heard his story and he himself had told me about his hobby of torturing, so those things certainly didn't shock me to see. One thing did, however, give me pause, and I very nearly stopped drinking from him. I saw him cradling a folding picture frame in his hands, looking lovingly at the picture, and slamming it closed as Dardanos approached him. For something so simple as a vision of him looking at a picture frame to be leaking from the memories of his dying brain, it must have been very important to him. I watched as he stuffed the small frame into an inside shirt pocket, on the left side, near his heart.

"I'm sorry for...belladonna. Wasn't meant for you...for Rachel. I thought...scare you...make you leave. Never wanted to hurt-" Osborn slurred as if drunk, "Mistakes...I made. You...always you."

Everything started to fade, the last images flooding his mind were of me, then my vision went black and I knew he was dead.

When I opened my eyes Malika was crouching next to me, half supporting me. Without a word I unbuttoned Osborn's shirt and found the pocket in which he had hidden his picture frame. I pulled it out and opened it.

I gasped and very nearly dropped the picture frame.

Malika explained in confusion, "That is Elizabeth Cranford."

I looked down at the picture. The woman looked identical to me, as I looked as a vampire, except of course the style of clothing was much more conservative and her hair was darker. Although the picture seemed to be black and white, Elizabeth's hair was painted a deep shade of red. I assumed the miniature portrait was actually a daguerreotype, a picture made on a copper plate, because along with her blazing hair, her cheeks seemed to be painted a pale pink as well. Not exactly accurate for a portrait of a vampire, but common for such pictures in the Victorian Era. The picture frame must have belonged to Dardanos, but I couldn't think why Osborn would be carrying it around. Looking at the picture I was startled once again by the uncanny likeness between Elizabeth Cranford and myself.

I shook my head at a loss. "Why would he keep a picture of Elizabeth in his pocket? He couldn't have known her."

"No," Malika said, smiling sympathetically, "but he did know you."

I stared back at Osborn's now lifeless face. How could such a disturbed killer have been harboring secret feelings for someone he didn't know, and what had he meant about the belladonna? Had he really been the one that had planted the poison? Was that why he had taken care of me after the poisoning? I tried not to think about it. Maybe he had said it as a last ditch effort to save himself.

Finally Malika brought me out of my thoughts.

"We've been searching for you all night. Where did he keep you?" Malika asked.

I looked at her not understanding what she meant and realized the reason all the council's had moved so quickly had been because of me. They had traveled to England thinking I was being held at OPTS headquarters. This had been a rescue mission, not the siege on Dardanos we had been talking about before my kidnapping.

I bit my lip guiltily. "I wasn't brought here by Dardanos. His hunters took me to an estate in North Carolina. He turned me there, but the next morning before I had fully turned Dallen-"I paused remembering Dallen. I jumped to my feet and ran to him. "Dallen! Dallen, please be alive!"

I held his face in my hands and kissed him as tears fell off my cheeks onto his face.

"He is still alive," Malika stated calmly, "though he is a traitor and, as such, his fate is sealed."

"No," I pleaded, "he's the one that rescued me. He broke into the estate and got me out. He returned with me to Lex's mansion and we found Sylvia there and he led us here to fight Dardanos. The only one he has betrayed is Dardanos. He has done nothing but protect me this whole time. He shouldn't be punished. Please save him." I stared at Malika in anguish, because I knew I couldn't go against whatever decision she ultimately made, but I could try to change her mind.

She seemed to be considering things and then she bent down on Dallen's other side. "Very well," was all she said before cradling Dallen's head in her arms and sinking her teeth into his throat.

For a moment I panicked thinking she meant to give him a quick death as a reward for his behavior, but then she drew back and I heard a sound like a sigh escape Dallen's lips. He was still alive. Malika ran her fingernails across the left side of her neck and pulled Dallen up, pressing his lips to the deep cut she'd made. Within seconds Dallen was wrapping his arms around Malika and greedily lapping at the gift she'd given him. Although it certainly was not as intimate as my exchange with Dardanos, I certainly felt like I was intruding by watching them. Finally Malika pulled him away and forced him to lie in my arms.

"He'll be weak for a while, until he has fully turned. This is a gift, Lillian, I trust you will not make me regret it," Malika explained sternly. "Now...I must get back, and help those still alive. I will try to spread the word for everyone to drawback. We cannot win this fight and dawn is approaching."

I laid Dallen down on the roof and stood. "I'll help you. There has been too much death because of me, let me do what I can."

I leaned down and whispered to a still half-conscious Dallen that I would be back soon for him and that he should hide himself until I returned. I pulled my poetry book out of the back of my corset, removed the moonstone pendant from around my neck, and slid the black moonstone ring off of my finger.

"I want you to hold these things for me. If anything should happen to me-"

"Nothing is going to happen to you," Dallen protested, "You are going to come back to me."

I smiled weakly, whispering, "Should anything happen to me, I want you to keep them. At least they will survive if I don't. The book is...my thoughts and ideas, the necklace..is my love, and the ring...is my revenge."

Before I could rise Dallen grabbed my arm and whispered, "I think he was in love with you. Osborn I mean. From the moment he met you he seemed...distracted, and his mood swings became more extreme. He stole that picture of Elizabeth from Dardanos even before he met you; I caught him looking at it a few times. I think he despised me for abandoning my

317

orders to be with you. I think he desperately wished he could have done the same. He certainly had issues, perhaps even some kind of genetic mental illness, but I can't fault him for forming an attachment to you. It was probably his best quality."

I smiled, relieved to hear Dallen's voice, but I found what he said disturbing. I touched his face and repeated assuredly, "I will be back for you."

"Lillian, I should have done more," Dallen stammered, holding me from getting up. "I should have protected you better. I knew the moment I met you that I was going to betray Dardanos for you, but I waited, I waited too long."

I bent down and kissed his dry lips lovingly. "You couldn't have known what Dardanos was willing to do to get to me. No one is to blame for what he's done. I have to go and help the others. Promise me you'll stay hidden, and if you have the strength to get out, just go, but be careful. I can't imagine living in this world and knowing that you're not in it."

Dallen grabbed my hand tightly and assured me, "We will be together again, *that* I will promise you. You are the love of my life, and I won't feel complete until I have you in my arms again."

I kissed him firmly once more on the lips before I left him to hide himself from vampire hunters and vampires alike. I worried that one of The Seventh Council members would find him and attack him not knowing that he was on our side, but I had to trust that he could take care of himself. I had to help Malika get anyone left alive out of there, too many lives had been sacrificed to recover me from Dardanos's clutches.

"There's something else you should know," I uttered regretfully to Malika as we made our way toward the door leading back into the building. "Demetrius, Una, and Kara aren't dead. It's worse. They've betrayed us. I saw them here, just before Sylvia was killed. I don't know how long they've been on Dardanos's side, but they are certainly on it now."

Malika took a deep calming breath. "That is not news that I wanted to ever hear, but I will know how to deal with them when I find them. Let us hurry, before any more lives are lost."

I turned to leave with Malika and saw Dallen putting all his energy into standing up, obviously taking my advice and finding a dark corner to rest in while I went off to fight some vampire hunters.

❧22☙

I followed Malika back through the manor house of OPTS, hoping there were still allies to find and send home. The first floor we walked down was uncomfortably quiet and I assumed it was the floor on which Dallen and I had been held. I felt a small pang of uselessness to know I had only had the will and strength to carry Dallen and me one mere floor higher. I couldn't help but be amazed that Dardanos hadn't found us immediately. We had been so close; he could have finished us easily.

As I ran after Malika, I also found my thoughts sliding to what Dallen had said about Osborn. How could someone so emotionless, so cruel, have felt love, and have felt it for me? We had barely exchanged more than a dozen words. Then I stopped short realizing what Osborn's last words had meant.

Malika turned suddenly, noticing I wasn't right behind her and gave me a quizzical look. "What is it?"

"I just realized, Osborn was the one that poisoned me, but it wasn't meant for me," I said with tears in my eyes.

"Who was it meant for?" Malika humored me.

"I think he had meant to give it to Rachel."

Though we were in a hurry, Malika took a step back toward me. "Why would he want to poison Rachel, I thought he had been in love with her?"

I shook my head. "It had all been an act. His orders were to stay away from me so he used Rachel, but it was painfully obvious he was pretending to be interested in her from the very first day. With the poison, I don't know, maybe he thought if Rachel was dead I would leave Lex. Maybe he thought in my distress I would leave with him. I don't know, it's all so strange. He never wanted to hurt me he said, but once Dardanos turned me I think he felt there was no hope, and that was why he'd been so cruel."

Malika put her hand on my shoulder and patted it gently in sympathy. I looked up at her and nodded my head, understanding we did not have time for this right now. I let out a deep sigh and gave Malika another quick nod to let her know I was ready. We continued our descent into the manor house looking for any of our kindred.

The next two floors were relatively quiet as well. We ran into four or five hunters, but we easily overpowered them, and I was able to practice my feeding technique. I was beginning to think that perhaps we were too late; perhaps everyone had already fled...or had been killed. Then suddenly on our descent to the ground floor Malika slowed down and pointed to the bottom of the staircase.

"Turin," she whispered to me.

I recognized him from the council, though we'd never spoken. He was struggling to walk. Not more than ten feet behind him were three hunters with weapons drawn. They seemed to be toying with him, giving him the chance to flee, though he barely had the strength to stand upright. I was trying to decide how we were going to sneak up and surprise the hunters when I heard Malika's voice above me.

Malika was suspended from the ceiling on hands and knees. I was too shocked to say anything as she explained, "I'm going to try to go above their heads and get behind them. When I jump down be ready to attack and try to shield Turin."

I just nodded in awe and decided I would have to practice walking on walls and ceilings once we got out of there. I tried my best to walk down the stairs without being noticed, but decided my best course of action would be to jump from where I was. Malika was able to quickly and quietly make her way behind the hunters and dropped silently to the floor. As soon as she called to them I jumped. I heard the shots from their guns going off, but didn't see if they hit anyone. I landed less than a foot behind one of the hunters and snapped his neck. As I did so Malika grabbed one of the others, and the last one I quickly sank my teeth into. When we turned back toward the staircase Turin was lying there grasping his leg. Malika tore open her wrist and let thick droplets of blood spill over the bullet wound on Turin's leg. Within minutes the Necro-Aim bullet popped out as if it had been pushed from inside.

Malika pulled Turin up to stand and stated firmly, "You must get out. The fight is lost. You know where to go."

Turin nodded to Malika and then turned to me seeming to take in the transformation that had occurred by becoming a vampire. He gave me a sad smile, as if he understood their efforts had not been enough to stop

Dardanos's plans, before running in the opposite direction of the front door to leave as he'd been instructed. Without thinking about it, I started heading for the front door. I was scared of what I would find, but after searching every floor of the house and only finding Turin a few hundred feet from the front door I was fairly sure that was where we would find the others. I was also fairly certain that as soon as we set foot out the front door we would come face to face with the massive bonfire that had been set to burn vampires.

Before we crossed the threshold of the door Malika put her hand on my shoulder. I turned, surprised to see her hesitancy. I was shocked to see her in such a weak state, though she didn't command the strict worshipful devotion that Vasile did, Malika had always seemed to me to exude an effortless power over those around her.

She lowered her head, admitting, "They are probably all dead. You should follow Turin."

I was confused, "What about you? What are you going to do?"

"I am their leader. It is my responsibility to lead them and protect them, and I have failed. I will try to save those they have not burned, but I cannot say what will happen. It would be best for you to leave."

I shook my head resolutely. "I can't. I have to know if Lex and Ben are still alive. They're my family and I can't abandon them, and the others, they've risked so much for me. I have to do as much for them."

Malika gave me a smile which I thought looked something like the look a proud mother would give to her child, though, I had little experience with such looks so I couldn't be sure. Maybe she just found my sense of obligation to be somewhat naïve, and had smiled at my stupidity. After all she herself had said it was a losing battle, throwing oneself into the thick of it didn't exactly show great judgment on my part, but sometimes I'm stubborn like that. So I smiled back at her pretending that it had been out of pride that she'd smiled at me.

"Let us go, and see what we can do," she said simply.

The scene we encountered when we emerged from the manor house was the most grotesquely evil thing I have ever beheld. The bonfire was off to the left, surrounded by armed hunters on all sides. Every so often one of them would aim at the fire and shoot. I didn't understand why at first, but then I watched the fire and realized there were bodies trying to escape the flames. There were vampires, probably those that were a bit stronger than average, that were not dying immediately from the fire. They had enough strength to attempt escaping from the bonfire, but every time one attempted it they got shot by a Necro-Aim bullet, sapping their strength and pushing them back into the flames. The hunters laughed as they hit their targets and watched them finally succumb to the fire.

That wasn't even the worst sight.

Wrapped up and lying on their backs one after the other on the ground, as if they were in line for something, were perhaps thirty or forty vampires. If my estimate was correct the total number of vampires that would have joined us in our fight would have neared eighty or ninety; if that was even close to the right number, then we had lost more than half our numbers. Though a few vampires seemed to be struggling weakly with their bindings, most were completely incapacitated. They were all wrapped in the same chain-like Necro-Aim I had been, but some also had the metal collar around their necks, and others looked as if they'd been shot in various places.

I quickly ran my eyes along the line of bound vampires saying a silent prayer that I might see Ben and Lex. Finally, about ten bodies from the end I recognized Ben's unconscious form, but I couldn't find Lex. My heart sank as I looked at Malika for support.

Malika didn't look back at me, but placed her right hand on my shoulder. "I know. He must be alive. If I know Alexander, he is still alive."

I wanted her words to be true, but I didn't believe it looking at the carnage in front of me. The only way Lex would still be alive is if he'd run and he just wasn't the running type. I could see from Malika's reluctance to even look at me that she too was upset by Lex's absence. He may be a handful at times, but I could see that he meant a lot to her. Then I realized that we had yet to come across Tor, Malika's companion and male elder of our council.

I turned to mention this to Malika, but she seemed to know what I was going to say and answered, "He is there."

I turned back to the line of vampires on the ground and shook my head as I was unable to find him. "I don't-"

Now I could see that there were tears streaming down Malika's face as she pointed to the bonfire. "He is there," she repeated.

I whipped my head around in disbelief at her words. There, in the flames, in the very center of the bonfire was a figure pacing, as if it were bored with this game. We watched as the figure tried rising upward out of the flames, but multiple gunshots rang out, hitting the figure, and sending it crashing back into the fire. Within seconds the figure was on its feet again, pacing.

"How long can he survive like that?" I asked horrified.

Malika shook her head. "I don't know. He is very strong, very old, but not as old as I am. This weapon they have, Necro-Aim you call it, I don't know what our limits are with it. As for the fire, I think eventually it will consume him. It could take days, perhaps a week. That along with the sun and the Necro-Aim, eventually he will perish. One thing I do know, even if he is still alive he is in excruciating pain. You cannot even imagine what he must be feeling."

I thought back to Lex's description of being burned by sunlight and my recent experience with Necro-Aim. "I can imagine, but I'm sure it doesn't even come close."

My eyes drifted across the scene before me and for the first time I noticed Dardanos was standing among the hunters. He was surrounded on all sides by hunters, some running up to report to him, and others apparently there to protect him from every possible angle. Then I noticed who else was standing close to him and I knew it was going to be trouble. I didn't even get the chance to point out to Malika that Dardanos was standing on the opposite side of the bonfire from us within a circle of hunters, and within that circle with him were Kara, Una, and Demetrius. Suddenly I heard a growl escaping Malika's lips. When I say growl I don't mean a low, animalistic sound only heard by me; I mean a loud, carnal exclamation which echoed across the entire estate, and made your hair stand on end.

You know the saying *like a deer caught in headlights*, that was exactly how I felt, because every cognizant body on the front lawn turned in our direction. I was so unprepared for Malika's announcement of our presence that at first I felt so awkward I was going to explain what we were doing there. Before I could find the right words to explain our unintended predicament to our enemies Malika lunged out across the bonfire. I knew her aim was at Kara, Una, and Demetrius, but I also knew she wouldn't get very far with Dardanos standing there. Without reconsidering what the best course of action was I bounded after her, half flying and half jumping my way to where Dardanos was.

Although everyone had been so fortuitously notified of our position, Dardanos and those around him were in somewhat of a daze as

Malika and I both penetrated the circle of hunters surrounding them. Malika dove straight for Demetrius, obviously the ring leader in his little group, and I started to head off Dardanos. I stopped, before I even took a step further into the circle of hunters. There at the feet of Dardanos, Demetrius, Una, and Kara was Lex.

He was tied up with the chain Necro-Aim, had the metal collar around his neck, looked as if he'd been shot in several places, and seemed to be healing slowly from what looked like scratches and bite marks.

Lex looked up at me wearily, but when he realized it was me staring down at him I saw a flash of menace in his eyes. Malika must have noticed what was going on and instead of focusing on our three traitors she ran at Dardanos unexpectedly and pushed him so hard he flew backward some hundred feet or so. That was all I needed. I didn't even think of the hunters surrounding me, somehow I knew Malika was going to cover me while I did what I had to. Like Dardanos had done to me, I started unwrapping the Necro-Aim chain from around Lex, ignoring the searing pain in my fingers. I then unclasped the collar, all the time hearing my skin sizzle from the burning cold of the Necro-Aim. Lastly, I did what I had seen Malika do, and as I held my breath in anticipation of the pain I ripped at my wrist. Contrary to what I thought it really didn't hurt, or at least not in the way I thought it would. Just as I had watched Malika do, I let droplets of my blood fall onto Lex's wounds, healing him quickly and extracting any Necro-Aim embedded in his body.

Lex stared at me in awe, as if he were just seeing me for the first time. I suppose after being turned I had changed a little so it was kind of like he was seeing me for the first time, but it was more than that. The look of pure love and adoration on his face was so different from any other look he'd ever given me that it made me wonder if he too were mesmerized by my resemblance to Elizabeth Cranford. I decided right then was not the time to ask him if he was thinking about Elizabeth and instead grabbed both his hands to pull him to his feet. As I pulled him to stand he continued moving forward and pulled me back into him, kissing me ardently, as his lips drifted away from mine he seemed to be transfixed by my eyes.

Before Lex pulled away from my stare I heard Malika yell, "Go! Free the others! I will handle these four!"

I knew she meant for us to free the other vampires, but I also knew there was no way she could handle Demetrius, Una, Kara, and Dardanos on her own. As much as I wanted to help her I also knew she would not allow it. Lex and I set to work freeing the bound vampires and making them retreat. As much as I wanted to free Ben first I knew he would take up too much valuable time arguing with me to leave and so I told Lex that we should start with those closest to the bonfire, but I didn't tell him why.

A few vampires refused to leave while we were still fighting and went to help Malika while we freed everyone. Finally, we were down to the last twelve and Lex saw that I kept glancing over at Ben.

"Lillian, go, I'll get the rest. Help Ben," Lex urged.

I started unwinding the Necro-Aim from around Ben's body and was relieved to see he had no other signs of injury. Almost immediately his eyes shot open and he nearly jumped at me to embrace me.

"Thank God. I was so worried," Ben gushed, pushing me back to look at me. "So he did it? He turned you? I thought we would get here in time to stop him." He lowered his eyes as if in guilt.

"Ben," I began. "He turned me two nights ago, and he brought me to North Carolina, not here. Dallen actually found me and got me out. Then we followed you here. I was afraid I would lose you."

Ben had tears in his eyes and I could see there was more he wanted to say, but instead he just embraced me again.

We were interrupted by Lex's sarcastic quip, "I do hate to break up this family reunion, but we've got a war going on."

I looked over at where we'd left Malika fighting. There were five others fighting with her, but I could also see that there had been more. There were at least four ash covered areas of grass resembling vague human outlines. Those ash covered spots had been four vampires that we had freed and told to leave that had instead stayed, fought, and died. Ben didn't even lecture me about the dangers I would face but helped me to my feet and led the way to join in the fight.

As crazy an idea as it was I decided to step in for Malika and face Dardanos. I was able to pull Malika aside as Dardanos volleyed attacks from three vampires. Lex was focused on going after Demetrius and Ben was trying to take out as many hunters as he could.

I had to put my hands on Malika's face so that she would focus on me as I shouted, "You have to go get him! You have to save Tor and get him out of here! We'll follow you as soon as we can!"

Malika took a desperate look at the bonfire where the figure we'd seen pacing before was now struggling to pull himself up off his knees. Without looking back at me Malika shook her head and agreed, "Yes, I must go to him. He is fading much faster than I estimated." She then turned back to me, concern in her eyes. "As soon as I have him, you must all get out. Do not try to win this night, it is beyond that now. Promise me you will not do anything foolish."

"I promise," I whispered, feeling a sense of dread deep down inside as if I'd just cursed myself to do the opposite. *Foolish, me? Of course not.*

Malika turned and moved so quickly into the bonfire that she was a blur. I watched as she hefted the almost lifeless body of Tor into her arms and shot straight up into the sky with not one shot fired at them from the hunters. I exhaled a sigh of relief as I heard a deafening scream from behind me.

"Nooooo! You fools, you let them escape!" Dardanos cried as his anger was manifested into a physical wind that knocked those within five feet of him backward.

At almost the exact same moment another scream erupted from the right of Dardanos. There stood Lex, holding what looked like someone's head in his hands. Lex's blue eyes seemed electrified as he stared down at the bloody head in his hands. Given different circumstances I would have been repulsed, but the current situation only made me curious to see who he had beheaded and how much joy I would get from that knowledge.

"There's only one place for traitors! Go home, Demetrius!" he yelled as he tossed the still animated head into the bonfire.

Before anyone knew what to do Lex grabbed up Demetrius's body and threw that into the bonfire as well. Kara and Una seemed to silently agree it was time to leave and took off before any of us realized what they were doing. Finally, Dardanos seemed to wake up to what was happening around him and pushed through the three vampires that had taken over for Malika, aiming himself right at Lex.

I screamed to the vampires still fighting, "Get out! Now! Everyone retreat!"

Unfortunately everyone listened and when I looked around again it was only Ben, Lex, Dardanos, perhaps five hunters, and myself. Dardanos caught Lex by the throat lifting him off his feet. I ran to help him as Ben was trying to fend off the hunters and their Necro-Aim. I dug my fingernails straight into the side of Dardanos's throat and ripped his flesh back, leaving a gaping hole and torrents of blood flowing down his side. He immediately let Lex go as he whipped around to defend himself from his unseen attacker. When he saw it was me, he stopped dead in his tracks, and a look of absolute anguish flooded his face.

"Elizabeth! You would attack me to save him?" he asked with such heartbreak I almost felt guilty and apologized, but then I remembered who I was dealing with.

I clenched my fists and scowled at him. "My name is not Elizabeth! And I will attack you a thousand times to save him, if that's what it takes!" As I realized Dardanos's focus was on me I shifted my eyes to Lex and shouted, "Go Now! Don't wait for me!"

Before Lex even had time to react to my command another voice bellowed behind me, "Lillian, look out!" It was Ben running toward us and away from the hunters that were still left.

As I heard him yell I turned my head to the right and caught a glimpse of a figure moving exceptionally fast toward me. I didn't have time to move. The figure caught me in its arms and drove me straight into the bonfire. The initial heat of the flames was enough to shock me into unconsciousness, but I held tight to the figure that had pushed me. The figure didn't expect me to take it along, and when we stopped in the center of the bonfire I could see the terrified face of Kara staring back at me. Evidently she had not meant to sacrifice herself in her effort to kill me, but I certainly was not going to let her victory be complete. I held onto her, though the pain was the equivalent of being shot with a hundred Necro-Aim bullets, until my embrace actually crushed her as her body turned to ash. I looked down at my own body expecting to see it falling away, but it looked completely unharmed. As painful as the bonfire felt, it didn't seem to be affecting me otherwise.

I turned back toward where Dardanos still stood and watched, helplessly, as he drove a sword through the center of Ben's body. The sword must have been made of Necro-Aim, because the skin surrounding the sword seemed to be withering. Dardanos yanked the sword upward as far as he could, slitting Ben up to his clavicle. The pain from the fire and the disbelief of what I was seeing had shocked me into not moving, but I finally commanded my feet to move and tried desperately to run to Ben's aid. Unfortunately, I stumbled over the accumulated ash within the bonfire, landing flat faced into what was left of probably about forty vampires. When next I looked up I saw Lex giving the fire a mournful look, obviously thinking I had perished, just before he grabbed hold of Ben and shot off into the night.

Dardanos turned worriedly back toward the bonfire, still holding out hope that I was alive I suppose. I threw myself onto the ground and tried to cover myself with the mounds of ashes. I wasn't sure how thoroughly Dardanos would inspect the fire to find me, but I lay there for what seemed like hours. It must not have been that long, though, because the sun hadn't risen yet. I decided that I would have to chance an escape, because the sun was sure to rise soon and I certainly did not want to test my stamina to that as well. I lifted myself just enough that I could get a good look around. When I was satisfied that at least no one was within the surrounding area of the bonfire I pushed myself up as hard as I could and took to flight.

I'd like to tell you that I fled and reunited with everyone and everything turned out happily ever after. I'd like to tell you that Ben didn't die, that Dallen made it out just fine, that Lex forgave Dallen for everything. I'd like to say that Dallen and I are together and still in love. I'd like to say that we've reorganized The Seventh Council, found a new safe-house, and are planning a new strategy to go after Dardanos. I'd like to tell you all that...but I can't.

The truth is I didn't even know where to look for those that had survived. I had assumed the meeting place would be back at Lex's mansion, but after arriving there and seeing the place burned to the ground I realized what a silly idea that had been. Of course they wouldn't meet back at a location that had been compromised. As for Ben and Dallen, I don't even know if they survived. For that matter, I really don't know if anyone had survived. I had lost sight of Dardanos and the remaining hunters after Dardanos had resigned himself to the idea that I had simply burned in the bonfire, and it was perfectly reasonable to assume that they had gone after the escaping vampires. If not all of them, Dardanos would at least have gone after Lex. After all I had attacked Dardanos to save Lex, and I'm sure that did not do anything to lessen his hatred for Lex.

After fleeing OPTS I had found a wretched little cottage to sleep in during the day. Amazingly I had sustained no wounds from my submergence in the flames, and felt as strong as when I'd ingested Vasile's blood when I awoke. As soon as I left the cottage I chanced flying back to the rooftop of the manor house, but as I expected there was no sign of Dallen. I wasn't sure if he'd been found by the hunters or if he'd escaped on his own. I did, however, find my poetry book, necklace, and ring lying in the dark corner where I'd seen Dallen headed to hide. I searched the pages of the book, hoping there would be some kind of message for me, but there was nothing that I hadn't written myself. Dallen had most likely dropped it in his escape or had simply been too over-powered by hunters to even be concerned about it.

With a sad heart I returned to Florida, to Lex's mansion. When I saw the rubble I knew no one would be coming back there, but I stayed. I found a way into one of the safe-rooms Lex had built under the house and I stayed there for two months praying someone would come back. At night I hunted and searched the nearby cities and towns for any hint of other vampires. During the day I would retreat to an underground safe-room buried under piles of debris, feeling like a monster, like a corpse returning to its final resting place. I thought horrible, wretched things during that time, I thought, perhaps, I wouldn't go on. I had nothing and the loneliness was very nearly unbearable.

Finally, I realized my best option was to go looking for the others. It would at least give me purpose, a reason to keep living. I traveled the country for years, probing people and vampires for any clue that someone had survived, that my family was out there somewhere. I even found my way back to Vasile's council, but they had vacated. Rumors in the town painted the old vampire to be a cult leader, practicing black magic, and devil worshiping. Some thought they had gone north, perhaps Canada. I keep telling myself I'll give up looking for Ben, Lex, and Dallen and venture into the North to seek out Vasile's council, but I just can't let my hope of finding them go...yet.

Twenty years passed in this way. Moving from town to town. Seeking out vampires and mortals obsessed with the occult. I only ever found vampires that lived secluded lives, pretending to be mortals, and who didn't seem to know anything of the councils or of those that I searched for. If any of them were still alive they kept themselves well hidden from the common vampires I came across. Eventually, I decided to head back home. Not exactly to Wilmington, but back to North Carolina at least.

Strangely enough I moved into an apartment with a view of the estate I'd been held captive in and given The Immortal Fate. It was my way of going back to the beginning. I could see the surrounding, mist covered mountains and that imposing house that was now a draw for tourists. I was haunted by the sight of it from my apartment, like a great hovering ghost calling me. Perhaps Dardanos still owned the property; perhaps he still used some of its rooms. Would I find him there? Did I just want to go back to the last place that I had been when I was still mortal? Did I want to give in to Dardanos? The loneliness was, at times, intolerable, and I found myself longing to go to the great house to see what was there. Maybe the real reason I had come back was because I secretly wanted him to find me. I knew I had to do something to keep my mind from such thoughts.

With nothing else left I felt I had to write my story, all of our story. I had to immortalize all those I loved, because maybe, just maybe, they were gone forever and this is all I will ever have of them. My every night has been filled with memories and endeavors to finding even just one of those that I had lost, and I have failed. Not even a rumor or hint of any of them has found its way to me, and I'm not sure that my heart can stand any more disappointment. Now that I have finished my story I don't know what I will do or where I will go. I have become lost in this world and know not how to move on.

I miss Ben, my true father, Lex, my irresistible companion, and Dallen, my undeniable love. I still wear the moonstone pendant Dallen had given me in hopes that its magic will bring us back together, and as I've mentioned I still wear the black moonstone ring upon my right hand, reminding me of my obligation for vengeance. I cannot continue on the way I have anymore, looking for signs of my loved ones, and finding nothing. I must find a new purpose; I must find something to occupy my mind so that I don't slip into the vampire madness and lose all hope. I must find something to give my life meaning again.

Perhaps it is now time to finish the past. I have become tired of hiding, and living in anguish over those I've lost. If I am to live in the world it must be without fear and resentment. Perhaps it's time to finally face Dardanos, and put an end to one of us. If I am to never see those I have loved again, then at least I might avenge them...or die trying.

A NIGHT IN THE UN-LIFE...

Lillian cupped her hands around the steaming cup of coffee, staring at the swirls of smoke rising from the boiling hot liquid. She loved having warm things pressed against her skin. It didn't feel the same as it had when she was human, but it still felt...like something, especially after she'd fed.

"It's so sad," Ash commented, looking up from the pages he was reading. "Is this how you feel? Is this what you wanted to show me?"

Lillian smiled weakly, not sure what she had expected Ash's reaction to be. He had met her as he had promised at the diner, and upon sitting at the counter Lillian had simply handed Ash her finished story to read. All she had told him was that it was "her story, her life". He obviously thought she had meant it metaphorically, but Lillian really couldn't blame him. If she were in his shoes she would have thought the same thing, or most likely worse.

Lillian placed her hand over the pages and pleaded, "Everything I have written is true. This is my story. This is my tragedy. I know it's hard to believe. I don't expect you to accept any of this, but I had to tell you. After I saw your studio...you need to know that I am no goddess. I'm immortal, but I don't deserve to be worshiped. I don't even know if I deserve to be loved." Lillian paused as she sensed the waitress coming by to refill their coffees. She again smiled weakly at Ash and continued, "I am a vampire. I know how crazy that sounds, but it's the truth."

Ash stared hard at Lillian, trying to decide if this was some kind of joke or test, but he could see that she was earnest in her declaration. No matter what the truth was, Lillian seemed to believe she was a vampire. Out of blind love Ash decided he would try to get to the bottom of Lillian's delusion.

"Why do you think you're a vampire?" he asked softly.

Lillian's heart sank as she mumbled, "Of course, you don't believe me."

Ash looked down at Lillian's story and countered, "I want to, it's just..."

Lillian smiled triumphantly as an idea occurred to her, and she took Ash's hand. "Come with me."

Ash threw money on the counter for the coffees and scooped up Lillian's book, stuffing it into his messenger bag. He followed her obediently, hoping she was going to lead him back to her apartment. Instead she led him down the alley that ran alongside the diner.

"So, is this where you show me you're really a vampire and scare me out of my mind?"Ash asked somewhat teasingly as he followed behind Lillian.

Lillian stopped and turned around. "Yes," she said simply.

Without warning she ran at Ash with unnatural speed, and stopped short in front of him baring her fangs. For a moment he seemed stunned, but then laughed.

"That was amazing. Did you have fangs put on just to play a joke on me?"

Lillian tried to figure out how she could convince Ash, without having to actually sink her teeth into his neck. "Hmmm, that would be much easier," Lillian mused to herself.

Ash knotted his eyebrows. "What would be easier?"

Lillian answered nonchalantly, "Drawing out your blood. That would certainly convince you." Lillian paused momentarily thinking it through and then another idea occurred to her.

She smiled slyly at Ash as she stepped in close and wound her arms around him.

"Hold on as tight as you can," she instructed softly. Then added, "Pretend your life depended on it."

Then she shot straight up into the sky.

The rush of wind in her ears had half drowned out Ash's desperate screaming, but once she leveled off just above the buildings he seemed to only be capable of small whimpers. Lillian held tight to him, confident that she now had his full attention.

"Do you believe me now?" she asked smartly.

All Ash could muster was a small nod. Lillian shot off toward the east and the ocean. Ash was quiet the whole time as Lillian softly told him, though he'd already read about it, things from her past. She included her connection to Dardanos, and what she planned to do. Ten minutes later she gently set down on a beach on the east coast of North Carolina.

Ash fell into the sand, a little thankful to be back on the ground, and sat. "How can you possibly go after this guy by yourself? If he's as powerful as you say, you have no chance."

Lillian knelt in front of Ash and explained sadly, "I don't have a choice. Either I go after him, or I wait for him to find me."

Ash smiled weakly at her and commented, "So it's true, everything in your book?" Ash gestured to her right hand asking, "And you still wear the ring he gave you?"

Lillian nodded her head guiltily. "Yes, until it's finally over, I feel I must. We're connected whether I like it or not and I must destroy that connection, and the ring is my reminder."

Ash bit his lip nervously, obviously uneasy about what he was going to say. "I noticed in your book you said your last name was Thorne, and there was a character, or I guess he's real, with the last name Gray. Did you...are you..."

Lillian laughed lightly and explained, "Did I what? Get married? No," Lillian added sadly, "His name was Dallen Gray and I am still in love with him. After I started traveling, and especially when I wanted to publish my poetry, I realized it wasn't smart for me to continue using my real name. I wasn't sure what kind of legal action had been taken when Rachel and I had disappeared and I really didn't want my family finding me, so I had my name changed. It's surprisingly easy when you have the ability to influence people's thoughts. Gray just seemed to fit, and I thought if he was looking for me maybe he would see the name Lillian Gray and know it was me."

Ash and Lillian talked for hours. For the first time since she'd been turned Lillian felt she could relax with someone. Ash was genuinely concerned for her, and seemed to still be in love with her, even though she was a vampire and still harbored feelings for someone else. She told him absolutely everything she could remember about her life, and he in turn made her laugh with stories about his life as a struggling painter.

Eventually, Lillian knew it was time to go.

"We have to get back. It's getting close to sunrise," Lillian said unhappily.

Ash stood and helped Lillian to her feet. "Whatever you decide, I'm not going anywhere. I love you as much as a vampire, as I loved you as a goddess."

Lillian smiled and again wrapped her arms protectively around Ash for their flight back to her apartment.

"Would you ever think of turning me?" Ash asked gently just as Lillian began her descent toward a park two blocks from her apartment.

Lillian set down in the darkest part of the park before answering Ash in a whisper, "I don't know. I hadn't really thought about it. I actually thought you would either never believe me or be scared to death of me, I didn't think past those prospects." Lillian thought in silence as they walked, and in time offered, "It would make my existence easier, to share it with another."

Ash didn't say anything more about it. He just put his hand in Lillian's and walked her back to her apartment, completely content with how things had turned out. Ash felt strange suddenly, as if time had slowed and each step seemed harder than the last. Something wasn't right. He looked at Lillian and could see she felt it as well. She was staring at him with a strange look in her eyes as if she were waiting for him to explain what was happening. They were perhaps thirty feet from the door into Lillian's hall, but Lillian stopped in her tracks.

Her heart beating uncontrollably, she whispered, "I feel someone near."

Ash didn't understand what she meant and just shook his head, but he could feel the very air felt heavier. Lillian saw the confusion on Ash's face, but pulled him forward roughly.

"I can always feel when another vampire is near...and this one is very powerful," she explained anxiously.

"Lillian, the sun," Ash warned, pointing at the brightening sky.

Lillian almost felt relief to see the coming gray morning, most vampires, no matter how strong they were would retreat once daylight was approaching. As Lillian was focused on the horizon she felt Ash's hand pulled out of hers. She turned around abruptly to see why Ash had pulled away so hastily and saw the last person she had expected to show up there at that very moment.

"Dardanos," Lillian sneered, with hatred in her eyes and hands clenched into fists.

Dardanos was standing in the middle of the desolate street, his right hand clutching Ash's throat, holding him out at arm's length. Ash was futilely scratching at Dardanos's iron grip as his feet barely touched the ground.

"Still trying to replace me, Elizabeth?" Dardanos said humorously.

Lillian looked at him in tired agony. "Please stop calling me Elizabeth. I'm not her. You've already taken everything I have ever loved from me, why can't you just let me suffer in peace." Lillian stumbled slightly, feeling the first bitter rays of sun fighting to reach her on the ground.

Dardanos too was beginning to feel the power-diminishing effects of the sun, but pretended to not notice and offered, "All you have to do is come with me. I will release your..." Dardanos paused giving Ash a wrathful look. "...friend, if you come with me willingly. Elizabeth, look at what happened last time you chose another over me. You were left alone. Do you think I don't know the anguish you have endured these past twenty years? I know, because I felt it as well. I would never have left you alone."

"No, Lillian! Don't listen to him!" Ash managed to shout to her in his agony.

Lillian looked up at the ever brightening sky in panic, and back at Ash. "Let him go. I will go with you, if you let him go," she conceded, lowering her head sadly.

"Lillian, I love you and I won't let you do this. You're going to have to kill me, because I will not let her willingly go with you," Ash announced bravely.

"So be it," Dardanos said simply.

Lillian raised her head, eyes wide, as she saw Ash's face contort to shock as he realized what Dardanos meant. Quicker than Lillian could even take one step, Dardanos pulled Ash toward himself and sunk his teeth greedily into his neck. It usually took Lillian at least two minutes to completely drain a victim, Dardanos was done in less than thirty seconds. He let Ash's body fall uselessly to the ground, and looked up at Lillian licking his lips.

Lillian thought perhaps she would just let herself burn in the coming sunlight. She looked down at Ash's lifeless body, tears streaming down her cheeks, and silently berated herself over and over again for putting him in danger. She looked back at Dardanos, feeling empty and unconcerned with what he was going to do to her. He started to walk toward her, but stumbled again, this time actually falling and catching himself on the ground with the palms of his hands.

The sight of Dardanos, weakened and half fallen, was all it took for Lillian's mind to scream at her to move. She took off as fast as she could toward her apartment. She could feel Dardanos behind her, but dared not look back. Suddenly, just a few feet from the door, a hand caught Lillian's shoulder. Lillian spun around with such force that Dardanos actually lost balance and fell backward. She saw that he was holding something. Lillian recognized it as the Necro-Aim chain used to bind vampires.

With the sun slowly starting to burn her skin, Lillian yanked the Necro-Aim from Dardanos's unprepared hands, and quickly wrapped the lethal chain around his neck.

Fighting the pull of unconsciousness, Lillian stood, gazing down at the weakened and now wounded Dardanos and snarled, "I will never go with you. Not if I have to face a thousand sunrises, not if I have to endure a thousand years alone. I will destroy you. I promise you that."

With that Lillian turned toward the door into her hallway, stumbling toward it like a drunk, but the sun was rising faster than she anticipated. Her entire backside began to burn, and she was sure she would collapse right there, dying in the harsh rays of sunlight and never fulfilling her promise to Dardanos, whom she assumed would live through such an ordeal. The sound of her flesh sizzling and the dimming of her vision spurred Lillian to throw herself, yet again, at the glass door leading to her stairwell.

Realizing she was no longer burning, Lillian lifted her head lazily to find herself safely in the darkened hall leading to her stairs. She forced her near unresponsive body to turn around so she might at least see Dardanos suffering in the light of the fierce sun. As she looked at him, struggling to stay awake, another figure approached.

Lillian shook her head to wake herself. What she was seeing could not be happening. A cloaked figure approached Dardanos, though the figure seemed to be burning worse than Lillian herself had, and was actually helping him up. Lillian thought she must be dreaming, but she could still feel the blistering heat that had singed her skin. As the figure pulled Dardanos to half stand the hood of the cloak fell back.

Lillian gasped so loud the figure heard her and turned in her direction. For a moment they locked eyes. Lillian felt her heart about to beat out of her chest as the figure hardened its expression to indifference and put Dardanos's arm around its neck. Giving Lillian one last hateful glare, the figure helped the weakened Dardanos to his feet as it seemed to encourage him, almost lovingly, to get up.

"No, it can't be..." Lillian said in disbelief.

The figure, still burning uncontrollably, led Dardanos away from Lillian, until Lillian could no longer see either of them. The pull of unconsciousness was too great, and Lillian felt confident that, at least, Dardanos would not be attacking her that day.

Lillian's eyes again filled with tears, and she put her hand to her mouth to silence her uncontrollable sobs as she slowly slipped, unwillingly, into her day-sleep muttering, "Rachel...Rachel...alive. Rachel helping Dardanos."

Also Available
By J.M. Merillo

Immortal Dreams: Poetry by Lillian Gray

(companion book to The Immortal Fate)

Waking the Sleeping Soul
(The Immortal Fate Book 2)

J.M. Merillo

was born in Medina, NY. She fell in love with writing poetry at the age of ten and soon after found a passion for creating stories. J.M. spent her childhood moving every few years to a new place, continuing to write to cope with the constant upheavals. *The Immortal Fate: Lillian's Story* is her first novel. She also wrote a book of poetry titled *Immortal Dreams: Poetry by Lillian Gray* as a companion book to *The Immortal Fate*.

J.M. lives in Florida with her husband and two children.

For more information visit:
www.facebook.com/authorjmmerillo
www.twitter.com/jmmerillo
www.jmmerillo.wordpress.com

www.ingramcontent.com/pod-product-compliance
Lightning Source LLC
Chambersburg PA
CBHW080836250626

47160CB00009B/2961